"Ahhh!" I said, my eyes taking in the discarded jars lining the counter top. A dusting of fine powder covered the floor. "This room's a mess. It'll take hours to clean."

"They must've taken a sample of everything." Deena piped up behind me. "What's on the floor?"

Billie Jo bent down and ran her finger over the floor, leaving a thin trail. "It looks like oatmeal. Carla said she mixed everything she could get her hands on into that death mask."

Mama stuck her head in the door. "Don't touch anything and get out of there right now. We need to get over to the hospital. Jolene, if you don't come out of there this instant, I promise you that when the roll is called up yonder, you'll be there!"

Deena backed out of the room. "She's right; the hospital is expecting me."

"I'm ready to leave, too," Billie Jo said, joining Mama and Deena in the hallway.

There wasn't any need to try and argue my point with them—my vote would be vetoed immediately. The facial equipment was unplugged, so I turned off the lights and shut the door. A loud crash sounded from inside the room. Quickly, I flung open the door, flipped on the overhead lights, and screamed with every ounce of my being—for there, on the facial bed, sat the faint, ghostly image of Scarlett Cantrell.

Dixieland Dead

by

Penny Burwell Ewing

The Haunted Salon Series

This is a work of fiction. Names, characters, places, and incidents are either the product of the author's imagination or are used fictitiously, and any resemblance to actual persons living or dead, business establishments, events, or locales, is entirely coincidental.

Dixieland Dead

Cover Art by *Angela Anderson*

The Wild Rose Press, Inc.
PO Box 708
Adams Basin, NY 14410-0708
Visit us at www.thewildrosepress.com

Publishing History
First Fantasy Rose Edition, 2016
Print ISBN 978-1-5092-1092-3
Digital ISBN 978-1-5092-1093-0

The Haunted Salon Series
Published in the United States of America

Dedication

For my mother, Dixie Lee Joiner,
who inspired the creation of Jolene
and her unwavering dedication to family.

Cast of Characters

Jolene Claiborne—The oldest Tucker sister wants Dixieland Salon to be the best full-service beauty shop in Whiskey Creek, Georgia. Nothing, or no one, had better stand in her way.

Deena Sinclair—Is this Tucker sister really the shy one? Or is the pretty brunette hiding something more sinister behind her demure, sisterly smile?

Billie Jo Hazard—Bold and outspoken, no one dares to push around the youngest Tucker sister. Such a mistake could find you staring down the barrel of a gun.

Annie Mae Tucker—The matriarch of the Tucker clan is smart, sassy, and dead serious when it comes to protecting her family.

Harland Clayton Tucker—The patriarch of the Tucker clan played badly on the roulette wheel of life and came up with the losing hand.

Scarlett Cantrell—Destiny dealt a deadly blow to Channel Ten's beautiful TV star.

Mandy Brown—Blackmail is a dirty word. How much will it cost this savvy nail tech?

Anthony Vogel—His secret could destroy Dixieland Salon. How far will he go to keep it silent?

Carla Moody—A facial with Dixieland's aesthetician could be a dangerous undertaking. You might wake up on the Other Side.

Robert Burns—the CEO of WXYB is on Scarlett's hot list—but if you play with fire, you'll get burned.

Cherry Hill Burns—This socialite isn't sharing her millionaire husband with a younger woman—she has too much to lose.

Henry Payne—Whiskey Creek's mayor will do anything to get the vote—maybe even commit murder?

Linda Payne—The mayor's wife is desperate to keep her place in society. Does madness mask itself behind those serene eyes?

Samuel Bradford—This Whiskey Creek detective has more women on his trail than a blood hound has fleas.

Chapter One
The Dead Don't Speak, Right?

In a small town like Whiskey Creek, Georgia, where the statue of a local Confederate war hero still stands tall in the courthouse square, there's a strong sense of community for the living and the dead. The old wrought-iron gates at Peaceful Valley Cemetery were open year round for residents wishing to celebrate birthdays or holidays with family members who'd passed over to the Other Side.

The Easter holiday had brought me here to visit my father and grandparents this early Saturday morning. Looking around, it seemed I had the place to myself, so I exchanged heels for flats and climbed out of my Mustang convertible. Armed with several fresh bouquets of Easter lilies, I picked my way through the gravestones until I stopped beneath a timeworn oak, its heavy branches dusted with shades of leafy green.

"Good morning, my dears," I said, placing the bouquets on a stone bench beside their graves, and bent down to remove the wind-beaten silk flowers from the bronze vases. "The rest of the family will be stopping by later on, but I wanted some private time alone with y'all."

My father's parents had both taken the journey to their final reward when I was just a young child, but I remembered them well. Grandpa Tucker always smelled of sweet pipe tobacco, and Granny Tucker, well, I remembered her soft, comforting voice, most of all. And then, four years later when I was only twelve, we lost Daddy. He was killed in a bank robbery attempt in Atlanta while on a business trip. One moment he was standing in line to cash a check and the next, gone forever. The thing I remembered the most about that time was Mama's strange behavior. She refused to talk about the shooting with me and my two younger sisters, Deena and Billie Jo. And because of that, deep down inside, I've always felt as if there was some dark secret surrounding his death.

Daddy used to say that secrets were like candy. At first, they're sweet on the tongue and bring such pleasure, but then with time the decay sets in, and you find yourself wishing you'd left that bonbon alone.

I brushed away my depressing thoughts and finished arranging the lilies in the vases. Once finished, I sat down on the bench to enjoy the beauty of the warm morning before I had to rush off to work. Hopefully, the chocolate-covered donuts I'd picked up earlier from the bakery would be okay for a little longer in the front seat of my car. I didn't want them to melt before the staff meeting at the salon, but I wasn't ready to leave yet.

I closed my eyes as birds sung overhead and took a deep, relaxing breath, wishing I could hear Daddy's voice once again.

"*Jolene honey, open your eyes.*"

My eyes popped open at Granny Tucker's voice. Startled, I studied my surroundings, but no one lingered nearby. Feeling a little silly, I stood up from the bench and went to stand over her grave.

Okay. That was weird.

Again, I cast a quick glance over my shoulder. A family had congregated nearby, and I could just make out a couple of words as they placed flowers on the grave, so it must've been them I'd heard and not the voice of my long-dead grandmother.

Which made perfect sense. According to Pastor Inman over at the First Baptist Church, once we'd left behind our fleshly homes, we weren't allowed to cross back over into the land of the living. The dead can't speak, only the living. Right?

Briefly, a long-buried memory of another disembodied voice from my childhood flashed into my consciousness and then fled as quickly as it had surfaced. Now completely weirded-out, I said a hasty goodbye, put the discarded silk flowers in my trunk, exchanged shoes a second time, and headed for the salon.

On Main Street, I passed a cluster of shops where tourists and local residents strolled down the tree-shaded, rustic brick sidewalks, peering into storefront windows or entering the establishments in search of the best sales. Farther down, restored Victorian homes offered respite from the heat with broad, covered porches filled with decorative wicker furniture. Tall, ancient magnolias branched out like sentries, and beneath their leafy canopies, bright swaths of azaleas, hydrangeas, camellias, and roses dotted the well-manicured lawns.

I zipped past Colonel Nathaniel Taft, keeping his ever watchful eye on the town from the courthouse square. Two streets over, I pulled onto Love Avenue and drove around to the rear of Dixieland Salon where I usually parked and spied my two younger sisters gesturing toward the back of the shop. When I pulled my car into a vacant space beside Billie Jo's old Dodge Charger, I saw the back door standing open, splintered wood littering the walkway.

Oh, no, not a break-in. Not today!

I joined my sisters at the front of my baby sister's car. "I knew there was a rash of break-ins in the neighborhood, but I never expected this to happen to us. How bad is it? Did you check to see if anyone is still in there?"

"No, Deena wouldn't let me," Billie Jo said. "So I called 9-1-1. The dispatcher advised us to wait out by our cars until an officer arrives and checks out the inside."

Deena pushed a damp strand of hair from her eyes. "I wish they'd hurry. It's awfully hot for April. I believe my makeup is melting."

Several more minutes passed without help arriving. Impatience made me antsy. "Is the property insurance up to date?" I regretted the words the moment I uttered them. At times, Deena was as touchy and snippy as her Chihuahua puppy, Gator Bait, and the expression on her face said I'd smashed her self-esteem *again*. I sighed inwardly. The slow economy had me fretful about the future. We'd even expanded the salon to include skin care in hopes of attracting more business. A scary move in these times, and I kept my fingers crossed that it would pay off.

"I'm sorry, sis," I said, backpedaling. "You're the best manager Dixieland Salon has ever had."

"Sounds right since I'm the only one we've ever had," she said, rolling her eyes but looking mollified.

Just then, a police cruiser pulled up, and a young,

fresh-faced officer climbed out. Warning us to stay put, he disappeared through the broken doorway.

I dabbed a Kleenex across my brow. "This heat is murder, and I have a dozen chocolate-covered donuts in my car."

Several minutes later, he emerged from the rear of the shop where we joined him.

"Well, someone broke into your cash register, ladies." He slipped his gun back into its holster. "Everything else looks undisturbed, but I'll let you go in and check the premises shortly."

I craned my neck around him to peer into the shop. "How long is this gonna take? I'd like to see the damage before the staff arrives."

This morning, I'd squeezed into a low-cut jean dress that emphasized my ample curves, and as I dabbed the tissue on my abundant cleavage, I noticed the officer's gaze riveted there. I gave him a raised eyebrow, and he flushed.

"There's the backup now, if you'll excuse me." The officer started toward the arriving squad car, but then he stopped, turned back with a smile. "Oh, and the name's Clark, ma'am." He tipped his hat. "Officer Charles Clark."

Officer Clark headed off to greet the uniformed man retrieving a large silver box from the back seat of his squad car. Both men disappeared inside the rear entrance leaving us to wait, again, in the thick, humid air.

Deena's sharp gaze locked onto my attire. "You know why he did that, don't you?"

I answered with a sisterly smile. "No, but I believe you're going to tell me."

"You're spilling out of that dress. *And* it's entirely too tight for a woman of your advanced age. You look like Barbie's mother."

Billie Jo's smile turned into a chuckle. "I wish I looked like Barbie's mother."

I gave my youngest sister a beaming smile. Billie Jo and I share many similar characteristic traits, although physically we're very different. She'd been born blonde and petite, whereas I'd inherited Mama's large frame and kinky, dark blonde hair. Deena, two years younger than I am, at thirty-five, fell through the cracks somewhere in the family gene pool. She had a nice figure and glossy brown tresses—from Daddy's side of the tree.

Thankfully, Officer Clark's reappearance cut off any further discussion of my questionable attire.

"You ladies need to take a quick look around to see if anything other than the cash from the register was taken."

I pushed past him into the hallway leading to the main salon and looked inside the dispensary where we kept all our chemicals for processing and dying hair—its usual disarray completely normal and no cause for concern. I moved to the opened door of the facial room and peeked inside. It, too, appeared untouched by scavenging hands.

"The hundred dollars starting cash is gone." Billie Jo's voice came from the front of the salon.

I closed the facial room door and headed to Deena's office where my sisters had gathered at the threshold. At the reception desk, Officer Clark stood next to the other officer snapping pictures of the opened register.

"So what's next?" Billie Jo asked him.

Officer Clark glanced up from his notepad. "Other than the hundred dollars, did you find anything else taken?"

"Not that I could see," I said. "The staff will have to check their stations before I can be sure."

"I found something strange." Deena moved into her office. We followed and stopped beside her desk where she picked up a dark green bank bag. "This was left untouched."

"Is that yesterday's deposit? There's over a thousand dollars in there!" I couldn't believe that much cash had been left overnight in the salon.

Deena nodded. "I know I'm supposed to drop it off after closing, but I feel like a sitting duck at the night deposit slot."

"Well, that's going to change," Billie Jo said. "You need to either embrace the gun movement, or Jolene or I will accompany you from now on. We both carry guns for protection."

"Ladies, I need to see your weapons and licenses, before we proceed," Officer Clark said.

I pulled a pink holster from my shoulder bag and handed it and the license over to him.

He pulled my .32 caliber snub-nosed revolver from the holster. One eyebrow lifted. "Never seen a pink gun with pearl grips before," he said as he turned it over in his hand. "Seems to fit you though." His gaze once again rested on me.

I rewarded him with a brilliant smile. "I named her 'Mini Pearl'."

Officer Clark examined my permit to carry license. He did the same thing with Billie Jo's Cobra derringer.

Satisfied that we were in compliance with state gun laws, he handed them back and took the bank bag from Deena. He pulled out the contents and quickly counted the money. The amount matched the deposit slip. "You said this was left here overnight in an unlocked drawer in plain sight?"

"Yes." Deena opened the top drawer of her desk. "Right here on top of this file folder. Why would burglars take cash from the register and leave this much money behind?"

"Maybe something or someone spooked them and they took off before they had a chance to search your desk," Billie Jo said.

I agreed with her. "Sounds to me like kids broke in here."

"There's been a rash of break-ins with the same M.O. in the area." Officer Clark closed his notepad and shoved it into his shirt pocket. "I'll let you know if we get any leads, but there's not much to go on. Call your insurance company and have the damage fixed as soon as you can."

"I'll walk you out," I said. "There are a dozen chocolate-covered donuts melting in the front seat of my car."

"I could take those off your hands, ma'am," he said with a flirtatious wink.

Oh, what the hell. I winked back. Perhaps destiny had stepped in to save me from the gazillion calories I was sure to consume if those donuts made it through the back door.

****

I emerged from the rear entrance to see our staff had arrived. Upon viewing their horrified expressions at the damage to the door, I assured them the situation would be explained in a meeting first thing. Carla Moody, our aesthetician, dabbed her watery, blood-shot eyes with a tissue.

"Are you okay?" I paused to check on her. A recent graduate of beauty school, Carla had been having a hard time working in a professional setting. After several minor incidents, I stepped in to guide her with skin care decisions for her growing clientele. With time and experience, I believe she'll make an excellent skin care specialist.

She avoided my gaze. "Yes, no need to worry." Her voice was weepy.

That struck me as odd, and I made a mental note to speak with her later. Retrieving the box of donuts from my car, I handed them over to Officer Clark.

He tipped his hat. "The boys in blue thank you."

I watched him drive off and walked back inside for the staff meeting, glad I'd given the donuts away. Given the chance, I'd have consumed half the box by the time the meeting wrapped up. I nibble when I'm anxious, and the break-in had ramped up my stress level several notches.

Ten minutes later, after offering the information I had, the meeting broke up. Deena stopped me in the hallway outside the facial room. "I photographed the back door and the broken register for the insurance claim. Roddy's sending a crew over to fix the damage right away. He told Billie Jo they'd inspect the front door lock also."

Roddy Hazard, Billie Jo's husband, was a general contractor and the go-to guy for all the salon's maintenance issues, and we depended heavily on him to keep the salon in tiptop shape. He'd also been great about coming over to the house for repairs since my divorce a couple of years back.

"Good. That's one less thing to worry about…" My words trailed off as Cherry Hill Burns, one of my clients, waved at me from the reception area. "There's my first appointment now."

Grabbing my apron from the dispensary, I greeted Cherry, who waited for me in my stylist chair. She immediately zeroed in on my new four-inch red heels. "Very nice. Mind telling me where you got them?"

I preened under the compliment and gave her the name of the shoe boutique on Second Street. After a quick shampoo, during which she chatted about all the latest gossip, I sectioned and cut her coarse brown hair.

"I swear I'm telling you the truth," she said. "Lila saw her husband sneaking into the neighbor's yard in the middle of the night."

"What was he doing?" I asked, our eyes meeting in the mirror as I distributed a generous amount of mousse through her hair.

"What do you think? Lila told me she waited until he snuck back over there a couple of nights later, and then she nailed the front and back gate shut. When he scaled the fence to get back home, she was waiting for him. He caught his britches on the pointed fence post and split 'em clean down to his birthday suit."

"Ouch. That's one splintered relationship."

We both burst into laughter. The pastor's wife looked disapprovingly our way, and it took a minute to regain my decorum and resume rolling Cherry's hair. "Any weekend plans?" I asked, hoping a change of subject would help dispel the picture of Lila's husband explaining to his doctor how he loaded his backside with painful splinters.

"No, Robert's in Biloxi on business this weekend."

"I'd like to drive down there and try my hand at roulette. Has Robert ever taken you?"

"No, but he promised to one day." Cherry stiffened. "Here comes *trouble*."

The front door swung open, jingling the bells above it, and the subject of her remark sauntered to the reception desk and arranged herself over its curving granite surface like a bobcat on a low hanging branch.

Crap. Scarlett Cantrell, darling of Whiskey Creek society. *Scarlett's Top Spot*—a TV show—had made her a local celebrity. She was the former Miss Pecan Festival Queen, Miss Whiskey Creek *and* Miss Georgia, president of the Cherokee Rose Club, a member of Daughters of the Confederacy, and active in the Journalist Network. She was an adjunct faculty member of Whiskey Creek Community College, and most recently appointed to the Mayor's Advisory Committee. Scarlett had the four B's of success— brains, beauty, bucks, and boobs.

"I don't know why you put up with her after she broke up Deena's marriage," Cherry said. "One day she's going to get what's coming to her."

I make it a habit to stay out of these kinds of matters as I need Scarlett's continued patronage at the salon, but I can see why Cherry felt threatened. Her husband, Robert, was CEO of WXYB Channel Ten television station, and Scarlett's employer. Affairs happened all the time in that intimate setting. My own husband had fallen victim to it.

Before I could respond, a commotion at the desk

grabbed my attention. "Calm down, Scarlett," Deena said in an aggravated voice. "Holly made a slight error. Anthony will work you in sometime today."

The sound of Scarlett's high heel shoe stomping the floor was the first sign of trouble. "Deena, *dah*-lin can't you ever do anything right?" Scarlett screeched. "Like hire a competent receptionist? Anthony will not squeeze me in. I'm not *worked in* anywhere in this town."

"How would you like me to work your important butt out the door?" Deena's voice ground out. "I'm sure I'm capable of doing that."

"You wouldn't dare!"

"Try me."

Here we go. I excused myself and hurried over to divert a disaster. Holly cowered behind the desk, intimidated by Scarlett's overpowering presence, and Deena wore the look of a constipated feline.

"Carla will be with you soon," I interrupted. "And Anthony is always at your disposal. We're very sorry for the misunderstanding. Right, Deena?" I gave her a nudge with my heel.

"Right," Deena said through clenched teeth.

Upon hearing his name mentioned, Anthony Vogel' swung his head in our direction. He frowned then scurried over. "I can't squeeze you in," he lamented, checking his morning appointments. "I'm booked until three. I can do you then."

Perfectly sculptured nails tapped on the counter. "Is that so, dear boy? Perhaps I should reconsider our last conversation."

He frowned but made the change in his book. "I'm sure Mrs. Walters won't mind waiting a few minutes."

"Good boy. Don't let it happen again." Scarlett brushed an imaginary speck of dust from her white, silk designer suit before taking a seat in the reception area. "I would like my tea now, Jolene." She picked up a magazine. "Make it hot and sweet."

I looked around for Holly, but she'd disappeared. Showing no outward impatience, I made my way to the kitchen, popped a cup of water into the microwave, and found Scarlett's personal tea canister filled with her own special blend of imported tea. "If I had another set of hands, they'd be around Scarlett's scrawny neck."

The door banged open. I looked over my shoulder at Deena standing in the doorway.

"If she calls me *dah*-lin one more time, I'm gonna barf in her Hermes handbag. I hate it when she acts as if she's some kind of modern day version of Scarlett O'Hara."

The microwave dinged, and I removed the steaming cup. "Well, you gotta admit that she looks a lot like her, so it's only natural that she'd try to act like her. Take my advice and grin and bear it. We can't afford to offend her. Besides, think of all the free advertising we receive from her show."

"And the manner in which she spoke to Anthony. You'd think he was a puppet on a chain, but I could tell she pissed him off. Poor guy."

"Her bark is worse than her bite, but that was an odd exchange."

"She delights in rubbing me the wrong way," Deena continued, "and I'm tired of bowing down to her. Sometimes I wish I'd killed her when I caught her in bed with Calvin."

"Holy cow, Deena. Don't let anyone hear you say

that! You know how folks around here can distort the truth to suit their needs. God, don't go digging up old bones."

The ringing phone interrupted us, and she ducked out of the kitchen. Muttering to myself about the stupidity of loose tongues, I dropped the tea bag into the cup, added three lumps of sugar, and rushed back to the reception area.

I handed Scarlett the cup and saucer. "Hot and sweet, as ordered."

"Is it my special blend?" She set down the magazine and sipped the tea. Her face wrinkled up like a prune. "I can't drink this witch's brew. Did you add sugar?"

"Three lumps."

"It's still bitter."

I gritted my teeth. "Deena, bring the sugar. Scarlett wants more lumps."

"Gladly. I'm just the person to deliver them," came the reply from behind the front desk.

"I have better things to do than to watch you cater to this woman's silly whims," a voice said from behind me.

Scarlett flashed a mercurial smile. "Well, if it isn't Mrs. Robert Burns. And where is your fine husband this fine day?"

I turned to see Cherry gazing with undisguised contempt at Scarlett. Her usual unflappable demeanor was notably absent, which surprised me. Cherry was known for her impeccable manners. Rarely did she lose her composure.

"My husband is out of town," she replied. "Not that it's any of your damn business."

"Hmm." Victory radiated from Scarlett's blue-green eyes. "That's strange. I saw him just this morning having breakfast at Merry Acres Inn. *And,* he wasn't alone."

"Drop dead." Cherry turned and stomped back to my chair.

I heaved another weary sigh. On top of everything else, I now would have an angry client to deal with when I was finally able to return to my station. Out of the corner of my eye, I glimpsed Mayor Henry Payne and his wife, Linda, walk through the front door, but before I could greet them, Scarlett sailed past me in a perfumed cloud.

"I've been trying to reach you, Mayor," she said. "It's urgent that I speak with you about a most pressing issue. This can't wait."

"Hello, Miss Cantrell," Linda greeted her.

Scarlett ignored the mayor's wife, and I fought the inclination to deliver a good hard kick to her skinny shin for her rudeness. How wonderful it would feel to release some of the stress that'd been building up since this morning's break-in.

The mayor tightened his hold on his wife's arm. "My secretary informed me you'd phoned. I've instructed him to clear a place on my schedule later today. Now, if you'll excuse us, Billie Jo is waiting for me, and Mandy is ready for my wife."

"Don't keep me waiting, *dah*-lin'," Scarlett cooed. One hand reached up to touch the diamond brooch pinned to her blouse. "Oh, and my condolences on your miscarriage, Mrs. Payne. Unfortunately, motherhood isn't for everyone."

Linda staggered against her husband as if

physically struck by an unseen hand. Dead silence fell over the reception area at Scarlett's vicious reminder of the couple's recent loss. Pain and fury splashed across the mayor's face. I didn't blame him for his anger. Scarlett was the kind of woman who burrowed under your skin like a parasite, leaving you itching with extreme frustration and half-crazed with the desire to murder her.

Chapter Two
A Special Mask for a Special Lady

The next thirty minutes passed without further incident. Relieved that the worst was over, I began removing rollers from my next client's silvery hair. Mrs. Eisenberg seemed determined to continue the discussion about Linda's recent miscarriage.

"My heart bleeds for the mayor and his wife." She sighed. "She's frantic to have a child, you know. And such a gentle creature and loved by the whole town, she is. Did you know that she's had three miscarriages? I heard the mayor is making her go to grief counseling. Good thing too. Her mother struggled with depression for years, bless her heart, and Linda has spent some time at Magnolia Manor. You know that private mental institution in Macon—very fancy, I've heard."

"Which is understandable under the circumstances," I said. "My sisters and I had counseling after Daddy died. Our world collapsed, which sent us into a tailspin." The emotional repercussions of that day left a trail of bad decisions through my life that I was still working to overcome.

Mrs. Eisenberg clucked her tongue. "Your mama was a brave soul after losing Harland Tucker. I remember a small, closed-casket ceremony. Not much in the paper about what happened. Of course, back then, the *Gazette* only came out once a week. And at that same time, there was an explosion over at the fertilizer plant. The town was in an uproar. Your father's accident took backstage to the disaster."

"I have so many questions that Mama won't answer." Could Mrs. Eisenberg shed any light on the subject?

Mrs. Eisenberg patted my hand. "That was a long time ago, Jolene. Best to look forward not back."

The strange incident at the cemetery flashed through my mind. The words—*Jolene, honey, open your eyes*—had come right after I wished I could hear Daddy's voice. Could it be that my subconscious mind was pointing me to the mystery of Daddy's death in the guise of Granny Tucker's voice? Why now after so many years?

Lost in thought, I had just removed the last roller from Mrs. Eisenberg's hair when Carla drew close and whispered in my ear.

"What do you mean the mask is stuck?" I asked, doubting what I'd heard. "Did you use plenty of water? Get back in there before Scarlett starts screaming her bloody head off. She's caused enough trouble for one day."

"You don't understand, Miz Claiborne. The mask is supposed to easily lift from the skin after it cools."

"Then get in there and fan it off," I said, my eyes glued on Carla's anxious face. She was frozen to the spot. "Would you excuse me for a moment, Mrs. Eisenberg? There's a minor problem I must see about."

"Take your time, honey. I'm in no rush. Mr. Eisenberg is on the golf course for the day."

I stepped away from the stylist chair, concerned at the thought of a mask stuck to Scarlett's face. "Is this a late April Fools' Day joke?"

"I'm not joking," Carla whispered. "This is serious. Please tell me what to do."

My grin faded. "How long has she had the mask on?"

"I think about twenty minutes."

"And you're just now coming to me?"

God, could this day get any worse? Fear for Scarlett's well-being set in. Not to mention the salon's reputation that my sisters and I had spent years building. Not wasting a second, I bolted around the corner to the facial room and eased open the door to the soothing melody of spa music and the soft, ocean breeze scent permeating the shadowed room. Scarlett lay face up on a massage table. "It's me, Jolene. Forgive me for disturbing your rest, Scarlett, but may I speak with you?"

No response.

"Scarlett? Are you okay?" I slipped into the room. Carla, on my heels, shut the door, and flipped on the overhead lights. My stomach somersaulted as I focused on the thick, pasty white mask covering most of Scarlett's face and neck. Her eyes were closed, and her lips were partially open.

Drawing near, I gave her a gentle shake. No response. My gut clenched. Oh, crap. I pressed my fingernails into the mask and felt its rubbery surface give under the pressure. Then I checked her wrist and found a weak pulse.

Relief flooded through me. Thank God she was still alive. I inhaled a calming breath to keep the panic at bay.

"Carla, tell Deena to call 9-1-1." A strangled cry

sounded behind me. "And do it quietly. Try not to alarm the other clients."

A jumble of voices resonated from the salon as Carla slipped out of the room. Alone, I directed my attention toward the mask, my fingers probing for the softest spot in order to pry it from Scarlett's face. No luck. Had Carla thought to try steam or ice-water?

A mumbled sound issued from the bed, boosting my confidence, and I sprang into action. Grabbing a towel lying by the sink, I turned on the hot water, soaked the towel in its steamy spray, and squeezed the excess water out before wrapping it around her face, all except for the nose and mouth. Scarlett moved beneath my hands.

"Be still. I'm going to try hot towels to soften the mask."

After a few seconds, I removed the towel and shoved it back under the hot water. Patches of reddened skin peeped through the dissolving paste, so I knew I was making headway. My hands were on fire from the hot water, but I ignored the pain as I once again wrapped the towel around her face.

"Someone...trying to kill...me," Scarlett said in an agonized whisper.

"No, it was an accident, I swear."

"Find...jade...elephant. Explains everything."

Scarlett's jagged, choking words ended with a long, shuddering breath reminiscent of air seeping through a punctured balloon. Taking a deep breath, I moved away, nervously wringing my hands. Panic threatened to overcome my calm. Black spots danced before my eyes as I continued to hold my breath.

The door opened, and Deena burst into the room.

"What's going on? Carla said there's a medical emergency with Scarlett. I brought my camera and notebook to document for the insurance company what's happened."

I gulped down a breath of air. My vision cleared. "Ever see a dead body, Deena? Well, you're gonna if help doesn't get here fast. We're gonna lose our panties on this one, mark my words. Scarlett would like nothing better than to skin us down to our skivvies."

Deena paled as she stood over Scarlett. "What's on her face?"

"A special mask Carla whipped up. I'm using hot towels to loosen and break it apart."

"Did she use the wrong products?"

"She must have," I cried, holding my temples. "Haven't you noticed how strange she's been acting the past several weeks? Quiet and withdrawn. And this morning her eyes were watery and blood-shot, like she'd been crying. And what about all those phone calls she's been getting? We should have paid better attention to her. This isn't the first mistake she's made. We're in serious trouble with this one."

"Then we'd better gather as much information as we can before the authorities get here." Deena bent over the bed, snapping pictures, zeroing in on the smallest of details.

"I don't believe the insurance company will need pictures of Scarlett's clothes," I said as she moved over to the wall where white linen slacks and blouse hung on pegs.

Setting the camera down on the counter, Deena pulled out a small notebook and began writing. "This is how it's done on *CSI*."

"You watch too much TV." I grabbed another towel and left it under the running cold water as I gently scraped off the remaining mask. "I'm not sure the salon can weather this, but if we do, the entire staff is going to learn emergency first aid and CPR." I stared down at red, angry skin that was puckered and blotched. The famous peaches-and-cream complexion had disappeared with the mask.

"Deena, squeeze the water out of that towel in the sink and hand it to me."

I looked up to see the worry in her eyes. Taking the towel from her, I wrapped the cool cloth around Scarlett's face.

"God, I hope she's going to be okay," she said.

"Better start praying for good measure."

She groaned. "Our insurance rates are going to skyrocket for sure. The police are going to be crawling all over the place. Georgia OSHA will investigate. We could be facing a lawsuit, too. And then there's Mama to deal with."

Oh crap. I'd forgotten about Mama. Her reaction to this was sure to cause me an ulcer. As co-owner of the salon, she'd have to be told, but it wasn't gonna be easy. We were a tight-knit family. Really tight. Mama hadn't cut the apron strings yet, even though we were grown women with families of our own.

Wailing sirens sliced through the air. The door opened, and Billie Jo stood framed in the doorway, scissors in hand. "Hell's bells. What's going on? There's more buzzing than a beehive out there."

I pulled her into the room. "Explain it to her, Deena. I'll show the EMTs in."

When I rounded the corner, I saw two uniformed

officers standing by the reception desk. "Officer Clark," I said, breathlessly, recognizing him from this morning's break-in. "Thank God, you're here. Follow me."

He turned at the sound of my voice. "What's the problem this time?"

Another wave of apprehension swept through me. I wiped my sweaty palms down the front of my apron. "There's been a mishap in the facial room. Where are the EMTs?"

"En route. We were close by when the call came in." He turned to his partner. "See that no one enters or leaves but the EMTs. I'll assess the situation before calling for backup."

The mayor stepped abruptly toward him. "What the hell is going on? My wife is terribly upset, and I'd like to get her home."

"I'm sorry, but no one's leaving just yet," the officer said. "If needed, your wife will be checked by the paramedics. I'll fill you in as soon as I know the details." He swung back to me. "Show me the way, ma'am."

Dashing back to the facial room with Officer Clark close behind me, I jerked open the door, eliciting a cry of alarm from my sisters, both of whom were bending over the bed.

"Back away, ladies." Officer Clark pushed past us and felt Scarlett's wrist. "No pulse." He removed the towel from her face. "Good Lord, her face looks like raw hamburger."

I started to explain what'd happened, but he hit the dispatch button on his shoulder radio, requesting backup. My sisters and I continued to stand in nervous silence as he worked to find a pulse on Scarlett's supine form, pausing to talk into his radio.

"Where's Carla?" I whispered into Deena's ear.

"I left her in my office with Holly," she whispered back. "She's so torn up about this that I was afraid to leave her alone."

Suddenly two paramedics rushed into the small room, shoving us farther into the corner. Feeling a sharp sting, I looked down at Billie Jo's scissors pressing into my arm. When I touched her, she jumped away, crashing into Officer Clark. He frowned, as if just noticing we were still in the room with him. With a quick assessment of the confining space, he steered us into the hallway where a stretcher was being wheeled toward the room. He spoke into his radio again. Turning to us, he said, "Where can we speak privately? I have a few questions."

"We can talk in the kitchen," I said.

Following us into the empty room, he pulled a small pad and pencil from his front uniform pocket. "Have a seat, ladies."

Silently, we complied. Anxiety poured off the three of us like water from a hose. I tried to reassure my sisters with a quick smile, but failed, and pushed my trembling hands under the table.

"You're bleeding," Deena said.

"It's a small nick from Billie Jo's scissors. I'm fine. Stop worrying about me."

Deena turned to Officer Clark. "My sister needs to clean up that cut. Those scissors could be contaminated."

"The first aid kit will suffice," I grumbled. "It can wait until he's finished with questioning us."

"No, ma'am." He nodded toward the door. "Take one of your sisters to help you tend to your arm and then return."

Before we could leave, one of the EMTs came through the door, requesting to speak with the officer.

"This isn't going to turn out well," I said the instant the door closed behind them. "Of all the people for this to happen to, it had to be Scarlett. God, she's gonna make our lives hell when she recovers from this." The EMTs would bring her back to life. They had to.

"We have to remain positive," Deena said. "Negative energy attracts negative results."

"I'm positive I've got a bad feeling about this," I repeated. "It started with the break-in and then Scarlett breathing fire down our necks and provoking hard feelings with our clients, and now this. What's next?"

"Scarlett's gonna sue, and I wouldn't blame her if she did," Billie Jo said.

"Well, if that's the worst of it, then I'll be thankful," I replied. "Paying higher insurance premiums is a small price to pay for a disaster of this magnitude."

Billie Jo made a face. "If you recall, I was against hiring Carla, but you and Deena were dead set on having her join the team."

"Carla was the top graduate in her class. She came highly recommended by her instructors. Accidents happen in this business," Deena pointed out.

I held up my hand to silence them. "All three of us agreed to hire her, so we all share the blame."

Before I could say more, the door opened. Officer Clark stood just inside the doorway. "I'm afraid I have bad news for you, ladies. The paramedics were unable to revive Miss Cantrell. I'm sorry, but she's dead."

Chapter Three
Murder in Dixieland Salon!

A flutter began in my belly. The thought of a dead body lying just feet away from where we sat scared the hell out of me, and I could see by my sisters' pale faces that they were having the same reaction. Bitch or not, Scarlett didn't deserve to die like this.

Billie Jo grabbed my hand, squeezing hard. "Dead. Man, this has gone from bad to really, really bad. Dead. Damn."

Deena shivered. "Dear God, how did this happen?" Tears pooled in her eyes.

I handed her a tissue from my apron pocket. "Hang in there. We'll get through this together."

Officer Clark cleared his throat. "I need to take a brief statement from each of you. The Crime Scene Unit will be here shortly."

"Why would you need the crime scene investigators?" I asked. "Carla wouldn't intentionally harm Scarlett."

"Miss Cantrell died under very unusual circumstances. This is standard procedure in unattended deaths. We're going to treat this as a homicide until proven otherwise."

Murder in Dixieland Salon! My mind floundered at the implications. All I wanted was to run my business and support myself and my sisters in a peaceful, productive way. Leave it to Scarlett to throw a wrench in my well-laid plans. My sisters and I exchanged worried looks and gave our statements to him. Afterward, we joined the other staff members and clientele in the reception area.

A tense silence fell over the salon as the paramedics wheeled out Scarlett's body. We now sat in small groups whispering among ourselves as we waited to be questioned further or released to go home. The murmur of solemn voices drifted throughout the room.

After an hour of anxious fidgeting, the front door opened. The man entering immediately caught my attention. With a tall muscular build, he had to be six-feet-two, I'd guess, and the way he stood there assessing the scene told me he missed little of what occurred around him. He wore a black western-style blazer over a white shirt and jeans. When he pocketed his sunglasses, his steely gaze zeroed in on me and my sisters huddled together on the sofa.

Beside me, Deena tensed. "Good Lord, that's Sam Bradford. It's been years since I've seen him. I heard he'd joined the military after high school. What's he doing here?"

"I suspect by the way he's looking at us that he's here on behalf of the WCPD," Billie Jo said under her breath. "Whatever his past, your old high school squeeze is now definitely a cop."

I drank in his tall form. Up until now, I hadn't contributed to the conversation, not being able to peel my eyes from his powerful gaze. I know I shouldn't have been, such dreadful circumstances and all that, but I was instantly attracted to my sister's old love interest.

"I wonder if he's married," Deena said in a low

voice.

"When he comes this way, I'll check for a wedding ring," Billie Jo whispered.

"Do you think he recognizes me?"

"He knows who you are," I said with certainty.

Bradford stepped over to speak with Officer Clark who stood next to the reception desk scribbling in his notepad. They spoke for a moment before he headed over to the mayor and his wife, seated in a couple of chairs from the kitchen in the make-up and retail section on the far side of the salon.

From where I sat, I had a clear view of the conversation, although I couldn't make out what they were saying. The mayor's waving hands made it easy to guess that he wasn't happy. He kept pointing at his wife and screwing up his face as if he'd swallowed a sour ball.

After a few minutes, Bradford allowed the Paynes to leave. He then questioned each of the morning clients one by one, and then let them leave. I glanced at the clock on the wall—almost one in the afternoon. My stomach rumbled with hunger.

Finally, he turned toward us where we had gathered with the rest of the salon staff in the reception area. Everyone looked paralyzed, unsure of what to expect. We'd given our statements earlier and now, according to Officer Clark, there'd be a formal investigation, presumably conducted by Detective Bradford. Well, at least we knew his reason for being here.

Bradford nodded an acknowledgement at Deena. "I know this is difficult, but I understand you're the one who placed the 9-1-1 call, so I'll begin with you."

"Of course," she said.

"Could you give an account of what happened this morning?"

"Carla came into my office and told me there was a medical emergency in the facial room. I immediately called for help."

"Did she specify what kind of emergency?"

"No, she was so hysterical I couldn't make any sense of what she was saying. She kept crying, so I left her in Holly's care and went to see for myself."

"You then proceeded from your office to the facial room?"

"Yes. I found Jolene applying hot towels to Scarlett's face, and she explained the situation."

Bradford looked down at his notes. "So Jolene was already aware of the problem and was attempting to assist Miss Cantrell?"

"Yes, that's correct. As master cosmetologist, my sister is the go-to person when there's a technical problem in the salon."

"I understand you've had quite an unpleasant history with the deceased."

Deena's face paled. I opened my mouth to protest, but Billie Jo grabbed my hand, squeezing my fingers hard, indicating with a negative shake of her head to keep quiet.

"I hated her for breaking up...my marriage...but not enough...to...kill her."

Bradford studied her for several moments. He turned to Carla. "Start at the beginning and tell me what happened."

Carla stared at the detective and then at me. I nodded encouragement, knowing she was nervous.

Tension blanketed the room.

"Well...er...after performing microdermabrasion, I applied a moisture mask. Miss Cantrell fell into a deep sleep before I'd finished. The mask has to rest on her face for a full twenty minutes, so I used the time to call my mother from the kitchen."

He made a note. "How long where you gone?"

"About twenty minutes. When I returned and tried to remove the mask, I knew something had gone wrong. It shouldn't have dried to a rubbery crust."

"Could you explain what kind of products you used?"

She nodded. "There's seaweed and collagen powder. I added oatmeal and clay powder to bind it together, and of course, distilled water. I've used it many times and never had a problem before today. I must've mixed it incorrectly or one of the products came defective from the manufacturers."

"So you believe this was an accident caused by your negligence or the manufacturers?"

Suddenly Carla broke down, sobbing gently. "I can't...believe...this happened. I was...so careful."

Bradford scribbled in his notepad. He looked up, and his gaze roamed over each of us. "Did any of you witness any other person besides Miz Moody go into the facial room?"

"No," we all chorused.

He turned to me. "I understand you were first on the scene, Miz Claiborne. Tell me what happened, beginning when you were first notified of a problem in the facial room."

My tongue froze when he said my name in his husky, southern drawl. His powerful gaze clung to mine. Heat surged to my face as my internal thermostat shot up a few uncomfortable degrees. Deena shifted beside me.

He gave a slight frown. "Please answer the question."

I released a pent-up breath. "Mrs. Eisenberg was in my chair when Carla told me a mask was stuck to Scarlett's face."

"The time?"

"Approximately ten-twenty or so."

"Okay, what happened next?"

"Well, I immediately checked it out. I couldn't have Scarlett waking up with a mask stuck to her face. She didn't respond when I tried to wake her. I found a weak pulse and sent Carla to tell Deena to call 9-1-1. I started applying hot towels to soften the mask. I removed what I could and applied a cool towel to her face to soothe the blistered skin."

"All right, go on."

"There's nothing more to add. Officer Clark arrived and took over, and the paramedics soon after."

He studied me for several seconds and then turned back to Carla. "Could you tell me why, as a licensed aesthetician, you failed to try all ways to remove the mask, such as the hot compresses Miz Claiborne spoke of?"

"I panicked."

"A witness reported hearing an argument coming from the facial room," he continued without pause. "A woman allegedly threatened to kill the victim if she didn't back off from her husband. Would you have any knowledge of this?"

Carla sprang to her feet. "I…didn't…mean to…kill

her," she said in shallow, quick gasps. The color drained from her face, and she slumped to the floor, hitting her head on the edge of the coffee table.

Officer Clark rushed over from the reception desk to join the rest of us bending over the crumpled girl.

"Holly, get a wet cloth," I ordered sharply. "Carla, honey, wake up." I patted her pale cheeks.

"Who would've thought our little mouse capable of devouring the big, bad cat?" Anthony said.

"Shut up," I hollered. "Carla wouldn't harm a soul. Not on purpose."

"Maybe you should share your *true* feelings about Scarlett with the detective," Mandy Brown snipped at Anthony from her position on the floor beside Carla.

Anthony glared at our nail tech—his lips thinned into a tight, angry line. "And how many times have I heard you call her a man-stealing bitch?"

Antagonism spread like wildfire on a hot summer day. The other stylists joined in with their own negative responses.

Bradford yelled for quiet. "Clark, get a bus down here."

Deena climbed to her feet. "We've had a terrible shock." Her voice quivered with emotion. "We are all strung out and frightened by Scarlett's brutal murder."

"Deena!" I rose from the floor as if propelled by an explosive force, horrified that it might be murder. "Don't say another word."

"Keep quiet," Bradford ordered. "Go on, Miz Sinclair, and tell me why you suspect foul play."

Quiet stole over the room as the faint wailing of the ambulance grew stronger and the seconds ticked by. As soon as the moment presented itself, I was gonna give my sister an earful. To suggest to a homicide cop that Scarlett's death had been anything other than an accident was asking for more trouble than we already had.

Thank God, help arrived before Deena could do further damage. Several police officers joined Officer Clark, and we sat silently as the paramedics checked Carla's vitals. After several minutes of working on her, they told Bradford she would be transported to the emergency room for treatment.

"Jolene."

I spun around in the direction of Deena's soft voice, bristling like a porcupine. "Thanks to your big mouth, the police are going to think one of us killed her."

"Well, one of us did," Billie Jo said as they loaded Carla onto a stretcher. "I knew something was gonna happen sooner or later. That girl shouldn't be mixin' so many products together. This isn't a chemist's lab, you know."

Anthony snickered. "So you're psychic now?"

Billie Jo flushed. "Pack up your things, Anthony—you're fired." Her expression made it clear we dared not oppose her decision.

There was a chorus of enthusiastic assent from the staff. Anthony Vogel wasn't well-liked among his peers. His competitive nature made him obnoxious, overbearing, and nasty even as he declared his innocence of ever stealing another stylist's client. Which he did on a regular basis.

The EMTs carried Carla out of the salon. Another officer came from the back of the shop, camera in hand. "CSU is finished in the facial room. The area is taped off and secure."

Bradford nodded. "I need everyone's attention, please."

Our gazes fastened once more on him, but not before we exchanged anxious glances.

"We're moving this party to the station where you will be fingerprinted and questioned further. I know I can count on your cooperation."

Loud moans sprang up from the staff at his unwelcome announcement.

"We can answer any questions you might still have right here," I protested. "Please don't drag us down to the station."

"Until an autopsy is performed to determine the cause of death, and all questions answered to my satisfaction, this case will be handled as a homicide. The salon is closed until further notice."

My stomach bottomed out at the thought of further financial losses. "You can't do that," I said in a defiant tone. "This will kill our business. We're barely hanging on."

He slipped on his Stetson. "I have a job to do."

Curious stares from the windows of the adjoining shops followed us as my sisters and I were handed into the back of a squad car. Envisioning tongues on fire regarding our entourage, I shot Deena an I'm-gonna-kill-you-the-first-chance-I-get look. Dang, if the rest of the day continued on the same path, I might end up behind bars for committing murder after all.

Chapter Four
Mama Ain't Happy

"Stop, I say! I want to talk with my daughters," a woman hollered out as we entered the police station.

I turned around at the sound of Mama's voice, speechless as she sashayed toward us in a costume from the 1930's era. The vintage ensemble consisted of tea length, black lace over a satin dress, a large black velvet hat with an ostrich plume and veil, black stockings, black patent leather shoes, and the long, fat string of black pearls Daddy had given her on their tenth wedding anniversary.

Deena groaned. "What's Mama doing here?"

"How'd she find out is what I'd like to know," I said.

"I called and left a message on her cell phone earlier," Billie Jo said. "She must have come straight here from dress rehearsal. Riverside Theater is putting on *Arsenic and Old* Lace in November. For the Pecan Festival." She continued to rattle on in spite of the scowl I directed at her. "Oh, by the way, Deena, Sam isn't wearing a wedding ring."

"You're babbling," I said.

"I'm nervous."

A door across the hall opened. Bradford stepped out. "What's the holdup, Clark?"

The officer pointed over his shoulder. "It's their

mother. She wants to talk to 'em."

"Oh, dear God, what's next?" Bradford moaned as Mama barreled her way through the others until she stood toe to toe with him, cocked her head sideways, and lifted the sheer veil to study him with brilliant green eyes.

"Is that you, Samuel Bradford? Why you grew up into a real good-lookin' man, I must say. Could you spare a moment of your time?"

"I'm always at your service, Mrs. Tucker."

Mama giggled and fluttered her eyelashes like a schoolgirl with a teenage crush. "I didn't expect to see you when I came down here to assist my daughters in their unfortunate incarceration."

"No one's being incarcerated, ma'am," Bradford said. "Your lovely daughters, and their staff, are here to answer some questions regarding an incident at their salon. Nothing more. As soon as that's done to my satisfaction, they're free to leave."

"I'm beholden to you," she said. "You know that they really are good Southern girls. It's just sometimes," Mama paused to look at us with a pained expression, "they act like they checked their common sense out at the library." Here she bowed her head, ostrich feather dipping gracefully. "Deena sure showed a lack of judgment when she dumped you back in high school."

Deena flushed beet red. "Mama, everyone can hear you."

Bradford threw an amused look at us, tucking Mama's hand in the crock of his arm. "Don't you worry, Miz Tucker. You can wait in my office while Officer Clark escorts the girls down to the interview rooms. They won't be long, and then you can take them home. I'll personally escort you to be fingerprinted."

"And why would I need to be fingerprinted? I wasn't even there," she purred softly, deceptively. I knew she wouldn't relish being fingerprinted, even by this great big hunk of a man who had the ability to make a woman wish his blue eyes were smiling down on her.

"They will be compared against the prints taken at the salon," I heard him say. "We wouldn't want to drag you back down here for that. I'm thinking of your comfort."

"Should I contact the family attorney?"

"It's not necessary, but if it would make you feel better, then by all means do so."

"Since you explain it like that, I'm all yours. Now could I bother you for a cup of coffee?"

"It'll be my pleasure, ma'am."

"Are you married? Deena's divorced now."

I rolled my eyes at Mama's audacity and watched in silence as she disappeared down the hall on the arm of the detective, her giggles echoing behind her. Yep, those apron strings were being tied tighter than Dick's hat band.

"God, what a performance," Billie Jo said. "Mama's a fine actress. No wonder she landed the role."

Leaning over closer to Deena, I whispered, "I'm sorry she embarrassed you in front of the others. If he's still single, she'll have him calling you for a date. You know how determined she can be when she sets her mind to something."

"Oh, I hope not," Deena whispered back. "I lied

about dumping Sam all those years ago. He dumped me."

I patted her arm in sympathy. "He's a good guy for not speaking up. If he calls, it might be kind of fun to go out on a date with him for old time's sake."

She giggled. "He is dreamy, isn't he?"

Officer Clark poked me in the arm. "Sorry to interrupt, but the detectives don't like to be kept waiting."

He led us down the hallway to a small waiting room. "Have a seat. Officer Graham will be right in to escort each of you to the interrogation rooms. Miz Claiborne, you come with me."

I followed him to a room where a squat, overweight, middle-aged man with watery brown eyes and meaty features stood up when I entered and introduced himself as Detective Larry Grant. I disliked him on sight. Sitting down in the chair he pulled out for me, I tried not to wrinkle up my nose as the scent of coffee and stale cigarettes drifted over me. He offered me a glass of water and pushed it across the table to me when I accepted.

As I fidgeted in my chair, uncertain what to expect, the detective raked his hand through thinning hair and opened a file. Once every few seconds, his liquid gaze lifted from the report to eye me across the table with speculation before dropping back down to whatever the page detailed. The plunging neckline of my blue-jean dress acted like a magnet for the creepy detective's swimming eyes.

Finally, he pulled out a pen and legal pad. "Now, give me your account of the incident this morning in your salon."

"But I've already given my statement to Officer Clark and been questioned by Detective Bradford," I complained, wanting to get out of this room and away from him.

He tapped the file folder. "I've read their reports. I want to hear it again—only this time from you."

I saw no way to avoid the question. "Would you like me to start with the break-in?"

"The report is here in front of me. I'm interested in what happened afterward."

Giving him the condensed version of my morning, I started with the staff meeting, the awkward exchange between Anthony and Scarlett, her confrontation with Cherry, the mayor and his wife, and ended with Carla showing up at my station requesting help with a problem in the facial room.

"Do you have any knowledge of the victim's relationship with the aforementioned persons? Any reason why there'd be hard feelings?"

"No, I have no such knowledge." I did, but let the detective do his own detective work. Besides, my opinion hadn't changed. Once an ass, always an ass.

"How long was Miz Moody into the service before you were aware of the problem?"

"I'm not sure. Carla marked out a ninety minute block of time for Scarlett's facial starting at nine-thirty. Scarlett arrived around nine. She likes to have a cup of hot herbal tea before her appointment. Holly wasn't available, so I made the tea and served it about nine-fifteen. It was around ten-twenty when Carla showed up at my station frantic about the mask stuck to Scarlett's face. I remember the time because I was finishing up with Mrs. Eisenberg's roller set."

The pencil stopped. "Explain 'stuck'."

I thought about it for a moment. "According to Carla, the moisture mask contains seaweed, collagen, oatmeal, and clay powder mixed together with distilled water. It lifts from the skin after it completely cools, but for some reason, this one wouldn't. She said it was as hard as cement. I was able to remove the mask from Scarlett's face with hot, steamed towels."

He raised a bushy eyebrow. "Carla Moody is a licensed aesthetician, correct? Why didn't she know to do the same?"

"She told Detective Bradford that she panicked."

His line of questioning changed. "What kind of relationship did she have with the victim?"

"That's a question for her," I said. "But I assume she maintained a professional relationship with her clients. In the time that she's worked for us, I've never heard a negative word come from her regarding any of the clientele, including Scarlett. Carla is a happily married woman with two adorable children. She's a good person."

"And your relationship with the victim?"

"I tolerated her," I answered truthfully. "Scarlett is the reason my sister is divorced. An adulterous affair, to be precise. Scarlett seduced Calvin." A flicker of interest came into his watery eyes. "Having said that let me assure you, neither me, nor my family had anything to do with this unfortunate accident," I emphasized. "Deena exacted her revenge in good old-fashioned greenbacks. In the divorce, she got the house, half of Calvin's retirement, child support, and alimony. And when Dixieland Salon landed a contract with WXYB to provide beauty services for their newest star, the free advertising brought in new business. So you see, Detective, Scarlett was worth more to us alive."

He scribbled something on his legal pad. "You were in the room alone with the victim?"

"Yes, I remained with Scarlett while Carla left to alert Deena to call 9-1-1."

"You told Detective Bradford that she had a weak pulse when you checked her upon entering the facial room. Was she able to communicate with you at all during this time?"

Closing my eyes, I thought back until a faint memory surfaced. My eyes snapped open. "Yes, she thought someone was trying to kill her. She asked me to find the jade elephant."

He gave me a long, searching look before asking, "Do you have any knowledge of this 'jade elephant'?"

"None whatsoever."

He slid paper and pencil across the table. "Okay. Can you sketch out the salon with everyone in his or her place? Including clients?"

Reluctantly, for I'm no artist, I drew a rough draft, placing the staff and clients where I'd last seen them. I slid the finished drawing across the table.

Grant surveyed my sketch while scribbling notes. Finally, he looked up. "Thank you for coming in. You're free to leave now, but keep yourself available for further questioning."

I made it to the door before the memory of this morning's break-in resurfaced. "Wait a minute." I swung around to face him. "What if this morning's burglary was a cover-up?" I hurried back to the table. "You know, for the real reason? What if the mask was sabotaged? Maybe someone has a grudge against the salon and wanted an accident to bankrupt us. What if one of the staff, or my sisters and I, were the real targets and Scarlett got offed instead?"

"I've gone over the report personally with the responding officers, and I can't see a connection between a minor burglary and Miss Cantrell's death. I remind you of the recent break-in of the establishment next door to your salon."

I started to protest, but he held up his hand to silence me.

"Listen to me good, Miz Claiborne. The official statement you and your sisters gave stated nothing was taken or disturbed other than the money from the register."

His dismissal of my theory annoyed me. But what if my reasoning had merit? I shivered at the thought of a faceless person, or persons, out for revenge against me, my family, or even my staff and clients. Instead of Scarlett lying dead in the morgue, it could've been one of us.

"But what about the thousand dollar deposit left in Deena's unlocked office desk drawer? If it was a simple burglary, why was it overlooked?" I tried to sound casual.

Grant leaned back in his chair, fitting his hands together. "Teenagers broke into your salon. Before they could search the office, they were spooked by passing car lights or something of that nature. Don't go scaring yourself or others with tales of conspiracy. Unless something unexpected turns up in the autopsy, or in the samples taken from the facial room, this is going to be a classic case of accidental death in my professional opinion."

I stared at him in hostile silence, considering the possibility that I could be wrong. This cop had years of investigative experience under his belt. As for me, the only crime I could solve was fixing others' mistakes when they attempted to cut and color their own hair.

****

Mama was wiping fingerprint ink from her stained fingers when we joined her in the front waiting room of the station. Her green gaze narrowed in on me. "I want to let you girls know how upset I am with the present state of affairs. How did this happen, Jolene?" Her voice raised a notch. "Murder! What are people going to say when word gets out?"

"Please stop saying murder. We'll talk about this later when we don't have an audience," I said, angry with her questions after what I'd been through with Detective Bulldog Grant.

Billie Jo touched Mama's shoulder. "Who cares what anyone thinks or says?"

"I care. You should too. This scandal could do irreparable damage to the salon, not to mention our reputations."

"I don't give a hoot about our social acceptance," Billie Jo retorted.

"No one asked you," Deena snapped back. "I agree with Mama. We have a reputation to protect."

As the middle sister, I knew Deena enjoyed being the center of attention, a place usually occupied by me, as the eldest, or Billie Jo, as the baby of the family. Daddy had treated us all the same, but Mama wore blinders when she looked at Billie Jo, which accounted for our fierce competitive nature. There were times when I was tempted to shine the spotlight on my baby sister's earlier explorations off the path of proper Southern manners, but since my own past was littered with questionable behavior, I decided that now wasn't the time or place for such enlightenment.

I stepped in between them. "Y'all are both right, but we really should be getting outta here." Tilting my head toward Dixieland's staff listening to every word, I visualized the wheels turning in Anthony's head as he soaked in tidbits of information to be sold or bargained off to the highest bidder. Since he'd come to work for us, I learned how much he prided himself in his ability to bounce out of bad situations with his pockets padded. Recognizing this repulsive personality trait, I'd hesitated reprimanding him because he was one of Whiskey Creek's most sought after stylists. Women loved him, and his appointment book showed it. Too bad Billie Jo had fired him. Replacing him and his clientele was downright unthinkable in this economy. The salon desperately needed the greenbacks this silver-tongued devil brought in.

"I'm in the mood to shop," Mandy said. "Can I catch a ride back to the salon with you?"

Was she kidding? Shopping? After what we'd been through? Mandy must have a heart of stone to be unaffected by Scarlett's untimely demise. Casting a dubious look at her, I thought about my earlier suspicions of a faceless person harboring a grudge against us personally or the salon. Could the despicable individual be one of the staff?

"I'm parked close by. There's plenty of room for everybody." Mama's voice dispelled my thoughts for the moment.

Deena's cell phone rang, and she moved a short

distance away to speak in private. A minute or two passed before she rejoined us.

"That was the hospital. Carla's being admitted for a psych evaluation," she said. "When she regained consciousness in the emergency room, she was confused and delusional. She also suffered a concussion from the fall. She's been sedated and is resting now, but they haven't been able to reach her husband. My number was listed as her work contact, so they called me to see if I could come down to the admitting office and bring her insurance information."

"Poor child needs her mother at a time like this," Mama said, pulling out her cell phone and scrolling down her list of contacts. "Beth Stevens is on a committee with me at church. I'll see if I can reach her."

After several unanswered rings, she left a short message for Beth to call her as soon as possible, leaving out any information which might cause the woman unnecessary worry.

"Can we leave now?"

We turned at Holly's voice and followed Mama out to her SUV. She drove to the salon and pulled into the crowded parking lot, staring for several seconds through the plate glass window at the empty salon that should've been open for business.

The employees were anxious to leave, so Deena instructed them to check with her on Monday evening as she was unsure just how long the police intended to keep the salon closed for the investigation. They agreed and climbed into their cars, driving off in different directions.

After the employees scattered for the weekend,

Deena turned to Mama. "Do you suppose it would be all right to inspect the shop? It won't take but a minute. I'm sure they left a mess, and it'll need to be cleaned before we reopen."

Mama vetoed the suggestion. "Sam gave me strict instructions to stay out of the salon. He promised to do everything in his power to have us back in business on Tuesday. Besides, there isn't time. We need to get over to the hospital."

"We need to be sure the electric appliances have been turned off and unplugged for the weekend," Deena cautioned. "They are the first thing the stylists turn on in the morning after they arrive. Those flat irons can start an electrical fire if they short out. It won't take but a second to double check. The last thing we need on top of everything else is a fire."

"Deena's right, we need to inspect the salon," I added to the argument. "If we don't, I won't be able to sleep a wink for worrying."

Mama started to protest, but Billie Jo cut in, wiping perspiration from her upper lip. "Let's get on with it. It's hot as Hades out here, and I'm thirsty. There's a pitcher of sweet tea in the refrigerator."

"Oh, all right," Mama finally conceded. "But hurry up. You have five minutes to do your inspection."

Deena dug keys out of her purse, unlocked the door, and led the way inside. Eerie silence greeted us as the outside sounds of cars speeding by and shoppers chatting ceased when the front door closed behind us.

Mama glanced at her watch. "Make it quick."

From where I stood in the reception area everything appeared normal, other than the polished hardwood floors needing to be swept from all the extra traffic and the hand-smudged mirrors in the make-up section needing cleaning. The retail shelves stocked with all the best-selling, name brand hair products were all in order. Nothing seemed amiss. At the reception desk, the computer had been left on, so I turned it off as Billie Jo headed in the direction of her barber station, saying she would inspect all the workstations. Deena headed into her office, and Mama shuffled off in the direction of the kitchen.

The facial room pulled at me like a magnet. Where did the human life energy go after departing this life? Could Heaven and Hell truly be our last destination, or could we linger here trapped in the last peaceful or hellish moments of our life? Thoughts like these had troubled me since Daddy died. For years afterward, I'd studied books on the afterlife, religious teachings from various faiths, the great philosophers, the occult, and even the ancient alien theorists, always trying in vain to contact him.

This morning's strange incident at the cemetery resurfaced. I removed the yellow crime-scene tape, the door vibrating under my hands. Call it déjà vu or precognition, but I suddenly *knew* something monumental waited on the other side. Slowly, I turned the knob. The hairs on my nape prickled as a voice whispered in my ear, "You can't go in there."

I snatched my hand from the door knob. "Crap, Deena, you scared the hell outta me. Must you sneak around?"

"I never sneak. You simply weren't listening."

The kitchen door swung open. Mama stood in the doorway. "What's going on out here? Stop horsing around. Go find Billie Jo. I'm ready to leave."

"Jolene's going in there." Deena jerked her thumb toward the closed facial room door.

Billie Jo rounded the corner. "What's all the commotion?"

"Jolene's going in there," Deena repeated.

"No, she's not," Mama said. "The police will accuse us of tampering with evidence. We'll go in when Sam gives the okay."

"We can't leave before making sure that multi-function Skin Care Station is properly shut off," I said. "It cost over fifteen hundred dollars."

"No one's going in there," Mama huffed. "Got it?"

Billie Jo reached out and tested the knob. "It's locked anyway."

"That's strange. It wasn't a moment ago," I said, twisting the knob to find it locked. "Go get the key, Deena."

"We lost the key years ago."

"Wait," I said, excitedly. "I'll get a butter knife from the kitchen." I turned to leave, but Mama grabbed me by the arm, causing me to stumble against the door. With a thump, it flew open, propelling me into the room. As I stumbled for balance, something white fluttered in the semi-darkness. Regaining my balance, I quickly flipped on the overhead lights before Mama could protest.

"Ahhh!" I said with vexation, my eyes taking in the discarded jars lining the counter top. A dusting of fine powder covered the floor. "This room's a mess. It'll take hours to clean."

"They must've taken a sample of everything." Deena piped up behind me. "What's on the floor?"

Billie Jo bent down and ran her finger over the

floor, leaving a thin trail. "It looks like oatmeal. Carla said she mixed everything she could get her hands on into that death mask."

Mama stuck her head in the door. "Don't touch anything and get out of there right now. We need to get over to the hospital. Jolene, if you don't come out of there this instant, I promise you that when the roll is called up yonder, you'll be there!"

Deena backed out of the room. "She's right; the hospital is expecting me."

"I'm ready to leave, too," Billie Jo said, joining Mama and Deena in the hallway.

There wasn't any need to try and argue my point with them—my vote would be vetoed immediately. The facial equipment was unplugged, so I turned off the lights and shut the door. A loud crash sounded from inside the room. Quickly, I flung open the door, flipped on the overhead lights, and screamed with every ounce of my being—for there, on the facial bed, sat the faint, ghostly image of Scarlett Cantrell.

Chapter Five
Earthbound

"Scarlett?" I yelled out, all at once frightened and excited. The moment I'd been hoping for since my father's death had suddenly presented itself. But instead of Daddy's ghostly image, Scarlett smiled back at me, red slippers swinging happily over the side of the bed, hands posed serenely in a lap of white cotton organdy.

Okay. This was really getting weird. First, Granny Tucker's voice in the cemetery, and now I was seeing ghosts. Not altogether sure I wasn't hallucinating from tremendous strain, I checked my pulse to rule out the possibly of an anxiety attack. Blinking several times didn't make Scarlett go away, so I concluded that, yes, I'd either had a nervous meltdown or I had finally broken through to the Other Side.

"What's going on in there?" Mama hollered from the doorway.

Scarlett brought her fingers to her lips. "Shhh, they can't see or hear me—only you."

"Why am I the only one who can see you?" I whispered.

She pointed heavenward. "I don't know. I'll ask next time I go up there."

I turned to my mother and sisters. "You don't see her? Hear her?"

"Who?" they asked in unison.

"Scarlett! She's sitting on the facial bed talking to me."

"Stop joking and come out of there," Mama ordered.

"I'm not joking."

Deena groaned. "Jolene's lost her mind."

"No, she had imaginary friends as a child," Mama said. "Perhaps the stress brought on a relapse. Jolene, honey, you come on out of there, and we'll take you home. Rest will get rid of those invisible people."

Well, that explained a lot. I grinned at the impact of her words. At least I wasn't crazy, which was a relief.

"Or a shot of tequila," Billie Jo added.

"Hush," Mama admonished. "Your sister is just traumatized by that poor woman's death. I told y'all this was a bad idea."

I turned at the sound of rustling petticoats as Scarlett climbed off the bed, smoothing down yards of ruffles and lace.

"Do you recognize the gown I'm wearing? It's the prayer dress Vivien Leigh wore in the opening porch scene in the movie." She spun around, smiling gleefully at her flying skirts. "I always wanted to be like her. Can you believe she loaned it to me? We're neighbors on the Other Side, you know. In the south side of heaven," she twittered. "Hey, I think I'll modernize the dress. You know, raise the hem, and lose the petticoats. Add a few tucks here and there. And new red heels would be perfect, don't you agree?"

"Deena's right. I'm losing my mind," I said out loud. Heaven is not where I expected her to end up. "This is definitely not the Scarlett Cantrell I knew and despised. Why don't you be gone with the wind of my imagination?"

Scarlett lost her smile. "Just pretend I'm one of your imaginary friends. Things are different over here, and I'm new at this, so don't push me, or I'll make your life miserable. And I *ain't* gonna be gone with the wind as you so put it, missy, so you'd better watch it."

I shivered as a shaft of icy air goosed me, and I made the sign of the cross over my heart for protection. Not being Catholic, I wasn't sure it would help, but the unholy expression on Scarlett's face left me with few options, and I wasn't taking any chances with the ghost of a dead client.

"Jolene, get out of there right this instant, or I'll come in and get you myself."

Still dazed, I jumped back from the facial bed at Mama's angry voice and stumbled toward the door, my gaze glued to Scarlett, who continued to scowl at me.

"Where do you think you're going?" Her tone deepened with anger. "Help me find justice, or I'm earthbound."

"Did you say earthbound?" My head started to throb. Oh, great, now I had a headache coming on.

"Yes, and you're the one I'm stuck with."

Her words died away as I ducked out the door, closing it softly behind me to face my anxious family. Mama grabbed me by the arm.

"I don't want you to worry about what you think you saw, Jolene. Let's get over to the hospital. While we're checking on Carla, it wouldn't hurt for a doctor to take a look at you. Sometimes there's a delayed reaction to trauma." She hauled me out of the salon and placed me in the front passenger seat of her SUV.

I spent the entire ten minutes as we drove to the hospital convincing Mama and my sisters that I didn't require medical attention. Only a passing anxiety attack, I assured them, was to blame for my neurotic behavior. They finally seemed to accept my explanation and left me alone with my swirling thoughts. And I mean swirling. I felt like a hen with a rooster hot on my tail. I clung to my shaky composure, hoping that nothing of what I felt, thought, showed in my expression. Unfortunately, I wear my heart on my sleeve.

My watch read four when we stopped at the information desk and asked for Carla's room number.

"Mrs. Moody is in room two-eleven," the courteous young woman said, directing us to a nearby elevator.

The corridor teemed with hospital staff and visitors, and when the elevator doors opened, we scooted in together. I'm sure doubt still lingered concerning my state of mind, and I could just bet that, at this moment, Mama and my two loving siblings were watching for the slightest hint of a relapse from me. I stepped confidently off the elevator when we reached the second floor.

Muffled voices resonated behind Carla's closed door as we approached.

"Probably the doctor," Billie Jo said.

Deena paused before entering the room. "Or the admitting clerk wanting her insurance information."

A passing nurse stopped in front of our group. "May I help you?"

"We're waiting to see Carla Moody," I said. "We didn't want to barge in if the doctor is with her, but we brought the health insurance information the admitting office needs."

"Her visitor is a police detective."

"Perhaps we should visit with her later," Mama suggested.

Deena backed away from the door. "Can you tell us how she's doing before we leave?"

The nurse opened the door. "I just gave her a mild sedative, but you can go on in. Her family should be with her while that detective is interrogating her."

"We're not her family."

Mama shot Billie Jo a heated look. "We're the closest thing to family that child has until her husband and mother can be reached."

The nurse eyed us closely. "Five minutes." She preceded us into the room. "Mrs. Moody, you have more visitors." She reached over to smooth the covers down before turning her attention to the man beside the patient's bed. "Your time's up, sir."

The notebook snapped shut as the man turned around. Detective Grant. Carla's teary face spoke volumes.

"You have no right to question her without her doctor or attorney present," I said hotly. "She's had a terrible shock and doesn't realize what she's saying." Those watery brown eyes raked over me.

"Miz Moody is aware of her rights," he said in a tone of voice one might use to reprimand a disobedient child. "I'm here in an official capacity. Stand down or I'll arrest you for interfering in a police investigation."

Rebellion runs deep in my blood. My family can be traced back to a long line of Confederate fighters— male and female. Nothing garners my defiance more than a man trying to intimidate a woman. Apparently, this bulldog of a man disliked me. The feeling was mutual but I couldn't afford to further antagonize him. No, better to bide my time and wait for another opportunity to put the detective in his place. Taking a deep breath, I said, "Sorry. I overreact in times of stress."

Mumbled agreements sounded behind me. Mama walked over to the bed and picked up Carla's hand, rubbing it briskly to restore warmth.

"Pay no attention to all this fuss, honey. Everything's gonna be all right. I've called and left several messages on your mom's home and cell phone. Deena hasn't been able to reach your husband at home, and we don't have his cell number."

Carla turned drugged eyes to Mama. "Frank and I are having marital problems. He and the kids are in Florida for a couple of days."

Hmm. That explained a lot—the weird phone calls, her inattention to her job, the weight loss, her weepy appearance, and her inability to think on her feet. Carla's domestic problems had turned into the perfect storm and resulted in Scarlett's messed-up face and premature death.

Quietly, the nurse slipped past the bed, gestured to Detective Grant, and together they left the room.

Gathering around in a show of support, we each in turn picked up a weak, limp hand, encouraging Carla to remain calm. As her thin, icy fingers closed over mine, I stared down at her pale, strained face, assuring her we would be there for her in her time of trouble.

Her dazed eyes focused over my shoulder. "Scarlett. Oh my God." She began to shake uncontrollably. "I didn't mean to kill her!"

"Hush now, honey. Everything's gonna be okay," Mama said, and with a wave of her hand pushed me out of the way to sit on the bed.

"God, help me," Carla cried. "I killed her!"

At her wild, terror-filled words, my nape hairs rose, and I got goose bumps.

Deena's gaze met mine across the bed. "I'd better go get a nurse."

"I told you we shouldn't have hired her," Billie Jo said, staunchly moving toward the door. "You stay here; I'll get the nurse. I need a breather."

A ghostly breath brushed my neck, alerting me to Scarlett's unwelcome presence. Anxious to get away from prying eyes and talk with my ghostly tag-a-long, I said, "No, Billie Jo, I'll go. Deena, give me the insurance card, and I'll take it down to admitting after alerting the nurses to the problem in here."

Deena fished the card out of her wallet and handed it to me. Without waiting for further comments from the others, I darted into the hall. Three nurses congregated around a massive desk down the corridor, and I explained the situation. Two nurses rushed to Carla's room while the other paged the doctor. Using the distraction to slip away, I stepped into an empty room, closed the door, and turned to face the ghostly pest who had trailed after me.

"Please tell me that I'm hallucinating," I said.

"Just think of me as one of your imaginary friends."

I frowned at her snarky tone. "Okay, you've got my attention. Start explaining what you're doing here and why you scared the bejesus out of me in the facial room. I don't like being threatened—by the living or the dead."

Scarlett struck a haughty pose in a form-fitting, above the knee, green flowered muslin dress. "This is the afternoon gown Vivien wore in the barbecue scene at Twelve Oaks. Of course, I put my own modern touch on it."

I reached for her arm but encountered only empty space. "Yes, I can see your hatchet work. Now, tell me why you're still here. Don't you see the light? You know, the one that you're supposed to cross, or whatever it is you're supposed to do when you bite the dust?"

Her perfect eyebrows pulled together in an affronted frown. "I see you've forgotten my warning. And FYI, I do see the light." She adjusted the wide-brimmed straw hat with green ribbons tied under her chin. "Vivian wasn't wearing it to the Chancellor's Ball, so she said I could borrow the dress. You should see the size of her closet."

"Never mind Vivian's closet. Why don't you stay over there with all the other hellions?"

"I told you, I'm earthbound."

"Then how'd you get the dress?"

"I have a travel visa."

"What on earth is a travel visa?"

"Not on earth. The Other Side. A travel visa allows me to pass between dimensions until my celestial trial is over. Which begins in two weeks, so I don't have much time to investigate my death."

Now I really was confused. "Celestial trial? This is the first I'm hearing of a celestial trial. And you're not earthbound, so scoot."

"I told you about the trial. Earlier, in the facial room."

I shook my head. "Ah, I don't think so. I believe I would remember you mentioning something so crazy."

"I need information. Fast."

I sighed. "It seems to me that the powers that be would have the information you're seeking. They have a bullseye view of everything happening down here on this blue rock, so they would know all about it."

Sighing dramatically, Scarlett untied the ribbons, removed the hat, and tucked several dark strands back into a perfect chignon. "I know who killed me, smarty-pants, but Carla Moody isn't the one on trial. Heaven's Department of Corrections has the idea that I wasn't a nice person during my lifetime. They want to know why she killed me."

"Probably for the same reason half the women in this town wanted to get rid of you," I reasoned.

"For gracious sakes, I wasn't that bad."

"Yeah, right. You spread a path of pain and destruction as wide as an eight lane highway through downtown Atlanta. Considering your record, I'm surprised they allowed you even temporary entrance through the pearly gates."

"You're still upset about my part in Deena and Calvin's divorce, aren't you? I tried to give him back, but Deena didn't want him. And I said I was sorry."

"Please go away," I pleaded. "All I want is to get my life, and business, back to normal."

"I can't rest in peace with my eternal residence in question."

She looked so forlorn and dismal sitting there fingering the altered gown that I seriously considered her request, knowing one's eternal resting place was mighty important here in the South. Most Sunday sermons were dedicated to keeping us out of the hot seat and away from hell and damnation. As a result, I'd given my life to Jesus so many times that I'd learned to swim in the baptismal pool.

"Detective Grant believes your death was accidental, but I'm not so sure," I thought aloud. "I'm suspicious of the timing between this morning's break-in and your 'accident'."

"You've got to help me, Jolene. I have the best angel attorneys, but I have to do all the legwork. Kind of like what a private investigator would do. My abilities are really limited, you know."

We stared at one another in mutual consternation. Finally I said, "I'm a hairstylist, not a cop. I don't know the first thing about investigating—especially a *possible* homicide. And I mean possible homicide. Nothing's concrete at this point. I'm not sure what I can do to help."

"All you have to do is gather information. I promise you'll be safe. Besides, what about that gun you carry?"

I gnawed on my bottom lip. "In light of this morning's events, I'm inclined to disagree with your reasoning. Pokin' a stick at a hornet's nest is liable to be dangerous. Mini Pearl is strictly for self-protection. However, I do have a lot of questions. And I don't believe Carla is capable of murder."

"Thank you. You won't regret helping me."

"I'm not doing this for you, Scarlett. I have my own reasons for digging into this. Mama took out a second mortgage on the farm to finance our business.

There's a lot more at stake than your eternal residence. But with the finger of suspicion pointing directly at one of my employees, well, if we lose the shop, we'll all be in a precarious financial position."

Scarlett leaned closer to peer intensely into my face. "There's one more thing I need to mention. If I lose my case, Dixieland Salon will become my permanent place of residence."

I sputtered with indignation as her misty figure began to evaporate. "Wait. Come back here. I'm not finished! Have you seen Daddy over there?"

Looking about the empty hospital room, I dismally shook my head. How could I convince my sisters to help me investigate Scarlett's death? Billie Jo, always on the lookout for adventure, would be the easiest to persuade. Deena, unfortunately, was another story altogether. The only spark of adventure I'd seen in her had been when Bradford strode through the front door of the salon and fastened those glorious blue eyes on her.

"That's it. I can use him as bait," I said aloud. "If it works, I can have access to the case."

Patting myself on the back for my quick thinking, I made my way into the corridor and down to the admitting office where I dropped off Carla's insurance information to a harried clerk, and rushed back to the second floor.

Mama and my sisters were waiting for me outside in the hall when I walked up.

"I'm sorry it took me so long, but I ran into a lot of traffic downstairs. How's Carla?"

Mama, clearly upset, said, "They're going to move her to the psych floor for her own safety. The doctor is with her now. That poor child needs her mother. I don't understand why Beth isn't returning my calls."

"She may be out of town," Deena suggested.

"Even if she is, wouldn't she respond to the voice mails on her phone?" I asked.

"Not if she's in an area without service," Billie Jo put in. "Roddy runs into the same problem when he's working on projects way out in the country."

"Well, until she's reached, we'll take turns checking on Carla," Mama said. "Let's go home. There's nothing more we can do here today."

Mama dropped us back at our cars at the salon. Waving goodbye, I pulled onto Dalton Road and headed in the direction of my house but decided at the last minute to detour over to the main library. Although snatches of memory from my childhood association with the dead had resurfaced, this job would require some research—a little refresher course to sharpen my skills.

The librarian shot me an aggravated look when I came through the double doors into the cool air-conditioned building. "We close in ten minutes."

"Can you tell me where to find books on mediums and the paranormal? Also on conducting investigations," I asked with a straight face.

The woman looked at me curiously but gave me explicit directions on where to find the books and again reminded me the library would close in ten minutes. With little time to waste, I located the section marked paranormal and found several interesting titles on mediums, psychics, and communicating with the dead. With the volumes tucked under my arm, I moved to the section containing police and private investigator manuals and selected *The Simpleton's Complete Manual to Private Investigating*. I checked out the books with a minute to spare and left the library with my weekend reading material with high hopes of solving Scarlett's murder and ridding myself of one pain-in-the-ass ghost.

Chapter Six
Post-Traumatic Murder Syndrome

My daughter's car was parked in the driveway when I pulled up to my house on Pinecone Lane. Weary and hungry, I parked under the carport and went inside through the kitchen door to find Becky eating pizza. My orange tabby cat, Tango, was chewing on a pilfered slice of pepperoni under the table.

Placing the books and my purse on the counter, I plopped down on a chair Becky pulled out for me. Kicking off my heels, I reached for the plate of pizza she pushed across the table.

"Wow, you look terrible," she said. "It's all over the news about Scarlett's death. Why didn't you call me? I would've come down to the salon."

I gazed at my twenty-year-old daughter, with her father's dark hair and my brown eyes, her rounded belly pushing against the edge of the table. "Now that you're in the last two weeks before your due date, I wouldn't have wanted you to be around the stress, honey."

"I'm fine, Mom. Oh, I forgot to tell you that Daddy called."

"What'd he want?" I asked with a mouthful of pizza. I got up and went to the refrigerator for a cold Coke and sat back down at the table.

"He wanted to know if you were still coming over to the barbeque tonight. Melinda is dying for you to meet her wealthy doctor cousin who came all the way from Savannah to make your acquaintance. Jacob is meeting me over there. Please say you'll come."

Kenny Claiborne and I had parted on good terms after fifteen rocky years of marriage. We'd married young, seventeen to be exact, and had become parents that same year. For Becky's sake, we'd given it our best but finally admitted we just didn't mesh, and he'd remarried last year to his attractive secretary. Through Becky, I found myself thrown together with them on many social occasions, and a friendship had developed between the three of us.

However, for some reason, Melinda had adopted me as her very own special matchmaking project. In her mind, I wouldn't be completely happy until I too had remarried. Thus, I'd been subjected to more blind dates than I could count. In short, I wasn't going to the barbeque.

"Your father and stepmother will understand if I skip the party, but I'm glad you stopped by. It's been a strange day."

"Do you want to talk about it?"

I took a sip of Coke. "No, I'd rather talk about you and your plans for nursing school. I know there's been a delay with the baby coming, but I don't want you to ignore your education."

Becky rubbed her swollen stomach. "I'm registered for the winter semester. Jacob's mother is going to watch the baby while I'm in school."

"Your mother-in-law is a sweetheart. You know I would do it if I could, and, well, even though I plan on spoiling my grandchild, I'm not the nanny type, like Ruth."

She nodded, bangs bobbing. "That's okay, Mom. My friends in high school envied me for having such a young, cool mother. I hope I can do as well with my child."

Basking in the warm glow my daughter's comment brought, I struggled to push back the weariness settling over me. Even after a ten-hour day at the salon with every bone aching, I hadn't felt this weary. This tiredness was different—stemming on the remembrance of every detail, the anxiety, especially the fear of Scarlett having being murdered. But most of all, the memory of her disembodied spirit drifted eerily in the back of my mind.

"Mom, you look tired. Not to mention worried," Becky said. "It would help if you told me about it. I insist."

Becky listened, not interrupting as I retold the horror of the morning's events, being hauled down to the police station to be questioned, seeing Scarlett's ghost, the disembodied voice in the cemetery, and lastly, the revelation of my childhood imaginary friends.

"It's all very simple, Mom. You have PTMS," she said after several silent minutes.

"That sounds awful. What's PTMS?"

"Post-Traumatic Murder Syndrome."

I laughed. Leave it to my crazy, wonderful daughter to simplify what I had previously perceived to be a life-changing encounter. The more I thought about it, the harder I laughed.

"No, Mom, I'm serious. There is such a thing as PTMS."

"You're pulling my leg."

"Look it up in the medical book I gave you for Christmas. I'll bet you'll find it referenced in there."

The pizza had cooled when I finally stopped laughing enough to take a bite. "The first page was so full of mumbo jumbo, I couldn't decipher it. I don't know why you gave it to me."

"You re-gifted it," Becky accused. "Who'd you give it to?"

I shrugged, feeling only a little guilty. "Your grandmother for her birthday."

"Mom, you didn't."

"I did."

Becky pressed a hand on the small of her back, sighing. "My back is killing me. Dr. Griffin suggested I use hot and cold packs to ease the discomfort until the baby is born."

"That's good advice," I said, rising from the table to retrieve the ice bag from the pantry. "I had back pain when I carried you. When is your next appointment?"

"Monday morning. You know, Mom, I don't know if I mentioned it to you but about three weeks ago, I witnessed a strange confrontation between Scarlett and the mayor's wife in my OB/GYN's office. Mrs. Payne appeared to be awfully angry with her. They were yelling at one another, and then Mrs. Payne grabbed her stomach. The nurses immediately rushed her to the back. Do you suppose that terrible scene could've contributed to her miscarriage a week later?"

I filled the bag with ice and handed it to her. "No. I don't believe so, honey. Do you know what they were arguing about?"

"No, but I got the impression that something bad had transpired between them."

Thinking back to the scene between the two women this morning in the salon, and the hostility radiating from Scarlett, I had to wonder why Linda had been so friendly. I would've ripped Scarlett's head off, but then again, I have an extremely different personality. Linda was a well-bred, proper society lady and I wasn't. I grew up on a peanut farm. I wore more dirt than clothes as a child.

"Not surprising. Scarlett was a heartless, self-centered woman," I said.

"I don't believe that. You have to look below the surface to see the hidden hurt. It's there, trust me."

"You're a wise and beautiful woman. You see sunshine when I see rain."

The phone rang, and Becky answered it, listened silently, her face wrinkling. "It's MeMaw," she said, her hand covering the receiver. "Why didn't you tell me she's expecting us for Easter dinner?"

"I forgot."

"Jacob's gonna be disappointed. He had other plans. Well, I guess we'll see you guys tomorrow." She said goodbye to her grandmother and handed me the phone. Then she leaned over to brush a light kiss across my forehead, grabbed her purse, and disappeared out the kitchen door.

"Hello," I said into the receiver.

"What took you so long? I was just about to hang up and call back. Becky's not very talkative. Is she feeling okay?"

"Becky's fine, just antsy. I'm sure you remember how uncomfortable pregnancy is."

"The memory has faded somewhat. Anyway, I just called to remind you about Easter dinner after church."

"Church is the last place I want to be tomorrow. I'll meet you at the house later."

"Aren't you feeling well?"

"Truthfully, I'm not in the mood for the stares and whisperings. Scarlett was a popular member, and the finger of blame will be pointed directly at us. I know these people. Someone heard it from so and so and then so and so tells this one, and before you know it the buzz is all over town."

"Don't be ridiculous." The words had an indignant ring. "If we don't show up, everyone will believe we've got something to hide. I know these people better than you, and I have a plan in mind to stop all gossip. You will be there along with your sisters. Understood?"

The call waiting signal beeped. "Hold on, Mama." Not waiting for her response, I hit the button and said hello.

"Hi," the deep voice rumbled over the line. "I hate to call you at the last minute."

Crap. I'd forgotten I had a date with Steve Elliott from singles class at church.

It was five forty-five, and I had just enough time to shower and change. "I'm looking forward to our date," I said in a light, carefree tone. What I didn't say was that all I wanted to do was shower, change into my pajamas, crawl into bed, and watch TV until I fell asleep. Going on a date was the last thing I was interested in after today's fiasco, no matter how sweet and handsome the guy. Bradford's face popped up. Shaking my head to mentally dispel the picture, I continued, "I'll be ready at six-thirty."

"Well, that's why I'm calling. Something's come up, and I can't make our date."

"What a shame. I hope everything is all right with your parents? Your kids?"

The reply was slow in coming. "They're fine. I just can't make our date."

"I suppose you heard the news about Scarlett?"

"Yeah, my mother was shopping in the boutique next door to your shop. Again, I'm sorry to break our date in this manner, but I'm sure you understand how it is when something unexpected comes up. I'm going out of town, so I won't see you at church in the morning."

Of course I understood. Steve wanted a polite excuse to back out of our date. He'd probably never ask me out again. I tried to analyze my feelings. Truthfully, I really didn't feel like going out tonight, but the rejection hurt nonetheless.

"Don't worry about it, Steve. I'm tired from being down at the jailhouse anyway. Have a safe trip."

I slammed down the receiver, went into the pantry, and found a box of Duncan Hines double chocolate cake mix. The phone rang. I ignored it, instinctively knowing it was Mama, angry that I'd hung up on her, but I wasn't in the mood for conversation.

The phone continued to ring as I mixed the cake, poured the batter into two round cake tins, and slipped them into the oven. While they were baking, I took a hot shower and dressed in loose pajamas. The oven timer buzzed just as I came into the kitchen, the delicious aroma of baking chocolate permeating the room. I dumped the warm cake halves on wire racks to cool and dug through the pantry for a can of ready-made chocolate fudge frosting behind a box of Cheerios.

I chopped a cup of pecans and frosted the still

warm cake, sprinkling lots of nuts between the layers and on top. Pouring a tall glass of milk, I sat down at the table and cut myself a large slice of the still warm cake. With the books I'd checked out from the library in front of me, I first chose the one entitled *The Science of the Soul and Communicating with the Dead* and began reading.

The book turned out to be fascinating, although some of the methods suggested for summoning spirits wouldn't work so well with Scarlett. For one, apparently she wasn't at my beck and call and would show up only when it suited her needs—not mine. Secondly, sitting cross-legged in the middle of the kitchen floor late at night with my eyes closed, calling out to the dead turned out to be a bad idea. Instead of attracting ghosts, I ended up with a cat in need of a manicure in my lap. Talk about having the bejesus scared out of me.

But on a happier note, by the time I climbed into bed, I had refreshed my understanding of the accumulated evidence of human souls and how mediums communicated with them. From the yellow pages, I'd located the phone number of Madame Mia, a local psychic medium/palm reader whose advertisement promised advice and help on all problems at a reasonable rate. First thing Monday morning, I'd drop in on her and see if she could give me some pointers on handling my wayward ghost. For a fifty dollar initial consultation fee, of course.

Also, I now had a working knowledge of basic private investigative skills thanks to the simpleton's guide from the library.

Oh, and I consumed half the damn cake and a quart

of milk, but I felt better and Steve Elliott was now a distant memory.

Chapter Seven
The Mole

Just as I had predicted, First Baptist Church was
packed the next morning. Evidently news of Scarlett's
death at our salon had spread through the large
congregation. Whispers of speculation began the instant
we entered the lobby. Mama, resplendent in a blue satin
pantsuit, led the way into the sanctuary with my sisters
and me close behind. Roddy and Lynette, Billie Jo's
husband and teenage daughter, brought up the rear. Of
course, smiles and nods greeted us down the aisle, but
as soon as we passed, the murmurs started anew.

"I never should've let Mama talk me into this.
Everyone's staring at us," I whispered as I sat down
between my sisters on the cushioned wooden pew.

They nodded in agreement.

"Let 'em stare," Billie Jo whispered back. Several
heads rotated quickly in the opposite direction when
they met her unflinching gaze.

"I'm embarrassed." Deena slumped down farther
on the pew. "I can just imagine what they're saying."

"Let 'em talk." Billie Jo's tone dripped with
sarcasm. "Everyone here has their own skeletons. Ours
just happens to be on display."

Every head in the congregation turned to stare at
us, some with pity, most with anger. From the
uncharitable comments I heard, the locals were

threshing the straw, so to speak, at our expense. Deena scrunched down as far as she could and buried her face into a hymnal, commenting to herself that this was most definitely a mistake. I shrugged. Really, I admired Billie Jo's gumption. Most people didn't realize her gruffness was meant to keep them at a distance. Billie Jo savored privacy.

Roddy reached over and laid his hand gently over hers, immediately defusing the situation.

"Sweetheart, stop fretting. We're all plagued with the human condition. They mean no harm. Take a deep breath and relax, love."

Billie Jo grasped his hand, smiling. "You're one in a million, and I'm a lucky woman. Now tell Lynette to stop texting until after the service."

The whispers stopped as the praise team mounted the steps leading into the choir loft. All heads turned toward the front as Pastor Inman stepped out from a side door and onto the pulpit platform. During the momentary quiet, I leaned over Deena's lap and tapped Mama's knee.

"Why are we really here?" I whispered.

"Damage control and information," was the whispered reply.

"Information on what?"

"Not what, dear. Whom."

"Stop with the grammar lesson. Just tell me."

She gave me a condensed version of her plan. "Now be quiet. Pastor Inman has taken his seat."

Sitting back in the pew, I contemplated all she'd told me. Her knowledge of private investigating was limited, to be sure. As was mine, but I'd skimmed through two books last night and had at least a smidgeon of familiarity on the subject. Mama's best bet in this crowd would be to tap into the gossip grapevine and see if anyone was in the mood to talk.

As the hour progressed, I dutifully sang each song, listened without hearing the long sermon, and watched without seeing the sinners answer the altar call, while each person in sight came under my questioning scrutiny.

Finally church ended. The doors opened, allowing the warm, humid air in and churchgoers out. A crowd had gathered on the front lawn when we emerged. Mama made a beeline to a large woman extravagantly dressed in a billowing caftan which appeared to be made out of several layers of soft, shiny silk, each layer a different pastel color. I immediately thought of the Butterfly House at Calloway Gardens. Had one of the glorious specimens escaped and flown south? But as we drew closer, I recognized Diane Downey, *grande dame* of Whiskey Creek's elite citizens. She was president of the Women's League, First Baptist Church Ladies Auxiliary, and a number of other higher establishments I couldn't name.

"Diane, darling, where did you find that sumptuous dress? I know you didn't buy it here in town," Mama gushed.

The woman beamed. "Pierre's in Atlanta. It's a copy from Hollywood."

"It can't be. You look glorious. I'm so jealous. Not every woman can carry off your unique fashion style. Right, girls?"

The matronly socialite grabbed Mama in a bear hug, burying her in yards of the flowered silk tent. Curious as to Mama's method of extraction, I didn't have long to wait before she emerged from the depths of the dress, looked morosely at her friend and said, "Have you heard the dreadful news?" She paused and then glanced at us, her three daughters, one granddaughter, and a fidgeting son-in-law. "We're devastated by the tragedy."

As if on cue, we all appeared miserable and down-hearted.

"Oh, you poor dears," Diane said. "Kayla Winston told me last night. Her husband's the coroner, you know. Such a terrible loss. What are you going to do?"

Mama took a tissue from her purse. "This could destroy our business. The police are investigating, but we just don't know what to do next." She dabbed her eyes with a tissue.

A veil of authority settled over Diane as she considered our dilemma. "The first thing we should do is put our heads together and see if we can't come up with something useful. I'm sure the girls will help stop any negative gossip about your salon."

Mama blew her nose into a tissue as Diane gathered the lingering ladies into a tight net around us.

"I heard Scarlett was robbing the cradle," one woman said.

"Oh, she dropped him for a rich, powerful, and very married man," said another.

"But that's not the worst part," a woman in red whispered. "She was pregnant!"

"I heard the wife found out, and the man dumped her," another added.

Diane drew herself up. "Well, I heard the man asked his wife for a divorce and proposed marriage to Scarlett."

"And WXYB wasn't renewing her contract," another woman spoke up.

"Well, that's nothing. I heard that she was selling drugs out of her house!"

The information dropped into my lap like gold nuggets from a prospector's bag.

I smiled at each of them. "Would any of you ladies happen to know the names of these men?"

They didn't have any names but said they would check their sources and get back with me. On and on the women chattered until someone's husband complained about the lateness of the hour and the circle broke up. I had a feeling the gossip milked from this loose-lipped social circle would prove valuable in the coming days.

****

Forty minutes later when I stepped through the back kitchen door at my childhood home, a cloud of tantalizing aromas wrapped its enticing fingers around my nostrils. My rumbling stomach sent me straight to the stove where Mama stood frying chicken. I closed my eyes, inhaling the rich scents. Happy memories of years growing up in this large rambling house flooded my mind. Impulsively, I reached my arms around her, squeezing hard.

"Honey, watch out for hot grease," she admonished as I dropped my arms and backed away from the hot oven.

Tongs in hand, she lifted another piece of chicken from the boiling grease, placed it on a paper-lined platter, then turned around, wiping her hands on her apron. "What's the hug for?"

I pinched off a bite of warm, sweet cornbread on

the counter. "Just thinking about old times."

Mama shot me a disapproving look. "I wish you wouldn't pick at the food before it's on the table." She turned back to the stove, picking up the tongs. "I miss those times, myself. What's got you thinking about that?"

"The smells in this kitchen always take me back to when Daddy was alive. You guys were the best parents a girl could have." The sound of slamming doors echoed through the kitchen. "Where is everybody?" I asked.

"Your sisters are setting the table, and the men-folk are down at the barn checking on that busted tiller. Becky is taking a nap in the front bedroom, and I believe Lynette is in the den on her phone." Mama turned around. Her eyes were misty. "I miss your daddy too. It's been so long since he went away."

"I know it's painful to talk about what happened, Mama, but we're alone, and I have so many unanswered questions about his death," I said softly. "I've always felt like you didn't tell us the whole truth."

She let out a heavy sigh. "I knew this day would come. There is something you girls need to know," she said. "And I will tell you soon. I need more time."

"You've had a lot of time to think about it. However, I'll drop the subject for now, but we're concerned about you living out here by yourself. We've even discussed you selling the farm and buying a smaller house in town, closer to us. We love this place, but what if something happened? It's a twenty minute drive out here."

She swung back to the stove. "You girls have been making a lot of plans behind my back." Her tongs quickly transferred chicken from the grease to the platter. "This is my farm, and I'm not leaving, you hear? The fields are leased to the Cassidy brothers, and they're bringing in a decent income. Now start dishing up the rest of this food into bowls and get it on the table. And tell Deena to put the ice in the glasses."

Both subjects were closed, so I left the kitchen, following the sound of laughter into the dining room to find my sisters finishing up with the table.

"Hey, there you are," Deena said as I entered. "What took you so long? I'm usually the one who's fashionably late for Sunday dinner."

"I ran home to change out of those pantyhose. And I wanted to jot down what the ladies at church had to say about Scarlett. There are a couple of leads I'd like to follow up on."

"What do you mean, leads?" Deena asked. "Like investigating? Leave that for the police."

"I wish it were that simple." I paused, debating whether this was a good time to enlist their help. Investigating Scarlett's death would require teamwork. Just as it would saving the salon. Upon further thought, Easter dinner wasn't the best time for a pow-wow with my sisters. Maybe tomorrow.

"I couldn't believe some of the things those old bats said," Billie Jo piped up. "Made me wonder what they'd say if someone asked about me."

Deena wrinkled her nose. "They'd say that you're as crazy as a polecat in winter."

Billie Jo placed napkins beside each plate. "Yes, that's true, but I guess that's true about the whole family. Including you."

I sat down at the table. "Remember when we

promised not to push Mama to sell the farm? Well, I opened my big mouth and made her mad. I know she's hanging on to this farm because Daddy loved it. Leaving here would be like losing him all over again."

"Don't beat yourself up about this." Deena sat down beside me. "It was just a matter of time before one of us slipped up and said something. I'm glad it's out in the open. The acreage is leased out, but this house requires a lot of maintenance. Roddy and the boys are trying to fix her tiller so she can put in a garden, for God sake."

I smiled at her outrage. "That's what she told me. And guess what else I learned?"

"What?" Deena asked.

Billie Jo looked up from the table setting. "No more bad news I hope."

"That remains to be seen," I said. "But I did get her to admit that she's been keeping something from us concerning Daddy's death."

"Good Lord, what could she possibly be hiding?" Deena pressed.

"I don't know, but I'm going to find out."

"I don't like this one bit," Billie Jo added. "All of a sudden, everybody's got a secret."

"Well, not everyone," I said. "Just our mother." I pushed back my chair and stood. "Come on. I hear her hollerin' for us now."

Mama, fussing under her breath when we entered the kitchen, lifted the lid of a pot and stirred the contents. "Get me a bowl for these mustards, Jolene. Deena, get on down to the barn and tell those men I said dinner's on the table. Billie Jo, get Lynette off that phone and tell her to get in here and help."

Becky strolled into the kitchen as I pulled down a large bowl from the cabinet and handed it to Mama.

"Need some help, MeMaw?" Becky asked.

Mama spooned up the mustards. "You can set up the dessert cart for me. There's a coconut cake there on the counter and a pecan pie ready to come out of the oven. And don't forget the strawberry pie I brought from Shoney's. It's in the ice box. Get Jacob to help you get the dessert cart out of the garage." She passed the steaming bowl to me. "Place these on the table."

Booming male voices coming through the back door echoed back to the dining room. Retracing my steps, I stood in the doorway leading into the kitchen.

One of the deep bass vibrations belonged to Sam Bradford. He stood just inside the door, cowboy hat in hand. My gaze swept over his dark wavy hair, just graying at the temples, eyes as fathomless as a cloudless sky, and his expressive mouth underneath a luxuriant mustache turned up in an audacious smile.

Does his mustache tickle when he kisses? The thought hit my brain like a bullet to its mark. An unwelcome surge of excitement goosed me. I *couldn't* be attracted to this man. He was bait to lure Deena into helping me investigate Scarlett's death. Hadn't I planned this out last night while stuffing my face with milk and chocolate cake?

"Come on in, Sam. Dinner's on the table," Mama said from the stove.

"Thank you for the invite, Mrs. Tucker." His gaze swept the room. "It's nice to see that some things never change."

Billie Jo took his cowboy hat from him and hung in on the hat rack. "Would you like to wash up before we eat? The bathroom is down the hall on the right."

"I remember where it is."

Waiting until he'd disappeared down the hallway, and out of earshot, I joined Mama at the stove. Billie Jo left to find Lynette, and Deena had disappeared down the hall. For the moment, Mama and I had the kitchen to ourselves.

"I'm not complaining, but I'm curious to know why you invited Sam to dinner."

She handed me the platter piled high with fried chicken. "Mind your manners and put this on the table. Sam's a lonely bachelor in need of a wife. He and Deena were such a cute couple back in high school and can be again with a little help."

So that was the reason for the invite. Mama wanted to play matchmaker. But wasn't this exactly what I wanted? I set the platter of chicken back down on the counter. "What if Deena has other plans?"

"Sometimes Deena can't see what's right in front of her."

"And Sam is perfect for her? Have you thought to ask him what he thinks about your plans of marrying him off to Deena?"

Her gaze held mine. "Please tell me you're not wanting him for yourself. I can understand the attraction, but you're not Sam's type. I invited him here to get reacquainted with your sister. I'm depending on you to help this romance along."

I frowned slightly, a tad offended by her comment. What did she mean by saying I wasn't Bradford's type? Besides, I *could* be his type. She didn't have all the answers. Not yet, anyhow.

The sound of the squeaking dessert cart being

wheeled into the kitchen stopped our conversation. Jacob steered it over to the counter.

Becky grabbed a wet dishcloth from the sink. "We found it, MeMaw. It's covered in dust, but I'll wipe it down good before we stack the desserts on it."

Maintaining a brittle smile, I picked up the platter of chicken and left them to finish up. In the dining room, the table was laden with steaming dishes. Mama came in behind me with a plate of deviled eggs, and Becky and Jacob behind her with the dessert cart. We sat down at the table, and Roddy offered thanks.

By unspoken consent, we avoided mentioning yesterday's tragic events at the salon. Instead, the conversation centered on the high cost of employee health care, the town picnic in July, and the price of a new tiller versus repairing the old one.

Several times, I looked up to find Bradford watching me, his razor sharp gaze seeing through me as if I was as transparent as the glass I held in my hand. Confident of my ability to shrug off the conflicting emotions his attention brought, I encouraged Deena to entertain us by reliving her prom night with our guest. Bradford joined the merriment, laughing as they recalled the fun they'd had with their friends at the dance. Deena beamed under his radiant smile when he told us how afterward at breakfast, just at sunrise, he'd given her his class ring and asked her to be his steady girlfriend.

Mama nodded her approval, and for the rest of the meal, I listened half-heartedly to Deena's excited chatter and Bradford's murmured replies as they continued to reminisce about their last year of high school and the mysterious hand of fate bringing them back together.

From where I sat, it appeared that Mama's wish—and mine—had come true. But victory left a sour taste in my mouth. Drinking down the last of my sweet tea, I excused myself from the table, having no appetite for dessert at this time. Besides, I had half a chocolate cake waiting to be polished off later at home.

Chapter Eight
The Mysterious Madame Mia

Monday morning, I drove to Madame Mia's House of Psychic Vision on Fifth Street. Not sure what to expect, I arrived fifteen minutes ahead of time and parked across the street from the beautifully-restored Victorian home. I had expected to find the fortune teller in a crumbling, rundown building in the older section of town not in this fabulous setting. The "Queen Anne" house, painted a soft yellow with black shutters, and tall, towering chimneys, dormers, and gables, had a wraparound front porch, gingerbread details, and a white picket fence. Perhaps this wouldn't turn out to be so bad after all.

Gathering my courage, I pushed open the car door, hurried across the street, through the gate to the large front porch, and rang the doorbell. Several minutes passed before the door opened, and I had my second surprise of the morning.

"Please come in." The woman's accent was heavy and exotic, her ivory linen business pantsuit looked expensive. "I've been expecting you."

Madame Mia was lovely. Cleopatra lovely. Helen of Troy lovely. Dark. Mysterious. Foreign. And certainly unusual for South Georgia.

I followed her into a foyer with inlaid wood floors, stained and shining. Scattered here and there, colorful woolen rugs formed a path to a simple yet intricately-carved staircase leading to the second floor. A huge, ornate chandelier hung high above my head. The twelve-foot coffered ceiling gave the house a feeling of grandiosity and in a time before air-conditioning, would have allowed the cross breezes from opened windows to cool the house.

At the end of a long hall, we entered a small parlor with velvet sofas and chairs pushed against wallpapered walls. A small round table covered with a delicate lace tablecloth occupied the center of the room. Warm, yellow sunlight spilled in from three tall windows. The room smelled faintly of lemon furniture polish.

Not a crystal ball in sight.

"Sit down, my dear," Madame Mia said. "I was intrigued by your call. Now, that we've met, I can see that you are yourself, a psychic."

I perched on the edge of an antique chair opposite her. "Ah, yeah, about that. This is new territory for me, and I'm flying blind here. Uh, I really didn't know who else could help me. You're the only, uh, person in the tri-county area who specializes in my problem."

"A dying art to be sure."

"Uh, yeah."

"You said you had a problem with a departed soul?"

"I'm being haunted by a dead client." I fingered the tablecloth. "She died in my beauty shop."

"I see."

"I read a couple of books on communicating with the dead. My ghost is kind of special and not cooperating. She won't come when I call."

One ringed hand reached up to brush a strand of

dark hair off a creamy cheek. "I see."

I hesitated, perturbed. This consultation cost fifty bucks—good money for advice—and so far all she could say was, "I see" in that cultured, silky voice. I was beginning to suspect I had wasted my time. I started to rise.

"I could try to contact her."

Excellent suggestion. "If it wouldn't be too much trouble," I said, relaxing back on my chair. "Although I should warn you about Scarlett—"

"Scarlett?" Dark, startled eyes bore into mine. "Just last Friday, I had a late night appointment with a woman by the name of Scarlett Cantrell. Her tarot reading told the end of a phase in life which had served its purpose. The beginning of a new life. A transformation—abrupt and complete. A crossroad. Such a lost soul. Haunted by the tragedy of past events."

"Yes, she died yesterday. And now, she's haunting me," I said. "She fed me some cockamamie story about a cosmic trial, angel defense lawyers, and her eternal residence being in jeopardy if I don't help her find justice. I need answers, Madame Mia. Fast."

"I see."

Oh crap. We've circled back to two word responses again. I twisted my fingers through the lace tablecloth. "Can you help me or not?"

"Give me your hands."

"What for?" I asked, struggling to free my fingers from the tablecloth.

"You're her point of contact. If you want me to connect with her, I must use your energy to do so."

I joined hands with her across the table. Madame

Mia closed her eyes and recited foreign words, a mantra. I'd learned this was a method of contacting the dead from the books I'd checked out from the library.

Quietly, I studied her as she continued to sing the strange words over and over. Her breathing became shallow. Red lips tightened. Her face grimaced. My hands grew warm, and a tingling began in the pit of my stomach as the singing became softer until it stopped.

Madame Mia opened her eyes. "The spirits are silent."

I shook my head. "I'm having the same trouble at home."

"The spirits will speak when they are ready."

"Can you tell me anything?"

She looked down at our clasped hands. "Only that the answers will only come after much struggle. Look to the past. Your answers are there." She handed me her card. "For emergencies," she said and stood.

That was it. My time had run out. I plunked down the fifty bucks and left Madame Mia's House of Psychic Vision with more questions than answers.

****

Late that afternoon, Deena called with the welcome news that the salon had been cleared by the police. Her excited voice left me with no doubt she'd been talking with Bradford.

"Sam cautioned us to be available for further questioning," she said. "I told him we'd cooperate fully with the investigation."

"Did he happen to mention the cause of death?" I asked, trying not to think about Mama's comment that I wasn't Bradford's type. I wondered about that.

He, being a cop, probably gravitated toward the

classic damsel-in-distress kind of woman—like Deena. I never needed Prince Charming to come to my rescue, because I wanted to be the one holding the reins, or be the first to cross under the checkered flag, or to bag the biggest fish in the pond. I'm not a missionary-minded woman in the least. To my way of thinking, the best position is on top, in control.

"The autopsy hasn't been completed," Deena replied. "He said they're waiting on the toxicology report before making the call."

I snapped back to the conversation. "How long will that take?"

"He didn't say, but foul play is suspected. He suggested we refrain from leaving the state until this is cleared up."

"I tried to tell Detective Grant the break-in and Scarlett's death are connected, but he wouldn't listen. That mask could've been sabotaged. What if we're the real targets, and Scarlett was accidently killed instead?"

"Your imagination is working overtime."

"You have to admit that it's a possibility. Have you ever heard of a person being killed with a moisture mask? Aren't you suspicious?"

Deena's sigh made me frown. "I don't think I'm going to like where you're going with this. Sam said it was an ongoing investigation, and until an official determination is reached, we should carry on with our lives as normally as possible. I intend to follow his advice."

"Did he happen to mention if they had any leads?"

"Carla is a person of interest, but that you already know. What are you suggesting?"

"Not anything dangerous. Only a little snooping

around for tidbits of information the police might not stumble onto. We have to do this."

"Why? Snooping around can be dangerous. I don't want any part of it."

Sigh. Not an adventurous bone in her body. Surely, she'd been switched at birth and branched off another family tree entirely. Her association with Bradford was having the opposite effect from what I'd hoped for.

"Do I have to spell everything out to you?" I asked. "We're the main suspects. Well, one of our employees is. What about the financial cost if we're sued for wrongful death. If we lose the salon, Mama loses the farm. Remember the fifty thousand dollar second mortgage she took out to finance the salon? It's not paid in full yet."

"How could I forget?" She paused for a couple of seconds. "Okay, I'm willing to help out, but only if it involves gossip and non-dangerous missions. Understood? No shoot-outs or car chases or dramatic scenes—agreed? But why me? What about Billie Jo?"

I grinned into the telephone receiver, savoring my triumph. "She's already on-board."

"This is a bad idea. Sam isn't going to be pleased with us."

"You're not going to tell him. Your job is gonna be to find out everything you can about the police investigation and feed the information back to me."

"You want me to be a mole?"

Her outraged voice made me laugh. "Yes, you're the snitch in this operation. When are you and Sam getting together?"

"We're driving over to Albany tonight to meet a couple of high school friends for dinner. I'm not sure I can do this, Jolene. He'd be awfully mad if he finds out I'm a snoop."

Guilt washed over me at the prospect of Deena being hurt a second time by this man. As casually as I could manage, I cautioned her to move ahead slowly with the budding relationship.

"Some things are beyond our control," I added.

She laughed. "You're warning me to be cautious in one breath and encouraging me to take risks in another. You can't have it both ways—but I'll be careful." She sighed. "Look, I hate to cut our conversation short, but I need to run down to the salon. Sam gave the all clear, so we can clean before we open in the morning."

"I'll do it. I'm five minutes away. Besides, you have a date to get ready for. Have fun and I'll talk to you in the morning."

I hung up the phone and slipped on a pair of old ragged jeans and sneakers and drove down to the shop. The silence of the empty building wrapped around me with warm familiarity as I let myself in through the rear entrance and made my way to the dispensary to collect cleaning supplies, half expecting Scarlett to pop up and say "boo".

"Yoo-hoo, is anyone here?" I called out as I came out of the dispensary with the cleaning supply caddy.

No answer.

Some of the books I'd checked out from the library had suggested finding a spot where one could concentrate without distraction. Well, the facial room was definitely quiet, and since I would be in there anyway, I decided now would be a great time to practice my psychic conversation skills.

I groaned at the messy room. There was a fair

amount of work needed to put the room in order before I could settle in for a ghostly-chat practice session.

Thirty minutes later, I dumped the dirty water from the commercial mop bucket out the back door and stored the cleaning supplies in the dispensary. Back in the facial room, which now smelled like a pine forest, I pulled the chair from against the wall to the center of the room and sat down.

Okay, if I remembered correctly, the next step in spirit communication involved holding an item belonging to or having some kind of personal connection to the deceased person with whom you were trying to make contact. Nix that part. I had nothing. The police had taken the remnants of the mask and Scarlett's personal tea canister from the kitchen.

On to step three, four, and five. I closed my eyes and thought about Scarlett, picturing her sitting on the facial bed in her antebellum garb. I called out her name as if she was right next to me, asking her to let me know if she was there.

Nothing.

Feeling positively stupid, I opened my eyes and said, "Damn it, Scarlett, get your skinny ass down here."

The room plunged into darkness. An eerie greenish light flashed, and thunder cracked directly overhead. The hair on my arms stood on end as a hideous howling echoed from the walls. I shivered in the warm, stuffy air and bolted for the door. The uproar ended almost as quickly as it started. The overhead light switched on, the silence was loud in the still room.

"You cleaned my room," Scarlett said in a voice that seemed to come from a long way off.

The words brought me around to face her. Costumed in a green velvet dressing gown, she lazed upon the facial bed, relaxed and seemingly satisfied with my state of unease. "I would've answered your summons sooner, but you caught me at a bad time."

My fists clenched. "What was all that?"

"I'm sure I don't know to what you're referring."

I waved my hands in the air. "That—that ghoulish display. You scared the life out of me."

Her smile turned into a laugh. "Oh, that. I was practicing my ghostly antics in case I'm stuck here. Your beauty shop will be the best haunted salon in town, I promise." She fanned her face. "Phew. Being a ghost is hard work. Now, tell me why you wanted to see me."

Since I really hadn't expected to see her at all, I decided to feed her a hastily made-up progress report. "Only two days have passed since your death, so don't expect a lot, but I do know you had a falling out with one of your lovers before you died. Are you able to remember his name?"

"Are you saying I had more than one?"

"According to the ladies at First Baptist Church, you had several. Oh, and there's a rumor you were pregnant. The autopsy's not finished, so whether the gossip is true I can't say. One woman reported you were selling drugs, and another said WXYB wasn't renewing your contract. Does anything sound familiar?"

"It's true that WXYB wasn't renewing my contract."

I sat down in the chair, facing her. "Why?"

"Robert is a pompous ass."

"You wanted my help, so answer the question."

"I wanted a bigger piece of the pie. *Scarlett's Top Spot* wasn't cutting it any longer. I wanted to cover important stories, like the major networks, but Robert only wanted a pretty face to represent his station. I wanted to prove him wrong, so I decided to dig up a story on my own."

"Okay, that's a good start. Tell me why you thought someone was trying to kill you."

"I was in over my head from the start." Her voice was resigned. "This town holds a lot of secrets. I should've left them buried."

"What story were you working on?"

"The recent mayoral election. That and several others that seemed to be tied together."

"You must've found something."

"I did—fraud. Unfortunately, I died before I could prove it."

I paused in my questioning, trying to digest the information. I had one more important question for her. "Scarlett, you said that the jade elephant would explain everything. What is it and where is it?"

Her face went blank. "My memory is so foggy in places, but it will come back to me in time."

I nodded my head. "Try to remember. I'm working on the theory that the break-in at the salon is somehow tied to your death. The police believe it's a separate incident because there have been a couple of similar break-ins with the same M.O."

"You sound very knowledgeable. I've a good feeling about hiring you."

"Hiring me? You begged me to help and then threatened to haunt my salon if I didn't. But thanks for the compliment. I've been reading a couple of books about conducting a private investigation so I can get rid of you faster."

Her eyebrows lifted in disdain. "You're lucky to have a ghost of my quality haunting your dinky hole-in-the-wall salon."

I laughed at her snobbery. "Always the belle, huh, Scarlett?"

She stretched, blinked sleepily, and yawned. "I haven't quite adjusted to materializing. Could we continue this discussion at a later time? I'm drained and need my beauty sleep."

I, too, was dead on my feet and ready to head for the house for a hot shower and an early supper, but I had something on my mind that I needed to air. "Ah, Scarlett, I'm exploring the possibility that you weren't the intended target."

Twin chips of green ice bore into mine. "I died ahead of schedule?"

Waves of psychic anger rolled off her. I stepped behind the chair, placing a little distance between us. "Well, sort of. Your demise could've been premature if the death mask was intended for someone else—a staff member, one of my sisters, or even possibly me."

"This is most distressing." Her image flashed several times, becoming more and more transparent until she faded into nothingness.

Looking around the silent, empty room, I shivered with dread. If what I suspected proved true, a faceless killer would try again for the real intended victim. Spooked by my morbid thoughts, I grabbed my purse from the dispensary and rushed out the back entrance, looking several times over my shoulder into the deepening shadows as I locked the door and raced for my car. Out of my driver's window, I glimpsed a thunderstorm on the western horizon.

Gathering my courage and determination around me, I drove the few miles to my house before the tempest could release its downpour. Once again locked safely behind closed doors, I jotted down a few additional notes from my conversation with Scarlett. Now, more than ever, it was up to me to find the killer before he or she could strike again.

Chapter Nine
Dixieland's Resident Ghost

Dixieland Salon opened on Tuesday morning to a packed reception area. Five walk-ins came in together wanting last-minute appointments.

"Would you look at this crowd?" I exclaimed.

Mandy overheard my comment to Billie Jo. "Packed in like sardines," she said. "Sightseers will gladly pay for whatever gory details you spill, which is all right with me because I'll sell my soul to the highest bidder. It won't last though so get it while you can is my mantra." She headed in the direction of her manicure table.

Restless and jumpy after a sleepless night, I turned back to Billie Jo. "What about Anthony? He's in the back packing up his equipment. I know you fired him, but we really need him today." Billie Jo's frown deepened with each word. I knew the look. This wasn't going to be easy. "I'm booked and can't help with the overflow."

Background sounds of the salon infused my consciousness—a wave of chatty customers entering the shop, clicking irons, whirring dryers, running water. Someone had turned up the volume on the radio and its rhythmic beat blared through the speakers. Deena came out of her office with Holly, speaking loudly and gesturing with her hands.

Billie Jo looked over her shoulder at the crowded reception desk. "I don't trust Anthony. Something about him just doesn't add up."

"I agree with you, sis. He's definitely hiding something, but until we can find a decent replacement, the salon is understaffed."

Holly stepped over to us. "Mrs. Hart and Mr. Turner are here."

I gave her a quick nod. "Thank you, Holly. Please escort them to our stations and let them know we'll be right with them. And see that Mrs. Hart is draped and shampooed, please."

"Will do."

Billie Jo released a heavy sigh. "I believe it's a mistake to keep Anthony. Yet, I'll give him another chance for the sake of the business. Just tell him to show respect for the other stylists and do the job he was hired to do and to keep his mouth shut. That's all I ask of all the employees, including myself."

I breathed an inward sigh of relief. At least for the moment, Anthony would remain close by and under my surveillance until his secret came to light. I gripped her hand, squeezing gently. "I'll talk to him, Billie Jo. If he breathes a peep, he's gone."

She made no further comment, just nodded in agreement and headed off to her workstation. I made a quick stop to tell Anthony he still had a job and warn him to behave himself, then stopped at the reception desk to check my afternoon appointments, instructing Holly not to add any last-minute appointments if I had cancellations.

"Mrs. Hart is shampooed and ready for you," Holly reminded me.

Annabel Hart was draped for a chemical service and seated in my stylist chair. "Good morning, Annabel. Are you ready for your perm?"

The older woman smiled. "I've been looking forward to getting something done with this mop. Elmore, that's my husband, is threatening to ship me off to Bora Bora if I don't stop complaining about my hair. He's right, you know. I can't help it though." She picked up a limp section of salt-and-pepper hair. "No body, no curl, no life. Work your magic, Jolene."

After consulting her chemical service card, I gathered the supplies needed and arranged them on the workstation counter. Quickly, I set to work on the towel-dried hair, wrapping each section with alternating blue and yellow rods. One side was completely wrapped when she inquired into the strange events that took place in the salon over the weekend.

"Scarlett's death came as quite a shock to the neighborhood," she said in a casual voice.

Stunned by the revelation, I paused. "Scarlett was your neighbor?"

"Yep, I live next door to her white two-story house she laughingly called her 'Tara.' Beautiful home and well maintained for a single woman's residence. She kept odd hours though. Cars comin' and goin' at all hours of the night. Very busy lady, if you know what I mean."

"Well, she was a local celebrity. I heard she threw some pretty wild parties."

Her eyes twinkled with mischief. "I could tell you some shocking stories about her famous parties."

"Do tell, Annabel. I've heard a few wicked tales myself," I coaxed. The books I'd been studying on private investigating all agreed the best way to obtain pertinent information was to find a common interest to share. Be charming and witty, they'd advised.

"Orgies," Mrs. Hart declared in a low voice.

"I beg your pardon?" I asked, totally blown away by her response.

"Oh, you heard me right. Elmore witnessed some bizarre behavior several times—even got an eyeful of Scarlett and some man in the raw."

I couldn't believe my ears. "They were nude? Were they outside?"

"No, in her bedroom. Elmore had his binoculars out and could see exceptionally well into her windows. The other guests were enjoying a lovely buffet downstairs while Scarlett and her friend were foolin' around upstairs."

I didn't know whether to laugh or cry. The thought of this woman's husband peeping into Scarlett's windows with a pair of binoculars didn't sit right with me, but I needed to know the name of her paramour, so I had to keep fishing. Boy, I had no idea what I was getting myself into.

"Did Mr. Hart recognize Scarlett's friend?"

"No. He said he was a young man with light brownish-blond hair and mustache. A good-looking kid—tall and muscular."

Hmm. I looked over at Anthony. That description matched my employee all right. And Anthony had a secret that apparently Scarlett had knowledge of. Anthony could very well be one of the men rumored to be sleeping with Scarlett at the time of her death. Could he be the mastermind behind the break-in and ultimately be responsible for her death? Highly unlikely, but I couldn't leave any stone unturned.

"Is that all your husband, uh, observed, Annabel...just questionable behavior behind closed doors? Anything else stick out as strange?"

"Now that you mention it, I observed two men in black casing her place."

"Casing her place?"

"Yeah. They were parked in a dark SUV across the street several nights ago. For hours they were there. Then, about two in the morning, the neighbor's dog started barking something fierce, so I got up to see what'd stirred him up. That's when I noticed those same two men get out of their car and disappear into her back-yard. I called the police and woke up Elmore."

"What do you mean when you say 'men in black'?"

She scowled. "These men wore black business suits, extremely sharp dressers. I believe they were FBI or some other government agency. I've seen their kind on TV. Distinct appearance those government people. Do you suppose Scarlett could've been an undercover agent? Those men didn't look like ordinary criminals, but I called the police to be on the safe side."

I cleared my throat, uncertain how to respond. The suggestion that Scarlett could possibly be a secret government agent had caught me off guard. But in reality, I knew very little about her, and anything was possible. *Be prepared for the unexpected—things aren't always what they seem*, the PI books had said. Annabel's observations certainly were unexpected, but welcome. I would document and analyze all information for further investigation.

"Could you describe these men to me, Annabel?"

"I thought I just did."

"You gave a general description of their apparel. Were you able to get a good look at their faces?"

She swiveled around to face me, her face mirroring curiosity. "You're asking the same questions as the police, and I'll tell you like I told them. Even as they passed under the bright streetlight, they were too far away for me to see their features clearly. They were big and bulky men—one black, one white."

"Were the police able to apprehend the men?"

She righted herself in the chair so she faced the mirror. "Naw, they took off when Elmore started waving his spotlight into Scarlett's back yard."

"Did you or your husband think to take down their tag number for the police?"

"And leave the safety of my house? We're young at heart but old in body. I forbade him to risk his life for a tag number."

"Where was Scarlett during all the commotion?"

"Asleep, I assume. I could see the cops knocking on her door from my front living room window. It took her a few minutes to answer. They disappeared inside, so we went back to bed."

For a few seconds, I digested the information and thought of possible questions, but her expression showed she had nothing further to pass along. I allowed her to fill the empty space with useless chatter as I doused her hair with perm solution and secured a plastic bag around her hair.

When I handed her a magazine, a subtle atmospheric change occurred around my station—like the air pressure had suddenly compacted into a tiny square space. The background salon noise disappeared.

My ears popped, causing me to blink several times to dispel sudden dizziness. Through my hazy state, the screeching voice of Reverend Leroy Masters rose to a keening wail. The magazine fell with a smack on the hardwood floor. Annabel's startled expression clashed with mine in the mirror.

Whirling in confusion, I ran over to the reception desk where Deena screamed at Holly to turn down the volume on the radio or shut the dang thing off.

"I can't shut the dang thing off," Holly yelled, her hand involuntarily turning the volume higher.

And, not surprisingly, superimposed over the receptionist's hand were the ghoulish fingers of Dixieland's resident ghost.

"Oh great," I said. "Scarlett's back."

****

The shop was quiet when I stepped through the back door juggling a box of pastries with one hand and shutting out the early Wednesday morning humidity with the other. With an hour to spare before the salon opened, I hoped to prevent a repeat of yesterday's fiasco by having a chat with Scarlett if she'd show. At home last night, I'd tried every trick to persuade her to materialize. My psychic development had suffered a serious setback when I'd failed to produce even a whisper from her. I had a call in to Madame Mia for more advice, but I hadn't heard back from her yet.

Yesterday morning, the whole salon had been in an uproar after Scarlett's wicked antics. Odd events kept happening, and I knew she was behind it all. And now everyone was upset with one another—Holly with both me and Deena, Billie Jo at Holly for lost clients, and so on.

Onella, Anthony's client, now had cotton-ball hair because Scarlett had set an additional ten minutes on the timer during perm processing. Anthony, frazzled, accused Mandy of the crime, and she in turn accused him of being a lousy hairstylist. The two had to be separated by Billie Jo, who stopped them before the first punch could fly.

Then, to really set things off, a curious client had decided to peek inside the facial room at the exact moment Scarlett decided to rearrange the room. The woman had run through the salon screaming that the salon was haunted before collapsing in a dead faint by the hair dryers.

The fire station across the street responded in record time, and the ambulance carted away another spooked client. One of the firemen dared to ask me if we were going to make this a habit. They were even taking bets on how long it would take before they had to respond to another call at the haunted beauty salon. He even boasted about the size of the pot as fellow firefighters around the city wanted a piece of the action.

And all this before lunch.

I flicked on the light switch by the back door and made my way into the kitchen to start a pot of coffee to go with the pastries. Sitting down at the small dinette table, tucked in the corner, I pondered yesterday afternoon. For that was when it'd started again—a minute past noon.

Scarlett had saved her best antics for last.

Just thinking about it gave me a chuckle. I'd just finished cutting long layers on a new client's hair when I happened to glance over at Anthony applying color to his client's hair.

My jaw had dropped open with astonishment at the scene. Scarlett, clad in what appeared to be a tight, white corset with sheer stockings, pressed every inch of her ghostly body against him. With featherlike caresses, her fingers sought out his torso. Phantom kisses rained on his sweating brow. Unconsciously, he began to moan, and his strong fingers caressed his client's scalp in the same circular motion the invisible vixen applied to his body. All of the air in his lungs expelled in one wild gasp—his erection was shameless, instant, and total as it pressed against his tight jeans.

By this time, however, I wasn't the only one to notice Anthony's strange behavior. His client, who'd been gaily chatting away with him, fell silent, and her face flushed a deep red. The other stylists and their clients stopped to stare also. The only one who apparently hadn't noticed was Billie Jo. I had to stop Scarlett before my sister became aware of Anthony's dilemma.

Tossing my comb onto my workstation counter, I'd excused myself and started toward Anthony when Billie Jo's clippers buzzed to a halt. Erotic moans filled the void. Unfortunately, my baby sister turned curious eyes at the intrusive noise. As expected, she turned beet red with anger and exploded.

Better her than Anthony!

Billie Jo excused herself from her client, stomped over to Anthony's station, and requested he accompany her to Deena's office. Her angry words could be heard behind closed doors, and when they emerged several minutes later, both went in separate directions to everyone's relief.

The rich aroma of freshly-brewed coffee

interrupted my musings, and I poured myself a cup. I sat down at the table and mentally prepared myself for the confrontation to come with Scarlett. When the mug was empty, I set it in the sink and went to find my trouble-making denizen of hell.

I found her polishing her nails at the manicure table. She flashed me an infectious smile as I sat down in the chair across from her. "You look tired this morning," she said. "Not sleeping well?"

"Thanks to you, I'm not. Look, we've got to talk. My employees are ready to walk out, and I've had to call 9-1-1 twice because of your destructive pranks. You were particularly cruel to Anthony, and Onella doesn't deserve cotton ball hair. Stop messing with the volume on the radio. You can't increase the temperature in the pedicure bath. And please, for God's sake, stay out of the restroom. What's up with that?"

The brush in her hand paused over a bright red nail. "I'm a ghost. Ghosts haunt the living. Rules are rules you know."

I scrubbed a hand over my face. "Why am I just hearing about the rules? You could've warned me on the first day."

"Sorry. I'm a newbie and haven't had a lot of practice at being dead. I was given a manual, but I haven't gotten around to reading it yet. And another thing, I don't like Deena. She needs her claws clipped."

"You'd better learn to like her. She's agreed to help and has the lead detective's ear"

"Deena's agreed to help me? Really? She hated me so much when I was alive."

"You remember that tidbit of information but can't recall the jade elephant? Really, Scarlett, I can't help you unless you try harder. And FYI, you gave Deena reason. Look, we don't have time to rehash the past now. Go easy on the haunting. My sisters don't know that you're still here, and I haven't figured out a way to explain it without sounding crazy."

Her face brightened. "The Department of Family Relations might have a brochure that might help explain my existence. I'll be right back." She disappeared through the wall into the facial room.

I jumped up, following her into the empty room. "Wait, I'm not finished. Geez, I wanted to ask you about an incident Annabel relayed to me yesterday."

"Jolene?"

The sound of my name being called brought me rushing into the hall. Deena came out of the kitchen as I closed and locked the facial room door.

"I thought you might come in early." She pointed to the closed door. "How Whynell managed to get into the facial room yesterday is a mystery. I've kept the door locked since Roddy installed a new lock."

I glanced over my shoulder for our resident specter. There was no mystery to how a client had entered the locked room. Scarlett had unlocked the door and waited for someone to wander into her invisible black widow spider web.

Jiggling the knob for Deena's benefit, I said, "It's locked up good and tight now. We don't want another client wandering in by accident."

"I don't believe I could survive it." Deena motioned for me to follow her into the kitchen. "I see you made coffee." She retrieved a mug from the cabinet.

I fetched mine out of the sink, holding it out for her

to refill. "So how did your date with Bradford go last night?" I grabbed a pastry from the bakery box.

Deena joined me at the table. "Fantastic. We met some of our old high school chums out at Logan's Steak House. I really need to keep in touch with them. I'd forgotten how much fun we used to have together. Sam entertained us with stories of his time in the Navy. He was military police. After his stint, he became a civilian cop."

"Interesting, but not what I hoped you'd be telling me this morning. Were you able to find out anything about the investigation?"

She set down her coffee mug. "I didn't ask."

"Why not?"

"Because I need more time to work up the courage, that's why. I'm not pushy like you."

"Are you seeing him again tonight?"

"No, not tonight. I'm going to prayer meeting at church. Aren't you? The pastor is preaching a series on facing the giants in your life."

"Sundays are enough for me," I said. "So, when are you seeing Bradford again?"

"He's taking me to dinner and a movie Friday night."

"Try to find out what you can, okay?"

Deena's golden brown eyes twinkled. "I'll do my best for you. However, small it may be I might add."

Footsteps sounded in the hallway. Holly waltzed into the kitchen, followed by the rest of the staff, cutting off any further discussion between us. They headed for the coffee and the box of pastries on the counter.

"Has Billie Jo arrived, Holly?" I asked.

The receptionist nodded, her mouth stuffed with half-eaten pastry.

"I believe Robert Burns came in with her," Mandy volunteered.

"He did," Anthony said, without turning from the coffee pot. "I heard him say he was in a hurry so he came early. They were headed for her station."

Since there were still a few minutes before the salon officially opened, an impromptu meeting got underway. Seated around the table, the staff, minus Billie Jo, hashed out a couple of trouble spots needing attention. Anthony apologized for yesterday's outrageous behavior. Although, he added, his reaction was a natural consequence of being massaged by hot, pressing, invisible hands. Laughter erupted as he came to a stuttering stop.

"Well," I said, glancing up at the clock on the wall. "Now that that's settled, let's go to work."

Chairs scraped across the hardwood floor as the meeting broke up. Mugs were placed in the sink for washing at the end of the day. Holly had just pushed open the kitchen door when a man's bellow of rage pierced the early morning silence.

Deena turned startled eyes to me. "Oh Lord. What now?"

Afraid to voice my suspicions, for I had a pretty good idea that Scarlett was up to no good, I bolted for the door and ran in the direction of Billie Jo's workstation. How many lives did a ghost have? Nine, like a cat? If that's the case then she'd have eight because I was gonna send her back to the Chief of the Supreme Mystery with a return to sender note penned to her celestial backside.

Chapter Ten
You Can't Shampoo a Skunk

The clipper still buzzed in Billie Jo's stiff hand when I rounded the corner, Deena close behind. Where the staff had disappeared to, I had no idea, but I was relieved they had the good sense to make themselves scarce. This latest catastrophe would be better handled between us.

The CEO of Whiskey Creek's small TV station had a wide racing stripe right down the middle of his scalp, leaving two twin hedges of thick, glossy, silver curls. Most of his pride and joy lay on the floor.

He surged to his feet and whipped the cape from his neck. "I'm going to shut down this salon." Obscene words poured from his mouth.

Billie Jo stood in stunned silence, staring at his mangled hair. "I'm sorry. I can fix it—"

"Fix it! I wouldn't let you touch me after this. I'm going to call the State Board of Barbering and lodge a complaint against you."

Up until this time, Deena had remained quiet. Gently, she extracted the clipper from Billie Jo's hand, turned it off, and placed it upright in its stand. "Shut up, Mr. Burns," she commanded. "We don't like to be threatened. Your hair will grow back."

"But what am I supposed to do in the meantime?" he said. "I can't go out into public with my hair in shambles. I have a very important press conference this afternoon."

"Can you blend the layers so no one will notice?" I asked my sister, with my back to him.

"I've lost enough hair for one day," he responded, his gaze fixed on Billie Jo.

Billie Jo flushed. "I said I was sorry, Robert. The clipper motor must've malfunctioned. This has never happened in all the years I've been barbering."

"Your excuse won't restore my hair." He took a menacing step, thrusting his finger into her face. "I trusted you."

I whirled around to glare at him. "Accidents happen, Mr. Burns. We're trying to come up with a workable solution."

"Your salon is having a lot of accidents, Ms. Claiborne." His face twisted furiously. "Your sister is possessed. I could see it in those she-demon eyes."

"What's done is done," Deena cut in. "The problem now is how to repair the damage."

My watch read nine o'clock on the nose. "Deena, tell Holly to reschedule my morning appointments. If there's any fuss, squeeze them into my afternoon schedule." I turned to Billie Jo. "Go have a cup of coffee and calm down. I'll take care of this."

Burns looked uncertain. "What are you thinking?"

"I'm going to fix your hair."

"How? By super-gluing it to my head?"

I nodded. "Something like that. I'm the best in the business with hair extensions."

"This had better work. And it better look natural. Not like a wig or toupee—and what about them?"

I glanced over my shoulder at the staff gathered

close by. Clients were coming through the front door and they too, stopped to stare. "Pay no attention to them. They've seen weirder hair than yours in here."

With a towel wrapped hastily around his head, Mr. Burns followed me to my stylist chair. "How long is this going to take? I'm pressed for time."

I fastened a cape around his neck. "As long as it takes. Let me get my equipment and we'll get started."

His cell phone rang. He answered it with a sharp bark. "What...? This is the last time I'm going to tell you I had nothing to do with that. Someone beat me to it... No, I haven't found it yet... Yes, I'll get back to you when I have something to report—"

The distraction of the phone call allowed me to dash back to the dispensary. I located the last bag of curly gray synthetic hair and hot gun on the top shelf and hurried back to my station. Robert was still on the phone when I set the items on the counter and plugged in the gun to preheat. Opening the bag, I pulled out a handful of the silky strands to judge the color match against his curls. Satisfied with the results, I began dividing them into small piles.

"Tell the mayor everything is under control," Robert said into the cell phone as he watched me through the mirror.

When the hot gun reached the correct heat, I selected a pile of strands, winding them around a half inch section of hair, and applied the hot gun, locking them together.

He snapped his phone shut and slipped it into his front shirt pocket. "Explain what you're doing."

I picked up the gun and another swatch of hair. "The synthetic hair melts together, creating a strong clasp to hold the extension to your natural hair shaft. You can shampoo and dry it as you normally would do. A trim every two or three weeks will keep it looking nice until all the extensions are cut out and your natural hair is restored to the desired length. No one will ever know the difference."

He visibly relaxed. "I need to look my best for this press conference this afternoon."

"Oh? I hope it's good news," I said obligingly as I settled into a steady rhythmic flow, my mind focused on my work. The sounds of the salon ebbed away as my pace quickened.

"Henry Payne is announcing his bid for the governorship of this great state, and I'm pleased to endorse his candidacy."

I didn't comment. In my opinion, Payne would make a lousy governor. If he ran the state with the same inefficiency he ran this city, we citizens had best get ready for a substantial tax increase to pay for his over-inflated projects. Yesterday's conversation with Scarlett seared my memory cells. Here was an opportunity to broach the subject utmost on my mind, but I had to be careful how I handled the bear. I didn't want him to catch on that I was suspicious of him in any way. I opted for the dumb blonde routine. "How was your trip to Biloxi?" I asked casually.

"Why do you ask?"

I shrugged. "Scarlett told your wife that you skipped the business trip to Biloxi and was entertaining at Merry Acres instead." I raised my brows suggestively.

"Scarlett was a liar and a troublemaker."

"I heard WXYB wasn't renewing her contract."

"*Scarlett's Top Spot* wasn't enough for her," he replied. "I was already looking for her replacement."

"Oh, I'm sure you did the right thing. Scarlett struck me as greedy."

"Lust for the limelight. That was her biggest crime. She wanted what she couldn't have. I shouldn't have hired her in the first place."

I giggled. "She did crave attention. She even complained loudly to Anthony that she wanted to pursue a career in investigative journalism, and her TV show hadn't turned out to be the stepping stone she'd envisioned. How'd she take the news that she was losing her show?"

"Surprisingly, she took it well," he said, his lips pursed in a miserly line. "Hinted that she had a big story she was working on. One that would prove she belonged on the news anchor's desk. As if I'd ever replace a good man with a pretty face. What a laugh."

Scarlett was right about two things: Burns was a pompous ass, and you can't shampoo a skunk. Today, most networks, even the smallest, employed women in the highest positions. And not just behind the screen. I swallowed my disgust, and squeezed his arm in a show of admiration. "Did she tell you what kind of big story she hoped would impress you?"

At my question, he clammed up. "As I said before, Scarlett wasn't a model employee. I decided to cut my losses and replace her. It's as simple as that." His eyes narrowed with suspicion. "What's your interest in this? Are you trying to suggest that I had something to do with her death? There were numerous complaints filed against her at the station. But I believe the most likely candidate is your aesthetician."

"The police haven't finished their investigation," I reminded him. "There were plenty of people who wanted to do Scarlett in. You said so yourself." I secured the last pile of synthetic hair to the last patch of hair.

"I said there were numerous complaints filed against her. And Carla Moody had a motive for wanting her out of the way. Her husband was stalking Scarlett."

For the second time in two days, unexpected revelations left me speechless. He smiled knowingly at me in the mirror. "I knew that would get your attention. Frank made a first-class nuisance of himself. Flowers arrived practically every day from him, and I personally witnessed him accosting her in the parking lot on Wednesday afternoon with vows of undying love. Scarlett told him to go home to his wife and kids. That woman tore him to shreds."

Questions swirled in my mind as I dampened his hair. "What did you do? Did you call the police?" I picked up my scissors and comb and started cutting his hair.

"No, not at the time. I felt sorry for the guy. I know how Scarlett could string a man along, so I had a talk with him. He confessed he'd made a pass at her in a bar. He woke up the next morning at her house. He told her he loved her and wanted to marry her. After his divorce. She wasn't interested in marriage, but he was determined to change her mind."

Burns sounded as if he had firsthand knowledge of being one of Scarlett's has-beens. How else would he know how it felt to be strung along by her? One thing for certain: Frank couldn't possibly have been Scarlett's married lover. He wasn't rich or powerful. Robert was both. I pressed him for further information. "What makes you believe Carla knew about her husband's infidelity?"

"Because Frank told me he was going to ask his wife for a divorce that night."

Well, he was right about one thing—Carla had motive. And so did her cheating husband. Perhaps Frank couldn't cope with Scarlett's rejection. Or maybe he decided if he couldn't have her, no one would. My theory sounded good, but I needed a sounding board to spring it off of after I'd had a chance to organize my thoughts.

With my mind awhirl with questions and speculations, I finished the haircut. After Burns approved the completed style, I removed the cape and waited as he slipped on his suit jacket. Checking out his appearance in the mirror, he then turned to leave, but paused. "One thing I failed to mention," he said, studying me. "Detective Bradford was at the station yesterday afternoon with more questions. I told him everything, so don't be surprised when Carla is arrested for murder."

This time I kept my mouth shut, and he left an extremely satisfied customer. His cap of curls showed no signs of the previous destruction from the malfunctioning clipper. We'd dodged the bullet on this one, but how many more of Scarlett's destructive pranks would we have to endure before the salon came down on top of our heads?

A few minutes later, I was standing behind the reception desk when I spied both my sisters slipping into Deena's office. With a little free time on my hands, I grabbed a Dr. Pepper from the refrigerator and joined them.

When I entered the office, Scarlett was perched on the edge of Deena's desk, resplendent in a short ivory satin wedding dress and veil. Silently, I moaned.

"Vivian hates this dress," Scarlett said. "She thought it looked better on me. Of course, I raised the hemline a little." Her eyes blazed with a haughty, defiant air.

I ignored her. I was more than a little put out with her, especially since our discussion this morning hadn't produced positive results. I fully intended to have another talk with this rebellious lost soul as soon as I could corral her without an audience.

Billie Jo, seated in one of the chairs facing the desk, said, "Robert is going to sue the pants off us. Our malpractice insurance is already through the roof."

I took a seat on the plush sofa and slipped off my yellow heels, wiggling my toes to increase circulation. "I worked my magic, and he was very happy with the results. I asked Anthony to pick up the overflow. He needs the money, and I need a break. Boy, my feet are killing me."

Deena closed the supply catalogue on her desk. "I swear I don't know how you manage to work in heels, Jolene. Your back is going to give out one day and then what will you do?"

"Find a sugar daddy, if I'm lucky."

The corner of Deena's mouth twitched. "Billie Jo, do you feel like telling us what happened? What did Burns say to set you off?"

Billie Jo wore an expression of dismay. "That's the weird part. He didn't say anything out of the ordinary whatsoever. We talked about Scarlett's death, the new tax proposition slated for this week's county commission meeting and then—nothing. I don't remember anything from then on until Deena took the clipper from me. I felt so strange."

"Like someone or something had invaded your body?" I asked.

"Please, be serious," Deena said. "Now is not the time for jokes. The last several days have been enough of an ordeal."

Scarlett stretched as she slipped off the edge of the desk. "He's had it coming for a long time, you know." Smoothing her hands over the wrinkled, silky material, she looked over at me. "You wouldn't happen to have an iron, would you?"

I continued to ignore her and spoke to Deena. "Billie Jo was under the influence when she mowed down Robert's hair."

Deena's frown deepened. "What do you mean?"

The subject of the undead, ghosts, spooks, spirits, or in Scarlett's case—poltergeist—wasn't one I relished addressing, but Scarlett's continued noisy, mischievous antics made it impossible to disregard. How did one explain a ghost? A dead person who didn't appear dead? Scarlett sure appeared alive as she floated across the room, her angelic face highlighted by the sunlight streaming through the window.

"I know you don't believe in ghosts, but I'm still seeing Scarlett's spirit around the salon," I said. "She's responsible for the crazy accidents we're experiencing. She manipulated Billie Jo to do her bidding."

"What nonsense." Deena rolled her eyes. "There's a logical explanation for every incident. Anthony set the timer for a longer period and is too embarrassed to admit he over-processed Onella's hair. Same thing for Mandy—she accidentally turned up the heat in the pedicure bath." Her gaze was direct, level. "Mama isn't going to be happy that your invisible friends are back."

"Leave Mama out of this," I said. "But tell me, how do you explain all the clients who've witnessed strange phenomena here?"

She shrugged. "Suggestive hallucination. Whynell started the whole thing when she wandered into the facial room and imagined a ghost. She's such a sweetheart that everyone wants to believe her."

Billie Jo set her Coke on the desk. "Oh, you don't really believe that. I discussed this with Roddy. He believes when people die suddenly, or tragically like a murder, their spirit can't move on until someone shows them the way. He suggested that I research it and draw my own conclusions, so I've been watching those paranormal reality shows on TV, and I've checked out a few websites on the Internet. I'm more open to the possibility. It explains what happened with my clipper."

"Y'all are starting to freak me out with all this talk of ghosts," Deena said.

I could understand her anger and disbelief. Heck, I'd felt pretty much the same way the first time I glimpsed Scarlett. But after reading and studying about life after death, I was more accepting of my "gift". Actually, I wanted to grow as a psychic or medium so I could help Scarlett find her way into the netherworld and out of my beauty salon. After that, I was gonna concentrate on communicating with Granny Tucker and my father.

"Take Billie Jo's approach and see if you don't change your mind," I suggested, then went on to explain, as best I could, what I could remember of my childhood experiences with lost souls.

"Okay. I'll keep an open mind." Deena's voice betrayed her doubt

"That's all I ask," I replied, happy that at least she wasn't laughing at me.

Deena's intercom buzzed. "Yes, Holly?"

"Detective Bradford is here to see you."

"Send him in," she said into the intercom.

I slipped on my heels. "We'll give you two some privacy. Billie Jo and I need to get back to work anyway."

The door pushed open, and Detective Bradford strode into the room, cowboy hat in hand, his sharp gaze sweeping the room. My heart reacted immediately, and I dropped my eyes from his before Deena could detect my interest. Maintaining an emotional distance from this man was getting harder with every meeting.

Scarlett threw me a saucy look. "I'd do him if I were alive. Can you believe there's no sex in heaven? I ask you, how can paradise be paradise without sex?"

Deena rose, smiling. "Come in, Sam. We're just finishing our break."

I stood up, smoothing my sleeveless, plaid dress. "Billie Jo and I were just leaving. I'm sure you two have lots to talk about."

He laid a file folder on the desk corner. "I'm sorry to interrupt, but I needed to come by and talk with you ladies about a new development in the Cantrell case." He sat down in one of the chairs in front of the desk.

Resuming my seat on the sofa, I caught movement out of the corner of my eye. Scarlett was on the move. She perched on the side of Deena's desk. "Yummy. If you don't make a play for him, you're crazy."

Thankful that I was the only one in the room who could see and hear her, I shot her a keep-your-distance look before fastening my eyes on Bradford, curious to hear the new development.

The detective shifted uncomfortably in his chair. Could he feel Scarlett's hot ghostly breath fanning his face? He cleared his throat and shifted again.

Deena hit the intercom button. "We're going to be a little longer." She turned to him. "Can I get you a drink, Sam? It's a warm morning."

There was a rasp of excitement in her voice. A rush of pink stained her lips, her eyelashes fluttered extravagantly, and the tip of her tongue darted out to lightly touch her bottom lip.

The atmosphere tensed. Sexual magnetism pulsed. What the hell?

Billie Jo shot up from her chair. "There's a fresh pitcher of sweet tea in the refrigerator," she said with an ear-splitting grin, her fingers nervously brushing pale bangs out of her eyes.

He smiled at her. "Make that a Mountain Dew if you have one."

"Sure thing." Billie Jo practically danced out the door.

My God, it was contagious. Even Billie Jo was flirting—and she was happily married. We were behaving like three middle-aged housewives experiencing a mid-life crisis.

Wickedness shone in Scarlett's eyes.

"Stop it," I mouthed.

Ghostly fingers played with his shirt buttons. "I'm not doing anything."

My forehead furrowed as I pictured my own hands unbuttoning his shirt. My toes tingled with the cosmic sparks flying around the room. "Turn it off," I mouthed a second time, glaring fiercely at her.

"Jolene, did you say something?"

I jerked back to face Bradford. Deena also looked amused. "No, nothing... What were you saying?" I improvised.

He sighed heavily. "I'm afraid I have bad news. A witness has come forward swearing she overheard Deena confess that she wished she'd killed Scarlett when she'd had the chance. I'm here to take her downtown for further questioning."

"Deena wouldn't hurt a fly," Billie Jo said from the open doorway.

My gut bottomed out at the thought. "That's insane." I jumped up from the sofa, bristling with indignation. Which staff member or client had overheard and mistakenly come to the wrong conclusion? "Surely you can't believe Deena was serious. Frustrated, yes, but we all were put out with Scarlett."

He opened the file setting on the desk. "You took her seriously. According to the report, you said, and I quote, 'Holy cow, Deena. Don't let anyone hear you say that.'"

Out of my peripheral vision, I glimpsed Scarlett float over to sit in the middle of the desk. "I knew she was capable of murder, but I didn't figure the victim would be me." She blew icy air into my sister's face, causing her to shiver and pull away in confusion.

"Get away from her," I said. "Deena didn't kill—"

Hand raised, Bradford shook his head. "No one is

accusing Deena of murder. I would appreciate it if you would sit down and control your emotions."

Deena placed a hand on his arm. "Jolene's a tiger when it comes to her little sisters. She's like an angel watching over us. But, I promise, we'll fully cooperate with the investigation."

Billie Jo handed him the glass of Mountain Dew and plopped down on the opposite chair. I wasn't even sure she heard him when he thanked her.

He took a long sip of the soft drink. "I know this situation is hard on your family, but I have a job to do, personal feelings aside." He set the glass down on the desk and reached out and caught Deena's hand in his. "I believe you're still the same sweet girl I knew in high school. But I must investigate every lead even if it implicates you, understand?"

She nodded her head decidedly. "I'm ready to leave when you are."

"Wait. What about Frank Moody?" The words punched out of my mouth. "He was stalking Scarlett according to Robert Burns. He wanted to divorce Carla and marry Scarlett, but Scarlett didn't want to marry him. Frank also told him that he was gonna ask Carla for a divorce on Wednesday night. I hate to believe she might be capable of murder, but revenge is a powerful motive."

Bradford's eyes were sharp and assessing as they settled on me. "My point exactly. Adultery hits hard and takes no hostages. Revenge is a powerful motive. It's the central thought floating around at the station about Deena. She's a person of interest along with the Moody couple."

"Does Deena need a lawyer?" I asked, uncertain

how this was going to play out. What if Deena was arrested for Scarlett's murder? She wouldn't be the first innocent person jailed for a crime she didn't commit. The niggling guilt of my own inadequacy washed over me.

"It's her right to have a lawyer present if she wishes one."

Deena flung out a hand. "I'll be fine. I trust Sam, and this shouldn't take too long. And please don't call Mama. She'll worry." She shot me a look that said I'd regret it if I did.

It's a good thing she couldn't read my mind, because those were my intentions as soon as the door closed behind her. With the finger of suspicion pointed directly at my sister, the time for extreme action had arrived. And I knew just who to call to get the pot boiling.

Chapter Eleven
A Meeting of the Minds

The door had no sooner slammed shut when a worried look creased Billie Jo's face. "Now what do we do?"

I shot to my feet and dashed over to the desk. "Call Mama, what else?" I punched in her number and waited for her to pick up.

"But Deena told you not to," she cautioned. "She's upset enough without Mama showing up at the police station."

Mama picked up on the fourth ring. "Hello."

"Mama, listen to me without interrupting, okay?" I continued talking over her reply. "Something important has come up, and I need for you to get me a copy of Scarlett's preliminary autopsy report. Detective Bradford was just here, and he took Deena in for further questioning."

"We've got to do something!" Her voice cracked over the line.

"I know Mama—I know that. Keep your panties on."

"Just how am I supposed to get a copy of Scarlett's autopsy report? This isn't some TV show, you know."

"Yes, I know that. I'm going to tell you how to get it if you'll let me talk. Call Diane Downey and explain to her that we need a copy of the report." I held the receiver away from my ear as she blasted her response on the other end.

"Good Lord Almighty, Jolene. Diane's gonna think I've lost my mind!"

"Kayla Winston adores Diane, and you know it," I replied as calmly as I could. "She'll jump at a chance to impress the Queen Bee."

"That's illegal," Mama pointed out.

"Yes, I know, but a witness overheard Deena telling me she wished she'd killed Scarlett when she had a chance to get away with it."

"I see what you mean. It shouldn't be too hard for Kayla to get her hands on that report. She's mentioned several times that her husband has a home office. Maybe his home computer links up with the one down at the coroner's office."

"Call me when you know something, okay?"

I hung up the phone, sat down heavily in Deena's chair, and crossed my fingers for good luck. "Now all we have to do is find out a way to obtain a copy of the police investigative report. Deena's not a reliable spy."

Billie Jo's face reflected skepticism. "You've crossed over to the dark side. First, you finagled church ladies into stealing from the coroner's office, and now you're suggesting we steal from the cops? One trip downtown was enough for me."

"I'm not suggesting we physically steal from the cops. Maybe something more along the lines of computer hacking."

"Equally undoable. What are we looking for?"

"The composition of the mask and their list of suspects. We need to find any information that will point us in the right direction in our own investigation."

Billie Jo smacked her hand on her forehead. "I forgot about the jars in the facial room. Why don't we have them analyzed? Then we'll know exactly what's inside them, and we can forget about getting arrested for computer hacking."

I beamed at her. "That's a brilliant idea. Now all we have to do is pray Mama works her magic with Diane."

"I've got a friend who owes me a big favor, and he just happens to be a lab technician for the coroner. I'll give him a call and see if he can help us. If he agrees, I'll run the samples over to him," she said, then left the office.

After the door shut, I joined Scarlett at the window hoping for a chance to talk to her now that we were alone. Waves of sorrow and frustration radiated from her. I wanted to both console and scold her for the continued bad pranks. My hand passed through her satin encased shoulder so I let it fall to my side. "I thought you'd be happy with the progress we're making on your case."

She turned haunted eyes on me. "That police detective said Deena murdered me for revenge. I guess you feel I had it coming, don't you?"

"Bradford never said Deena murdered you. Be reasonable."

"One act of revenge deserves another." Then she glanced out the window and vanished from sight.

Oh, good grief. Now I had an angry, vengeful ghost on my hands on top of a murder investigation. There were some days I wished I'd stayed home in bed.

****

Precisely three hours later, I looked up from my client's hair to see Bradford's unmarked police car pull up at the front curb. Deena climbed out, waved at him, and waltzed through the door with a huge smile on her face, and a half-eaten ice cream cone in her hand. Without so much as a how-do-you-do, she disappeared into her office, shutting the door before I had a chance to motion her over to my station. Her wide smile made me believe she'd gone on a date instead of to the police station for questioning. Removing the cape from my client, I followed her up to the reception desk and waited as she paid her bill.

"Your next client cancelled," Holly said. "She rescheduled for Tuesday."

"How much time do I have before my next appointment?"

She brought up my appointment book on the computer. "About thirty minutes. I could call her and see if she can come in earlier."

I shook my head, anxious to talk with Deena. "No thanks, I need a break. I'll be in Deena's office if anyone's looking for me. And tell Billie Jo to join us when she's finished with her haircut if she has time."

The office door was closed, so I knocked once and opened the door. Deena looked up at my entrance and promptly ended her phone call—but not before I heard her tell the caller she'd see him later. Probably Bradford, I reasoned by the happy look on her face.

"I won't ask who was on the phone," I said. "That Grand Canyon smile you're wearing speaks for itself. Now, tell me what happened at the police station."

She finished the last bite of ice cream cone, licking

her fingertips. "Detective Grant went over my statement again and again, trying to catch me in a lie. Finally, he gave up. I swear he's like an angry battering ram."

I shook off my tight heels. "You were gone for three hours. Did it take that long?"

She reached for her purse, removed a compact and a tube of lipstick and applied a peachy shine to her lips. "We grabbed a bite to eat afterward at the Dairy Queen."

"You could've called and said you were okay. Billie Jo and I were worried about you, and I had to skip lunch to help Holly out at the desk." A hint of jealousy crept into my voice as I pictured them together at a small table, burger and fries forgotten, as they laughed over a remembered incident from their high school days.

Right then, the door burst open, and Mama rushed in. "I got it, Jolene. Kayla said it was easy. She found a copy in the file cabinet in her husband's home office and made a copy on his copier and ran it over to Diane's, and I met them for lunch at Ruby Tuesday's and voila, here I am." She flung out her arms in a grand gesture. "Are you okay, Deena, honey? They didn't slap handcuffs on you, did they, honey? I swear I don't know what the world's coming to."

I felt my eyebrows stretch toward the ceiling. "How many cocktails did you have with your lunch?"

Mama flashed me a dour look. "We shared a carafe of wine with our seafood. I was worried about my daughter being hauled to jail." Her eyes narrowed. "Are you questioning my choices?"

"Yes. Now, let me read the autopsy report you're waving around like a flag on a stick."

Deena gave me a sharp glance. "I told Jolene not to call you. Sam took me in to answer some additional questions regarding some foolish remark I made. I wasn't hauled to jail. Now, would someone please explain what's going on around here?"

Mama just smiled. "Ask Jolene. She's the one with the harebrained ideas. She called me this morning, scaring me half to death with tales of your imminent incarceration if I didn't do what she wanted." She waved the paper just under my nose. "This is Scarlett's preliminary autopsy report, lifted by the coroner's wife."

I grabbed the paper and shooed away her hand as she tried to retrieve it. "Let me read this." I smiled sweetly to soften my voice.

The door opened, and Billie Jo paused on the threshold. "Hey, Mama. Glad to see you back in one piece, Deena. I took those samples over to Paul. He said he'd get back with me in a day or two at the most, when he's finished analyzing them."

Deena gestured to Billie Jo. "Join us. Our big sister is going to explain what's going on since she's the catalyst of all this activity."

I quickly scanned the report while Billie Jo closed the door and settled on the sofa. I looked up to find all three of them staring at me. From the stony expression on Mama's face, I suspected she was still stewing. Vivacious Billie Jo tried not to appear curious, and Deena had that silly grin back on her face. I guessed she was using the time to daydream about her time with Bradford.

Pushing aside that thought, I cleared my throat. "I'm trying to pin down the facts regarding Scarlett's death so we can clear our name of any wrongdoing and save our business. Now that Deena's a person of interest, we have to obtain the information by any way available to us to clear her and hopefully, Carla. Mama obtained a copy of the preliminary autopsy report through her connections. The report indicates the mask constricted Scarlett's throat muscles. She choked to death on her own vomit. The coroner has it unofficially as a suspicious death."

"Does it say what made her sick?" Deena asked.

I glanced back down at the report. "I'm not sure with all of these medical terms, but he obtained samples of her stomach contents for toxicology. He put a rush on it."

"Detective Grant kept asking me about the mask. Like how much I knew about the products. What to mix together. He really focused on my knowledge of chemistry. I informed him that, as manager, I have to have a working knowledge of all the products used in the salon."

Billie Jo made an impatient gesture. "Jolene wanted to hack into the police computers to copy their investigative reports, but I thought it was a dumb-ass idea. I suggested we take samples of the facial room jars and have them analyzed instead. That way we stay out of jail longer."

"Stop staring at me like I've sprouted another head," I said. "We need to know what evidence the police have so we can plan our next move."

Mama huffed. "Plan our next move? I believe we should gather all future information from the grapevine and stay out of jail like Billie Jo suggested."

I turned to Deena. "Do you have the pictures of the

crime scene?"

She opened the top desk drawer, and withdrew a packet of pictures. "Yes, here they are. I looked at them, but nothing stands out other than that ghastly mask." She handed them to me.

The intercom buzzed. "Mrs. Hazard and Ms. Claiborne's clients are here."

"Thank you, Holly. They'll be right out," Deena said.

I shoved the fat envelope back across the desk. "I'll look at these later." I kissed Mama's cheek. "Perhaps you should have a cup of coffee before you attempt to drive home. Or better still lie down on the sofa until some of the alcohol dissipates out of your system. We wouldn't want to have to bail you out of jail for driving under the influence."

Mama gave a quick cackle of laughter. "Go on with you. I'm fine. But perhaps a fresh cup of coffee is a good idea before I hit the road."

Billie Jo and I left the office together. The rest of the afternoon progressed smoothly, other than the occasional problem with Scarlett's ghostly moods. I swear once or twice her lamenting must've pierced through the veil, for I witnessed several clients jump up from their seats and plop back down in another, all the while scanning the salon wide-eyed. The commotion created havoc among the staff and clientele alike. Deena caught most of Scarlett's pranks, but she refused to admit anything supernatural had taken over the salon. Everyone's nerves were frayed by the end of the day. If I didn't solve this soon, we wouldn't have a salon left.

****

The salon had closed, the staff had left, and the

welcome silence washed around me after a long day behind the chair and smoothing ruffled feathers. Telling my sisters I had unfinished work on several wigs, I locked the doors and went into the kitchen for a glass of iced tea. Scarlett and I needed to talk.

My wait wasn't long. I'd just sat down at the dinette table when she materialized over by the refrigerator, Civil War tatters and all—altered, of course.

"Your face's puffy," I said. "Mine does the same thing after a good cry. Feel better?"

She sighed. "Crying does help."

"Want to talk about it?"

"Hearing all those negative comments people are making about me struck a memory. When I was alive, I never really cared about anyone's feelings but my own. I came first. If I saw something—or someone—I wanted, I just went for it, regardless of the outcome. I never realized I was destroying lives along the way. No wonder Deena murdered me."

"I thought you said Carla did you in."

"I was wrong. Deena did it."

"You need to get that notion out of your head. Deena isn't capable of murder. She won't even kill a bug. Although, I wanted to strangle you—"

"Ohmigod. *You* murdered me? I'm alone with my murderer?"

Her reaction amused me. "You're all ready dead, so settle down. The only thing I'm guilty of is wishful thinking. The killer is still at large."

Scarlett adjusted her tattered dress and sat down across the table from me, looking so alive I had a hard time believing her body rested on a cold slab in the morgue.

"Sorry I accused you, but it sounded like a confession to me."

I finished my sip of tea. "Your apology is accepted. I'm glad your memory seems to be working well. I need some questions answered, like the names of the men you were sleeping with. Mr. Hart observed you messing around with a man whose description sounds an awful lot like Anthony."

"Old man Hart spied on me?"

"Yep. With binoculars. Mrs. Hart too. She witnessed two men casing your house one night. She described them as dressed all in black like the FBI." I laughed. "Annabel believed you might be an undercover agent. She woke up her husband and called the police. The men drove away before they could be apprehended."

She looked thoughtful. "Damn nosey neighbors. Believe me when I tell you that I wasn't having an affair with Anthony."

"Okay, what about the jade elephant? It's important, or you wouldn't have asked me to find it. Try to remember. Even the slightest hint. Nothing is too small or insignificant."

She stared through me as if lost in the past. A golden glow pulsated around her. Not a halo, but a warm, loving light. Suddenly, her ethereal beauty struck me full in the face.

"Death becomes you," I said. The words were out of character, but I felt as if I looked upon an angel. Surely, Scarlett was no angel—just a misplaced ghost with an overactive aura.

"Perhaps you might find this jade elephant in my

house?" she said off-handedly. "That would be the logical place I would hide something."

This wasn't the first time the thought had occurred to me. However, thinking about it and actually breaking into her house was something else entirely. That was very dicey. Also, a scary kind of dangerous. I voiced my doubts. "Oh, I don't know. The police know about the jade elephant. By this time, they've gone over your house with a fine-tooth comb. What if I get caught?"

"What if you don't?"

"The police are probably watching the house."

"My father had an elephant figurine from the Orient."

"Made of jade?"

"Could be."

"The police would have found it by now," I reasoned out loud.

"I think I'll go have a look-see."

"By yourself?"

"Well, you won't go, so I have to," she said, sounding exasperated. "Come with me."

I hesitated, instinctively knowing that to take this drastic step would mean that I'd crossed the point of no return. At this moment, I had enough demons on my tail without adding possible jail time, and prison orange wasn't my best color.

Scarlett must've seen the indecision written on my face because she pressed me further by saying, "I'll have your back. And you do have a gun in case we run into trouble."

I stood up, still feeling uncertain. "I've never shot anyone in my life, and I don't plan on starting, so nix the gun thing."

"Got it—no guns. Stop worrying, you'll be fine. I promise."

A second later, I made my decision. "Okay, I'll drive out to your house late tonight. See if I can locate any clues to identify the jade elephant or anything else that might solve this mystery."

At my words, she glowed brighter. "Do you have my address?"

I shielded my eyes from the bright golden glow. "You're not going with me like that. Turn it off. Or stop doing whatever it is causing you to light up like a Friday night high school football game." I held up her client information card. "I have it right here. Ashland Drive in Westgate."

She floated over the dinette table. "I'll ask Vivian how to turn it off when I change into something more appropriate for house haunting, or whatever it is you said we'd be doing tonight. This is going to be so much fun. See you later." She vanished through the wall.

Fun? This wasn't meant to be a pleasant outing between friends. I'd be undertaking a dangerous mission. What if the Harts started snooping around and alerted the police? Or worse yet, what if the killer showed up? Someone could end up hurt or—heaven forbid—dead. Wait a minute. That someone could be me!

Chapter Twelve
Speaking of the Dead

I locked up the salon and headed straight home to a hot shower. I emerged from the bathroom feeling refreshed and slipped into a pair of black jeans and T-shirt. In the kitchen, I made myself a peanut butter and jelly sandwich, fed Tango, and went into the den to relax and eat my supper.

Wheel of Fortune had just started when I switched on the TV. Settling back into my recliner, I ate my sandwich and drank the cold milk as I formulated a plan for later tonight. With daylight saving time in full swing, it wouldn't get dark enough to sneak around undetected until nine o'clock or later. Tango jumped up onto the recliner, settling in my lap. His purring lulled me to sleep.

The shrill ring of the phone woke me close to 9:25. Tango, angry at being disturbed, hissed at me when I dislodged him from my lap. The kitchen phone ID indicated the caller. Not really in the mood for conversation, I started to ignore it, but thought better. Mama would just keep calling until she reached me. And there was the slightest chance she might drive into town looking for me and I didn't relish the thought of her on the roads after dark. I picked up the receiver.

"Hello, Mama."

"Did I wake you?"

I smothered a yawn. "Yes, but I'm glad you did. What's up?"

"Merriam called with a wild tale about the salon being haunted. Deena suggested I speak with you."

"If you've spoken with Deena then you know the whole story. We're experiencing some random incidents. There's nothing to worry about."

"So your invisible friend has moved on?"

"What invisible friend?"

Mama's sigh echoed over the line. "That's real good news. Now, the other reason why I called was to tell you Diane phoned. Scarlett's body has been released for burial."

That little bit of news was surprising. "Who claimed the body? She was an only child, and her parents are dead. I didn't realize she had any other living relatives."

"Wrong. Word from Kayla is a cousin from Dothan claimed the body this afternoon. A short memorial service is planned for Sunday afternoon at Beulah Hill Funeral Home."

"Wow. I thought there'd be more of a fuss. She is a local celebrity of sorts. Why isn't WXYB more involved? There hasn't been a lot of coverage on the news about her death. Who's this cousin? Scarlett never mentioned having a relative in Alabama."

"I can't answer your questions. Diane's trying to find out all she can."

"Is the cousin male or female?"

"Female. The grapevine spit up a doozy. Seems Scarlett was not only sleeping with a married man but also with a much younger man. Rich-and-married found out Scarlett was two-timing him, and that's why they fought. Or so they speculate."

Hmm. This information warranted consideration. Had rich-and-married killed Scarlett in a crime of passion? I grabbed a pencil and scribbled the question down on a notepad I kept by the phone for emergencies. "I don't suppose the ladies have been able to come up with any names, have they?"

"Not yet. They have feelers spread throughout the tri-county area. Oh, before I forget, I expect the staff to attend the funeral."

"They'll be there. Have you heard from Carla's mother?"

"Yes. She was in Florida and didn't offer any explanations as to why she'd been unable to be reached. She's home now. She did mention Carla was being released from the hospital tomorrow or Friday. Her doctor advised against her attending Scarlett's funeral. She needs time to adjust."

The clock over the stove read nine-thirty. So far, there'd been no further sign from my wacky ghost. Perhaps she was knee-deep in Vivian's heavenly closet and had forgotten about my undercover excursion.

"Is that all, Mama? I'm in a hurry."

"Beth asked me about Carla's employment status, and I told her we'd discuss it another time. 'Bye."

With those parting words she hung up. Anxious to get started, I slipped on black sneakers, fished my ankle-holster out of a drawer, strapped it on, and secured Mini Pearl with a snap. Grabbing up my purse and keys from the counter, I headed out the door into the dark, cloudy night—a night perfect for undercover work.

Dalton Road wasn't crowded when I pulled into

traffic off Roadrunner Drive. I was traveling west when I noticed a late model dark blue sedan tailing several cars behind. The car seemed vaguely familiar, but I couldn't place where I'd seen it before. But I had seen it. And recently, of that I was certain. With my eyes glued to the rearview mirror, I shifted lanes, speeding up to put a little distance between my Mustang and the blue sedan, not exactly knowing why I felt the need to lose the tail.

I had just swung off onto a side street when, without warning, Scarlett's dark form appeared in the passenger seat, decked out in a mourning dress and veil like a great black vulture. Screaming with fright, I swerved into the opposite lane, which promptly sent a white van careening into the shoulder of the road. The driver shot me a bird, and I returned the gesture.

"Don't do that," I yelled. "I could've been killed."

She raised her veil. Blue-green eyes snapped with glee. "I'm in a jovial mood."

"Jovial mood? Ha. You're planning my demise. Don't you have enough neighbors on the Other Side?"

My transient specter flashed a wicked smile. "Are you fishing for your heavenly address? I know it if you're interested."

Swinging left at the intersection, I turned onto Virginia Court, checking the rearview mirror for any sign of the blue sedan. "Can I have a rain check?" I asked, relieved that I'd lost the sedan.

The veil dropped back into place. "Well, I don't know. Depends on my mood at the time."

"Fair enough. Are you in the mood to answer a question or two for me?"

"If it'll help my case. I'm getting tired of all this

back and forth."

"The word around town is you were having multiple affairs. Can you name any of them?"

"There was only one man in my life. The others were merely pawns to obtain my goal." She spoke with some bitterness.

"Uh huh. So, who was the man?"

"The mayor." Her voice had softened, and a dreamy expression crossed her face.

I gasped with the impact of her confession. "Crap, Scarlett. Talk about sleeping with the enemy!"

"It started out innocently," she answered defensively. "Those long, boring meetings…"

"The Mayor's Advisory Committee." I understood at once. Scarlett had purposely positioned herself to be appointed to the group—a cunning, but superb camouflage maneuver. Once inside, she had access to the big wigs of Whiskey Creek. And a lot of under-the-table dealings that would serve her purpose well.

"Yes. At first, I kept my mouth shut and my ears open, and I made good connections. Henry was so mixed up about his marriage that I just naturally took advantage of the opportunity." She stopped, her sulky red mouth pulled tight.

"So you used any means at your disposal to get what you wanted."

"At first I did."

"And then you fell for him," I added.

"Hard."

In silence, we passed Westgate Country Club and made a left onto Lovers Lane Drive and drove around to the back of the neighborhood. "Your cousin from Dothan is burying you at Peaceful Valley Cemetery," I told her.

Finally, she glanced in my direction. "I'll be there. Are you doing my hair and makeup?"

I shivered at the thought. "No, I'll leave that to someone else."

"Why not? It's a special day."

"I believe it'll be a closed casket ceremony. You wouldn't want folks staring at your wrecked face, would you?" I shivered again.

"I'm glad you told me."

"Speaking of the dead, have you seen Daddy over there? On the Other Side, I mean?"

Scarlett tapped her cheek as if in deep thought. "No, can't say that I have. Would you like me to track him down?"

"That would be great if you can."

"Hey, we're having a bonding moment."

I smiled at her observation and turned onto Ashland Drive which butted up against a huge wooded area and would afford some much-needed concealment. Slowly, I approached her two-story white house. I slowed down and pulled my car off onto the dirt alleyway leading to the back of the row of houses and turned off the headlights.

"We'll have to drive in the dark. Better to be safe. I'll park a ways down from your house so the neighbors don't become suspicious."

Scarlett's laughter was low, throaty. "I see quite well in the dark. It's one of the benefits of being dead."

I inched the car down the alley toward her back yard. I'd just pulled under a giant oak and killed the engine when the moon peeked out from behind a cloud, bathing the two-story white house in silvery light. "It looks eerie. And haunted."

"Don't be afraid. The house isn't haunted—you are."

I reached for the door handle. "Thanks for reminding me." I glanced over at the passenger seat. "Let's get this over with fast."

The seat was empty.

"That's just great," I muttered. "I'm a haunted woman without a ghost."

Uneasiness settled over me, and I felt a reluctance to leave the safety of the car and go off into the unknown reaches of the empty house. Gathering my limited courage, I left the car and crept along the dense tree line banking the alley. Scruffy clouds passed over the moon, blocking the muted light, and I stumbled over ancient roots littering the dusty, alleyway. A warm breeze stroked the leaves overhead, rustling the branches as I cautiously picked my way toward the shadowy house.

I paused at the back gate, my hand on the latch. The eeriness of the night hadn't helped my frayed nerves, and I was strongly tempted to flee before the phantom winds of fate had a chance to fling me forward into this creeping, whispering house. What waited beyond the gate? Answers? More secrets? A homicidal maniac waiting for his next victim? Before I could change my mind, I took a deep, shuddery breath, and pushed open the gate.

Chapter Thirteen
The Break-In

The front and back doors were locked. No surprise there. I slipped on a pair of latex gloves from the salon and tried several windows before the kitchen window eased open under heavy pressure. I managed to slip in with only scratched elbows, landed with a thud, and scrambled to my feet noiselessly. The small flashlight pinched my side when I landed, but thankfully, there was no real harm done.

I switched on the pencil-thin flashlight, and the tiny beam struggled to break through the wall of darkness. Wispy shadows shifted and swirled like a stalking alley cat ready to pounce on the slightest movement. With so little light, this was going to be much harder than I'd planned.

I started with the kitchen. The cabinets contained beautiful dinner and stemware. It looked like delicate porcelain and probably designer, knowing Scarlett's expensive tastes. After I'd rifled through the kitchen without finding anything of interest, I moved on to the formal dining room.

Here the pattern repeated. The china buffet held more pricey china and crystal. An antique silver coffee and tea set dominated the heavy Sheraton sideboard. From what I could discern in the semi-darkness, the room was exquisite. Custom-made white wooden plantation shutters with paisley silk toppers dressed the floor-to-ceiling windows, matching the rug underneath the large table. Landscape paintings lined the ivory walls. A quick search revealed nothing of interest.

"Scarlett?" I called softly as I exited the dining room, and entered the foyer. My voice echoed through the cavernous entryway. Not receiving an answer, I found my way to the library. The walls were lined with built-in bookshelves overflowing with heavy volumes and covered in family portraits. I recognized Scarlett's parents staring out from their gilt frames. Both had been tragically killed five years ago in a plane crash, which had left Scarlett a very wealthy woman according to the gossipmongers. At the time, she had been happily planning her wedding to a millionaire, but after the fatal accident, she broke off the engagement, disappearing from society. Two years later, she reappeared, footloose and fancy-free. That's when she started husband poaching.

Sitting on the end tables were figurines of every kind and variety. I examined each one carefully, but there wasn't an elephant figurine in the room. The bookshelves were extensive. Could the jade elephant be the title of a book? Had Scarlett hidden something vitally important between the pages of one of the hundreds of books? God, I hoped not. I'd need an army to help me go through the heavy, dusty volumes.

A cabinet under one of the shelves contained family albums. I was leafing through one when a slight breeze brushed my face. "Is that you, Scarlett?" The hairs on my arms stood up as the breeze shifted in the opposite direction. "Stop, you're scaring me."

The grandfather clock standing in the corner

chimed. I jumped, spooked. Crap, now I had to pee. Where was the downstairs bathroom located? And where was Scarlett? A tree branch tapped against the window. I leaped away in alarm, colliding with the square coffee table, and knocked several magazines to the floor. Feeling completely vulnerable and scared out of my wits, I bent down to pick them up. Creaking sounds echoed from the front of the house. This investigating idea wasn't working out. God, I had to find the bathroom real quick.

Chills skittered up my spine as another breeze goosed me. I returned the magazines to the table and the photo albums to the cabinet.

"Come see what I found," Scarlett said from behind me.

I peed my pants. "Aaugh! Look what you did!" Ready to strangle her, I stood there in my wet jeans feeling foolish and disgustingly unclean. Complaining all the way to the kitchen, I snatched up a couple of paper towels and wiped the hardwood floor clean, dumping the soiled towels in the trashcan under the sink.

Scarlett kept up a running commentary the entire time, and I made a point to ignore her. If she hadn't startled me, this wouldn't have happened. "Where's your bedroom?" I grumbled.

"Just down the hall, why?"

"I need something to wear, that's why." I explored the rest of the downstairs until I found the master bedroom. A huge walk-in closet afforded a bevy of choices for a super-thin woman. I discarded most of the clothing until I found a dark, wraparound skirt large enough to cover my size twelve figure.

Everything in me rebelled at the thought of wearing Scarlett's panties, so I'd go home commando. She followed me back to the kitchen to watch me rifle through her pantry until I found the zip-up baggies and a plastic sack for my wet clothes.

With supplies in hand, I headed into the master bath. With guidance from the small beam of the flashlight, I removed several items from beneath the vanity cabinet, and cleaned myself, dumping my soiled things into a plastic sack. With my ankle holster reattached, I dressed in the skirt and pulled on my damp sneakers.

While replacing the items I'd removed from the vanity, I knocked a small, square box to the floor. Passing the beam over it, I stared down at the opened home pregnancy test. I dumped the box's contents onto the marble counter. With a tissue, I rolled the test stick over and trained the tiny flashlight beam down on it.

Not pregnant.

Why hadn't I noticed that important information on the preliminary autopsy report?

Scarlett stood by the white claw-foot tub watching me, hurt and longing spread over her face.

"I'm so sorry. I had no idea you wanted a child." I was at a loss for words.

"I didn't either until it was too late." She faded from view.

Taking a few calming breaths, I stood on wobbly legs, the box still in my hands. I scraped the contents back into the box, returned it to the vanity, grabbed the sack, and headed back into the master bedroom.

Darkness closed around me. Now disoriented, I wasn't sure how to escape the house. I raked the room with the tiny light. The plastic sack rustled loudly. I moved slowly toward the door in front of me and stepped out of the bedroom, making my way down the hall. The soft click of a door closing reached my ears. I froze.

Footsteps approached the foyer. I backtracked to the bedroom. Hopefully, I'd be able to open one of the massive windows before the intruder realized I was in the house. The plastic sack under my arm crackled with each step. I had to get rid of it, so I tossed it under the bed thinking I'd retrieve it later and ran to one of the windows. It wouldn't open.

Now, footfalls sounded in the hallway. Out of time, I dashed to the walk-in closet, burying myself deep between the layers of clothes. Removing Mini Pearl from her holster, I waited with bated breath to be discovered. From my silken coffin, I heard muffled sounds and detected a crack of light coming from the bathroom.

The grandfather clock struck midnight before I heard no further sounds coming from the bedroom. I holstered Mini Pearl and emerged from the closet. As quietly as I could, I eased into the bedroom. Faint sounds filtered down from upstairs. Tiptoeing around to the other bedroom window, I struggled to lift it. After several attempts, it moved slightly. The prospect of escape gave me courage, and I pushed with all my strength until it slid open. The screen fell out with a whoosh.

As quietly as I could manage, I climbed out the window, landed on the lush grass and dashed for the cover of the trees and my car parked under the massive oak down the alleyway. In my haste, I tripped and landed face down on the hard red clay, and my skirt flapped open. Sweat poured down my face, stinging my eyes as I got up and raced for cover.

"You! Hey, you! Stop," a male voice hollered at my back. I ran harder. Ducking into the line of oaks, I tripped again, landing on a soft mound of plants, my ankle exploding with pain.

My black Mustang loomed ahead. Lumbering to my feet, I yelped in pain as I applied weight on my injured ankle. Limping the last couple of steps, I jerked open the car door, slid in, and fished for the keys in my pocket. Although I couldn't see my pursuer, I could hear him ordering me to stop. That I wasn't gonna do. Gunning the engine, I slammed into reverse, did a quick turn, and sped off down the dirt alleyway. The twenty mph speed limit in the neighborhood necessitated that I slow down. Keeping my eyes peeled to my rearview mirror in case my pursuer tracked me, I painstakingly wound around the twisting streets until I reached Old Dalton Road. After a mile of nothing but dark road behind me, I relaxed my grip on the steering wheel and the gas pedal. Immediately a shaft of fear shot through me as fearful images of the break-in and pursuit built in my mind. My heart pounded, and my eyes watered. My hands began trembling, so I pulled over to the side of the road to calm my breathing and fight for control over my swirling emotions. Without shame, I gave into the tears, and had a good long cry at my foolish actions.

After the initial shock wore off, I again started for home. As I drove, questions circled through my mind. Who had been in the house with me? Could the intruder possibly be looking for the jade elephant? What other secrets did the house hold? How many people had

Scarlett pissed off? Who were the men in black? Was Scarlett the intended target that day in the salon? Carla? Me? My sisters? Crap, what had I gotten mixed up in?

Ten minutes later, I pulled into the carport of my darkened house and killed the engine. The streetlights pooled golden light on the street. Through my rearview mirror I noticed the same late model, dark blue sedan that had trailed me earlier parked in front of the house across the street. A man sat smoking in the driver's side. His face lay in shadows, but a heavily-muscled, arm rested on an opened window frame. From the tilt of the cigarette tip, I knew he was watching me.

Again, adrenaline caused my blood pressure to skyrocket. Grabbing my purse, I withdrew my cell phone to call 9-1-1 and then stopped. What if this wasn't the same car and the driver was innocently waiting for my neighbor to return home? I had no proof to substantiate my suspicions.

Keep cool, I reminded myself as I snapped my phone shut and reached for my gun. With Mini Pearl tucked securely in my hand, I exited the car and backed to the kitchen door, fearful of turning my back to the man. I unlocked the door and stepped inside, locking it behind me. I hit the light switch and Tango immediately yowled as the room flooded with brightness.

Quickly, I reset the alarm system in the hallway. With muted light spilling through the door from the kitchen, I positioned myself by one of the windows in the living room, and peered out from a slit in the heavy damask draperies. Relief washed over me. The car was gone. Taking a deep breath, I relaxed now that the danger had passed for the moment.

I holstered my gun and made a painful round

through the house on my aching ankle, checking every door and window until satisfied the house was secure. I turned off the front and back porch lights, and went into the kitchen, poured Tango a bowl of milk to stop his crying, and then limped down the hall to my bedroom.

When I emerged from my shower, Tango was cleaning himself at the foot of the bed.

Exhausted, I fell into bed and tried to sleep, but my thoughts and assumptions of the night's events circled nonstop in my head. Disturbed by the implications of being in such close proximity with a possible killer, I imagined every night sound as a signal of danger. Restless, I tossed and turned, tangling the sheets about my body. My ankle throbbed, and I felt the slightest urge to scratch my face and nether regions.

Tango protested loudly, so I abandoned my efforts at sleep. Rolling over, I switched on the bedside lamp, swinging my legs over the side of the bed. Perhaps a cup of hot chamomile tea would aid in relaxation. In the kitchen pantry I found a box of Sleepytime Tea on a back shelf. With steaming cup in hand, I settled at the kitchen table with pen and notebook. Hastily, I jotted down my discovery at Scarlett's house. Fact 1: The negative pregnancy test. Evidently the rumor had proved untrue. Had Scarlett been the one behind the lie? If yes, what would she accomplish by lying? I'd ask her at our next meeting—whenever that would be. Fact 2: There had been a man in the house with me. I knew that much from the masculine voice that had ordered me to stop as I had fled the scene. He was searching for something.

Finally, the soothing effects of the tea kicked in. I yawned several times, rose from the table, and started back down the hall to my bedroom. As I passed through the living room, a strange outside noise caught my attention. As a precaution, and to assure myself all was well, I peeked through the heavy drapes. The dark blue sedan had returned.

Quickly, I stepped back from the window, and allowed the drape to drop back in place. The calming effects of the tea seemed to dissolve with the mounting tension. Who was this man? What did he want? And more importantly, how much danger was I in? Burning questions continued to swirl in my mind as I paced the length of the living room until finally, pain from my injured ankle, and exhaustion drove me to the couch. My last thought was of Scarlett's mangled face and the frightening possibly that her murderer watched from the dark blue sedan.

Chapter Fourteen
Consequences

The early morning light beaming through the crack in the draperies pierced my closed eyelids. I fought to wake from the deep sleep of emotional and physical exhaustion. As the events of last night came rushing back, I wind-milled off the living room sofa and stubbed my big toe on the oak coffee table. Cursing my bad luck, I hopped to the window on my uninjured foot and peered out into the bright sunshine. The man in the blue sedan had disappeared—sometime in the pre-dawn hours, as best as I could figure. My last time check of the wall clock had been at four a.m. I must've dozed off.

A pounding headache, and itchy, stinging skin, forced me into the bathroom. One quick look into the mirror confirmed what I'd suspected last night: I'd fallen into a patch of poison oak or ivy while fleeing the scene of my crime. My face, covered with red bumps, looked like an adolescent breakout. Even my mouth had yellowed where I'd smacked it on the hard ground when I fell. And lo, even my butt and lady parts itched.

"What's next, for God's sake, Jolene? You look awful."

Pulling out a bottle of aspirin and calamine lotion from the medicine cabinet, I popped two pills and doused my face and body where the poison had touched with lotion-soaked cotton balls. Grabbing an Ace bandage, I limped into the kitchen and wrapped my sore ankle. Tango sat next to his bowl, expectantly.

I filled the food bowl with cat food and then made coffee. The clock over the oven read 7:32. My cell phone lay next to the stove. I picked it up and dialed Deena's number.

"Hey, I know it's early, but I wanted to call and tell you I'm feeling a little under the weather and won't be into work today," I said when she picked up. "Can you have Holly reschedule my appointments or see if any of the other stylists can work them in?"

"Do I need to come over and take you to the doctor? Billie Jo can supervise if needed. Anthony called out also, but I'm confident the other stylists can pick up the slack."

"No thanks. I'll be fine after a day's rest."

"Oh, you poor dear, call me and tell me what the doctor says, okay? Promise or I'll worry."

I rolled my eyes. Crap, now I'd have to consult with my doctor because Deena, a natural born nurturer, would hound me until I did. She would've made a fabulous nurse or doctor. Instead, she chose to come to work with Billie Jo and me in the beauty shop. Oh, well, while I was out I'd make a quick stop and see if I couldn't get some answers to a few questions circling in the back of my mind.

"I promise to call you later. Since I'll be in the neighborhood, I'm gonna stop by the hospital and see Carla, if she's still there. Mama spoke with Beth Stevens. Carla is expected to be released today or tomorrow."

"Mama and I discussed her employment last night

on the phone. How do you feel about it? Oh, hold on a minute, I've got another call."

"No, I'll talk to you later," I said, breaking the connection before she could object.

An hour later, I had showered and rubbed down with witch hazel. To help the itch, I sprinkled liberally with Gold Bond Medicated Powder. Even though I smelled funny, I refrained from using my usual floral body mist. Makeup helped my face a little, but not much. The rash continued to worsen with each passing minute. I suspected blisters would soon be popping up over my nose and cheeks, both facial and buttocks—just my luck.

With my long, curly hair twisted in a decorative barrette, I dressed in black, loose-fitting slacks and a white silk scooped-neck blouse. Lastly, I slipped into my brown alligator flats and grabbed a matching shoulder bag from the top shelf of the closet.

I cranked up the air-conditioning in my Mustang and headed for the hospital. Already, the infamous Georgia humidity added a new level of misery to my itchy skin. Luckily, the hospital parking lot wasn't packed, and I parked close to the main entrance.

The clerk at the information desk flashed me a 'damn-what-happened-to-you' smile when I limped in. She tried to give me directions to the emergency room. Before I could stop her, she flagged down a passing nurse to take a look at my ankle and spreading rash.

Embarrassed by all the attention I'd garnered, I ducked into the elevator and punched the second floor button, all the while keeping my head downcast. The elevator stopped with a soft jolt, and the door opened with a ping.

Detective Grant stood outside Carla's room when I stepped off the elevator. My nose protested as I drew close, but I couldn't avoid him, since he blocked the door. His disheveled appearance reeked of stale cigarettes and coffee.

"You look real pretty this morning, Miz Claiborne. Nice blouse."

My flesh crawled as his watery brown eyes roamed over my figure, making me wish I'd chosen a less revealing neckline. "Excuse me. I'm here to visit Carla."

He reached out and ran his finger down my cheek. "Looks like you've been crawling in the bushes."

Shocked by his unprofessional behavior, I jerked my face away from his hand and stepped back. "Is there something you want?"

"Yeah, but you won't give it up easily."

Confused by his words, I counterattacked. "You're way out of line. Now move back or I'll report your behavior to your superiors."

A gleam of interest shone in his eyes. "Bradford is a lucky man. I see the way you look at him. I bet you'd give it to him if he asked for it."

My hand moved of its own accord, but was caught in his iron grip before it could connect with his face. "Be careful, or you'll find yourself behind bars for assaulting an officer." He squeezed down tight on my wrist. "I don't take kindly to threats. Remember that and stay out of my investigation."

I cried out in pain, and he released me. Grabbing my bruised wrist, I watched with trepidation as he strutted down the corridor, his laughter loud and clear. Shock quickly yielded to anger as the elevator doors closed behind him leaving me to weigh his threats.

One thing I knew for certain, I had gotten under his skin in a dangerous way. He would take great delight in bringing me down. Why? What could possibly be his interest in me? Did I remind him of someone he disliked—a divorced spouse? That would account for his animosity. His strange behavior puzzled me almost as much as his out-of-place Rolex watch. How could the detective afford such luxury on a policeman's salary? Something smelled rotten, and it wasn't just his hygiene.

Shaking the thought aside, I pushed open the door to find Carla getting dressed. "Good morning. Feeling better?"

She turned at the sound of my voice. Her eyes were clear and she appeared to be lucid. "I'm fine now. What happened to you?"

"Long story. Was Detective Grant harassing you?"

"No, he had permission from my doctors to question me, although I wasn't much help. My memory is still so fuzzy. My doctors diagnosed me with severe depression and anxiety. I'm on drug treatment now, and they're confident I'll make a full recovery. They're releasing me today."

"Do you remember what happened on Saturday?" I asked gently.

She shook her head. "Not clearly. I've been under a terrible strain lately. My mother has been diagnosed with lung cancer. Added to that, Frank started sleeping around. He'd asked me for a divorce just days before. I know I should've gone to Deena when all this started, but I was so ashamed. For what it's worth, I no longer believe that I killed Scarlett. The police, according to

Detective Grant, seem satisfied that I'll be cleared of all charges, but until then I'm still a person of interest. Please help me. I don't want to go to jail for a crime I didn't commit."

"I'll do what I can, Carla, but where's your husband? Shouldn't he be here with you?"

She gave a revealing, melancholy sigh. "He doesn't like hospitals." Her eyes were tortured. "He says he can explain his involvement with Scarlett. I know I shouldn't have, but I let him come home. God, am I a fool for giving in?"

To my way of thinking, Frank Moody was a skunk. Personally, I'd divorce him so fast he wouldn't know what hit him. Then again, a broken heart could make you do unspeakable things.

"Honey, we're all fools in one way or another, but your problem isn't a broken marriage, it's a possible murder charge. I wouldn't place too much stock in what Grant says. You need an attorney."

"My mother contacted Ian Garrett. I have an appointment with him in the morning."

"I've heard he's really a top-notch lawyer. Expensive, but good. You were lucky to retain him."

The door opened and a nurse came in. "I have your release papers, Mrs. Moody."

As Carla conferred with the nurse, I stepped over to gaze out the big plate-glass window. The bright mid-morning sunshine highlighted a late model, dark blue sedan—the same automobile that had been parked outside my house last night—parked a row behind the Mustang. I shivered at the implications.

Now, for certain, I knew this guy was following me. But why? Where did he fit into the scheme of things? The connection was Scarlett, of that I was certain. He'd only shown up on my doorstep after I started digging into her past. Could he have the mistaken belief that I had uncovered evidence, and now wanted to silence me as he had Scarlett? The thought slammed into my brain, leaving me frightened and shaken. I'd rather be alone with a rattlesnake than with my faceless stalker.

The nurse suggested I leave so Carla could sign her release papers and finish packing. I could tell by Carla's closed expression that she'd finished answering questions for the day, and in light of my discovery, I felt incapable of continuing. I wished her well and slipped out the door and down to the elevator. How I arrived home without wrecking the Mustang, I'm not sure. My mind whirled with questions, speculations, and possibilities. I could hear the phone ringing as I parked under the carport and shut off the ignition. Tango met me at the door, tripping me as I rushed in. "Hello?" I could now add bruised knees to my growing list of ailments.

"What'd the doctor say? I've been trying to reach you but your cell phone goes straight to voice mail," Deena accused.

My cell phone lay on the table where I'd placed it after my earlier call with her. "I forgot to take it with me. I told you I'd call you later." My face and other body parts started itching. "What's got you so riled up?"

"Sam was in to see me this morning. Someone broke into Scarlett's house last night!"

My neck started burning. So Bradford was suspicious? Just my luck. "Is that so? What'd he want?"

"I do declare, Jolene. You're getting ornery in your old age."

"Look who's ordering me a cane. You're only two years younger, so you'd better get one for yourself while you're at it," I shot back, my knees and ankle stinging. "Tango tripped me coming in and now my knees hurt. Tell me what Bradford wanted or hang up the phone."

"You'd better be glad I'm not Mama or you'd be listening to dead air right about now."

"Damn, Deena, I *am* listening to dead air."

"Fine," she huffed over the line. "Sam came to question us and the staff on our whereabouts last night. He wanted to know how to get in touch with you since you weren't answering your phone. I told him you were out sick. He said he'd stop by your house. Listen, I'm leaving work early today. I have a date—"

"He's coming here?" I slammed down the receiver. Pausing at the counter, I stood frozen with indecision. Bradford would take one look at my swollen, itchy face and know he'd found the guilty party. I had to get out of my house before he showed up and carted me off to jail. With no time to waste, I grabbed my purse off the floor, spilling the keys. Scooping them up, I limped to the door and stopped as I looked through the glass kitchen storm door at the car pulling into the driveway.

Think fast, old girl. I needed an alibi—one that explained my beat-up condition. The usual stand-by flu excuse wouldn't work. I looked like I'd been in a boxing match. Nothing came to mind. Throwing my purse back onto the table, I sprinted across the kitchen as fast as my crippled condition allowed, and jerked open the refrigerator door, pulled out a pitcher of sweet tea, and set it upon the counter. From the cookie jar I fished out half-a-dozen homemade chocolate chip pecan cookies and placed them on a platter. Maybe I could dazzle my way out of this with sweet treats.

I limped down the hall to the bathroom and patted an extra coating of loose powder on my red, bumpy face, retouched blush and reapplied lipstick. I was dragging a brush through my hair when the doorbell rang. Gathering the curls back with a clasp, I surveyed my image one last time in the mirror. My confidence plummeted—God, my skin looked like the Martian surface. How to explain it? I reached the front door just as it rang a third time.

Bradford zeroed in on my face the second I opened the door. I causally invited him in out of the heat. He remained silent as he followed me back to the kitchen, my flats click-clacking on the hardwood floor. I placed the platter of cookies on the table along with two glasses of iced tea.

"Deena called and said you'd been by the salon this morning," I said after we were seated. I grabbed a couple of cookies, needing something in my hands. A trembling had started deep down in my bones.

His sharp gaze passed over me. "There was a break-in at Scarlett Cantrell's house last night. You wouldn't happen to know anything about that, would you? The intruder climbed out the master bedroom window."

I took a long swig of cold tea. Had the police found the plastic bag with my wet jeans and panties I'd forgotten under Scarlett's bed? Heat flooded my face as the thought scorched my brain waves like burnt bacon. If they had, there was nothing to tie them to me. Yeah, right. Only DNA.

Bradford continued to stare at me from across the table. "I noticed you look kind of banged up. Deena said you were out sick, but it appears to me you've been crawling around in poison ivy or is it poison oak?"

Butterflies twittered around in my stomach. Good God Almighty—he knows! Now was the time to confess and climb off this fast-moving train I'd hitched my caboose to. I was a hairstylist, not a PI or a cop. Since taking on this investigation, I'd broken the law left and right. Sooner or later I was gonna end up behind bars for good. But I'd crossed the point of no return, and there wasn't any going back. I had to see this through all the way to the painful end.

I crossed and uncrossed my legs, fighting the burning itch between my legs. Words lodged in my throat as test phrases jockeyed for position. Taking a deep breath, I started to speak when Anthony's calm voice sounded behind me. "I can tell you how she came into contact with poison oak."

My head jerked around as he came into my full view. Fury blinded me at his unwelcome intrusion in my home. I reacted foolishly, bolting out of the chair and almost landing on my face as my ankle gave way. Anger kept me from being embarrassed as Bradford steadied me.

"Who do you think you are walking uninvited into my house?" I yelled as Anthony seated himself at the kitchen table as if it were an everyday occurrence.

"I knocked on the front door." He casually picked up one of the cookies from the platter. "I guess you didn't hear me. I really needed to talk to Deena, but she stepped out of the salon, so I came over here to speak with you. But I can answer your question, Detective. Jolene was with me last night."

Bradford looked at me to confirm his statement. When I didn't immediately answer, he looked back at Anthony. "You failed to mention this when I questioned you this morning." He flipped open his notepad. "You said you were alone, and now you're telling me you lied?"

"I didn't think it mattered since Jolene had been there earlier in the evening. She helped me with a shutter that'd torn loose in the storm last week."

Bradford waited for me to confirm Anthony's story. Torn, because I wanted to see Anthony exposed as a liar, I paused to consider several questions building in my mind. What was Anthony's true motive for being here in my house? It wasn't to give me an alibi. How would he even know I needed one? My mind wrapped around every reason...when suddenly I knew. The only way he would know I needed an alibi was if he'd been in Scarlett's house with me and not that guy in the blue sedan. That unlocked a number of questions. What was he searching for? The jade elephant? Or something else that would connect him to the murder? If it were a possibility, no way I'd sit here silent.

I looked Bradford square in the eye. "He's lying. I don't know what his game is, but he wasn't with me last night. I was breaking into Scarlett's house."

Bradford turned to look at Anthony. "Get out of here, Vogel. I'll deal with you later. Take notice. You're under surveillance."

Anthony shot daggers at me with his eyes then stood and retraced his steps. I breathed easier when I heard the front door slam.

"That was strange," Bradford said, his gaze never leaving my face. "You seem afraid of him. May I ask why?"

"I suspect he killed Scarlett."

He didn't seem surprised at my statement. "Anthony is a person of interest. Care to share your theories?"

"Why are you still sitting at my kitchen table eating cookies and drinking iced tea as if this were a social visit? Aren't you here to nab the perp?"

Bradford leaned back in his chair. "I still may arrest you. Convince me to do otherwise." He relaxed and actually smiled. My heart skipped a beat, and I thought I was gonna melt right there in my kitchen. He was one good-looking man, and I couldn't help but be attracted to him whether I liked it or not.

My sister's words echoed through my mind—*I'm leaving work early today. I have a date.*

Deena did have first claim on him. I'd even encouraged her to spend time with him. And she'd been wearing that silly grin ever since they'd lunched together. My smile died.

"I can explain what I was doing in Scarlett's house. You may not believe me, but I can explain."

He gave a slow nod. "First tell me why you suspect Mr. Vogel of killing her."

If it was possible, the itching increased tenfold. The witch hazel and calamine lotion were wearing off. I kicked off my flats and rubbed my feet together, hoping to ease the itch. It didn't work. Bending down, I scratched my toes. "Because I believe he was hiding in Scarlett's house last night."

"You weren't alone in the house?"

I sat back up in my chair. "I just said that."

Bradford scribbled on his notepad. "Why do you believe Mr. Vogel was also present in the house?"

"Why lie if you're not hiding something?"

"You have a point. Anything else of interest?"

I bent down to scratch my hot ankles. "Anthony was there for a reason. He was searching for something. Same as me."

"Such as?" Bradford asked when I righted myself again in my chair.

"You'll have to ask him."

"I'm asking you. What you were searching for?"

"The jade elephant."

"And what is the jade elephant?"

"I don't know," I admitted. "That's what I'm trying to find out."

"Let me get this straight. You broke into the victim's house to search for an object you know nothing about?"

I nodded. "That's correct."

He scribbled again on his notepad. "Okay, tell me where you heard about this jade elephant."

"Scarlett told me."

He frowned. "When did she speak of this jade elephant?"

"The day she died."

Bradford looked none too pleased at my answer. "Why did you withhold vital information? You should've disclosed this when you were questioned at the scene."

Beads of sweat gathered on my brow, which in turn made me itch more. "I did tell someone," I snapped, scratching my neck and face nervously, wiggling in the chair to relieve my nether regions. "I told Detective Bulldog, I mean Detective Grant."

His pen stopped, and his jaw tensed. "Start at the beginning and tell me everything. Don't leave out any details. Even if you think they're unimportant. Got it?"

And I did. I told him everything that'd happened from Saturday morning when Scarlett arrived for her appointment until my exit from the hospital an hour ago, not mentioning my continuing interaction with Scarlett's ghost. Some things were best left unsaid.

"Is that everything?" he asked when I came to a stop.

I nodded. "That's all of it."

"Good. Now listen to me. First, I'm going to forget the breaking and entering charge *if* you'll promise to stay out of trouble. Forget investigating. Let me and my boys do our jobs. Don't repeat our conversation. Not even to your mother or sisters. Strictly under wraps, understand?"

He was offering me an out. It was a chance to escape jail time, and I had no intention of wearing prison orange. Scarlett would have to wait for the police for answers. I was through sticking my neck out for her. I stuck out my hand. "You've got a deal. What about Anthony? He knows I confessed to breaking into Scarlett's house."

Bradford shook my hand. "You let me worry about him. Write out a detailed statement. Everything you just told me. Add anything you believe would help in the investigation. I'll pick it up in the morning, understood?"

I agreed to his terms and watched as his car backed out of the driveway without me handcuffed in the back seat. Mama says that the best lessons in life are the ones you learn the hard way. Boy, she'd nailed that one. For now, I wouldn't be wearing prison orange, but I wasn't sure how long that would last.

Chapter Fifteen
Good Ol' Fashioned Candied Secrets

After dodging the bullet yet again, I placed a quick call to the salon to check with Holly about tomorrow's appointments and then took another cool shower. A fresh coat of witch hazel, calamine lotion, and a liberal sprinkling of Gold Bond Medicated Powder eased my irritation.

General Hospital had just started, so I fixed a sandwich and sat down on the couch to watch my favorite soap. The dongs of the grandfather clock woke me at four. In the kitchen I called Mama to get her recipe for chicken and dumplings, my favorite fast food. Ten minutes to prep, ten minutes to simmer, and you'd be sitting down with good, old-fashioned, comfort food.

She picked up on the third ring. "Hello."

"Whatcha up to?"

"Are you feeling better, honey? Deena said you called in sick. What's the matter? Is it your time of the month?"

I made a face. "I wish Deena wouldn't call and tell you everything that's going on at the salon. It's just a bout of poison oak."

"How'd you get into poison oak? You know good and well what it looks like. It's all over the property out here."

"I fell into it helping a friend fix his shutters," I said, figuring I might as well use Anthony's lie—it being a good one—but I wasted my breath because she'd moved on to another subject.

"Deena said Scarlett's house was burglarized last night. She said Sam came by the salon to inquire about everyone's whereabouts."

"He came by here to question me, too."

"Humph. Strange happenings going on in this town. Makes me shudder to think about the future. So, what can I do for you, Jolene?"

"I called to get your recipe for quick and easy chicken and dumplings."

"What else are you making to go with it?"

"Confederate cornbread and turnip greens," I said. "And a Mrs. Smith's apple pie for dessert."

"That's a lot of food for one person."

"Scarlett's gonna join me," I teased.

"Ha ha, smart-aleck. Hold on,"—there was a clunk of the receiver being laid on the counter, the sound of movement, and finally—"You ready?"

I told her I was, and she rattled off a list of ingredients and instructions. It sounded easy enough. "Thanks for sharing. I know how much you hate to part with your special recipes. Which side of the family is this one from?"

"Your father's side, honey. Mrs. Tucker copied it off the side of a Bisquick box."

Sunday's brief conversation came to mind. "Speaking of Daddy—"

"You're not going to let this rest, are you?"

"I will as soon as you tell me what you're hiding."

"Telling the truth is like opening Pandora's Box."

Her voice trembled. "But I guess time isn't going to make it any easier." A long sigh echoed from her end. "Your father—"

Call waiting beeped on her line. "I need to answer that," she gushed. "I'm expecting an important call."

"But you were going to tell me about Daddy," I protested.

"I'll call you later."

The line went dead. I hung up, discouraged about ever learning the truth. The early news came on as I started cooking. I'd just placed the cornbread in the oven with the apple pie when I heard the anchorwoman mention Scarlett. I placed the pot of turnip greens on the stove and wiped my hands on the front of my apron so I could turn up the volume.

The anchorwoman reported there were no further leads on the death of the former WXYB employee at a local hair salon. A brief interview with Bradford followed, but there wasn't any pertinent information forthcoming. He stated that the investigation continued and if any tri-county viewer had any information to call the number at the bottom of the screen or call Crime-Stoppers. The anchorwoman gave the details of Scarlett's memorial service—in lieu of flowers, the family had requested a donation made in the victim's name to hospice.

With the burner on low so the greens could simmer, I grabbed a pen and paper and settled in the den with my notebook. As I wrote more doubts began to surface, and with them unanswered questions.

First, I made a list of Dixieland Salon's staff. Beside each name, I recorded their whereabouts as best I knew them, at the time Scarlett was in the facial room.

Then I jotted down a separate list of the salon's clients I remembered seeing that morning. I noted either a positive or negative mark beside each name depending on the person's known attitude toward the victim. Leaning back in my comfortable recliner, I let my mind wander over the last couple of months. Little incidents that seemed unrelated then now resurfaced with sinister implications.

Like the time I overheard Mandy and Scarlett arguing. It was a busy Wednesday before Thanksgiving last fall, and every chair had been filled with last-minute clients looking for a new look for the holidays. As I approached the dispensary to mix color, I heard loud voices coming from behind the closed kitchen door. Thinking there might be a problem, I cracked open the door just in time to witness Mandy handing Scarlett an envelope.

"Don't tell them, Miss Cantrell. They'll never understand."

Scarlett tucked the envelope into her purse. "This is our little secret. No one will know unless you miss a payment."

Neither woman had noticed me standing in the half-opened door. Not wanting to eavesdrop, I turned to leave and heard Mandy say, "How long must I keep this up?"

The door closed on, "Until I'm dead."

Blackmail seemed to be Scarlett's hobby. What I had wanted to do was confront the two and demand this injustice stop at once, but wisely, I refrained. This was none of my business. Whatever Mandy's secret, she was paying for Scarlett's silence.

I scribbled all this down, and several other

incidents involving Scarlett that had caught my notice in the salon. Then I made a list of questions that stuck out in my mind:

1. *Scarlett was blackmailing Mandy. What for? Scarlett didn't need the money. Or did she? (Check Scarlett's finances.)*

2. *Was Scarlett blackmailing Anthony? What was he searching for in her house? What's his motive for lying to Bradford to give me an alibi for the time of the break-in? What's Anthony's secret?*

3. *Who was the woman, or man—Scarlett didn't specify—that Robert Burns was seen with at Merry Acres on the morning of Scarlett's murder?*

4. *Was Carla involved in Scarlett's murder? Was her husband involved?*

5. *Cherry hated Scarlett. Why? An affair between Scarlett and Robert? Something else?*

6. *Scarlett was having an affair with the mayor. Did his wife know?*

7. *What about the strange scene Becky witnessed between Scarlett and Linda in the OB/GYN's office? Could Linda have harbored hard feelings for her rival?*

8. *Who broke into the salon? Was there a connection with Scarlett's murder?*

9. *What's up with Detective Grant and the expensive Rolex watch? Why did he fail to inform Bradford about the jade elephant? Does he have me under surveillance?*

10. *Who is the man in the blue sedan? Why is he following me?*

11. *What is the jade elephant, and where do I find it?*

On and on I wrestled with my thoughts, stopping

only to peer out of the drapes into the deepening night for any sign of the blue sedan. Hunger drove me to the kitchen for a quick supper, after which I returned to my notes with a sense of urgency. With only the sound of the ticking grandfather clock and Tango's soft padding across the hardwood for company, I wracked my brain for any further incidents that might shed light on this mystery. The truth was hiding in plain sight, and I had to find it before I was shackled with Scarlett's ghost, or worse yet, another death, and I wasn't ready to be headin' for the Gloryland.

****

"Deena, come see Jolene's face," Billie Jo said when I walked into the salon early the next morning. "She's been kissing a moving fan."

"Oh, Lord, what happened to you? Is that a rash on your face and neck? And look at your arms. No wonder you called in sick," Deena remarked as she looked me over.

Not being one for a lot of attention, I sidestepped their questions by using the same lie I'd used with Mama, figuring one lie was as good as another. No one questioned my story, but I could see the doubt in their eyes.

The morning remained busy for me since Holly had been unable to reschedule most of my appointments from yesterday and had to squeeze them in today. And, of course, my beat-up condition was the buzz for the day. I received more pitying looks than I cared for. Anthony avoided me completely.

Unfortunately, Cherry Burns turned out to be my eleven o'clock appointment. She took one look at me as Holly deposited her at my station and immediately started fussing.

"Please don't worry about me, I'm fine," I told her, fastening a shampoo cape around her neck. "Are we touching up the roots today?"

"Yes. Give me the works."

I leafed through the color cards until I found hers and set it on the counter. After sectioning her hair, I went back to the dispensary to mix her color. She was on her cell phone when I returned.

She snapped the phone shut just as I began applying color. "That was Robert," she informed me with a smile. "He calls throughout the day to check in with me, you know."

"No, I didn't know," I murmured half-heartedly, not really caring if he called her or not. I had other things on my mind.

"He's changed since Scarlett's death."

That caught my attention. "I believe change is good, don't you?" If my hunch proved right, Scarlett had found out about Robert's affair and had been blackmailing him. That spelled motive. Any information I gathered could be passed along to Bradford. Luckily, she was in a chatty mood.

"Not many people know this, but Robert and I were close to a divorce," she confessed. "I suspected him of having an affair. He denied it, of course."

"Scarlett?"

"Who else?"

"That's what you were trying to tell me on Saturday," I said with sympathy. "You believed Scarlett was after your husband?"

"Yes! God, I hated her. Robert accused me of driving him away with my unfounded accusations. He threatened to move out," she finished with a sob.

Hmm. That opened another possibility. Cherry could be the mysterious female voice heard in the facial room just before Scarlett's murder. Reaching for the tissue box, I encouraged her to continue. There was no better source of information than a hysterical woman who believed she'd been betrayed.

I wasn't disappointed. Between sobs, she told me the whole wretched story.

"Did you ask him about Scarlett claiming to have seen him at Merry Acres when he was supposed to be away in Biloxi on business?"

Cherry clenched her hands in her lap. "I confronted him about it when he arrived home Sunday morning. He confessed that he'd lied about his whereabouts. He took a room at the inn so he could work out a very serious situation with Scarlett. He said she was determined to catch the eye of a major network with an undercover piece she was working on. He was trying to protect me from the nasty fallout if she succeeded in her plans."

The story rang false, but I couldn't voice my doubts if I wanted additional information. "Did he mention the subject of this alleged report?"

She dabbed her eyes with the tissue. "He would only say that the report would hurt a lot of very important people in this town, and the state. Scarlett refused to listen. She wanted to make a name for herself at the expense of others. Even the mayor became worried about a scandal if the report was made public."

This I could believe. Wouldn't Bradford be surprised when I handed over my notes to him, plus this added bonus? Of course, I'd leave out the part about the filched autopsy report.

I flashed a playful grin. "This has all the makings of a great mystery novel. You say the mayor was concerned?"

She made a dramatic gesture with manicured hands. "Well, Robert came home late one night a couple of weeks ago, just furious. Scarlett had ruffled the feathers of some very important men, he said and if she wasn't careful she'd find herself at the end of a very long rope. I overheard him arguing with the mayor on the phone."

"Did he go to the police? You'd think so, especially if the mayor knew what was going on."

"I don't know. When I suggested he do so, he blew up at me and told me to mind my own damn business, so I did."

I finished applying color to the last section and set the timer for thirty minutes. "Who do you suppose those men were? And what connection does the mayor have with them?" I placed a plastic cap on her head.

"I asked myself the same questions."

"You don't suppose they could be responsible for Scarlett's death, do you?" I shivered at the thought of a bunch of hired thugs breaking into the salon.

Cherry shook her head. "Robert said your aesthetician—what's her name?—is the guilty party. And I heard Deena made another trip downtown."

Frowning into the mirror, I said, "Deena is no longer a person of interest. And Carla is out of the hospital and at home resting. She didn't deliberately cause Scarlett's death."

"Don't be too sure." She pushed herself to a standing position and followed me to one of the preheated dryers lining the wall. "You never know about people. Robert told me Scarlett broke up Carla's marriage."

This old news I was aware of, but I played dumb, hoping for more tidbits. "Seriously?"

"Robert said he tried to dissuade Frank, but the boy was bewitched."

"And you yourself believed Scarlett was having an affair with Robert which gives you motive."

Her eyes narrowed. "True. Killers come in all shapes and sizes. I would've killed her long ago if I had a mind to do so, Jolene. But thanks for thinking about me. I appreciate the vote of confidence."

I flushed at her sarcastic tone. I really had to watch my tongue if I wanted to keep my customers from walking out.

"At least Scarlett never dug her claws into that divine hunk," she added, nodding toward the front of the salon.

I glanced over my shoulder as Bradford strolled through the door. He stopped in front of me. Every feminine eye watched as he brought his hand forward and handed me the plastic bag with my soiled clothing in it.

"I presume these are yours?"

Mercifully, the poison oak hid the extent of my embarrassment as I took the bag from him.

Bradford merely smiled at my humiliation. "You have something for me, right?"

"In my car," I said, keeping my eyes averted. "Come with me."

Quickly, I pushed Cherry under the dryer and hurried away. Her cry of indignation fell on deaf ears as

I rounded the corner with Bradford behind me.

Holly signaled to me as we passed the reception desk. "Your next client had to cancel. She rescheduled for Thursday afternoon, but your next appointment is here a little early for his haircut."

"Thank you. Please take him to my station and tell him I'll be with him in a minute."

Bradford followed me to the rear parking lot. I unlocked my car door and threw the plastic bag into the back seat. From the front passenger seat, I retrieved the manila envelope holding the copied notes and handed them to him. Then I told him everything I'd just learned from Cherry.

"You seem to have forgotten your promise to stay out of this," he said, towering over me. "I appreciate the help you've given me, but no investigating from this point on, no matter what. We have a deal, remember?"

My mouth opened, closed. I nodded. He smiled. "Good girl. Oh, and I like your shoes."

With a wink, he turned on his heel and strode off in the direction of the front parking lot. Like a breathless girl of eighteen, I stood staring down at my lime-green heels with adorable yellow polka-dot bows.

He likes my shoes!

A zing of anticipation filled me, and I returned to work with renewed zeal. Deena may have hooked the best fish in the pond of eligible bachelors, but the look in Bradford's eye left no doubt that he hadn't been reeled in yet. And therein lay the problem. How to stop this growing attraction?

Chapter Sixteen
The Jade Elephant

"We have a business meeting at six with Robert Burns," Deena said. "He's looking for the right salon, and stylist, for Scarlett's replacement, Tammy Hodges. He advised me he was strongly considering other salons, so this is our only chance to convince him to give Dixieland another chance. No more mistakes. We need this contract."

Billie Jo and I were having lunch in her office. "Anthony will have a hissy fit if another salon is chosen." I took another bite of my peanut butter and jelly sandwich. "He's got it in his mind that the position should be his since he was Scarlett's stylist."

"Anthony's hiding something," Billie Jo said.

I looked over at my sister who was crunching a carrot stick. "You're right, but what?" After his unwelcome appearance in my house yesterday, I'd pulled him aside and threatened to introduce him to Mini Pearl if he ever pulled a stupid stunt like that again. Hopefully, I'd put the fear of God into him because I wouldn't want to follow through on my threat.

"Never mind," Deena said. "We're short on time and need to discuss our strategy for keeping our business in the media. The positive side, I would add."

We decided on the straightforward approach.

Deena would be our spokeswoman, and Billie Jo and I would answer any technical questions regarding styles and makeup.

The rest of the day passed in a blur as I permed, cut, and colored my way to exhaustion. My last client waltzed out the door precisely at five. I left the salon, promising to meet my sisters at WXYB in forty-five minutes, and raced home to shower and change into comfortable slacks and a short-sleeved blouse.

At 5:45, I pulled into the TV station parking lot. Billie Jo and Deena were waiting for me at the front entrance. I parked and joined them. The receptionist escorted us to Robert's secretary—a pretty brunette, who ushered us into his opulent office.

"Sit down, ladies." Robert motioned us to the chairs before his massive cherry wood desk. "I've been expecting you."

Tired beyond thought, I sank down into the pale ivory plush sofa, leaving the two wingback chairs for my sisters, as I preferred to stay in the background. Billie Jo scowled at me but followed Deena to the chairs facing the TV executive.

Since it'd been decided that Deena, as salon manager, would be in charge, I allowed the conversation to fade into the background. I laid my head back, and the comfort of the expensive fabric embraced me. The murmur of voices flowed over me like warm bath water. I slipped off my heels and plunged my toes into the lush green carpet. The lightest scent of vanilla wafted throughout the space and as I inhaled deeply, the mental picture of homemade sugar cookies popped into my mind.

My stomach rumbled loudly, and I opened my eyes

to find Billie Jo frowning at me from her chair. From the sound of the pleasant conversation, matters were under control and my presence wasn't required, so I excused myself and escaped into the outer office.

"The restroom is down the hall to the left," the secretary explained when I voiced my need.

"Thank you," I said, heading out the door. The hallway was long and branched off into a Y. Just as I reached the fork and started left, I paused, certain I recognized Scarlett's co-host, just down the hall to the right along the Y branch. After a moment's hesitation, I turned around and caught up with him midway down the hall, but it turned out to be the wrong guy.

I don't believe in fate, but after the man walked away, the nameplate on the door facing me gave me pause. Scarlett's office.

Get out of here. For several seconds, I stood in indecision. I'd promised Bradford I would stay out of trouble. No investigating, no matter what, he'd said.

"I'm not investigating—just seizing an opportunity to satisfy my curiosity."

Buoyed by my whispered but confident words, I pushed open the door. The small office appeared neat and feminine, everything in its place. A bookshelf filled with knick-knacks, books, and pictures of Scarlett posing with various people dominated one wall. Several awards for outstanding journalism hung on the wall behind a desk and chair. An inviting pink and green chintz chair sat in the corner of the room.

Somewhat surprised by the coziness of the office— I'd figured Scarlett for something a little less homespun—I wandered over to the bookshelf and picked up a picture of her parents. They'd been a handsome couple. Scarlett mostly resembled her mother, with the dark hair, but she had her father's remarkable blue-green eyes.

Curious now, I fingered several of the small figurines, hoping they might shed more light on Scarlett's upside down personality—a crystal unicorn, a porcelain squirrel gripping an acorn, and a hand-carved jade dragon. The latter jarred my memory, and I searched around for a jade elephant figurine, but to no avail. When I looked over the next shelf, filled with books, I spotted a small volume entitled *The Jade Elephant*.

Excited with my discovery, I grabbed the book off the shelf and leafed through it, looking for any pencil marks or notes Scarlett might've made on the pages that would give a clue to its meaning. Finding none, I studied the worn jacket cover and frayed binding. It was a collection of poetry by an unknown author. Nothing unusual caught my eye. I turned the book over, searching for any clue on the back cover jacket.

Several more minutes passed as I continued to examine the small volume. Perhaps the mystery lay in the content of the poems. Removing the book from the office wasn't something I wanted to chance, but what other option did I have? I couldn't study each poem here. Besides, would anyone even notice its absence? Probably not, since Scarlett's personal items hadn't even been removed. Opening my purse, I groaned, wishing I'd switched handbags. Mini Pearl, nestled in her pink holster, filled the crammed space. Time was running out. I had to do something fast, so I snatched off the jacket cover and examined the frayed and split edges of the binding.

One spot looked as if it had been purposely cut in an effort to hide something, so I slipped a finger down inside to feel the edges of something hard and flat. Turning the book upside down, I gently shook it to dislodge the item, but when that failed, I slipped two fingers back in to retrieve a small flash drive.

Approaching footsteps alerted me to possible discovery, so I shoved the thumb-drive into the tiny outside compartment of my purse, reinserted the book back into its jacket, and returned it to the shelf.

The door cracked open as I settled into the chintz chair in the corner. I glanced down and noticed the top edges of the thumb-drive sticking out. Crap, it didn't fit, but there wasn't anything to be done about it now. I pasted on a bright smile and waited for the woman who had stepped into the room to turn around and notice me.

She was petite, with curly red hair. Her movements were light and quick as she moved across the room, humming an unfamiliar tune. She laid a folder on the desk, hesitated for a moment, like she'd forgotten some minor detail, and then turned around as if to leave. That's when she spotted me.

"Oh! I beg your pardon—you startled me. I don't believe we have an appointment, do we?"

I stood up and approached her with an outstretched hand. "I'm sorry I startled you. I'm Jolene Claiborne. My sisters and I own Dixieland Salon."

Golden eyes flickered with interest as she shook my hand and, thankfully, she didn't comment about my messed-up face. "I'm Tammy Hodges. It's a pleasure to meet you. I've heard about your salon. I do believe in the context of murder." Her eyebrows rose politely.

"We did have an unfortunate accident in the facial

room," I said, trying not to show my displeasure in the way she'd worded it.

She tilted her head to the side. "Unfortunate accident?"

I let out a strained laugh. "You know how things get blown out of proportion in small towns. Give us a chance before judging. Lightning only strikes once in the same place." By now, I was pretty sure it'd been no accident—but I wasn't ready to admit that publicly.

"Gossip does tend to grow with each new telling," she agreed. "Please tell me what I can do for you."

I sat down in the chair facing her desk. "My sisters and I are here for a meeting with your boss. We're hoping to continue our contract with the station."

"Oh, yes. That dreadful incident is the reason I have this job. How did you know where to find me?"

"I didn't. This is Scarlett's office."

"It's mine now. The name plate is being replaced today." She gave me a suspicious look. "What are you here for if you're not looking for me?"

"I stumbled upon it while looking for the ladies' room and I was curious."

Tammy scowled at me from across the desk. "Curious? Why?"

"Scarlett was a local celebrity. Now you're in the same position and people will be curious about you. Including how your office is decorated."

My answer seemed to please her. "Did you find what you were looking for?"

"Excuse me?" I shot back. Her eyebrows raised a fraction at my tense tone, but I couldn't help it. I wanted to bolt out of the office and away from her probing eyes.

"Is your curiosity satisfied now that you've seen her office?"

"Oh, yes," I said, relieved she hadn't discovered my crime. "But I have to confess I'd pictured it differently."

"I must admit that I did too. It's small and simply furnished. From everything I've read and seen of Scarlett, she wasn't into simplicity."

"That she isn't," I said, picturing her in her latest modified creation from Vivian Leigh's heavenly closet. To me, Scarlett wasn't dead, just in another form, but very much alive.

A knock sounded at the door and Robert Burns stuck his head in, cutting short any further discussion. "I was hoping you'd be here, Tammy." He addressed the young woman, not seeing me. "I need to speak to you about a matter."

She indicated my presence. "Jolene and I were just getting acquainted."

Stepping into the room, he glared at me. "So this is where you got off to. We've been looking for you."

I apologized as my two sisters, stepped in behind him, gazing at me with questions in their eyes.

He introduced Tammy and then launched into a spiel, aimed at us, about not having decided which salon he'd chosen yet, but saying we would be considered with the others.

Tammy spoke out. "Do I have a say in this?"

"Of course you do, my dear," he said.

"Then I choose Jolene."

No one was more surprised by this announcement than me. The last thing in the world I wanted, or needed, was another demanding celebrity breathing down my neck—dead or alive.

****

"I don't know how you did it, Jolene, and I'm not going to ask. I've got to hurry," Deena said when we reached the parking lot. "If I don't get home and changed, I'm going to be late for my date. You can give us the details tomorrow. Come on, Billie Jo. I'll drop you off at your car on my way home."

I stood in the parking lot beside my car and watched my sisters leave. Deena was in a hurry. Not that I blamed her. I'd be, too, if I had a date with the sexy detective. Besides, the last thing I wanted was to explain to them how I'd landed a job I didn't want. Somehow, I'd find a way to steer Tammy to one of the other stylists. Right now, I was anxious to get home and examine the stolen flash drive.

The distant rumble of thunder sounded in the darkening twilight. Hopefully, we were going to finally get some much-needed rain before the night was out. I glanced down at my watch—6:50. My stomach grumbled again in protest of a late supper. Thankfully, traffic was light, and I pulled up into my driveway fifteen minutes later.

Tango's angry meow greeted me, so I fed him and then took last night's leftovers out of the refrigerator and placed them into the oven to warm. From my purse, I dug out the thumb-drive and headed to my small office. I kicked off my shoes and turned on the desk lamp to closely examine the object I held in my hand.

I booted up the computer and inserted the drive. Immediately, a message flashed on the screen saying it couldn't open the main file because it was encrypted and needed special software and a password. Uncertain how to proceed, I secured it away in one of the desk drawers, determined to find a way to access the files before turning it over to the police. Although, I'd promised Bradford not to meddle in the investigation, I reasoned that it wouldn't hurt to hold onto the flash drive for a day or two at the most. If I hadn't found a way to read it by then, I'd hand it over.

Now, I needed to get in touch with my troublemaking cosmic underling since I'd found the elusive jade elephant, which had produced even a greater mystery, in the form of the cryptic thumb-drive. Scarlett had questions to answer. Wasting no time, I sent SOS messages heavenward, but she, apparently, wasn't in tune with my psychic vibrations this evening. After thirty minutes, I gave up. The questions would have to wait, and I headed for a long, cool bath, and another coating of calamine.

With my itching back or buttocks under control, I settled in front of the TV and enjoyed my supper while watching reruns of *The Walking Dead*, which turned out to be a mistake as it brought Scarlett back to mind. She'd popped in on me earlier today while I was in the restroom at work to tell me that she'd had no luck tracking down Daddy. That bummed me out, but apparently, she said, he wasn't a resident of the Golden City, and therefore must be roasting in the devil's domain. My grandparents were there, and yes, Granny Tucker had taken a brief trip to Peaceful Valley Cemetery last Saturday. The meaning of her message would come clear with time, she had promised.

Restless with my thoughts, I turned off the TV and started a pot of coffee. Taking the morning newspaper I hadn't had a chance to read, I sat down at the kitchen table to wait for the coffee to finish dripping when the front doorbell rang.

I opened the door to see Mama standing on the porch, her face pale, but proud. "What are you doing here at this time of night?"

"It's time for that talk about your daddy." She stepped into the foyer, and I closed the door behind her. A sudden nervousness descended upon me at this unusual visit. Mama rarely left the farm after sunset because she detested driving in the dark, and by the break in her usual routine, I knew this was going to be serious chat.

"I made a pot of coffee," I said, and started for the kitchen. "Should I call Deena and Billie Jo to join us?"

"No, it's best I tell you first," she said somberly. "You're the oldest, and your sisters will take it better if you've got your emotions under control when they learn the truth. And you're gonna need a little time to digest the truth as well."

Okay. This wasn't going to be good. I clamped down on my bottom lip to keep from blurting out the burning questions blazing through my mind.

We entered the kitchen, and Mama took a seat at the table while I took two mugs from the cabinet. Tango jumped down from his perch on the refrigerator and wound himself around Mama's ankles, purring his welcome. Tango loved Mama. She showered him with attention each time she visited. Tonight, she ignored him.

I made quick work of putting the cream and sugar on the table. I poured coffee into the mugs and set one in front of her. Thus far, the only sound between us was Tango's purring and the soft chimes of the grandfather clock in the den as it struck ten.

With the hot coffee mug nestled in my hands, I waited anxiously for her to begin. Finally, she looked up from her cup, uncertainty etched on her face. "This is going to be hard, so please don't interrupt until I'm finished. Can you do that?"

I had a sinking feeling, but I nodded, and tightened my fingers around the mug.

She took a few sips from her cup. "It started the year we lost the entire peanut crop to white mold. The loss was heavy, and we were on the verge of losing the farm. Your father was frantic with worry. When the bank refused our loan application, he turned to a loan shark—a Mr. Blackstone. Everything went downhill from there. We struggled to make the payments. The first time Harland failed to come up with the money, Mr. Blackstone's hired goons worked him over."

I gasped. "I remember Daddy's shattered face. He said he fell off the peanut combine trying to fix something or another."

"Things got worse. As hard as we tried, we just couldn't keep up the payments and the expenses of the farm and household. Harland didn't want me to, but I went back to work teaching school. For a time, it helped, but we fell behind again, and that's when Mr. Blackstone threatened to kill you girls off one at a time, starting with Billie Jo, until the loan was paid in full."

Shock stole my voice. I sat in numb silence as she continued, "I thought Harland was going to drop dead of a heart attack that night when he got home and told me what the man had said. We'd burned through our savings long ago, so we decided to sell the farm to pay off the loan shark, and hopefully have enough left to start over. But that too fell through. Farms weren't selling fast at the time, and Mr. Blackstone got impatient for his money."

I took a quick breath of utter astonishment. "Are you saying that Daddy didn't die in that bank robbery? He was murdered by this loan shark?"

Mama bent her head and studied her clasped hands. "No, that's not what I'm saying." She looked up, her eyes green pools of appeal. "Jolene, your father is alive."

Chapter Seventeen
Back From the Dead? Again!

A feeling of helpless confusion swept over me at Mama's confession. I flushed hot with anger, then felt pain at the lies, and finally joy as the implications of those five spoken words slammed into me.

Daddy is alive!

I expelled a pent-up breath. "How could he be alive? He's buried in the Peaceful Valley Cemetery. I *saw* his casket lowered into the ground twenty-five years ago."

Mama got up from the table and went over to the coffeepot. "All that's true, Jolene." She poured another cup of coffee and sat back down at the kitchen table. "Everyone, but a select few, believes that Harland Tucker is in the sweet bye and bye."

"Including me and my sisters," I accused, tears of anger gathering in my eyes. With trembling hands, I grabbed a napkin from the holder and wiped them away. "My God, Mama, for all these years you've allowed us to believe that Daddy was killed in a bank robbery. Do you have *any* idea what growing up without a father has done to us?"

She reached for my hand, but I snatched it away, placing it out of reach. She sighed at my reaction and slowly retracted her hand, placing it again in her lap. "Yes, Jolene, unfortunately, I do. I've seen the damage our actions caused, but we had no other choice. Mr. Blackstone approached Billie Jo one day when she and her classmates were on the school playground. Her teacher spotted him, and he ran off. She reported the incident to the principal, and we were notified. Your father and I knew we had to do something. That's when we came up with the plan."

"Which was to deceive your daughters?"

"No, yes, but that was a consequence we couldn't avoid if we were to keep y'all safe."

"Why didn't you go to the police?" I asked.

"We did go to the sheriff, but he couldn't offer much help. Back then Whiskey Creek was a much smaller town. The only law enforcement consisted of the sheriff and his two deputies who did their best to patrol the entire county. He promised to keep his eyes open for Mr. Blackstone, but with the explosion at the fertilizer plant, he had his hands full. We were on our own."

"The family—"

"Didn't know, and had no money to lend us," she said. "And telling them might have placed them in danger."

"So what happened after you left the sheriff?" I rose for another cup of coffee. "What about the plan?"

"It's complicated," she replied.

"And everything you've told me so far isn't?" I sat down and reached for the cream and sugar. "I've been to Atlanta many times over the years searching for answers. No wonder no one could help me find an account of that supposed bank robbery. Go on, I need to hear the rest if I'm ever going to understand."

Mama dashed a tear from her eye. "From the

sheriff's office we went over to Pete's Funeral Home. He was terribly busy—three people had died in the explosion—but he heard us out and agreed to help. We bought a cheap coffin, planned a small funeral, and came up with the story of Harland's demise in a bank robbery attempt. He left town that same day for a job with a hauling company. The plan was for him to send me money each month. I leased the farm lands for extra income, and with my teaching job, we were able to make it."

"I don't understand," I said. "You faked Daddy's death to throw off Mr. Blackstone? What if he'd come after us as promised? Didn't this leave us completely vulnerable?"

Mama shook her head. "Harland and I thought about that when we came up with the plan. We got a couple of watchdogs, and your father taught me how to shoot his big shotgun. With the sheriff and his deputies on the lookout, we felt we'd be pretty safe until I could sell off that bottom land we weren't farming. With the proceeds, I was able to make a deal with Mr. Blackstone. I promised to pay him the rest of the debt in full, if he'd give me time, and take a smaller payment each month. I told him that was the only way he'd ever see his money. I guess he saw my point because he agreed."

"So he never asked to see the body? To verify your claims?"

"Under normal circumstances, he would have."

"What do you mean?"

"Mr. Blackstone lost his brother in the explosion. By the time he thought to ask, it was too late."

"And what about the family? How did you explain

the closed coffin to them?"

"That I was following Harland's wishes."

"I suppose you filled the empty coffin with rocks," I speculated.

"Sand bags."

"So where does Daddy call home now?"

"Fitzgerald."

I thought about the small town of Fitzgerald, just fifty miles southeast of Whiskey Creek. Daddy had been living so close, yet for me, a million miles away. I squelched back the resentment as it reared its ugly head once again, and said, "When can I see him? Can he come home now?"

"He's on the road, but he's scheduled to return to Georgia in the morning." Her voice sounded tired. "There's something else."

"There's more?" I asked incredulously, my overstrained nerves ready to snap.

"He took another name for precaution—Buddy Nelson."

I closed my eyes. "This is a lot to take in." My voice shook.

Mama's hand closed over mine. I didn't flinch this time, but allowed her soft touch to comfort me.

"That's enough for tonight," she said. "I need to head for the house, and you need to rest."

My eyes snapped open. "But you didn't answer my question. Can Daddy come home?"

She stood. "Tomorrow is soon enough to talk, Jolene. This is hard on me, too."

Her face reflected exhaustion, so I let her go, locking the door behind her. On automatic, I cleaned the kitchen, set the alarm, and turned out the lights. In my bedroom, I flung myself across the bed, gave into my warring emotions, and had a good cry.

It was midnight when I finally turned out the lights, but sleep evaded me. As hard as I tried, I couldn't get Mama's story out of my mind. Daddy had been living and working close by all these years. The story sounded like something straight out of Hollywood. My parents had outsmarted a dangerous criminal.

And that brought my thoughts to the stolen flash drive locked in my office desk drawer. What information did it contain? Whatever it was, I instinctively knew it was important. Was it related to Scarlett's demise? Could the thumb-drive be what Anthony had been searching for? The man in the blue sedan? No one knew it was in my possession. If they did, that would make me the target for a cold-blooded killer.

****

I woke with a start, momentarily disoriented by a sense of being watched. A slender thread of moonlight from the half-closed blinds cast its silvery glow across the bed. Pushing myself up on one elbow, I tried to discern what'd awakened me and looked over at the bedside clock. Four a.m. A slight movement in the corner of the bedroom stirred, taking shape, and tiny pinpricks of light slowly formed into the pale figure I recognized. Alarmed, Tango hissed and sprang from the bed.

"You aged me ten years with that stunt, Scarlett," I said, falling back on the pillows with relief.

She floated closer. "Sorry, I'm so late in getting here, but I was busy. FYI, there's some guy in a ski mask in your backyard. I believe he's looking for a way in."

I froze, straining to hear. After a moment, I heard the subtle rustling of fingertips brushing against the windowpane. The faint outline of a person painted itself against the shadows. Quietly, I grabbed Mini Pearl from the bedside table, emptied the cylinders and reloaded with hollow-point bullets from the drawer. Taking several deep, calming breaths, I eased out of bed.

For a long, tense minute, I studied the indigo shadow as it tested the window, and upon finding it locked, disappeared then reappeared at the other window. Confident with Mini Pearl in my grip, I crouched beside the bed until the shadow moved out of my line of sight, and then I darted out into the hall. Staying in the semidarkness, I double-checked the security system. Satisfied, I moved into the kitchen where I'd last seen my cell phone.

I found it lying next to my purse on the kitchen table. I snatched it up and dialed 9-1-1.

"What is your emergency?"

"Someone is trying to break into my house."

"What is your address?"

I gave it to her. "Please hurry. I can hear him on the front porch."

"Stay on the line until the officers arrive, ma'am. Are you alone?"

Heavy footsteps approached the back kitchen door from the carport. The door-knob rattled, and I could just make out the shape of a man through the glass. "Yes, I'm alone. He's at the back door now... Where's the freakin' police?"

"Stay calm. They're less than two minutes out." A pause, then, "Where are you in the house, ma'am?"

"The laundry room. Just off the kitchen. Better tell them to hurry, or I'll introduce the jerk to Mini Pearl."

"You said you were alone in the house, ma'am. Is Minnie Pearl your dog?"

"No. My gun."

"You're armed? Put the weapon down, ma'am."

"Not on your life. If that sucker takes one step in my house, I'm aiming south of the Mason-Dixon Line."

"Don't do that, ma'am. The police have arrived. They've requested you put down the weapon."

"I will when they identify themselves—not before."

A knock sounded at the kitchen door. "It's the police, ma'am."

I hung up with the dispatcher, holstered Mini Pearl, turned off the security alarm, and threw a robe over my shorty pajamas. When I opened the door, two large policemen stood there, hands hitched on the butts of their firearms.

"All you all right, ma'am?" asked a tall African-American officer.

I nodded. "Yeah, I'm fine now that you're here."

"We'll search the area," he said. "It's probably the same Peeping Tom who's been reported in the area. He's long gone."

The other officer, a slightly smaller version of the other, had smiling eyes that set me at ease, and I relaxed under his gaze. Apparently, knowing how to carry on a conversation with a scantily clad civilian in the early morning hours was one of the classes taught at the police academy. They seemed unaffected by my dishabille—unlike most men. "Keep your blinds closed," he advised. "That will discourage him in the future."

"It's nice to know he'll be back," I said to the two. "Have you guys thought about nabbing the jerk?"

"We'll keep that in mind and let you know if we find him. You can press charges then."

"I've heard that a lot lately."

The taller officer took out his notepad and wrote down my statement. His smile remained as he snapped the notepad shut. "We'll do a sweep of the area before we leave. Call us if you have any further problems."

"Thank you, I will." I closed and locked the door. Since I was wide awake with no chance of sleeping, I started a pot of coffee and sat down at the kitchen table, drained and achy, and in need of a caffeine infusion.

Tango ambled in, purring loudly and entwined himself about my legs. From his calm behavior, I knew the house was ghost-free, which suited me. Last night's revelation about Daddy resurfaced, but at the moment I needed to focus my thoughts on the would-be intruder, or "Peeping Tom" as the police had labeled him.

Retrieving my notes, I returned to the kitchen. The coffee pot had finished gurgling, so I fixed a cup and sat down at the table. Two cups later, I suspected the bungled break-in was related to the flash drive locked in my top desk drawer and not a Peeping Tom as the police had indicated. Someone knew I had it in my possession. Tammy came to mind, but I immediately discarded that thought. She hadn't known Scarlett. Or had she? What about Burns or even possibly Grant? Robert's eagle eyes might've spotted the top of the thumb-drive sticking out of my purse—and who knew the motives of the creepy detective? Anthony? The mysterious man in the blue sedan shadowing me? The idea terrified me, but I couldn't find another reasonable explanation to explain the strange events currently plaguing me. I had to find the answers quick or that ticking time bomb might claim me as its next victim.

****

An hour and a half had passed when the phone rang. I glanced up at the wall clock. 6:23. Caller ID indicated Mama's number.

"It's a good thing I'm up."

"I knew you would be. That's why I called. I have news about your daddy."

I set the coffee cup down with the clunk. "Where is he?"

"He just got in from the West Coast. He wants to see you this morning."

"Is it safe?" I asked, anxious for his safety. I had no intention of losing him a second time.

"He's willing to take the risk," she said. "Mr. Blackstone got his money, but he still might kill your father if he knows he's alive. For now, we have to meet in secret."

"Where and when?"

"Joggers Pond at eight. He'll be dressed in jeans, a red shirt, and an Atlanta Braves ball cap. Oh, and he has a beard."

"Deena and Billie Jo have to be told," I reminded her.

"You're right." Her voice cracked over the line. "How am I going to break this to them?"

"Just like you did me," I said, gently. "Billie Jo was so young when this took place. She doesn't remember much about Daddy, but she's strong and has Roddy to lean on. Deena's the one I'm worried about.

198

She's gone through a lot since her divorce."

"And you? How do you feel now that you know the truth?"

My eyes watered, and I swallowed the lump in my throat. "You know me. I'm fine now that I'm all cried out and have had all night to think about it. I'm just glad he's alive."

"You're not a brick wall, Jolene. You're a fine woman. I'm proud of how you've looked after your sisters all these years. I wish you wouldn't keep yourself walled up. You've got a lot of love to give if you'd just let yourself."

It took all of my willpower to hold back the raw emotions her words evoked, but if I started crying now, I'd never stop. Truthfully, I was a freaking mess inside. Daddy's return had stirred up all the insecurities I'd managed to bury all these years. "The best way to handle this is just to face it," I said. "Why don't you invite Deena, Billie Jo, and Roddy to supper tonight? I'll help break the news. They can tell their children later after they've come to grips with it."

"Sounds like a good plan. I'll see you tonight around six."

I hung up and rose from the table, coffee cup in hand, with Mama's disturbing words still ringing in my mind. *If you'd just let yourself love.* Impatiently, I pushed aside the knowledge of my inability to completely give myself to any man because of Daddy's disappearance. My inability to trust had caused my divorce and a number of other issues that crept up from time to time. Oh well, I wasn't in the mood to dwell on my growing list of faults this morning.

I fed Tango, and then puttered around the house,

trying to dispel the anxious nervousness and anticipation of seeing my father after a twenty year absence. After a quick shower, I slipped into an eye-popping floral print dress and yellow heels, pinned up my tangle of curls, and went to meet Daddy.

Chapter Eighteen
Another Dead End

The tall man outlined against the golden backdrop of water was feeding a small family of ducks when I stopped my car just out of his sight ten minutes later. From this vantage point, I could study him at my leisure without him being conscious of my appraisal. Thinner than I remembered, and his shoulders drooped slightly, but he still commanded attention. My breath caught in my throat when he threw back his head, roaring with laughter as a family of ducks competed for the bread he tossed into the water. The ceaseless hum of traffic disappeared as the booming sound replayed in my memory.

Satisfied that the man in jeans and red shirt was indeed Daddy, I drove until I was several feet from where he stood and parked my car at the curb. He swung around at my approach, flashing me a welcoming smile. With shaking hands, I turned off the ignition, climbed out of the car, and then hesitated, my feelings for him becoming confused. My pulse jittered as butterflies assaulted my stomach, and my legs became weak all at once with the jolt of anxiety and self-doubt that struck me.

Daddy, too, froze as if any sudden movement would cause me to bolt. Time slowed to a crawl as we continued to gaze at one another. The widening of his smile broke the spell, and I flew into his outstretched arms. After a moment, he held me at arm's length and quite openly studied my face.

"You're as beautiful as the pictures Annie Mae sent me," he said. "You favor her."

The rich timbre of his voice brought past recollections rushing back. Like the time I'd borrowed Mama's dressmaking shears and whacked off Deena's long chestnut hair. Mama hadn't appreciated my artistic flair and spanked me. Daddy had come home to a house of wailing females. He'd wiped away my tears, promised Deena her hair would grow long again, and kissed Mama so long she started moaning. Billie Jo thought he was hurting her and started crying. After supper, Daddy piled us in the car and took us to Dairy Queen for chocolate-dipped ice-cream cones. To this day, it was still one of my favorite memories.

"I have your brown eyes, Daddy," I said softly, my fingers aching to touch his lined face, to feel the silkiness of his salt-and-pepper beard.

Lightly, he fingered a loose tendril of hair on my cheek. "Blonde and curly like Annie Mae's when I married her."

I laughed. "You mean frizzy, don't you? Did she tell you about the time when I was in high school and she caught Deena trying to iron the kinks out of my hair? The iron was too hot and scorched my hair. She made me go to school with burnt, stinky hair. After that, I saved up my allowance and bought a flat iron."

"I wish I could've been there."

I reached for his hand, needing the connection. "Me, too, Daddy."

"I guess you have questions."

"I do. Mama did her best to explain things, but I don't want to go into that now—not here—you could be in danger."

"I checked the area out before you arrived," he assured me. "It's still early, and so far no one has recognized me, but we do need to be cautious—until I can come up with a new plan."

"You could go to the police," I suggested. "Deena's dating a nice detective."

His face tightened. "I need to be sure I can trust them before I open my mouth. No, for now, let's keep things as they are." He rubbed the back of his neck.

His agitation was apparent, so I shifted gears. "Agreed. Now, tell me about your life."

The minutes passed as Daddy shared his long-distance travels across the country behind the wheel of a big rig—the ups and downs, the loneliness, and camaraderie between truck drivers. He told me of the small, cramped apartment he rented in Fitzgerald, and how each time he heard one of his neighbors address him as "Buddy" or "Mr. Nelson" he longed all the more for his life with us here in Whiskey Creek.

Finally, he fell silent as we stood at the edge of the water, our shoulders touching. I looked out across the small lake to the Methodist church towering above the shady trees on the far bank. Only a few early morning fishermen dotted the crooked dirt path winding around the pond. The soft breeze felt heavenly on my skin. The air smelled pungent with warm earth and spring flowers. Joggers Pond was a peaceful paradise that I loved sharing with my father.

"Can I ask you a personal question?" I asked, breaking the silence between us.

"Of course, sweetheart." He placed an arm about my shoulders. "You can talk with me about anythin'."

"Do you believe in ghosts?"

Candid eyes stared back at me. "Yes, honey, I believe in restless spirits," he said without hesitation. "My mother called it the third eye. She said it was a blessin' and a curse in her life."

Granny Tucker. I smiled. "I heard her voice when I was placing lilies on the graves at Easter. I thought I was crazy."

"No, honey, you're not crazy," he replied. "I never said anythin' before now, but your grandmother started seein' spirits as a child. Her mother, my grandmother, told her to keep it a secret. Back then, the church came down pretty hard on what they termed as witchcraft. There was a lot of suspicion in them Alabama hills at that time. I found out about her ability quite by accident one day. She was talkin' to an empty chair in the kitchen. Thought she was crazy until footsteps sounded across the wooden floor. The back screen door opened and slammed shut. Funny thing, no one was there. She caught me spyin' and explained how God had given her a special gift to help his lost children find their way home. Did you know that at your birth she told me you had inherited the same gift? Remember your imaginary friends?"

"I remember Mama taking me to a psychologist. Soon afterward, I was able to block them out. Until recently, that is."

"Those imaginary friends were spirits seekin' help. I told Annie Mae you were fine and to leave you alone, but she wouldn't listen to reason. I tried one time to tell her about my mother, but she cut me off before I could explain. After that, I kept my mouth shut. I'm sorry, honey. I should've explained things to you a long time ago."

"I'm glad you told me now. Makes it easier to understand."

"So tell me what's goin' on that you would ask me about seein' ghosts?"

"I'm sure you've heard about what happened at the salon."

"I've been on the road for weeks," he replied. "Your mother didn't mention the salon when I spoke with her this mornin'. She kept saying that the chickens had come home to roost."

"It was in the newspapers and on the news—the death of a local TV personality? Scarlett Cantrell—she died in Dixieland's facial room."

"Vincent and Rowena Cantrell's daughter?"

I stared at him, startled. "You knew them? Mama never mentioned any connection. They died in a plane crash several years back."

"I didn't know them personally," he replied. "But I overheard Mr. Blackstone mention Cantrell's name one day when he paid me an unexpected visit. His goons were about to work me over when he received a call. That's when I heard the name. I never forgot it because back then Mr. Cantrell was a respected judge in the state. I believe he was heavily invested in many local businesses. He and Richard Payne—"

"The mayor's father?"

"Yeah, that's the one. Those men ran this county. They were both very powerful with connections in high places. Richard had just been elected mayor." He paused. "You say that Vincent's daughter died in your beauty shop?"

"She's the reason I brought up the subject of ghosts. You see, she was murdered in my salon, and now she's haunting me—she wants me to find her killer."

An expression of fear crossed his face. "No, Jolene. That sounds dangerous. I'm not convinced the politicians weren't somehow tied up with Mr. Blackstone. I would strongly suggest you back away and leave this to the police. It's their problem."

"I'm already involved," I said, leaving out the details of my adventures into investigating. It wouldn't be fair to worry him so soon after he'd come back into my life. I'd watch my step, and hand over the flash drive to Bradford as soon as I could arrange a meeting with him. Hopefully, I'd have discovered its contents before then.

Glancing at my watch, I was relieved to be out of time and couldn't debate his objections. "I've got to get to work." I kissed his cheek. "Mama's arranging a dinner so we can share the good news with Deena and Billie Jo. I'll see you there."

"How do you think they'll take it?"

I tried to reassure him. "Well, I'm not sure. Like me, they'll be shocked, but after they've had time for it to sink in, they'll be as thrilled as I am."

I left him standing at the water's edge and drove to the salon, replaying our conversation in my mind. I would keep Daddy's return a secret until tonight. Besides, I had more pressing issues on my mind. In light of Daddy's revelation about Vincent Cantrell's possible connection with Mr. Blackstone, I had burning questions that needed answering. And what about the mayor's father? Was he a part of the maze of confusion? I'd promised Bradford I'd stay out of the investigation, but now I wasn't so sure I could keep my promise.

****

My sisters were in Deena's office when I stuck my head in the open doorway. "Are you ready for a crazy morning?"

"Not really," Billie Jo said. "Everyone's on edge. Mandy practically bit my head off a minute ago when I asked if the coffee was ready. I have a bad feeling about today."

"Nerves," Deena said. "I'll just be glad when this whole murder business is over and the salon is back to normal. And I'm not looking forward to Scarlett's funeral tomorrow. I wish we could skip it."

My nine o'clock spied me standing in the office doorway and yoo-hooed to me from across the reception area. Holly intercepted her and escorted her to my station. Since it was a color correction service and would need my full attention, I left my sisters and hurried back to the kitchen to take an aspirin and call Mama about my meeting with Daddy before my hectic day kicked in. She wasn't in, so I left a message.

The kitchen door swung open. Mandy rushed over to the coffee pot. Good, just the person I wanted to talk to. "Good morning, Mandy. Got a minute to spare?"

At the sound of my voice, the spoon in her hand clattered to the counter, and she swung around to face me. "I didn't see you sitting there."

Her eyes shifted from mine as I motioned to the chair opposite me. Picking up her cup, she sat down.

"I'm sorry I startled you. I guess you were deep in

thought."

"I'm a little on edge these days." She forced a laugh. "So much has happened. I can't seem to settle down."

"Is everything okay with your family?" I looked closer at her. She did seem downright scared, but of what—or whom?

"Why do you ask about my family?" Her hands clutched the cup as if it'd shatter into a thousand pieces.

By the mounting tension in her voice, I deduced her family was strictly off-limits. Now that I thought about it, she never mentioned them, never recounted happy childhood memories like the rest of the staff so often did. Really, we didn't have a clue about her background. What sordid details did she hide—and possibly pay blackmail money to keep secret?

"I asked about your family because it's the usual thing to do when a person appears as upset as you. No offense intended."

She expelled a long breath. "I'm sorry for snapping. I didn't want to say anything, but the salon gives me the creeps. I've been freaked out since Miss Cantrell died. I keep looking over my shoulder every time I pass the facial room."

I gave her no quarter but dived right into the question bugging me. "But aren't you a tad relieved you don't have to pay her blackmail money any longer?"

She tensed at the question, her knuckles white against the black cup. "What do you mean?" Her eyes darted to the door as if seeking escape. "She wasn't blackmailing me."

"I witnessed an exchange between you two here in this kitchen last November. From the conversation, you were on the hook for a long time."

She looked at me, her eyes watering. "She was bleeding my family dry."

Her whispered reply almost derailed me, but I had to press on. "That's why you were so relieved that day outside the police station. You mentioned going shopping which sounded heartless at the time."

"Scarlett died before collecting her next payment. So why not take it and buy something for myself for a change?"

"What was she holding over your head?"

She frowned. "I'd rather not say."

"Would you rather I called the police? I need to know about criminal activity involving my employees."

"Please don't do that," she said, grabbing my arm. "It's my younger brother who's in trouble. He's a teacher, and Scarlett saw him outside school property with a female student. If it became public knowledge, he could lose his job at the high school, so he came to me for help. It was innocent, I swear. Donnie's not a pervert."

"That's for the police to decide."

"Would you give me some time to discuss this with my family? To hire a lawyer?"

I hesitated, unsure if I should agree to her terms. The thumb-drive locked in my top desk drawer came to mind. Wasn't I also withholding information? Even possible evidence? I could give them several days to come forward on their own. "Three days. After that, I'm going to the police."

Mandy's strained features relaxed. "Thank you."

A jumble of voices sounded outside the kitchen door. I recognized Mrs. Hawthorne's booming voice immediately. My face twisted in response to her braying.

"That's my first appointment now." Mandy bolted from her seat and sailed out of the kitchen.

Now, I had another burning question on my mind. Why did Scarlett need money? From appearances, that seemed to be the one thing she had plenty of. Big white house in an exclusive neighborhood, luxury car, designer clothes and handbags, and I suspected Mother Nature hadn't produced those basketball boobs. Nope. Store-bought, had to be.

Holly stuck her head through the half-opened door, halting my racing thoughts. "Your client is prepped and ready," she said.

The buzz of excited voices filled my ears when I left the kitchen and started down the hall toward the front of the salon. I glimpsed Holly folding towels as I passed the laundry room. Employees came and went like snowbirds in spring. We were lucky to have found such a good, hardworking receptionist, I thought, as I drew near the facial room. Suddenly, Scarlett stuck her head through the closed door, scaring the crap out of me.

"We need to talk," she said.

I stumbled to a stop, my feet frozen to the floor. "Yes, we do," I whispered. "But now's not the time."

Mandy, whose pedicure chair was in my direct sight, eyed me quizzically. I tried to smile reassuringly at her as Scarlett threatened dire consequences if I didn't get my overly large butt in the facial room right now, emphasizing *right now* in a low, rumbling voice. Mandy winced. Her hand trembled as she lifted Mrs. Hawthorne's fat foot out of the bubbling spa. Her gaze swept around as if expecting someone to jump out at her.

The second Mandy bent down over her client's chubby toes, I ducked into the facial room. I heard the click of the door lock, and a small light over the sink flipped on of its own accord. I stood face to face with a ghost outfitted in velvet ranging from dark green to chartreuse.

The curtain dress. Modernized, of course, to Scarlett's specifications.

"Look, I don't have much time," I said. "I know about the blackmail money from Mandy. Care to tell me why you were bleeding her dry? You didn't need the money."

"Wrong. I was left with a big house and lots of debts. Keeping up appearances costs a fortune these days. I saw an opportunity and I took it."

"Okay, moving on. I found the jade elephant in your office. Turned out to be a book. And guess what I found inside?"

"A flash drive with my files on it."

"You remember?"

"That's what I was going to tell you last night, but your midnight visitor distracted me."

"I have a problem. My computer won't read the thumb-drive. And I need a password."

"The password is moonpaddy."

"Any ideas about the software to open it?"

She tugged down her tight skirt which had bunched over her hips. "Yes. I—"

The doorknob rattled. "The door's locked, Holly." Deena's irritated voice filtered through the panel. "She's probably in the restroom."

"I checked there first. Her client is getting impatient." Holly's voice was equally agitated.

The knob rattled again. "Well, she's not in here, so check the restroom again. I'll look in the kitchen."

I waited until their footsteps faded before turning back to Scarlett. "The software?" I whispered.

"Try my office computer."

I sighed with exasperation. "Your *former* office is now occupied. How am I going to gain access?"

"Another nighttime visit," she suggested.

"Sneak into the station like I did your house?" My voice rose. "I promised to stay out of trouble."

"What choice do you have?"

Choices. The word held multiple outcomes. Bad choice—do as she suggested. Good choice—hand the thumb-drive over to Bradford—right now. I juggled the ball back and forth before I let out a long sigh of surrender. Scarlett's smile wasn't reassuring, but I gave her a quick nod. Now, all I had to do was come up with a good plan that would keep me out of jail or joining Scarlett in the hereafter.

Chapter Nineteen
Mama's Having Sex

The next several hours passed by quickly. At noon, I had a break in appointments. Deena brought me a roast beef sandwich from the diner on Main before she left for a lunch date. I'd just finished eating when Billie Jo came into the kitchen and sat down at the table.

"Paul dropped off the analysis report on the contents of the jars in the facial room. They had plaster mixed into them."

"Plaster? That's strange. Is he positive?"

"He's positive. He tested the paste on a small portion of skin on a cadaver, and the results showed it hardened slowly. He said it took thirty minutes for the paste to dry to the consistency of hard rubber."

"Carla said she was away from the facial room for twenty minutes."

"According to the test results, she lied to us."

"And to the police," I added.

"Maybe she's confused about the time frame. She's been acting strange lately."

"Her marriage is falling apart, thanks to Scarlett."

"That gives her motive."

"And Frank too," I said. "I'm gonna ride out to Carla's house before the funeral. I'd like to hear his side of the story."

"Deena and I are coming with you. We're in this

together."

I rose from the table and dumped my paper plate into the trash can. "We'll have a chance to talk about this tonight at Mama's house."

"What's that about, anyway? She was terribly mysterious this morning when she called to invite me and Roddy to supper—she sounded nervous. Has she met a man and intends to introduce us to him?"

I thought about Daddy. "You might say that, Billie Jo."

"Oh, so you know what's going on?"

"Yes, I know."

"So tell me."

"No, I think it would be best for you to wait until tonight," I said, picturing the aftermath of exposing this secret here in the salon. "This is a family matter to be discussed in private."

Billie Jo made a face. "She's not planning on moving some stranger into the house, is she? I don't want to think about her having sex in the same bed she shared with Daddy. I'm going to tell her she has to buy a new one. What do you think about Mama having sex?"

Thankfully, Deena came in and spared me from having to answer. "What are y'all talking about?" she asked.

"Mama having sex," Billie Jo said. "Jolene said the reason Mama wants us to come out to the house for supper tonight is to tell us she's moving some man into the house. I just think she should buy a new bed. That was Daddy's bed."

"I *didn't* say that, Billie Jo."

Deena smiled. "Mama's seeing a man? Wow, she's

never mentioned anyone to me. I think that's great news. Love keeps us young at heart."

"Who said anything about love?" Billie Jo said. "We're talking about sheet-wrinkling, heart-pounding, sex. Lust, pure and simple. You remember those days, don't you?"

I slapped Billie Jo's arm. "Stop bragging. And stop teasing Deena. She doesn't think like we do."

"Ha, she's fooled you."

The wall clock showed I had run out of time. "Well, back to work," I said and left them in the kitchen. The rest of the day, I avoided Billie Jo like the plague.

At six, I arrived at the farm to find Mama pacing in the kitchen. The smell of burnt food struck me in the face when I opened the back door.

"Get in here and help me, Jolene. I burned the roast and forgot about the peas on the stove. They're so scorched I had to throw them out."

I set my purse down on the kitchen table, took a bottle of blackberry wine from the refrigerator, and poured Mama a tall glass. "Sit down and drink this. It'll calm you down. Now, what's in the freezer for emergencies?" I opened the window over the sink to air out the room.

"There's homemade chicken vegetable soup."

"Where's Daddy?"

"He'll be here soon."

I went to the freezer, searched for a moment, and pulled out the freezer bag of soup. "I'll put on a pan of cornbread to go with this. We don't need much. Just enough for six." I placed the bag on the counter and preheated the oven. "Did you and Daddy have a chance to talk?"

"Yes, we had lunch here where it's private," she said from the table.

I looked over at her nursing the glass of wine. "Do you think it's safe for him to be here at the farm? What if Mr. Blackstone finds out he's back?"

"We had a long talk over lunch. He's going back on the road in the morning and will be gone for a week. When he returns, we'll drive over to Fitzgerald. It'll be safer over there."

"Thanks for telling me your plans this time."

"I regret the past, Jolene, but it couldn't be helped. Your father's foolish actions forced us into a dangerous situation, and I would've done anything to keep my girls safe and hang onto my home."

I withheld comment and stepped inside the pantry, thinking about the ticking time bomb stashed in my desk. What secrets had Scarlett uncovered? More blackmailing schemes that shouldn't get out into the public? Hopefully, tonight I'd know.

"Have you told Becky about her grandfather?" Mama asked.

"No. I'll drop by her house when I leave here and have a talk with her. Jacob will be home, and I'll feel better with him there. She's been so sick with her first pregnancy. I'd love to wait until after she delivers, but I'm afraid someone might call her and drop the bomb."

Mama was warming the soup on the stove when I came out of the pantry with the ingredients for the cornbread. I mixed them together and slid the pan into the oven. Deena, Billie Jo, and Roddy came through the back door.

Billie Jo flung her purse on the table. "Where's he

at, Mama?"

"And who are you referring to, honey?"

"The man you're seeing. The one we're here to meet."

"What man?"

Detecting a faint tremor in Mama's voice, I rushed to defuse the situation before it could take shape. "Would anyone like a glass of wine before supper?"

"Got any Scotch?" Roddy asked.

Mama pointed to the cabinet over the refrigerator. "Harland kept an old bottle up there over the ice box."

"Daddy's just the person I want to talk about," Billie Jo said. "Mama, how could you?"

"Give her a chance to explain," Deena suggested. "That's why we're here."

I handed a glass of wine to Billie Jo. "Drink up. You need to de-stress."

"Boy, you spoke the truth," Roddy said, tossing down his drink. He poured another. "She talked me to death on the way out here. I love her, but there's only so much a man can take."

"Shut up, Roddy, or I'll take my straight razor to your balls while you're asleep," Billie Jo snapped.

"Ohhh, I love it when you talk dirty to me," he said.

Deena rolled her eyes at me and took the soup bowls I pulled from the cabinet. "I'll set the table." She disappeared through the doorway leading to the dining room.

Sliding up next to Mama, I whispered in her ear, "Don't you think you need to tell them before Daddy returns from the fields? Now's a good time."

Mama nodded. "Deena, can you come in here for a

minute? I have something I need to discuss with you girls."

"Here it comes," Billie Jo said from the table. She took a long swig from her glass.

Deena poked her head through the doorway. "What's up?"

"Come on in and have a seat at the table," Mama ordered.

"But I'm not finished—"

"It can wait. Have a seat with your sisters."

Taking a seat beside me, Deena squeezed my hand. "I hope I like him."

"You will," I said.

Mama pulled out a chair and sat down. She cleared her throat, the room went silent. "Your father is alive."

Her shocking words had the effect of a gunshot blast on a quiet Sunday morning. Once spoken, they stung the air like the caustic smell of gunpowder. A dull flush spread over Billie Jo's face as if she too would explode. Roddy winced as her hand tightened on his. Deena's face took on a slight greenish tinge—Mama's, too.

"Good grief, Mama. I didn't mean for you to blurt it out like that. Now everybody, stay calm," I advised as my sisters turned their stunned gazes on me. "Give her a chance to explain."

"You knew this morning in the kitchen that Daddy was alive and didn't tell us?" Billie Jo accused.

"How long have you known?" Deena's voice broke.

"Since last night," I said. "I'm just as shocked as you are."

"Don't go blaming Jolene for staying quiet," Mama

said. "She's done the right thing. I should've told you girls long ago. I just got scared, and well, I take full responsibility for my actions." After a few expletives from Billie Jo, she quieted down, and Mama repeated her conversation with me from the night before. They deluged Mama with questions, and she did her best to answer, but tension mounted as we waited for Daddy to make his appearance.

The oven timer buzzed. I pulled the cornbread out of the oven and checked the soup, then uncorked another bottle of wine from the refrigerator and refilled my glass. Deena ambled off to finish setting the table, and Mama returned to her vigil over the soup.

She was standing at the stove, stirring the bubbling broth with a long wooden spoon when Daddy came through the back door. I gulped down my glass of wine, needing the fortification now that the moment of confrontation had arrived. I glanced at Mama. She stood frozen, her eyes taking in the drama. Billie Jo twisted in her chair at the click of the closed door, her wine glass paused in midair.

A flash of blue in the corner of my eye told me Deena had returned from the dining room. "Daddy!" She flung herself into his arms. Roddy set down his glass, pushing himself to his feet to meet his father-in-law, his hand possessively resting on Billie Jo's shoulder. She rubbed her cheek against his hand, her pained gaze transferring from me to Mama.

"I'm sorry for what I've done." Mama laid the spoon down on the stove top. "I was wrong in my judgment."

"*We* were wrong," Daddy said coming to stand beside her. Deena, still wrapped in his embrace, shuffled along beside him. "I won't stand by and allow your mother to blame herself for my mistakes."

Billie Jo stood. With slow, hesitating steps she approached him. When she reached him, she again hesitated. Releasing Deena, he gathered Billie Jo into his arms. "I know this is going to take time, honey, but give us a chance. We should've told you the truth long ago. Your mother and I made some mistakes for which we're awfully sorry."

"Yes, you did," Billie Jo said with a catch in her voice. "Those life-altering mistakes will take a lot of time and love to erase, but I'm willing to try."

From then on, things went well. After supper, I left my sisters to get reacquainted with Daddy and drove to my daughter's house. Becky took the news in her usual calm manner, expressing the desire to meet her grandfather as soon as possible. Emotionally tired, I excused myself and drove home to retrieve the thumb-drive. I couldn't put off going to the TV station any longer.

Thankfully, the lobby was deserted when I entered. In the distance, I could hear the soft murmur of voices, so I knew I'd have to proceed quietly to escape detection. Cautiously, I retraced my steps to Tammy's office, not seeing a soul in the empty hall, and slipped inside the unlocked door.

With the light from a small flashlight, I sat down at the desk and booted up the computer. When ready, I inserted the finger stick and typed in the password.

An incorrect password message flashed across the screen.

I retyped "moonpaddy" and hit the enter button.

The same message flashed across the screen.

Crap. What now? Sure that I'd heard Scarlett correctly, I tried again for the third time without success. The same message blinked from the screen. I even tried various spellings, but still nothing.

Discouraged with another dead end, I withdrew the flash drive and stashed it, and the flashlight, alongside Mini Pearl in my purse, then turned off the computer.

The empty hall was a welcome sight when I eased out of the office, my purse tucked at my side. I had made it part-way down the corridor when an office door swung open, and a man stepped out, hesitating when he spotted me. I swallowed the scream that'd risen in my throat, and gave him a friendly nod. Not daring to speak, I escaped down the hall, imagining his eyes burning a hole through my back.

Something clattered behind me, but I kept on going, not slowing down until I'd burst through the lobby door into the warm, night air. Exhausted, and shaking with adrenaline overload, I drove home and collapsed into bed fully clothed. The last thought I pictured before falling dead asleep were my hands nailing Scarlett's coffin lid down good and tight and chunking her into the deepest part of Whiskey Creek.

Chapter Twenty
A Green Funeral

Sunday morning dawned bright and early. My cell phone rang. The bedside clock read 7:48.

"Hello."

"Are you awake?"

Yawning, I answered, "What's up, Billie Jo? I thought we decided to skip church since we have Scarlett's funeral later."

"We did. Roddy and I are going to breakfast. Do you want to join us? Deena's tagging along."

"You guys go on ahead without me. I want to run over to Carla's before Scarlett's funeral."

"Oh, I forgot. Deena and I were supposed to go with you. We can do breakfast another time."

I swung my feet to the floor and padded down the hallway to the living room for a quick look see out the window. "Don't worry about me." My gaze swept the street for the blue sedan. All clear. The drape dropped back into place. "Why don't we meet up at the salon around three? We'll ride to the funeral together."

"And what are you going to do in the meantime?"

Thinking about my failed attempt to read the flash drive last night, and the potential danger attached to it, I said, "I've a few errands to run this morning. Talking to Carla and Frank Moody is one of them." As much as I wanted to know what was on the flash drive, I realized the sooner it was out of my possession and into Bradford's, the safer I would feel.

"Okay, but be careful. We'll see you at the salon around three."

After clicking off, I fixed a light breakfast and settled down to read the morning newspaper. Tango watched from the top of the refrigerator. Afterward, I puttered around the house straightening the clutter and doing deep housework that never seemed to get done during the busy work week.

At eleven, I showered and changed. Knowing today would be a long, hot day I dressed for comfort in a black cotton-lace sleeveless dress and matching pumps. With my hair piled high off my neck, I grabbed my keys, put the top down on the Mustang, and headed for Carla's house west of town.

Two vehicles were parked in the driveway of her single-story ranch house. I recognized Carla's red Honda and figured the blue pickup must be Frank's. I parked behind the Honda, walked up to the front porch, and rang the doorbell. As I waited for someone to come to the door, I looked around at my surroundings. Large pecan trees shaded the front yard, but the grass needed mowing, and the flower beds needed weeding. The house had a rundown appearance and was in desperate need of a fresh coat of paint.

Just when I was wondering if I should leave, the door swung open and Carla stood there, her eyes red and puffy, her face drawn into a tight frown.

"What are you doing here?"

"You asked me to help you. That's why I'm here. I have some questions for you and Frank."

She hesitated before inviting me in with a gesture.

"I was talking with my mother on the phone when you rang the doorbell. I'm so worried about her. I can't help but cry when we talk. The kids are in the backyard, and Frank is in the den watching a race."

"I hope he'll be open to talking with me." I followed her through the house to the back den, a nice space with a blue flowered sofa with large, colorful pillows. Family pictures lined the beige walls, threatening to take over the confined space.

A young, handsome, dark-haired man clicked off the blaring TV, and climbed to his feet from the recliner. Clad in jeans and a white T-shirt, Frank Moody reached out a hand when Carla introduced us and explained why I had dropped by.

"Thank you for agreeing to speak with me. If I'm to help Carla, I need to hear your side of the story." I shook his hand and sat down on the sofa opposite the recliner. Carla joined me on the sofa.

He resumed his seat on the recliner. "I don't see how I can help, but I'll do what I can. Carla and I are ready to put this behind us. She's agreed to marriage counseling."

"We have to try. For the kids," she said, confirming his statement.

"So this affair with Scarlett was a one-time deal?" I asked him.

His eyes narrowed. "I've gone over this with the police. I had nothing to do with Scarlett's death. Neither did Carla."

"Robert Burns said you were stalking Scarlett."

"That was a mistake. I've learned my lesson."

"He told me you asked Carla for a divorce just before Scarlett died. He said you wanted to marry

Scarlett, but she rejected you."

Red-faced, he jumped up and prowled the den, his hands clasped behind his back. "Are you here to completely destroy our chances of reconciliation? It's none of your business."

Carla eyed her pacing husband. "I think it's time you told her the truth."

He ground to a halt, facing us. "I lied about the affair. Me and Carla were having problems. Scarlett found me dead drunk at Cooter's one night. I made a pass at her. She took pity and let me crash on her sofa for the night. The next morning, she fed me breakfast and listened to my sorry story. She told me to go home and work it out. But I didn't listen. She tried to let me down easy, but I refused to back off and acted the fool. I hate being rejected, so I lied about the affair."

"That was the last time you had contact with her?" I asked.

He dragged his fingers through his hair. "No. We met Friday morning down at Joggers Pond. I begged her to give me a chance. I even promised to give up drinking, but she wanted no part of it. She had a man in her life. She said I loved Carla, not her. She understood because she'd ridden the same roller-coaster after her parents died. That's when she confessed to being a recovering alcoholic."

That's a new revelation.

"And then what happened?"

"I followed her advice and went to an AA meeting."

"You didn't try to contact her after that?"

He shook his head. "No, I realized she was right. All the time it was Carla I was missing, wanting.

225

Scarlett may have come off as a haughty, uncaring bitch, but deep down inside, she was a good person. I wouldn't be here today with my family if it weren't for her."

Becky had expressed the same opinion. Frank held out a hand to his wife. "Sorry you had to hear it again."

Carla rose from the sofa and went into his arms. "If we're going to make it, I have to hear the bad parts. And we are going to make it. I'm not going anywhere, and neither are you." She turned to me. "Are those all the questions you have?"

"I have one for you, Carla. Why did you lie to me and the police about the twenty minutes you said you left the mask on Scarlett's face? In the lab, it took thirty minutes for the mask to dry to the rubbery hardness it was on Scarlett's face."

"I must've lost track of time a bit while I was on the phone with my mother. God, I was so mixed up and confused that day that I don't remember much."

"So you weren't trying to cover up your own mistake?"

"No. But I did make a mistake. I allowed my personal problems to interfere with my job. I wasn't even aware of my mental state until the doctors diagnosed me. All I could focus on was my failing marriage and my dying mother. I'm sorry I caused so much trouble for your family."

A door slammed and the sound of running feet and giggling kids burst into the den. Two young children—an older boy I judged to be about seven and a girl around five or six—ran up to their parents.

"Tag, you're it," the boy cried, tapping his younger sibling on the arm.

The girl squealed with delight and chased her brother around the den. Frank reached out, hauling his laughing daughter to his side to swing her up into his arms. The boy grabbed his father's leg with both arms and looked up at him with adoration.

I smiled at the picture, knowing this young family would be okay with time and counseling. "I believe it's time for you and your family to get back to enjoying your Sunday," I said, hugging Carla and following her to the front door.

"Thanks for helping me. Your family has done so much. I can't thank you enough."

With my head near to bursting with the surprising revelations, I said goodbye and headed back into town—my next stop was Dixieland Salon. The empty parking lot told me I had the place to myself when I pulled around to the back. In case of rain, I put the top up on the convertible and let myself in through the back door. In Deena's office, I booted up the computer and slipped in the thumb-drive. I tried the password again. The computer flashed the same message I'd received at home—the thumb-drive required special software and a password.

I tried rousing Scarlett, but she wasn't answering my call. Discouraged and stumped with my lack of computer skills, I abandoned Deena's office for the kitchen and poured a glass of Coke. Then I grabbed the phone book off the counter, opening to the yellow pages. I found the computer consultant listings and punched in the first number. They were closed. I tried each of the others, but they were all closed. Now what?

****

Not too long after, Billie Jo showed up, wanting

me to cut and style her hair. Since we had some time to kill, I agreed. I shampooed and cut her short, blonde hair into wispy layers throughout, and blow-dried it into a cute pixie style. She wanted to reciprocate the favor. Having more time to burn, I consented, although I wasn't confidant of her skills being a barber with limited experience with ladies' hairstyles, but she was my sister, after all.

Loosening my hair out of its clasp, she let the thick, heavy waves tumble through her hands to settle at my waist. She picked up a hairbrush.

"How did your meeting go with the Moodys? Find out anything new?"

"Actually, quite a lot," I said. "Frank insists he never had an affair with Scarlett. Not for a lack of trying on his part, but she wanted no part of it. She had a man in her life and wasn't interested in another. She confessed to being a recovering alcoholic. How the gossip mavens allowed that juicy tidbit to escape notice, I'll never know."

She started brushing the tangles out of my hair. "How about an updo?"

"I don't care what you do as long as it's off my neck," I said, relaxing under the strong pull of the hairbrush.

"And Carla? What was her explanation for the time discrepancy with the mask?"

"She said she lost track of time when she was talking with her mother. Blamed it on confusion. It could be true."

Billie Jo picked up the curling iron and began curling my hair. "So do you still suspect them of doing Scarlett in?"

"Naw, not so much. I'm inclined to believe their stories. Neither one strikes me as a killer." I paused as another question came to mind. "Hey, tell me how you really feel about Daddy's resurrection."

"Well, I was certainly shocked and hurt, when the truth came out. But after all the trouble lately, I'm just glad he's alive. Does that make sense?"

"I feel the same way. But Scarlett's death has had a profound influence on me. Now I know for sure that my imaginary friends weren't a figment of my imagination. That's a good thing."

"Is she still hanging around the salon?"

"I haven't seen her today. She's probably getting ready for her funeral."

Billie Jo grabbed for a stack of bobby pins on the counter. "Speaking of Scarlett, I forgot to tell you Deena called, and she's gonna meet us at the funeral home."

I glanced at my watch. 2:45. "We'd better get a move on. It's getting late."

Billie Jo reached for a can of hairspray. "I'm done."

"Not too much spray."

It's a good thing my sister rarely applied hairspray because the way she waved the can around my head, there wouldn't be an ozone layer when she finished. The can finally fizzled out, and I looked open-mouthed at my reflection in the mirror.

"Well?" Billie Jo asked expectantly, her face openly proud of her accomplishment.

I hesitated, not knowing whether to laugh or cry. "You did a great job," I said, not wanting to hurt her feelings, and I reached up to pat down the small curls sprouting from my head like antlers, then gathered up my purse and followed her out to the back parking lot.

"I'll meet you there," I said as Billie Jo climbed into her Charger.

She waved from her car. "Don't put the top down on your car. The wind will mess your hair."

With my new updo, I had to duck my head to get my hair inside the vehicle and for a split second, I contemplated putting the top down anyway. The wind couldn't do any more damage than the convertible top pressing against my curls.

The ride to the funeral home took less than ten minutes, and as I stepped inside the cool lobby, the soft, gentle strains of soothing music washed over me. Billie Jo waited by the memorial book. I signed the book and ignored the strange looks thrown my way as we mingled with the crowd and finally found Deena talking with a group from our church. She did a double take when she spotted us and excused herself. Together, we found a couple of empty seats in front and sat down.

Deena touched my hair and whispered, "Having a bad hair day?"

I batted her hand. "Be quiet. The service is about to start."

"It's such a shame about Scarlett's beautiful face. That's why it's a closed casket, you know. I bet they couldn't fix it," Billie Jo whispered.

"Shhh. Have you no respect for the dead?" Deena whispered back.

Billie Jo tapped me on the knee. "What's up with the strange casket?"

"It's a green funeral," Deena said. "Scarlett's casket is made of one hundred percent bio-degradable cardboard." She waved a paper in front of us. "It's all explained here in this handout."

"Poor Scarlett, her cousin is burying her in an oversized shoe box," Billie Jo remarked in a low voice. "Roddy and I are going to have a serious talk tonight. I plan on staying high and dry when I bite the dust."

I looked away from my sisters to the coffin surrounded and blanketed in flowers and greenery, sitting a few feet from where we sat. "She's not gone," I whispered, apparently the only one who could see or sense her.

Crap. Scarlett's here. Not exactly the time for a chat. I'd have to wait until after the funeral. Hopefully, she'd clear up the password mix-up. I plucked a tissue from my purse. The scent of so many flowers made me a little nauseated. And the fumes from the hairspray didn't help. Scarlett glared at me from her flowery perch.

What was eating her? I was the one with reason to be steamed. Last night's wasted trip to the station hadn't brought results, and frankly, I was getting pretty damn tired of chasing my tail.

"Where's Mama?" Billie Jo wanted to know.

I sneezed. "She said she would meet us here." I sniffed into the tissue.

"Maybe she's in back with the others," Deena suggested.

"I wonder where the cousin is," I said from behind my damp tissue. "Do you think that wispy-haired redhead could be her?"

Deena perked up at this. "Whose cousin?"

Billie Jo leaned over me. Deena met her halfway. "Scarlett's," she said.

"Shhh." A man turned around, giving us an angry stare before his wife leaned over and whispered in his ear. He turned back around to soothe her after shushing us one last time.

"Do you hear me, Jolene?" Scarlett's angry voice sent warning chills down my spine. My bad feeling intensified. I had to tread carefully. Bradford usually kept a close eye on me, not to mention the creepy Grant. Surely, they were both here somewhere. And now would be the time to hand over the pilfered thumb-drive stashed in my purse. The police would have computer experts with special software. With my head cocked around, I surveyed the group of mourners, but I didn't spot Bradford in the crowd.

Finally, a man with a guitar stepped up to the front. A young woman joined him, and the lone strains of a melody flowed over the crowd. Deena shot me an expression of pure disbelief as the woman sang the simple lyrics of an old bluegrass gospel hymn—inappropriate for the successful professional woman I knew Scarlett to be. A quick glance at the coffin confirmed my evaluation—the deceased glowed ruby red with rage.

I held my breath as the song died, and an older black man, microphone in hand, launched into another bad song choice. Billie Jo speared me in the ribs. "Never seen a coffin bought from The Casket Store. Isn't this the strangest funeral you've ever attended?"

Not taking my eyes from the aforementioned, I whispered, "Yes, appears so." I wanted to tell her that if the black cloud gathering over the casket was any indication, the fun was about to begin.

Deena leaned over. "Scarlett must be turning over

in her eco-friendly coffin."

"You might say that," I said as the deceased climbed off her cardboard burial box in a slow, smoldering manner. The urge to get up and move back a couple of rows washed over me. My butt, however, remained glued to the chair.

As the song closed, a minister gave a short sermon on the delights of heaven. He finished his talk assuring the listeners they need not mourn Scarlett's departure, for she was at this very moment strolling the golden streets with her loving family who had gone on before her.

I rolled my eyes at the subject of his sermon, for she was at this very moment shouting curses at the redhead in the front row—probably the cousin who'd arranged the cardboard coffin and the dreadfully depressing music. Without warning, the woman wailed, cutting through the minister's words, bringing the funeral to a dead stand still. I could see by the satisfied smile on the deceased's face that she was very pleased to have gotten her message across to her unfortunate next-of-kin.

Next, a procession of mourners came forward to say a few kind words. First, Mayor Payne pontificated on Scarlett's virtue and talents, followed by his wife, who delivered a sweet eulogy on the deceased's beauty and love for mankind. Well, she was right about that one thing. Scarlett loved men—even if they belonged to someone else.

Then Robert Burns stepped up to the front. The room remained quiet, but for the soft background music and quiet crying. Someone must've muzzled the cousin. I glanced at my sisters. Their eyes were trained on the front in anticipation of what Robert would say about Whiskey Creek's local celebrity. I too was curious, because as far as I could tell, he'd shown no regret at her passing from the start. This might prove to be the most show-stopping performance of his miserable life. At least his hair looked nice. More than I could say for mine.

To give Robert his due, I must admit he spoke kindly and graciously about his former employee. He finished by announcing that a bronze plaque honoring her invaluable contribution—along with other Hall-of-Famers—to journalism would be placed in the front lobby of WXYB.

Cherry joined him. Together, they placed a single white rose on Scarlett's coffin while another bluegrass song about going to the lonesome valley played over the speakers.

A strong perception of disaster gripped me. A streak of green velvet descended on the couple. I was the only one to witness Scarlett plow into Robert, knocking him into Cherry. She flailed her arms, and together, they crashed into the coffin. It landed with the top open; corpse flung halfway out.

Screams filled the viewing room at the sight of Scarlett's mangled face. A mass exodus ensued, and I lost sight of my sisters in the melee. Keeping my seat, I watched in horrid fascination as funeral-goers scattered like leaves on a windy day. Only a few stragglers remained near the overturned coffin when Scarlett popped up at my side and said with a huge smile, "That popinjay reminded me that I have a laptop hidden in my house. It has software that'll read the encrypted flash drive. Oh, and I gave you the wrong password."

"I found that out last night in your office," I growled.

"Sorry. Won't happen again. You coming?"

"No. I've decided to hand over the flash drive to Bradford as soon as I find him. Let the police figure this thing out."

"He's not here. I promise nothing bad will happen." She crossed her hands over her heart. "I swear."

"Liar. That's what you said last time," I whispered.

"This time is different."

"I don't believe you. Besides, I'm being watched."

"I'll throw the dog off the scent."

"How?"

"Just leave it to me. Besides, you can't quit now. We're close to cracking this case wide open. Think, Claiborne. You have the flash drive in your possession, and I have laptop. This is your last chance to know for certain what's going on."

She was right about that, and since Bradford hadn't attended the funeral, the thumb-drive would remain with me until I could locate him. Still uncertain, I juggled the pros and cons on the risk for several more seconds before curiosity won out.

"I have a feeling that I'm going to regret this, but let's go," I said and headed toward the exit.

Chapter Twenty-One
Snuffed Out

The late afternoon heat bore down mercilessly, as I pulled my car into the back alleyway leading to Scarlett's house. I was still uneasy about entering in broad daylight, but Scarlett had finally recalled where she'd hidden an emergency key to the back garage door since I didn't have the automatic door opener. Making as little noise as possible, I located it under the indicated rock, unlocked the garage door, and parked inside.

The access door pushed open easily, and I cautiously moved into the small mud room leading from the garage. The gentle humming of household appliances closed around me. I slipped off my heels and, in stocking feet, trailed after Scarlett.

"Where's the laptop?" I whispered to her green velvet form. "I want to be out of here in five minutes."

"No need to whisper. You have my permission to be here."

"Very funny," I retorted in a tone heavy with sarcasm. My gut instinct screamed to cut and run because I'd made a colossal error of massive proportions. Bad vibrations surrounded me like fumes from a rotten onion.

Not making a sound, I followed her ghostly form up the staircase to the landing overlooking the family room, and then into a large guest room.

Scarlett pointed to a large dresser. "The laptop is in the false bottom in that drawer."

Quickly, I retrieved the laptop and placed it on the bed. Following Scarlett's directions, I inserted the flash drive into the computer and punched in the correct password. There were five files listed on the thumb-drive: Prototype-(Magnolia Manor?), Cantrell Plane Crash (mechanics report), Burns, Payne, and Brotherhood.

I clicked on the first file. After reading just the opening line of the investigative report, I was sure I'd found the motive for Scarlett's murder. I closed the file and skimmed though the others. I whistled.

"I can't believe this is happening under our noses," I said as I continued to scan the remaining file on the Brotherhood. "Man, this is going to blow this town apart. Who would've thought the Georgia Mafia has been working underground in this town for years? You've named some heavyweights—they won't go down easy—and there's a lot of money involved. Bingo. Here's Mr. Blackstone's name. I have to get this into Bradford's hands right away."

"Did you hear that?"

"What?" I said, caught up in the shocking report. "If this proves to be true, the mayor will be out of a job. He and Burns could go to jail for a very long time. The mayor's father too."

"Someone followed us here—get out, Jolene. Run!"

Suffocating panic gripped me as footsteps sounded downstairs. Scarlett vanished through the wall, leaving me alone with evidence that could get me killed.

Without wasting time, I gathered up the laptop and made for the stairs. The coast was clear, so I eased down them and ducked into the foyer closet just as the footsteps drew near. I waited until I heard an upstairs door closed and then, in stocking feet, made my way into the kitchen, retrieved my heels in the mud room, and went out the access door into the garage where my Mustang was parked.

Thankful that I'd left the garage door open, I slid into the driver's seat, dumped my purse and laptop into the back seat, fired up the engine, and threw it into reverse. The Mustang spun out of the garage, tires screeching on the driveway. I stepped on the gas and raced down the twisting road, my eyes glued to the rearview mirror for any pursuers. The wheels spun out as I turned onto the main road without slowing down.

My heart lurched as the familiar blue sedan shot out of the neighborhood and raced toward me. Flooring the Mustang's accelerator, I raced down the blacktop, with the other car close behind. Suddenly a shot rang out. Something pinged on the top of the Mustang. I ducked down low over the steering wheel. Another shot rang out, shattering the rear window. I screamed and jerked the steering wheel in reaction. The car rocked from side to side as I fought to regain control, the tires screeching in protest at such violent treatment. In the rearview mirror I saw the sedan behind me swerve, and then straighten. My teeth clenched as the Mustang careened around the curves of the road.

Sweat stung my eyes, making it hard to see. Up ahead, another car swung onto the road from a side street. Even from this distance, I could tell the car was traveling at a much reduced speed and if I didn't slow down, I would smack into its rear. My clammy hands slipped on the steering wheel, causing the Mustang to lurch sideways onto the shoulder of the road, half-losing it as the back end slewed around on the gravel. Jamming my weight hard on the brake, I spun the wheel in a last-ditch effort to regain control of the car. For an instant, deadly calm settled over me as the Mustang bucked like a wild bronco before slamming headlong into a tree. There was a sickening sensation of falling; a sharp and agonizing pain in my head, and then my body was hurled into nothingness.

****

"She's coming around," a voice said in my ear. "I believe she's turned a corner."

"Thank God," I heard Mama respond. "Did you hear that, Jolene? The doctor says you're fine."

"He didn't. He said she turned a corner."

Billie Jo.

"I told her she drives too fast."

Deena.

"Mom, Jacob and I are here."

Becky.

So the whole gang, all but Daddy, had gathered around my death bed. I cracked my eyes to see their somber faces. My mouth felt like cotton. "Water."

The nurse gave me a few sips. The relief was immediate, but I remained confused as to what had happened. A young man in a white coat stepped up to the bed and introduced himself as Dr. Hadley.

"You're in the hospital," he said in a kind, soft voice. "You were in a car accident."

The memory came flooding back. Shock stole my voice. I gasped for air and tried to speak. The monitor above me sounded an alarm, and the doctor placed his hand over mine. "Calm down." He increased the oxygen feed. "Breathe deep and slow. That's it," he said as the beeping quieted down. "You're very lucky. Thanks to the seat belt and air bag, you sustained no life-threatening injuries. But you do have a concussion, and I'm going to keep you here under observation for a couple of days. Your blood pressure and heart rate are dangerously high, and you're covered with scrapes and bruises."

"I have a few questions I'd like to ask you, Dr. Hadley," Mama said.

Dr. Hadley took Mama by the arm, propelling her toward the door. The others followed as the doctor said, "It would be better if we spoke in the hall. I've ordered pain medication with a light sedative for my patient. I want her to rest easy tonight. She's had enough excitement for one day, wouldn't you agree?"

Helplessly, I struggled against the fatigue weighing me down, but all I could manage was a squeak of protest at being left alone to the mercy of overworked nurses. I had to get the evidence into Bradford's hands ASAP, but the pleading movement of my hand went unnoticed by the others as they followed the doctor, leaving me alone with only the beeping sounds of the heart monitor for company. My heart skipped a beat as anxiety gripped me. An alarm sounded on the monitor, and a nurse came through the door a minute later.

Turning off the alarm, she turned to me and said, "Everything's fine, honey. Don't you worry none. I'm gonna take good care of you." A long needle appeared in her hand along with the smile on her face. "Dr. Hadley ordered you a cocktail to take the edge off."

No, damn it! The only cocktail I wanted contained a shot of Jack Daniels, not some clear liquid inserted in my IV. My lips were dry, but I managed to croak out another protest. A deep, warm, heaviness came over me as the medication entered my bloodstream. My eyelids fought to stay open. "Detective Bradford—"

"Will have to wait." I heard her say through the haze fogging my brain. "Dr. Hadley told the police they'd have to wait until tomorrow for any questions about your accident."

With difficulty, I continued to struggle against the drug-induced medication dragging me down into oblivion. Footsteps sounded, then briefly, a male voice filtered through the opened door before fading away.

I slept through the night, waking only when the nurses came into the room to take my stats and shoot additional medication into my IV. Early Monday morning, I woke with a splitting headache, my muscles stiff and sore as Dr. Hadley had warned. Before eating a bland breakfast, I called the police station only to be told that Detective Bradford was out of town and unavailable, so I left an urgent message on his office voicemail for him to come see me at the hospital as soon as possible.

After breakfast, Dr. Hadley stopped by to check on my progress. I could go home tomorrow if I continued to improve. He promised to stop by later and left for rounds.

The rest of the morning was filled with visits from the family. Deena and Billie Jo were the first to arrive.

Deena set a vase of flowers on the bedside table as they walked in. "Becky sends her love. She wasn't feeling well, so I suggested she stay home."

"The nurse says we can't stay long," Billie Jo added. "How are you feeling?"

"Like a semi-truck ran over me," I said. "And concerned about my car."

"We haven't seen it, but the police told us it was totaled," Deena said.

"Don't worry about that now," Billie Jo advised. "Wait until you're feeling better."

"Did the police recover my belongings from the car?" I thought about the laptop and flash drive, and my purse with Mini Pearl tucked inside. I wouldn't want them to fall into the wrong hands. God, I needed to speak with Bradford. Perhaps Deena could get a message to him. I nixed that thought. Deena would ask too many questions that I wasn't prepared to answer.

"One of the officers gave Mama your purse last night," Billie Jo said. "Your gun was inside, if that's what you're worried about."

"What about my laptop?" I asked.

"The officer said the purse was the only personal effect in the car," Billie Jo replied. "Your laptop will be covered under your automobile insurance. It can be replaced."

Not this one. Of course, Billie Jo didn't know that. I was the only one who knew of its importance, but I couldn't share that knowledge with them—or the attempt on my life. Speaking up might place them in danger. Someone had taken the thumb-drive and laptop from my wrecked car. I thought about my pursuer in the dark blue sedan. He would've had time before the first responders arrived on the scene. I licked my lips, my mouth and throat suddenly dry. Had witnesses kept him from finishing the job and murdering me?

Mama arrived. With my mind occupied with more pressing matters, I let Mama to do all the talking. Fortunately, Billie Jo could see that I wasn't listening and she suggested—strongly—that they let me get some rest. Before Mama could object, a nurse's aide came into the room for the exercise Dr. Hadley had prescribed for me.

I spent the next hour painfully parading up and down the corridor with my IV pole, nurse's aide in tow. By lunch I was exhausted, but beginning to feel better now that I was out of bed and moving my sore and bruised muscles. After repeating the procedure several times, the pounding headache returned, and the nurse gave me something for the pain so I could rest.

Unexpectedly, in the late afternoon, Linda Payne stopped by for a visit with a lovely bouquet of flowers. After placing them on the counter, she pulled a chair close to the bed and seated herself with a rehearsed smile. "The mayor and I were sorry to hear of your accident, Ms. Claiborne," she said in a bubbly voice. "We do hope you'll be up and about shortly."

Still groggy from the pain meds, I pushed myself to a sitting position. "Thank you for the lovely flowers."

"Henry begged his apology for not being able to join me in wishing one of his constituents a speedy recovery, but city business takes all his time, you understand."

I couldn't say I did, but the unusualness of her visit kept me quiet. The mayor's wife and I were hardly buddies, and I couldn't help but wonder why she was here.

She waved a delicate hand and her perfume wafted over me. "Henry and I were talking over breakfast," she said. "First, that dreadful funeral, and then, in the same day, your near-fatal accident. You must be more careful, my dear. One never knows when the unexpected will happen." She patted my arm. "And on top of everything else going on, you've got your hands full with the tragedy at the salon." Her hands fluttered. "A break-in *and* a murder. Poor Scarlett—to die in such a manner."

In an instant, my mind turned to the angry confrontation between the two women my daughter had unwillingly witnessed in the doctor's office. In light of this knowledge, her statement rang false. There was something I should remember. Something…

"Henry refuses to discuss the case with me," she continued in my silence. "He says I should concentrate on getting well, but I'm frightened by the thought that we were in close proximity to a killer. What if I'd booked a facial that morning? I would've suffered the same fate as Scarlett. Was it a random act of violence? To think that one of our citizens is a murderer." She shivered. "Now that Henry is mayor, he really must do something about the crime rate. I'm having nightmares about being murdered in my bed."

A wave of grogginess poured over me as she continued chatting. I closed my eyes to block out her morbid words.

"Oh my dear, I'm so sorry for bringing up such a distasteful subject when you're lying helpless in your hospital bed. Don't give my babbling another thought. I'm sure you don't have anything to worry about." She stood. "I must be going. Take extra special care, my dear."

As she left the room, I found her parting words

vaguely disturbing, but the visit had sapped my strength, and I allowed the lingering effects of the pain meds to claim me once more.

****

In the wee hours of the morning, I awoke to the sound of someone entering my room—probably the nurse. Her footsteps were light, shuffling, almost halting. Through my drugged state, I struggled to make out her wavering form in the muted light as she paused at the foot of the bed. Lightheadedness made it impossible to focus on her, so I closed my eyes once again, giving into the extreme fatigue plaguing me.

The steady *beep-beep* of the heart monitor seemed loud in the silence, and I could just make out her footfalls as she stopped beside the bed and fiddled with the IV bag. For several seconds, the comforting sounds of her ministrations lulled me back to sleep. As I sank deeper into slumber a slight pressure rested over my face. An alarm sounded by my head, and I struggled against the suffocating weight pressing me into the bed.

I fought to breathe. Another alarm screeched out another warning. Suddenly, the pressure lifted, and I flung the soft object from my face. Oxygen filled my lungs, and I gulped in great gasps of air. A light switched on overhead, and several faces swam into view as I continued to fight against the terrible blackness hovering about me.

"Calm down," a soothing voice advised as an oxygen tube was inserted into my nostrils. "Take a deep breath now. Slowly… That's it…another breath. Good."

I'm not sure how much time passed before my vitals steadied and I was able to sit up in bed. With the nurses and Dr. Hadley—who'd been called in—congregated around me, I tried to explain my terrifying ordeal with the nurse.

"You had a nightmare, Miz Claiborne," Dr. Hadley tried to assure me. "A rare side effect of the pain medication. I've seen it before. Not to this extent, but nonetheless, not unheard of."

"But—"

"Listen to Dr. Hadley," advised the head nurse. "No one is trying to kill you."

"But it seemed so real." My voice intensified as I grew more excited. "This isn't the first—"

"Yes, my dear. I've seen it happen before," she said, taking my hand in hers. "You're seeing things that aren't there. Certain medications can produce very realistic hallucinations in patients in a highly emotional state."

As I looked around me, I could see by their expressions that they were firmly convinced that my terrifying experience had been a product of pain medication and my overwrought emotions. But they were wrong. Twice now, someone had tried to snuff me out. As they continued to watch me, I stifled the whisper of terror clawing at my throat. Somehow, I had to keep it together until I could talk to Bradford. But where was he? And why hadn't he returned my calls?

Chapter Twenty-Two
Code of the South

The next morning, Dr. Hadley came in with a positive report. Briefly, he mentioned last night's commotion and said he wanted to keep me one more day in case I had another complication with the pain medication. I would be released tomorrow if all went well. He left for rounds just as the same nurse's aide from yesterday came in to take me for my daily exercise.

I had just finished eating a bland lunch when Bradford came into the room, accompanied by an attractive African American officer with beautiful, warm brown eyes. Admiration for him shone in those expressive eyes when he asked her to wait outside the room while he visited with me.

"Thank God, you're here," I said, jumpy and anxious from watching for another attempt on my life. "I've been frantic to speak with you."

Bradford sat in the chair beside my bed. "I'm sorry it took so long for me to get here, but I had a personal family emergency that took me out of town. I came as soon as I could. Grant filled me in on your accident. How are you feeling?"

"Lucky to be alive, which is saying a lot. Twice now, someone has tried to kill me."

"Start at the beginning and tell me everything."

247

"Well, I know you're going to be a little upset with me, but that's a small matter now in light of my discovery."

He dragged his fingers through his hair in a despairing gesture. "Perhaps you should start at the beginning and tell me what this is all about," he repeated.

"Scarlett was working on an investigative story involving a powerful cartel operating here in Whiskey Creek," I said. "She was also investigating her parents' plane crash five years ago. There was a copy of the plane's mechanic's report on a thumb-drive, along with a file on Robert Burns, the Payne family, and the Georgia Brotherhood."

"How did you come by this information?"

"Remember when I told you about Scarlett's last words—the jade elephant?"

He nodded. "Yes, I remember."

"Well, the jade elephant turned out to be a small volume of poetry I found in Scarlett's office. And guess what was inside?"

His eyes narrowed. "What were you doing in Scarlett's office? Remember your promise to stop investigating?"

Heat crept up my neck. "Do you want to hear my story?" I continued at his curt nod. "I found a finger stick hidden inside the cut binding of the book. I knew it was important, so I took it home."

"You didn't think to turn it over to the police?"

"I had every intention of turning it over to the police," I declared. "As soon as I knew what was on it."

"Sounds like your reasoning." His voice held a hint of mockery. "Go on and tell me the rest."

"Well, turns out my computer, or the office computer, didn't have the special software needed to read the thumb-drive. And I didn't know the password." I paused. I couldn't exactly tell him the whole truth. "Uh, that's when I got the idea that Scarlett had to have a computer with the necessary software either at her house or her office. Her house was closer."

"So you went there against my advice?"

"I looked for you at the funeral with every intention of turning over the flash drive. However, I didn't see you in the crowd."

"You went to Scarlett's house from the funeral," he stated flatly.

"I found the laptop in an upstairs bedroom. Just as I suspected, it read the flash drive."

"And the password?" He crossed his arms across his chest.

"I found it on a sticky note buried under a pile of magazines on her desk," I said, leaving out the part about Scarlett's help. Bradford wouldn't understand my ability to communicate with her. "The flash drive has five files—Prototype-Magnolia Manor, Cantrell Plane Crash, Burns, Payne, and Brotherhood—or in other words, the Georgia Mafia."

"Where are the laptop and flash drive located now?"

"I don't know." I fidgeted with the bed sheet. "While I was skimming over the files, I heard a noise downstairs. I knew I shouldn't have been alone in the house, so I grabbed the laptop and hid in the downstairs foyer closet, hoping to escape without detection."

"You thought one of them was in the house with you?" His tone was soft. His eyes never left me.

I nodded. "Some guy in a dark blue sedan has been watching me for days. I was terrified that he'd followed me to Scarlett's house. Turns out I was right—the creep chased me down with his car, with bullets flying. I swerved to avoid a car pulling onto the road and lost control of my car. The laptop was in the back seat of my Mustang. One of the officers returned my purse, but the laptop and thumb-drive are missing. I believe the jerk in the sedan snatched them before the first responders could arrive. That or someone in the police department is on the take."

"And the second attempt?"

"Someone came into my room last night and tried to snuff me out with a pillow. The doctors tried to convince me that I was hallucinating—a rare side effect from the medications—but it was real, all right."

"You're sure about it? Is it possible the doctors could be right about the hallucination?"

"Anything is possible, but I'm not willing to bet my life on it, if that's what you're asking," I said hotly. "Especially since the evidence have been stolen."

"Give me the details of the investigative report. There are names?"

I gave him a quick nod. "I didn't recognize most of them, and I only had a chance to skim over the document. Robert Burns' name caught my attention immediately. He's definitely involved, along with several high-profile lawyers and judges. The mayor is mentioned, and his father. I don't know their connection. There's also a tie with her parents' plane crash."

"Involved in what?"

"Money laundering and election tampering, and

possibly her parents' murder. Scarlett uncovered a conspiracy to change the recent election with vote-rigging software. You know…gangster stuff. Scarlett also suspected the Brotherhood had infiltrated the police department and the GBI."

Bradford whistled. "How is that possible? Those electronic voting machines are tamper-proof."

"That's what I read. Scarlett was trying to arrange a meeting with some guy who supposedly created a prototype for some big wig in this town."

"Where does Burns fit in?"

"Money? He's filthy rich and was strongly opposed to Sonny Carrollton becoming mayor. Said Carrollton's plan to curb city growth would send us back one hundred years. He believed Henry Payne was the man to transform Whiskey Creek into one of the largest and finest cities in Georgia."

"Is that it?"

"Do you have something I can write on?"

Bradford handed me a small notepad from his pocket along with a pen. I jotted down the names I could recall from Scarlett's notes. I explained the best I could about my conversation with Cherry on Thursday morning.

"So Robert Burns was determined to stop Miss Cantrell from airing her report?"

"Cherry told me that Robert came home late one night just furious. Seems that Scarlett had ruffled the feathers of some very important men. Scarlett refused to back down, and Robert seemed afraid. Cherry overheard him on the phone with the mayor."

"Are you sure she said Burns contacted the mayor? Did Burns mention the names of these men?"

"No, but Cherry said they were the kind you avoid. Boy, you were right to warn me away. Rest assured I won't make that mistake again. Oh, there's one other thing I suppose I should mention."

"I'm listening."

I told him Daddy's story. "And Mr. Blackstone is mentioned in the report. He must be tied to the Georgia Mafia."

Bradford didn't comment right away. He sat staring at me. Unconsciously, I reached up to smooth my hair and encountered a rock hard mess of tangles. Dammit—I probably looked like the hairspray queen with a crown of sticky knots.

"I don't want to frighten you, but you're in real danger," he said, effectively switching my concern from the sorry state of my hair to my life expectancy. "And it's my job to ensure your safety."

"Duh. What do you think I've been trying to tell you? And just how are you going to protect me? My address is in the phone book."

Bradford flashed a cunning smile. "If you're willing, I'm going to move into your house and become your lover, my dear Jolene."

I gave an anxious little cough. My face must've shown my surprise because Bradford grabbed my hand, his tone apologetic when he quickly added, "Just a pretence, you understand. I'm sorry for giving you the wrong impression. I'm placing you under protective custody."

"I don't see any way that we can manage that," I said, a warm glow flowing through me at the thought of sharing my home with this man. "My family wouldn't buy that tale." Immediately, I felt a pang of guilt. Deena had first dibs on him. She'd reeled him in fair and square, and there was no way I was going to flip this dish into my frying pan. Sisters didn't taste each other's catch. Code of the South.

"Let me start at the beginning," he started to explain when the door opened to admit a male nurse.

"Sorry to interrupt, but I need to check the patient's vitals." He took the blood pressure gadget from the wall above my bed and fastened it to my arm, then placed a thermometer in my mouth.

"No problem," Bradford said. "I was just explaining to Jolene how I'll take good care of her when she's released. We've been waiting to move in together, and this is the perfect time. Don't you agree, my sweet?"

The young man looked quizzically at me, and I shrugged. What else could I do with a thermometer shoved in my mouth and Bradford nodding like a bobblehead doll? The news would spread through the hospital—and then the town—just as Bradford planned.

"You did that on purpose," I accused as soon as the nurse exited the room. "Are you nuts? Word will be all over town by sundown."

"Precisely," he said. "If people believe that we're a couple, no one will question why I'm at your house all the time. Separate rooms, of course. My presence in your home will be above suspicion."

I was thoroughly confused. "We barely know one another, and now you're moving into my house? That's suspicious even to me. And what about Deena? How does she fit into all this? I won't have to wait for the mobsters to do me in—she will."

He seemed nonplussed. "Give me a chance to

explain my plan."

My mouth flew open to argue, but he raised a hand to stop me. "Deena and I have been out twice—as friends, nothing more. We're not dating so you can't use her as an excuse not to cooperate."

"You dumped her again?"

"Your outrage is touching, but I didn't come here to discuss your sister. I have a problem on my hands and little time to get control of it."

"Go on, then. I'm listening."

Bradford barked into a radio. Before I could comment, the young female officer with the inquisitive eyes came into the room.

"Officer Diamond Presley, meet Jolene Claiborne."

"I'm pleased to meet you, ma'am."

I accepted her outstretched hand and echoed back the greeting, then turned a questioning eye to Bradford.

"There is only a small group of officers in the department that I can absolutely trust," he began. "Diamond is at the top of the list. Her trustworthiness is without question. You're going to hire her as your assistant at the salon, and I'm going to move into your house."

He plunged on when I tried to sputter my objection to his plan. "But to be positively sure of your safety, no one, and I mean no one, is to know this is a ploy. Otherwise, your Georgia Mafia may decide to give one of us the same treatment they gave Scarlett. Officer Presley will be at your side during the day, and I, at night to ensure no harm will come to you. I need your cooperation until I nail these guys. In the meantime, one of us will be with you until you leave the hospital."

My head spun at the implications. "Well, that's

blessed assurance, but why can't you just arrest those men? Or lock me up in the jail where I'll be safe."

"I don't have the list or the evidence to make an arrest," he argued. "I can't lock you up in jail where one of the prisoners, or guards could be bribed. You're stuck with us. Right, Diamond?"

Officer Presley smiled at me. "It's in your best interest to listen to him. There's no changing his mind once it's made up. He's stubborn as a mule."

She's right, you know," he agreed. "Best give in."

I wasn't convinced, but the thought of those mobsters gunning for my hide swayed me a little closer to agreeing. "Tell me how I'm going to pass off Officer Presley as my assistant? My sisters know I'd never hire anyone who isn't familiar with the business."

"It's a good thing I was a dual enrollment student back in high school," she responded.

"Diamond worked in a salon before going into law enforcement," Bradford volunteered at my doubtful look.

"Very convenient," I said with heavy irony, annoyed by the two and their obvious scheming.

"Look, to ease your mind about my competence as your assistant, I'll do something with your hair if you have a brush and comb," Officer Presley said.

My hands automatically touched my hair. "It's a mess, isn't it?"

"Yes," Bradford answered. "But Diamond will have you looking great in a snap."

I frowned when he snapped his fingers in my face. "I'll agree on one condition."

"And that is?"

"We work together as a team."

Bradford's expression grew serious. "I don't like the sound of that ultimatum. Just what exactly did you have in mind?"

"I share what I know with you and vice versa. Partners, take it or leave it."

"What if I say no?"

"I'm not sure, but I'll think of something," I declared. "Those are the terms for sticking my neck out, Bradford."

"You're like a pit bull in heels. Grit and gumption. I've always liked that about you. But admiration aside, you'll be the death of me yet."

"More like the death of me. Deal or no deal?" I stuck out my hand.

He took it. "Deal—but you have to obey me."

"Obey you? This isn't a marriage, you know."

"Take it or leave it. And no one is to know about this crazy deal, agreed? Not your family or co-workers. No one. Understood? This is strictly under wraps. To all purposes, we are a happy couple."

"I can't tell Deena this make-believe relationship is a police arrangement?"

"No. Everyone has to believe we're lovers, especially Deena. If she buys it, then we'll be able to pass this relationship off as legit."

I stared at him, dazed and incredulous. "Oh no, I'm not going along with your plan unless she knows it's a ploy to catch Scarlett's killer and save my hide, especially now after you've dumped her a second time. It'll be hard convincing the rest of my family, but Deena has to know the truth. She can smell a lie from fifty yards."

He seemed to consider my argument. "Deena's

cooperation will help pull this off," he agreed. "She can run offense for us. But absolutely no one else is to know. I need to be able to keep you safe while I unravel this mystery."

"While *we* unravel this mystery," I emphasized. "Partners, remember?"

"Knock it off," Officer Presley told us. "Y'all sound like a married couple already. Do you have a brush so I can tame the savage beast on your head?"

Scowling at her remark, I reached inside the bedside drawer and retrieved the hairbrush Billie Jo had brought. "I don't believe you'll get a brush through it. There's enough hairspray in it to glue two boulders together."

"Call me Diamond."

"All right, Diamond, but take it easy. I'm tender-headed."

Bradford watched from his chair as Diamond tugged and pulled at my tangled hair. Try as I might, I couldn't keep quiet as pain radiated from my scalp. One quick glance at Bradford's amused face wasn't even enough to keep me still. Finally, I begged her to stop torturing me.

"If you'll just hold still, it'll only take a few minutes more," she said.

The brush dug into my scalp. "I can't hold still." I twisted away from her.

"Now look what you've done." She reached out and grabbed the brush handle, giving what I thought was a particularly hard tug.

"Ouch!"

"Be still. The brush is tangled in your hair."

Having had enough grooming, I threw Bradford a

nasty look when his booming laughter accompanied Diamond's scolding.

"Stop," I said just as the door opened to admit Deena.

Standing awkwardly on the threshold, her eyes took in the scene of Bradford sitting close by my bed, his face wreathed in a boyish smile, and Diamond struggling with the entangled brush. Her smile faded.

"I'm so glad you're here," I exclaimed with a laugh, overcompensating for the domestic picture we presented. I knew she imagined the worst.

Frosty eyes met mine as she crossed the room. "I'm glad to see you're feeling better." She bent over the bed to kiss my cheek then addressed Bradford. "How nice of you to stop by, Sam. Is this an official visit?"

Bradford stood and introduced Diamond. After the pleasantries were exchanged, he pulled up another chair to my bedside. Diamond lounged against the window sill, her expressive eyes watching as Bradford motioned to my sister. "Please have a seat," he said. "This is an official visit, but not what you're thinking. We need your help with a serious matter."

She slid gracefully onto the chair. "What's this about? Jolene, is there a problem you're not telling us?"

"I'm fine for now," I assured her. "Bradford will explain."

And he did without interruption.

After he finished, Deena looked at us in turn. "That's the most incredible story I've ever heard. Is someone really trying to kill her?"

I nodded. "Twice now. Not to mention there have been a lot of strange incidents lately. A prowler around my house—"

"Good Lord, why didn't you tell us?" Deena grabbed my hand. "You could've come and stayed with me."

"And expose you to danger?" I shook my head. "Never."

Deena turned her attention back to Bradford. "You're sure this scheme will work?"

"It will with your help," he said. "Officer Presley will protect Jolene during the day, and I'll be with her at night."

"And don't forget I'm pretty handy with a gun," I added.

"One day you're going to accidentally shoot someone," Deena said, scowling. "You and Billie Jo act like Whiskey Creek is the wild, wild west."

I returned her frown. "Well, considering the fact that gangsters are after me, I'd say that's a pretty good comparison."

Over by the window, Diamond gave a soft chuckle.

"Exactly what is my role in this scheme of yours, Sam?" Deena asked.

"We need your help convincing others we're a new and happy couple, and that my moving into Jolene's house might seem like we're moving fast, but we're in love."

"I told Bradford I won't go along with his plan if this causes you pain," I pressed, watching her expression carefully as it shifted from moment to moment.

"Strictly a police arrangement," Bradford added. "Jolene's life is in danger."

Deena took my hand in hers. "I'll do anything to

keep you safe." She smiled for the first time since arriving. "Now, if we're to convince the masses you're a couple, you'll have to follow my instructions." Her tone turned businesslike. "Sam, let me see you kiss Jolene."

That surprise almost sent me over the edge. "I don't think that's necessary," I sputtered, my eyes darting to Bradford who seemed amused by the suggestion. "We won't be indulging in any public displays of affection."

Deena frowned at me. "And how else are you going to convince Mama this is real? She's going to be expecting it. You asked for my help, and this is it."

"But I didn't have a chance to brush my teeth after lunch," I protested.

"He's not removing your tonsils with his tongue." Deena snickered. "I want to see how much work is needed to make this believable."

Diamond gave me a thumbs-up from her position by the window.

Heat crept into my face as Bradford leaned over the bed and lightly touched his lips to mine. The kiss, almost a whisper, lasted for a moment but felt like an eternity. As he lifted his head, his eyes were shuttered, unreadable. He resumed his seat.

"That'll do for a start," Deena said, unaware of the emotional aftermath the simple kiss had evoked. "The awkwardness will go away with practice. Just be natural with one another and for heaven's sake, relax, Jolene. Pretend you like it."

Pretend I like it! Damn, I wasn't dead—yet. I did like it, which presented the problem with this whole screwed-up plan. This contrivance would have lingering repercussions I hadn't counted on. I had to nix it before I lost my heart. "Perhaps Diamond could move in with me instead of Bradford," I suggested.

"Won't work," Bradford said in an even voice. "Diamond has her grandmother to care for at night, and she's the only female on the force, so you're stuck with me."

Resigned, I leaned back against the pillows. Living in close quarters with this man was liable to produce enough stress to induce a heart attack.

Deena dropped a sisterly arm about my shoulders. "Cheer up. It's only until Sam nabs the bad guys. I'm sure everything's going to work out fine. You'll see. But for now, why don't we let your new assistant begin by doing something with your hair?"

Events were moving way too fast in my life, and I was trying to mask my uncertainty and irritation when Scarlett materialized, clad in a blue velvet dressing gown, basketball boobs practically bouncing out of the plunging neckline. She plopped down on the bed and proclaimed in the haughtiest tone I'd heard from her yet, "Finally! I've been looking all over for you. Why's that brush stuck to your head?"

Deena released me and moved quickly away from the bed, her eyes wide and startled. Her brows drew downward in a frown as she positioned herself against the far wall, her purse clutched to her stomach as if frightened. That gave me pause. Like me, could she possibly sense spirits?

I gave my ghostly visitor a hostile stare. This was her fault, after all. If she hadn't convinced me to return to her house, I wouldn't have been in the wrong place at the wrong time, and landed in this hospital room—with a new assistant I didn't need or want, and a confused sibling who probably believed I'd cooked up this whole gangster story to snatch her old boyfriend right after he'd dumped her a second time.

Before I could piece together something to fill the sudden silence, a nurse marched in and ordered everyone out so she could change my bed. Bradford made a brief show of affection, promising to return by evening to take up guard duty. In the meantime, he promised I'd be perfectly safe with Diamond positioned outside my door. With a quick kiss on my brow, he and Diamond left the room. Deena cautiously approached the bed, leaning down to brush a kiss across my cheek. "Your secret is safe with me. No one will know from me that you and Sam are faking it."

"Thanks for going along with this craziness," I said. "Could you dissuade the rest of the family from visiting until I get out of here? I'm exhausted with all this drama."

"Sure thing, sis." Her gaze held mine briefly then she exited, leaving me alone with the nurse and Scarlett, who draped herself over my bed.

"You look terrible," Scarlett said.

"Thanks."

The nurse helped me sit in the chair beside the bed. "You're welcome, my dear. You've had enough company this afternoon. Dr. Hadley wants you rested before you go home tomorrow."

I lifted my gaze from Scarlett to smile at the nurse. "That's the best news I've heard today. I'm tired of lying around in this bed."

"Are you sick?" Scarlett asked.

"I had a car accident, remember?" I informed

Scarlett rather stiffly. Although I needed to talk to her, my anger hadn't cooled. She had abandoned me in my hour of need. I would've told her so if the nurse hadn't looked so confused.

"Dr. Hadley is the best doctor in town," the nurse said, clucking at me. "You're going to make a full recovery. I wouldn't worry." She quickly changed the linens and then helped me bathe and put on a clean nightgown, before settling me back in the bed.

"What's that?" I pointed to the needle she was injecting into the IV bag hanging over my head.

"Just a little sedative to help you rest."

"I don't need a sedative," I protested. "I wanna watch TV."

"Doctor's orders," she said as a wave of drowsiness hit me. Scarlett, who wavered at the end of my hospital bed, appeared wrapped in a fuzzy cocoon that obscured her features.

"Great balls of fire!" she hollered.

"Great balls of fire to you, too."

"You're a strange bird, Miz Claiborne," the nurse said as my eyelids slammed down, and I drifted off into a drugged slumber.

Chapter Twenty-Three
The Haunted Salon

The next morning, Mama sailed into my hospital room with a stern-faced expression and headed straight for Bradford, who sat in the same chair he'd spent the night in. Luckily, Diamond wouldn't report for guard duty until later, so we wouldn't have to explain her official presence to my agitated parent. Bradford had just taken my hand to assure me everything would be fine. I, in turn, was gazing gratefully into his face.

Evidently, we portrayed a loving couple to my overwrought mother. I braced myself for what was coming.

"I'm sure you'll understand my confusion in all this," she said. "Imagine my surprise when Deena shows up on my doorstep this morning with this outrageous story of how the two of you found love in the middle of a crisis. Horse manure. I don't believe it. What's really going on here?"

Bradford stood and dropped a light kiss on my forehead. "Now, I'm terribly sorry if you misconstrued my relationship with Deena, but I've been interested in Jolene from the start. Deena and I are just old friends."

"That's what she said, too. I don't believe it. There's more here than meets the eye."

He merely nodded. "If you say so, ma'am."

Luck smiled down upon us when the door opened to admit Deena and the assistant pastor from church, Bill Mahoney.

"Mama, I told you not to bother Jolene and Sam this morning," she said with a wide smile and crossed over to the bed to kiss my cheek. "I brought reinforcements," she whispered. "He knows everything."

I grabbed her wrist and twisted down hard when Mama turned to greet Bill. "Deena! You promised to keep quiet." I scolded in a soft whisper.

She grimaced. "I needed help. You know how Mama is. I had to be interested in someone else if she was to believe that you and Sam are for real."

"This better work." I released her.

"It will," she said, and turned to introduce her escort. "Sam, this is William Mahoney from First Baptist Church. Bill, this is Jolene's boyfriend, Detective Sam Bradford of the WCPD."

"Call me Bill."

They exchanged handshakes and carried on a light conversation. Mama kept a watchful eye on all of us. Finally, she seemed to relax her guard and even smiled when Bradford showered me with attention, which made me uncomfortable under the circumstances.

When this charade concluded, there would be hurt feelings and perhaps a broken heart or two. *Including mine*, I thought with regret. Again, I questioned the wisdom of Bradford's scheme.

A little after ten, a nurse interrupted our impromptu gathering with welcome news of my release. Dr. Hadley had signed my discharge papers, and they would be up from administration soon. The men excused themselves from the room while Deena and Mama helped me dress in a pair of jeans, cotton blouse, and flats for my trip home.

I'd just finished gathering my things together when another nurse came in with the papers. "All done. Just one more signature and you're free to leave. Follow Dr. Hadley's home care instructions and call his office for a follow-up visit. And only part-time work for now, okay?"

I nodded and sat down in the wheelchair. Deena and Bill excused themselves, promising to check in on us later. Mama walked with us down to Bradford's waiting car and then left to pick up a bakery cake from Potts' Bakery for a church ladies meeting.

After the nurse helped me into Bradford's car and closed the door, I waited until he'd climbed in beside me and pulled away from the curb before I turned to him. "There's something else I forgot to mention."

Bradford eyed me with interest. "Oh?"

"I believe Grant is spying on me. When we came down just now, he was in the lobby watching us. He even had the nerve to threaten me to stay out of his investigation. He's obnoxious and suspicious."

"He could be visiting a sick family member or friend. Don't jump to conclusions."

"I'm certain."

"And he threatened you? I've done the same."

"I'm dead certain. And it's not the same. He accosted me on Thursday morning outside Carla's room. He definitely tried to intimidate me."

"He accosted you in the hospital? Why didn't you report this to me?"

"Did you know he wears a Rolex watch?" I countered with a question of my own.

"What does a Rolex have to do with anything? It could've been a gift."

"Or it could be a payoff. Remember, someone stole the evidence. It could've been him."

"Hmmm. As a precaution, I'll keep my eye on him." He threw me a wicked grin. "And I believe you should call me Sam from now on if we're going to make this believable."

That smile almost derailed me. "Any sign of the missing evidence, *Sam*?" My tone came out harsher than I intended. Heat flooded my face, so I turned to look out of the window before he could see my confusion. Damn, I had to get a grip on myself.

"Not yet, but I'm working on it." We were sitting at the intersection of Third and Mississippi Avenue, waiting for the light to change. "Is plaster powder usually kept in the facial room?" he continued his questioning.

I paused, and then turned away from the traffic outside my passenger side window to look at him. "No, but I know it was in the mask."

"And how did you come by this information?"

"Billie Jo and I had the contents of the jars analyzed. I also know Scarlett choked to death on her own vomit."

"Of course you do, Jolene." Amusement flitted across his face. "You're in the wrong line of work, woman. Care to share how you obtained the information?"

Picturing the coroner's wife rifling through her husband's home office, I shook my head. "You don't want to know."

The light turned green and we continued down 3rd Avenue. "The toxicology report showed traces of arsenic in her stomach contents. The coroner believes it was in the tea she drank shortly before she died."

"Oh my God," I burst out. "I must've given her the poisoned tea. Not on purpose, of course."

"Someone knew about Scarlett's special tea canister and planted the poisoned bags, I suspect. There were only traces of arsenic in the bags and only enough to make her sick. It could be a completely separate incident. We just don't know. The District Attorney says there isn't enough evidence to convict Carla Moody. Anyone could've planted those tea bags."

"Did you find the plaster powder at the salon?"

"No sign of it," he said. "The perp must've ditched it after mixing it into the jars. Who could've known Scarlett was scheduled for that particular kind of service, other than the salon staff?"

We made a right onto Pinecone Lane. "Recently, we added a new feature to our website. The client can type in a date and the name of the stylist in order to view her or his appointments for the specified day. And we keep a handwritten appointment book in full sight at the receptionist desk." He frowned, and I added, "Have you considered that the arsenic-laced tea bags and plaster powder might've been placed there during the break-in?" We pulled into my driveway.

He switched off the motor, and climbed out. "We'll talk about this later," he said, handing me out of the car. "Right now, I need to get to the station." A white Chevy Volt pulled in behind us. "There's Diamond now."

The three of us went into the house. Diamond helped me get settled while Bradford placed his suitcase in the guest room. "I'll be back this afternoon," he said, and left for the police station.

Still not back to my usual buoyant self, I lazed around the house. Daddy called right after lunch. At the sound of his comforting voice over the line, I told him everything. And I mean everything. He threatened to come home, but I talked him out of it. His being here would only add to the problem, I told him. It took a while, but I finally convinced him to stay away. He warned me to be careful and hung up. Immediately, the phone rang. Deena. I relayed my conversation with Daddy to her.

"With all the confusion, I forgot to mention that Carla phoned," she said.

"What'd she want?"

"She and Frank have decided to leave Georgia. She won't be returning to work."

"I think that's best at this point. She needs to concentrate on her family. What are we going to do? Hire another aesthetician?"

"We'll have to at some point. There's a lot of money invested in that equipment."

"And clientele we've built up," I finished for her. "Have you discussed this with Billie Jo? Mama?"

"Billie Jo said that Scarlett's wrecked face should answer that question. She feels a massage therapist would be a better fit for the salon. Mama suggested we wait until things settle down and then reconsider what to do. We can't wait too long, Jolene. We're losing money every day that room remains unused." Her worried voice echoed over the line.

I didn't answer. Scarlett would be happy with the news. Earlier, she had complained about the stark décor. She visualized soft pink walls and pale pastel-printed chintz chairs with ruffles and decorative pillows for her comfort. But Scarlett's comfort wasn't my main concern. It was the possibility of another "accident" taking place.

"Jolene?"

"I'm here," I said into the receiver. "Mama's right. We should close the room."

"That's going to be a financial hardship."

"More costly than another client dying?"

Deena agreed and the matter was settled. Until the killer was behind bars, the facial room would remain Scarlett's domain. The thought gave me a headache. Owning a haunted salon in the Deep South went against all the rules in the Good Book, and everybody knows you don't break the rules written in red without incurring a little karma payback.

Chapter Twenty-Four
The Stalker

I spent the rest of the day puttering around the house under Diamond's watchful gaze. Bradford returned in the late evening so she could leave to pick up her grandmother from the senior center. I handed him a glass of white sangria when he plopped down on the sofa.

"How was your day?" he asked, sipping the wine.

"Just peachy. Carla quit her job. She told Deena she and Frank have decided to relocate to another state. They both need a fresh start."

We sat in compatible silence for several minutes before Bradford collected my empty glass and went over to the bar. "The Moody's had nothing to do with Scarlett's murder. Carla was an unknowing participant, and her husband's a blind fool."

"So who did?" I asked to his back.

When he turned around, his face bore an amused smile. "Give it a break, Jolene. I have some news. You're not going to have time to snoop." He handed me my refilled glass. "The mayor's father is opening his home for a black-tie fundraiser Friday night, and I'm working as undercover security. A lot of the names you mentioned from Scarlett's report will be in attendance, and this will give us the chance to check them out."

"Us?" I brightened at the thought.

"Can't leave you alone with a price on your head, now can I?" He grinned. "You're my date."

I sipped the wine. All thoughts of murder were immediately replaced with a new and, equally compelling thought—what to wear?

The basic black sheath hanging in the back of my closet wouldn't do. I'd worn it so many times, the material shone with wear. The red backless dress Kenny had bought me on a whim? Nope, it was a size five. What about the white silk—the newest of the oldest? Hopefully, the startling white hadn't yellowed with age, but with the infamous southern humidity, the odds weren't in my favor. I was still mentally digging through my closet when I heard Bradford's voice. "Hey, where are you?"

I looked over at him. "I have nothing to wear."

He shrugged. "Go shopping, but take Diamond with you. And be careful."

"Shopping. I never would've thought of that," I said, leaving all traces of sarcasm out of my voice, although I was already listing boutiques in my mind. And maybe even the big department store out at the new mall. With working part-time, a shopping trip would be possible tomorrow afternoon.

The prospect of hobnobbing with the upper echelon had landed me in a good mood, and it must've shown on my face because Bradford smiled back at me. "Lovely. You should smile more often."

Flattered by the unexpected compliment from this handsome, dynamic man, and excited about the upcoming weekend, I decided now was a good time to confess my latest infraction. I gave him another dazzling smile and said, "I have some news of my own."

"Oh, yeah? Good news, I hope."

"Well…"

"What'd you do?"

"Daddy called. I told him everything."

He chuckled. "I'm aware of your misdeed, Jolene. Your father called me—"

"What? How'd he get your number?"

"Your mother."

"Oh, I see."

"Lose the frown. We had a long chat, and I assured him you were safe in my care, but please refrain from telling anyone else."

Happy that I'd escaped a serious lecture, I started up from the sofa. "I'm starving. I'd better see about supper."

"I'll order a pizza," he said. "You should be resting, not laboring over a hot stove."

The pizza arrived, and we devoured the whole thing. Afterward, Bradford settled in front of the TV, and I went to take a shower, still riding a wave of happiness toward the sandy shore. True, all this coziness was just a lie, but his being here felt so good, so right. Even with the probability that I would wipeout at the end of this charade with a mouthful of gritty sand.

****

Tango peeked out from underneath my bed when I closed the bedroom door behind me. After several minutes of coaxing him onto the bed, I stepped into the bathroom, undressed, and eased under the hot spray, sighing with pleasure.

That's when Scarlett ambushed me.

"I need to talk to you," she announced in a light,

festive tone.

"Damn it," I squealed, opening my eyes which brought a string of curses as the shampoo burned my eyeballs. Groping for a washcloth to wipe the soap from my stinging eyes, all the while trying to twist my body away from her view, I ordered her out of the bathroom.

"Not until we talk," she said over my shoulder. "Here, take this."

"Geez, Scarlett, you scared ten years off my life." I grabbed the washcloth. "Knock next time. And would you please stop invading my privacy?"

"Hurry up," she said, and left me to finish bathing in private.

I finished my shower in record time. Draping a towel around myself, I stepped out of the shower to see Scarlett perched on the toilet seat, bone dry and dressed for afternoon tea.

"Kind of late for a chat, isn't it?" I motioned for her to turn her head so I could dry off and dress. She rolled her eyes but did as I requested. I pulled a blue silk short nightie over my head. "Why are you here? I'm really tired."

"Yeah, and I know why. That hunky detective is sucking up all your attention when you should be working on my case."

An abrupt banging on my bedroom door startled me. "Jolene, are you okay? I thought I heard a noise in your room."

Scarlett faded away.

Padding to the bedroom door, I opened it to Bradford's concerned countenance. "What's going on?" His eyes swept over my dishabille.

In my hastiness, I'd forgotten to slip on a robe.

Standing against the lamplight, I realized the thin nightie only amplified my ample curves. His breathing quickened. He tensed.

I froze as he continued to stare at me with indecision. Would he kiss me? I hoped so—this time I'd remembered to brush my teeth. The impulse to reach out and touch him became a tangible urge I couldn't ignore, and I watched my hands move as if on their own accord across the expanse of his chest. Almost as if it pained him to do so, he gathered me into his arms and we stood there locked in a tight embrace.

For a long moment, I floated on a warm sea of longing. His electric touch sent my nerves tingling as his hands roamed over my back and hips, pulling me closer until I pressed against his erection. Liquid warmth spread through my body.

"This is a bad idea," he said, starting to back away.

"Not my first, and probably not my last," I said, reaching up to bring his lips down to touch mine. He opened his mouth to accept my probing tongue. For one heart-stopping moment, I savored the feel of his unrestrained response before he tore his mouth from mine.

He dropped his hands and backed away. "That must never happen again. We can't afford to lose our focus. It could cost us our lives."

I heard his words, and I could see he was shaken also. My knees were trembling and I must've stumbled because he swept me, weightless, into his arms and carried me into the bedroom. Tango hissed and sprang from the bed as Bradford pushed the covers down and gently eased me onto the bed.

"You need your rest," he said, tucking the covers

around me.

"I don't believe I'll be able to rest now, Bradford. I'm wound tighter than a rubber band."

"Perhaps if I rubbed your shoulders for a minute," he suggested.

"Bad idea. I'd shoot off like a rocket."

He smiled at my attempt to lessen the tension. "I'm sorry, but I lost my head when I saw you in that nightie."

"It's not your fault. I started it." I hiccupped and let loose a giggle. "I think the wine has gone to my head."

"Yes, the wine has altered both of our good judgments. Perhaps I should take a look around outside before I secure the house for the night. I'll be on the couch in the living room if you need me," he said, and swiftly left the room.

Restless and edgy after the awkward encounter, I grabbed the romance novel I'd been reading out of my nightstand. Several pages later, I slammed the book shut, exasperated that the section was filled with a sensual sex scene that only fired up my imagination and had my insides quivering with suppressed passion. I turned off the lamp and settled down into the bed for what I knew would be a dream-filled night.

****

The next morning, I awoke to the smell of frying bacon and freshly-brewed coffee. I remembered to slip on my robe before padding down the hall and into the kitchen.

Bradford, dressed in his usual jeans and cowboy shirt, was lifting crisp slices of bacon from the skillet and placing them on a paper towel-lined plate. Tango watched from his perch on the refrigerator.

He nodded when I walked in. "Good morning. I trust you slept well."

I smothered a yawn. "Not really. Too much on my mind." I glanced at the food. "You didn't have to cook breakfast, you know. I usually have a bowl of cereal."

"I was up anyway," he said, setting a platter of bacon on the table. "Besides, I like to cook." He resumed his position at the stove, emptying a bowl of eggs into the hot skillet.

I poured two mugs of coffee and set them on the table. "From the chipper sound of your voice, I assume we had no nighttime visitors?"

"All was quiet. Your blue sedan failed to show."

We ate breakfast in silence, avoiding any mention of last night's encounter. Bradford cleaned the kitchen, while I took a quick shower and dressed in a cool cotton dress and matching lilac heels.

Bradford tailgated my car all the way to the salon and pulled into the back lot. Diamond waited next to her Chevy Volt.

Speaking briefly with Diamond, he then cautioned me to stay alert and warned me against making snap judgments. "If trouble walks in the door, let Diamond handle it," he added.

"Detective Bradford is a fine man. He's great husband material," Diamond said as he drove off and we entered the back entrance.

Choosing to ignore the obvious, I introduced her to the staff and started my day. I had just placed my client under the dryer when Nancy Chance tapped me on the shoulder.

"Got a minute?"

I glanced at my watch. "Maybe five. Diamond is

prepping my next client for her perm. What's up?"

"Who's Diamond?" Nancy asked on our way to the kitchen where we could speak in private.

I preceded her into the kitchen. "She's my new assistant." I motioned for her to take a seat. "Sam Bradford brought us together. He figured I might need an extra hand after my car accident." Her expression said she'd heard the rumors.

"Talk around town about y'all is fascinating," she said, faint amusement evident in her voice. "The grapevine is on fire with detailed speculations about your romance."

"You didn't come here to poke the embers, Nancy. I know you better than that, and I don't have time to chew the fat."

She smiled. "Then I'll get down to the reason I'm here. I need your help. Your sisters too."

"Whatever it is, we'll do our best."

"Good. We're including tours of Pineridge Plantation for the Pecan Festival this year. I'm seeking volunteers." She handed me a small booklet. "Here's the history of the place. There's even a story about ghost soldiers searching for lost Confederate gold. Y'all will look fabulous in antebellum gowns."

I had to agree with her there. Mama had made sure of that. She had worked overtime to cover the cost of piano lessons, dance lessons, and tea parties. Deena sucked up etiquette like dirt in summertime rain. Unfortunately, apart from looking the part, Billie Jo and I had turned out to be clay pigeons.

"Scarlett would've been the perfect docent." I pictured her strolling down the portico decked out in antebellum finery. "She belonged to the time."

Nancy gave a quick nod. "She would've had the tourists eating out of her hands with that refined southern accent and southern belle attitude. She was the real deal. I miss her sassy quips."

"I didn't know you two were friends."

"My husband Roger and I were good friends with her parents. After they died, we tried to stay in touch with her, but she avoided us. I had hoped she'd carry through with her plans to marry Delany Tyler, but she turned her back on him, too. Our relationship really never recovered. I ran into her about a week before she died. She acted strange…even for her."

"Define strange."

Her glance was speculative. "Paranoid? She kept glancing over her shoulder. When I questioned her about it, she apologized and said she was just in a hurry to chase down a source in Macon—at Magnolia Manor, that private mental institution. That's the last time I saw her alive."

I whistled. "That joint is only for the wealthiest of the wealthy. I wonder who her source was and what kind of story would take her there."

"I don't know, but she alluded to the mayor needing to take off his rose colored glasses and see the facts as they really are. I tried to question her, but she waved me off."

Okay, what was I missing here? Something tickled my memory—something I should remember. Could the source in Macon possibly be the man who supposedly wrote the vote-rigging software—a prototype paid for by a faceless person here in Whiskey Creek? Had Scarlett met with him? If so, where was the proof of her findings—on the missing flash drive? Possibly. No, probably. What if he was the one who'd killed her? And then again, what if I was wrong? Somehow, I had to find the last remaining pieces of this complex puzzle. But I had to hurry before the noose dropped over my neck and the killer kicked the horse out from underneath me.

Chapter Twenty-Five
Diamond is a Girl's Best Friend

True to her word, Diamond turned out to be a treasure, and it was apparent to the clients and staff that she was an excellent addition to the salon. Her steady presence and warm smile charmed everyone who came in contact with her. Perhaps, when this ordeal was over, I could lure her away from the police department.

By two, we'd finished my appointments for the day and headed straight for the new mall on the outskirts of town. Unfortunately, Scarlett popped in just as I looked in my rear view mirror and spotted a parking spot open up close to the side entrance. Her sudden appearance startled me, and I accidentally stepped on the gas, cutting off another driver who'd made a mad dash for the same spot. I slid my Mustang into the parking space, ignoring the offensive hand gestures from my disappointed opponent.

"I broke a nail on the dashboard," Diamond said. "Be glad I'm not in uniform. Otherwise I'd have to give you a ticket."

Scarlett materialized at my driver's side door, beautifully attired in a cropped blue dress with the sides charmingly gathered to the back. On her burnished curls perched dashingly over to one side, was a darling blue flat hat with a veil.

"Do you think I can find good quality green

281

ribbons for my new straw bonnet I plan to wear to my trial?" She quirked a smile. "I thought we might run into that little shop around the corner from the soap store. You know the one I'm talking about, don't you?"

I wanted to ask her how a ghost could use ribbons from the material world, but I felt certain Diamond wouldn't understand me talking into thin air. I'd come to respect her and wanted her to like me in return, so I ignored Scarlett.

"My foot slipped on the gas pedal," I explained. "I'm sorry about your fingernail. Mandy can fix it."

"There's no harm done," she said with a candid smile. "Just warn me the next time. Or perhaps, to be on the safe side, I should drive."

"Oh, so it's the silent treatment for me, is it?" Scarlett scowled. "You know being dead isn't easy. Do you hear me, Jolene?"

I heard the question but didn't answer. Instead I pushed open the car door which effectively passed through her ghostly form, bringing a screech of indignation. "Ghost abuse! Ghost abuse! This will go into your file for future retribution."

"I'm sure my file is bursting at the seams."

Diamond came around to my side of the car. "Were you talking to me?"

"No, just making an observation. Let's go shopping."

Diamond held onto my arm before I could move away from the car. "Give me just a second." Her eagle-sharp gaze surveyed our surroundings, her hand resting on the butt of the gun barely visible on her side. "Okay, all clear. Tell me immediately if you see anything suspicious or out of the ordinary. Stay close and duck if you hear me shout."

Uncertainty descended over me and I hesitated. Would a sniper take a pot shot at me here at the department store? What about innocent bystanders? Some of my earlier excitement faded as I noticed the dozens of nearby cars—they were the perfect hiding places for an assassin.

Diamond gave the all-clear, and a blast of cool, scented air swept over me as we entered the store and walked to the escalator leading to the dress department on the second floor. After ten minutes of fruitless searching, I enlisted the aid of a young, smartly dressed sales woman who introduced herself as Joye, promising I'd be the best-dressed woman Friday night. She selected several long formal gowns, then ushered me toward the dressing room. When I protested her selections, she urged me to trust her.

Diamond made a face and shook her head. "She's gonna look like my granny."

Joye scowled. "Classic designs never age."

I fingered the gowns, liking the silkiness of the materials and held one up, frowning at my reflection. "Diamond's right. No wow factor."

"You won't know until you try them on," Joye said, smiling politely.

I closed the dressing room door and shucked down to my skivvies. The first gown fit nicely but wasn't my style. It went on the rejection hook. The second gown followed suit. One by one they all went on the rejection hook.

Scarlett's reflection materialized in the mirror. "Too bad you can't borrow something from Vivian's closet."

I reached for my clothes. "I wish you wouldn't do that."

"At least you're talking to me and not trying to pass things through my body."

"You don't have a body," I reminded her. "Now please leave so I can try on more dresses."

"Ha. That woman has no style. Let me pick out something for you."

"How's it going in there, Miz Claiborne? I've found a couple more dresses I think might work."

I jumped at Joye's voice. When I opened the door, she stood there with an armload of stunning evening attire. The deep, rich colors immediately appealed to me, and I took one off the top and held it up to myself, admiring the neon blue silk in the mirror. "Nice."

She hung the rest on a hook. "I thought you'd like these styles better."

"It's a step in the right direction. However, I would be more comfortable in something snug and above the knee."

"I know just the dress. I'll be right back," she said, disappearing with the armload of rejects.

Scarlett positioned herself on the dressing room bench. "Don't trust her. Just look at what she's brought you so far."

To appease her, I said, "If you'll behave I'll take you to find ribbons for your bonnet as soon as I'm done here, okay?" I slipped into a pink satin dress with a pleated skirt before stepping out to the three-way mirror.

"What do you think of this one? I love the way the pleated skirt moves."

"The color is great on you," Diamond said. "But if

I had your great legs, I'd go for all out sexy."

My smile faded. "Not too sexy. This is a classy affair."

Joye returned with a garment draped over her arm. "You'll be sensational in this cocktail dress."

The dress she held up simply took my breath away. "It couldn't possibly fit," I whispered reverently, mesmerized by its silky ebony perfection. The neckline, edged in exquisite lace, plunged down to the base of the breast line, meeting a larger insert of sheer lace that cupped the mid-section to emphasize the breasts and slim the waist. Shimmering, midnight silk, gathered at the base of the insert, fell to short form-fitting pleats.

Here was a dress to die for—perfect for turning every head at the affair—man and woman alike.

"It's for a much slimmer, petite woman. Both I'm not," I said, immediately dismissing the glorious creation.

An exasperated smile flitted across Joye's face. "Nonsense. Trust me—you'll look smashing. All you need is shapewear." Turning on her heel, she headed for the dressing room with the cocktail dress.

"Well hello, Jolene," a voice said over my shoulder. "You look very snazzy and hip. You must be shopping for a new look."

I turned around. Cherry and her friend, Thelma Sands, were giving me the once over. Quickly, I introduced Diamond to the two women—of course, leaving out the fact that she was one of Whiskey Creek's finest and my bodyguard. That was need-to-know information, and they didn't need to know.

Thelma whispered into Cherry's ear. Since she wore a perpetual frown, it didn't take any brain power to deduce her comment was about me.

Cherry tapped her playfully on the shoulder, cooing in my direction. "Jolene knows she and Detective Bradford are a red-hot topic." Her courteous voice turned patronizing. "Be kind now. No embarrassing questions. Jolene is recovering from a car accident."

"Do you want me to slime her?" Scarlett asked from her perch on a dress rack.

I wanted to give her the go-ahead, but thought better of it. Bradford had warned me to expect nasty gossip. Our living arrangement had certainly brought out the town bitches. He'd suggested I take it in stride and have fun with it. "Don't let them suspect this is a ruse," he'd said. Well, that wouldn't be hard to do as Thelma's thin-lipped smile had condescension written all over it. Nothing would've given me more pleasure than to reshape her head, but I had to watch my blood pressure. Instead, I said with an exaggerated wink, "Sam says I'm more woman than he can handle."

She glared at me with burning, reproachful eyes. "Well, I never!"

"I bet you'd like to, though," I shot back.

My head spun with satisfaction when she gave me a black look and marched away telling Cherry she'd meet her in the jewelry department.

"I'm sorry," Cherry said as her friend disappeared down the escalator. "I shouldn't have poked fun at you. Please don't be offended."

Joye stepped out of the dressing room with my earlier rejects. "I'll be right back with that shapewear."

My attention shifted back to Cherry. "Will I see you and Robert at the fundraiser?"

"Oh yes. We'll be there," she declared with an enthusiastic hand wave. "Robert talks of little else these days. Richard Payne has high ambitions for his son. Being mayor is only the beginning of his career."

"You mean the governorship? Robert mentioned a press conference the other day at the salon."

"Yes, and hopefully, one day, the presidency."

"Wow, those are high ambitions. But speaking strictly between you and me, Linda Payne doesn't strike me as a strong candidate for First Lady. Her health is too delicate."

Cherry nodded in agreement. "I know what you mean. She looked positively terrible coming out of Dr. Graham's office the other day. She walked right past me without speaking."

"Dr. Graham, the psychiatrist?"

"Yes, that's the one."

"Mrs. Eisenberg mentioned Linda is in grief counseling."

"She is. Henry wanted to send her away to that exclusive medical retreat in Macon."

"The mayor is gonna need a lot of money to run for governor," I speculated out loud. "Is that where Robert comes in?"

Cherry's smile faltered. "Thelma's waiting for me. Ta ta."

"See you Friday night." I waved at her retreating back.

Diamond chuckled. "You sure know how to kill a conversation. That woman certainly didn't want you talking about her man parting with any money."

"I got the same impression."

As I stood there pondering my conversation with

Cherry, a creepy sensation crawled down my spine, as if I were being watched. I glanced over my shoulder, but observed only several women leafing through the racks—nothing unusual for the ladies' dress department. Quickly, before Diamond could notice my preoccupation, I turned back to the mirror.

I was in the dressing room trying to wiggle out of the pink satin when Joye returned.

She reached for the zipper. "Here, let me help you. I found this in the wrong drawer." She held up the black shapewear.

The zipper opened under her firm hand and dropped to pool at my feet. I stepped out of it, handing it to her. She placed the tiny garment in my hands and backed out of the room.

"I'll rehang these gowns." She paused at the door. "Holler if you need help."

"I'll need help," I said to the sound of the shutting door. Alone, I removed all my underclothing and picked up the tiny garment. A fine sheen of perspiration covered me when I finally managed to wiggle into the darn thing. The dress slipped over it like silk.

Joye was right. I looked sinful and utterly sensational. I bought the dress and the black monster underneath along with a new pair of black hose and heels. Scarlett harassed me about green ribbons during the entire transaction. Weary of her nagging, I finally suggested to Diamond we take a quick trip down the mall to the Dollar Store. As we were exiting, I again felt apprehensive—as if hidden eyes tracked me. I followed the curve of the clothes racks with my gaze, which is when I noticed a shadowy figure dart behind a purse display. Oh no... Oh, no. Not Grant again. I searched the crowd of shoppers desperately until Diamond stepped protectively into view.

"Is something wrong?" Her eyes clouded with suspicion. "You seem scared."

I shivered. It had to be a coincidence.

I blinked, pulling myself together. "No. Everything is fine. My overactive imagination is at work." My voice sounded guilty even to my own ears, but I smiled to lighten the mood, and we started down the mall.

The feeling of being watched persisted as we entered the Dollar Store. Once again, I turned around to see if we were being followed and again glimpsed a man duck into a small outlet store close by. I was able to get a good enough look at him to know that Grant wasn't tailing me. My fears of his leering face momentarily vanished, to be replaced by a new and equally frightening thought. Was this the same man in the dark blue sedan?

Spooked, I finally told Diamond my suspicions that we were being followed. With the quickness and skill of an experienced police officer, she ushered me out of the store and back to my car without frightening the other shoppers. Scarlett had a hissy fit, of course, but I was the only one to hear her screeching complaints.

Diamond drove back to the salon. Once I was safely ensconced under Deena's watchful care, she disappeared out of the office with a cell phone glued to her ear. I knew she was calling Bradford to alert him of my scare. It was a good thing too, because it appeared that I was still in a shitload of trouble.

Chapter Twenty-Six
The Dead Don't Haunt the Living

Bradford was waiting on me when I arrived home. The atmosphere between us became strained somewhat as night fell. He grilled me on the details of the suspected stalking until I was as angry as a snapping turtle on speed. Finally, he backed off. We ate a quick supper and then cleaned the kitchen. I went back to my room, leaving him to watch TV, or pace the floor, or whatever cops do when they guard important witnesses.

After a fitful night of troubled dreams, I woke up the next morning tired and cranky and feeling out of sorts with the world. On top of everything else, my menstrual cycle was screwed up. That accounted for my bitchiness. I swear to God, sometimes I wished for menopause to go ahead and catch up with me and rid me of bloating, painful cramps, and mood swings.

Bigfoot had nothing on me, I decided, as I gazed at my reflection in the bathroom mirror. The poison oak had started to heal, so I should be grateful that I no longer had a face that scared children. I showered and dressed hurriedly in slacks and heels, and found Bradford seated at the kitchen table munching on a cinnamon bun and drinking coffee.

He looked up from the morning paper. "Good morning, sleepyhead. I made coffee and cinnamon rolls for breakfast. Hey, are you all right? You look a mite droopy. I noticed your light on until well after midnight. Perhaps you should think about getting to bed earlier."

"I'm old enough to decide my bedtime, Detective Bradford." Tango sprang off the refrigerator, curling around my ankles. I went into the pantry for cat food and a box of cereal. I fed him then joined Bradford at the table with a bowl of cold cereal.

He shrugged. "Point well taken. Listen, I'm in a hurry. I have a meeting at the police station in less than twenty minutes."

"I'm capable of driving myself to work without being escorted," I responded without looking up from my cereal bowl.

"Look, I don't know why you're all tangled up like a barbed wire fence, and I'm not going to ask. Be ready to leave in ten."

His chair scraped across the floor, and I looked up to see his face drawn in a tight frown. Shame washed over me at my irrational behavior toward him.

"I'm sorry." My voice sounded flat, tired.

Some of the hardness seeped out of his face. "I know this arrangement is hard on you. On both of us, but we've got to keep a united front to pull this off. Please try to be patient, and I'll be out of your hair soon."

Yesterday's conversation with Nancy resurfaced. "You're right. We've got to work together. I came into some information you'll be interested in. I've been unable to follow the lead—you might have better luck," I said as a peace offering.

Bradford was brisk. "I'm listening."

"Nancy Chance ran into Scarlett about a week

before she died. Scarlett appeared scared, paranoid. When questioned, she waved off Nancy's concern. She said she was running late for a meeting with a source at Magnolia Manor—that expensive private sanatorium/mental institution. I'm wondering if the writer of the vote-rigging software works there or is possibly a patient. If so, his name is on that flash drive."

"I'll follow up on it," he said in a professional tone. "How much longer until you're ready to leave?"

"Give me five minutes."

I brushed my teeth in record time and grabbed my brown bag lunch I'd made the night before from the refrigerator. Bradford waited for me at the kitchen door, and we left together. So close, in fact, that he tailgated my rental all the way to the shop. Diamond took his place from there, practically breathing down my neck as we entered through the back entrance.

My first client arrived on time, and I went to work. The morning sped by, and the last time I noticed the time was around eleven when my client came in for her perm. She began talking the instant her butt hit my black leatherette stylist chair. I lost her somewhere between the high price of groceries and something about Medicare refusing to pay for her facelift. Silently, and with careful debate, I replayed my conversation with Nancy, seeking clues to the identity of Scarlett's source. From there I pictured my notes and list of suspects. What would Bradford find in Macon? A viable lead? I hoped so. We needed a break in the case.

"Hey, Jolene. What's wrong with you? You're a million miles away."

Slowly, Billie Jo's face came into view. I was no longer reliving my breakfast conversation with

Bradford, but under the glaring lights at the salon wrapping a permanent wave.

"Are you okay, honey?" Mrs. Butler laid her thin hand on my arm. "You've been lost in space since I've been here. I was telling you about Mr. Butler's bout with athlete's foot."

"I'm fine," I said with a smile. "Just daydreaming. It's been a busy week, and I've had a lot on my mind. I'm sorry I missed hearing about your husband's foot problems. My assistant, Diamond, will take over." I turned to Billie Jo. "What's up?"

She tapped her watch. "Are you ready for lunch?"

Diamond appeared with the waving solution and cotton strip. Expertly, she replaced me behind my stylist chair and began winding cotton to Mrs. Butler's hairline. I could hear their laughter as Billie Jo, and I headed toward the kitchen.

"Nancy called to thank us." Billie Jo swung open the kitchen door. "You should've checked with me before you volunteered my services. She wasn't happy to hear that I'm not volunteering to conduct tours at Pineridge Plantation or wearing one of those antebellum costumes."

I went straight for the refrigerator, fishing for my lunch, my stomach growling. I needed something a little more substantial than that quick bowl of cereal to get me through the rest of my day, which included two full head foils and another permanent wave.

"Hey, where's my chicken salad sandwich?" I said with my head inside the refrigerator.

"I saw Deena in there earlier."

"She ate my sandwich!"

"Didn't you say you wanted to drop a few

pounds?"

Deena's voice dripped sugar. I raised narrowed eyes over the refrigerator door to see her standing in the doorway. "Can't abide a food thief," I muttered.

"I'm just trying to help my big sister get into her snazzy black dress for the Friday night fundraiser *my ex-boyfriend* is taking her to." Deena walked over to the table, pulling out a chair into which she sank. "Make me a glass of tea, will you?"

Billie Jo's cell phone rang. "It's Roddy. I'll leave y'all to duke it out in private," she said, ducking out the door.

"Is there anything left for a starving woman?" I pulled out a pitcher of tea, set it on the counter, and grabbed two glasses from the cabinet.

"Funny you should ask. Anthony stashed a bag of Oreos in the bottom cabinet behind the paper plates and cups."

With goodies in hand, I joined Deena at the table, took out a couple of cookies, and handed the package to her. "I'm sure Billie Jo told you about helping out at Pineridge Plantation? She's not happy with me."

Deena nibbled on her Oreo. "I'll talk to her."

"She's pretty mulish, as you well know."

"We all are. I believe it's a family trait."

She was telling the truth about that. When we were young, Mama used to accuse Daddy of siring a bunch of jackasses. He'd just laugh and remind her from whose loins we'd sprung. After all the yelling and hollering, it'd get real quiet, and we'd hear Mama giggling behind closed doors. We never did figure out what they were doing until Billie Jo found a *Playboy* magazine shoved under their bed and showed it to

Mama. That night when Daddy got home, they shared the story of the birds and the bees with us right after dinner. I never did look at them the same way again from that moment on.

Deena, too, looked lost in thought.

"Whatcha thinking about?" I asked her.

"You wouldn't believe me if I told you."

"Oh, I don't know. Try me."

"Scarlett."

"What about Scarlett?"

Her face crinkled in thought. "I believed you'd lost your mind when you claimed to have seen her ghost in the facial room," she admitted. "But I've witnessed several strange happenings around here since her death. At first I thought someone was sabotaging the salon. But now, I'm not so sure."

I reached across the table for her hand. "I appreciate the support. What changed your mind?"

"I think I just saw a white mist go into the facial room," she said in a low, composed voice. "Promise me you won't mention any of this in Bill's presence. He'll think I'm a kook like you."

I jerked my hand away. "Well, that explains the odd look he gave me at the hospital the other day. Who else have you told?"

"I'm sorry, but I've been worried about you," she said. "I discussed it with Mama and Bill. I thought he could help us understand your strange behavior since this is along his line of work. With the invisible, you know?"

"And what did he offer in the way of explaining my strange behavior?"

"He said that the subconscious does weird things to

our vision under extreme periods of stress."

"So it's our subconscious conjuring up Scarlett's ghost?"

She nodded. "Bill said the dead don't haunt the living."

"Tell that to Scarlett," I said with a mouthful of cookie.

"Maybe Bill's right. Our nerves are shot from the trauma of her death."

I washed the cookie down with a swig of tea. "Daddy told me that Grandma Tucker had the third eye, Deena. Another family trait."

"Well, I don't want any part of it," she declared. "This could cause major problems with Bill."

"You really like him, don't you?"

"Yeah, I do."

"No more thoughts of Sam?"

"None. At first, I was jealous, but now with Bill in the picture, I'm okay with you guys dating. Besides, Sam and I don't mesh, and I could never be a cop's wife. What about you? I think there could be something between you guys if you'd let go and enjoy yourself."

"Thanks, sis, but I haven't thought about remarriage in a long time." With that, I pushed myself away from the table and went to check on Diamond's progress with Mrs. Butler's perm, not ready to share my feelings with my sister.

Searching for plausible answers to the questions about Scarlett's murder consumed all my brain power for the rest of the day, which ended up costing me a client. I had years of working with bleach, but with murder on the brain, I over-processed my client's long, golden curls, which to my horror, broke off and floated to the floor in frizzy puffs of cotton. "God, help me," I said, gaping down at the lost strands on the floor. This haunting business would drive me into bankruptcy if I didn't get control of myself and put a stop to it.

"Sure thing, Jolene."

Of all the stylists to come to my rescue, silver-tongued Anthony would've been the last on my list. Before I could bat an eye, he whisked my furious client out of my chair and into his, but not before she called me every name in the book. Dead tired and worried with time running out, I fled to the facial room, hoping to contact Scarlett about my conversation with Nancy.

No luck. Apparently, my cosmic tag-a-long was still pissed at me for not buying her a green ribbon for her bonnet and remained elusive. After several more minutes of sending out the universal signal for ghosts, I grew discouraged, and gave up. The clock kept ticking. Three days remained before Scarlett became earthbound, and then I'd be stuck with her until the day I died. Not a pleasant thought at all.

Chapter Twenty-Seven
Blackmail is Dirty Business

Thursday night passed without incident. Bradford and I were like two ships passing in the night. A light under his door signaled he was awake when I got up for a glass of milk. When I spoke to him the next morning at the breakfast table, he seemed preoccupied and answered my questions about the case in half sentences.

No sign of the flash drive.

Scarlett had visited Magnolia Manor, he mentioned. No new leads there.

"Do you know why she was there?" I wanted to know.

"That information wasn't provided."

"You explained that it was a murder investigation?"

He opened the refrigerator door, took out a carton of creamer, and set it on the table. "The administrator was adamant—no information without the proper subpoenas. I have a call in to the judge. What are your plans for the day?"

I poured myself a cup of coffee, sat down, and picked up the morning paper. "I'm getting the works at the salon." I found the sports section and passed it over to Bradford who immediately buried his face behind it. The society page had a write-up on tonight's fundraiser. Several of the names from the expected guest list promised I'd be rubbing elbows with a number of the names on Scarlett's list. Kind of like the bullseye coming to target practice. The thought made me a little apprehensive and ready to back out of the deal.

I left Bradford finishing breakfast. A hot shower later, I was dressed in jeans and flats and ready for my day of pampering. As a usual precaution, Bradford followed me to the salon, where Diamond waited to take up guard duty.

A cup of hot green tea waited for me at Anthony's station when I arrived five minutes later.

"Do you do this for all your clients?" I asked him as I sat down in his stylist chair.

"Only the ones I owe an apology to."

"I'm listening."

He draped a stylist cape around my neck and shoulders. "I have a confession to make—it was me you heard in Scarlett's house the other night." His voice dropped lower. "I didn't mean to scare you, but I thought the neighbors had called the cops."

I played it cool. Anthony remained a suspect, however low on the list. I would let him talk and then decide what to do with the information. "Me, too," I reciprocated. "What were you doing there?"

"So, what are we doing today?"

It took me a couple of seconds to realize he was referring to my hair. "Something simple and elegant."

He nodded at my refection in the mirror. "I know just the thing. First, let's shampoo, then I'll tell you my story—and Scarlett's."

Questions lit up my mind as I followed Anthony to the shampoo bowl. I kept silent as he shampooed and conditioned my hair, all the while chatting like a squirrel in mating season. With my hair wrapped in a towel, we returned to his station.

Briskly rubbing my hair with the towel, he leaned over my shoulder. "Scarlett was paying me a lot of money," he whispered. "That's why I was at her house—looking for the proof of our arrangement."

I met his serious expression in the mirror. "I don't understand. Scarlett was blackmailing you?"

"No. She was paying me a lot of money to obtain some information for her."

"Are you saying that you were spying for her?"

"Yeah. My half-sister works for the County Elections Board, and Scarlett believed I was the best way for her to obtain evidence she needed for a story she was working on. Scarlett would do anything, and I mean anything, to get what she wanted. Even greasing palms with a lot of greenbacks."

Would wonders never cease? Another unexpected revelation.

"What kind of information was she after?"

He pulled over the roller cart and began rolling my hair. "Anything regarding the recent, and past, city government elections. She wanted names and contribution amounts from each donating person, and organization."

"And were you able to obtain the information?"

"Nothing big. Just inconsistencies here and there. Scarlett was terribly interested in those. She pressed me to dig deeper, but my sister got spooked and refused to give me further access to the records."

"How did Scarlett react to the news?"

"I never told her," he said. "I kept feeding her false bits and pieces to keep the money coming. For a while, it worked, but then she started demanding viable info. She said she had to find the 'smoking gun.' Whatever that means. Man, that story was tearing her to shreds. When she ended up dead, I realized I'd be implicated in her death if the cops connected me to her. That's why I was in her house—looking for her notes."

"You realize this establishes a motive, don't you?"

"I'm many despicable things, but not a killer," he said.

"Did you share this with the police?"

"Most of it. I left out the money changing hands part. They interviewed me several times and warned me rather strongly to forgo the spying business. I assured them that I'd learned my lesson. However, I'll be leaving this small hamlet."

"Where are you going?"

"California. I have an aunt out there. The police shared my exploits with my father. Let's just say that he believes the West Coast has more to offer a male hairdresser with my talents. Hey, you're not going to tell the police about the money I took from Scarlett, are you?"

For a moment I thought about it. How many laws had I broken in the past two weeks? Quite a few. And I'd been given a second chance by Bradford. Could I do anything less for Anthony? "Do you still have the money Scarlett paid you?"

"I spent some of it," he admitted. "But my father made me donate the rest to local charities."

"Well then, your secret is safe with me. But Dixieland Salon will never be the same without you."

"Honey, you don't need me to liven up the place," he declared with a laugh.

The next hour passed pleasantly, and Anthony outdid himself. He was a natural, and I knew he'd be a success wherever he landed. By that time, Mandy was ready for my manicure and pedicure. With my hair elegantly styled, I gave him a quick peck on the cheek and a big tip.

Mandy had just finished applying the final coat of red polish on my nails when Deena came over to her station.

"Billie Jo and I are getting ready to have lunch in my office. We have an extra tuna fish sandwich for you if you're hungry."

"I'm starving."

Mandy stuck my hands under a nail polish dryer, and in five minutes, my nails had dried smudge-proof. I thanked her, gave her a generous tip for a job well done, and headed into Deena's office to join my sisters for lunch.

"I have some shocking news about Anthony," I said, taking a seat across the desk from Deena.

"What now?" Billie Jo asked.

After swearing them to secrecy, I repeated my conversation with Anthony.

Deena gasped. "I don't believe it."

"I do," Billie Jo said. "I knew he was hiding something. So he's off the suspect list?"

I bit into my sandwich. "Yes. I believe his story. He gave me notice, so we'll have to start looking for another stylist to take his place."

"I'll place a few calls this afternoon," Deena said. "I heard of a couple of stylists who are looking for a new salon. They're both good and have a strong client following. If you two approve."

I nodded and took a sip of Coke. "Now for my next piece of news—it's about Mandy."

The crease on Deena's brow deepened. "Is she leaving, too? We're not going to have any employees left by the end of the week."

"No, that's not it," I said. "Scarlett was blackmailing her. Mandy's brother is a math teacher at the high school. Scarlett ran into him one day outside school property with one of his students and jumped to the wrong conclusion. He was tutoring the girl, but Scarlett inserted a sexual twist on it. He came to Mandy for help, and she agreed to help him pay Scarlett off."

"I thought Scarlett was rich," Billie Jo said.

"According to her, it was all a façade," I replied. "She needed money to keep up appearances, but I suspect it was used to buy useful information."

Billie Jo let out a low whistle. "Damn, no wonder someone killed her. I'm surprised she lived as long as she did."

"No, I don't believe it's as simple as that," I said. "Scarlett was an investigative journalist and always on the lookout for a story. I suspect she started out right and simply lost her way. It happens sometimes in her line of work. Mandy's brother was a means to an end."

"Is Mandy a suspect?" Deena asked.

"I think it's safe to say our employees are in the clear," I said. "Mandy promised me she'd go to the police and tell them everything."

"Well, that's a relief," Billie Jo said.

I thought about the crime-scene photos Deena had taken. "I'd like to take a look at those photographs you took of the facial room again, if they're handy."

"What are you looking for?" Billie Jo asked.

"I'm not sure, but I'd like to take a closer look. I have time, we're not leaving for the Payne mansion until seven. Bradford has to be there a little early since he's working security. "Billie Jo, I would like to borrow your derringer."

"What for?"

"I need something light and compact. Mini Pearl won't fit in my black handbag. Your derringer will—or I could strap it to my thigh."

She nodded. "Sure. I guess that's okay."

We swapped guns and holsters. Deena rolled her eyes but withheld comment. She opened her desk drawer, pulled out the pictures, and slid them across her desk. I picked them up, shoved them in my purse, and stood. "I'm going to look at these at home. See you in the morning."

"Break a leg," Billie Jo said.

"That's not an appropriate statement for the occasion," Deena said. "The proper terminology would be to tell her to have fun."

"That's why Bradford dumped you, Deena. You're so perfect. Wait, that's not what I meant to say. You're not perfect."

I shut the door on Deena's reply, and Diamond and I drove over to my house. The answers to this mystery must be hidden in plain sight. I hoped I had them in my hands.

Chapter Twenty-Eight
The Mole and Mr. Blackstone

The white colonial mansion sat on a small rise, circled by ancient pines, in the center of the city historic district. When Bradford and I drove up to the Payne residence, I tried to remain calm and composed in the face of such grandeur. Bradford pulled around the circular driveway. He climbed out of the car and handed the valet the keys. Coming around, he opened the passenger side door and offered me his hand.

When we reached the house, the heavy wooden double doors stood open, spilling music and laughter out into the night. An immaculately dressed man I recognized as Richard Payne stepped forward to welcome us.

Here was one of the major players on Scarlett's list. I could see that he had aged well. His silver-lined, dark hair enhanced strong, vibrant features not yet distorted by age. He looked years younger than seventy and exuded enough sexual magnetism to make any woman glance twice.

"Detective Bradford, I'm so glad you could make it," he said, and then those fathomless, black orbs fastened on me. "And who is this beautiful creature?" he drawled, lifting my hand to brush his lips across my knuckles. I resisted the urge to shiver, and offered a plastic smile to hide my repulsion of the man.

Bradford disentangled my hand from our host. "This beautiful creature is my date, Jolene Claiborne," he said, his voice slightly amused. "I would remind you, sir, to keep that in mind throughout the evening. I would hate to haul the mayor's father to jail for grand larceny."

He laughed at Bradford's implication that I was a treasure worth stealing. "It's a pleasure to meet you, my dear. Please come in and meet my bride of fifty-plus years." He winked at me. "She'll want to know where you purchased that dress."

I thought my face would crack from smiling as I stepped through the front door into a large, ornate foyer with black and white marble flooring. An old Pre-Civil War chandelier threw tiny prisms of flickering candlelight upon the rich walnut paneling on the walls. Warm, yellow light danced into every corner, highlighting magnolia blossoms floating upon blue pools of water in sparkling vases resting graciously on antique tables. Immediately the arms of southern hospitality closed around me.

We followed our host to a magnificently-proportioned room with high ceilings and the same rich walnut paneled walls. An attractive older woman excused herself from a small circle of guests. I recognized Alice Payne from her many photographs that graced the society pages in the local newspaper, and I briefly wondered if she knew about her husband's activities. Richard reached out and drew his wife to his side.

"My dear, I would like to introduce you to Jolene Claiborne, Detective Bradford's lovely date."

Alice Payne dripped diamonds, and I couldn't help

but stare. She smiled. "Stunning dress, my dear." She turned to the men. "If you'll excuse us, I'd like to introduce Jolene to several of my friends."

I found my arm entwined in hers. With a quick turn, she steered me away from Bradford and in the direction of a group of ladies gathered in the far corner of the room. I snagged a glass of champagne from a passing waiter, doing a swift assessment of the whereabouts of additional trays of bubbly. From the looks of the female elite, an inquisition lay straight ahead. My joy took a nosedive at the prospect of fencing with the dragons. How little they knew of the true nature of my relationship with the dreamy homicide detective.

Thankfully, my thoughts were cut short when the mayor's wife appeared at my side. A light, ocean scent wafted over me.

"Everyone's talking about Sam's ravishing blonde. I can see why now that I've seen you." Her gaze devoured my evening attire. "You look smashing."

"As do you, Mrs. Payne." I sincerely meant the compliment. The deep blue silk of her dress heightened her red-gold hair, green eyes, and fair skin. Her throat was encircled with diamonds and earrings glittered at her ears, matching the diamond brooch pinned to her dress.

"Henry will be so pleased to learn you're Detective Bradford's date. He's counting on the local businesses to endorse his run for the governorship. I know he can count on Dixieland Salon for support."

Proper words failed me. In present company I couldn't express my dislike for her husband, but I wouldn't support him for dog catcher, let alone the governorship. The state of Georgia deserved better. I couldn't say that either, so I did the only thing I knew to distract her from the subject of politics.

"I've never seen such magnificent specimens—your diamonds, I mean," I said, staring at her diamond covered chest.

She gave me the most peculiar look, thanked me in a haughty voice, and excused herself, disappearing into the crowd the way I wanted to disappear beneath the floorboards.

Tammy Hodges, Scarlett's replacement at the TV station, swooped in just as the circle closed about me and took charge of the conversation. A wandering waiter replaced my empty champagne glass. After three, I began to relax and enjoy myself. Tammy seemed very pleased to talk about herself. However, as fascinating as she portrayed her life to be, I grew bored and drifted away to wander about the room—eavesdropping without drawing attention. Since I rarely traveled in these circles, I could casually lounge close by, and then move on when someone took note of my presence. An hour of milling around in my exquisite new heels had my feet begging for respite, and I looked for a quiet corner to sit down and slip them off.

A small alcove, sheltered by pony palms, presented the ideal place to rest. Unnoticed, I slipped behind the palms, sank down on the upholstered window seat, and pulled off my shoes, sighing as the throbbing subsided.

I was massaging my pinched toes when the sound of a man's voice nearby caught my attention over the piano music, voices, and laughter. Not ready to return to the party, I stilled my movements, so I wouldn't be discovered in my stocking feet. The speaker would move on in a minute or two, so I closed my eyes, picturing Bradford's strong arms around me and my toes sinking into the cool wet sand on a moonlit Florida beach.

Someone lit a cigarette and my beach evaporated. I stifled the immediate urge to cough, wanting to stay hidden for a few minutes more.

"I assume you have the package, Blackstone? The boss is most anxious to put an end to this business."

Blackstone! My heartbeat escalated at the thought that this could be the same man who threatened Daddy's life all those years ago. The man speaking sounded vaguely familiar, but I couldn't quite put a face to the voice, so I leaned closer to the screen of green palms.

"Yes. Our PD informant slipped it into my pocket a moment ago," was the rumbled reply.

"I'm sure he had an excuse for delaying delivery?"

"Circumstances. He didn't elaborate, and I didn't press."

"The boss will be very happy to have this in safe hands. He's meeting me in the library during Junior's speech."

Could the "package" be the missing thumb-drive? I'd bet my next breath the answer was a resounding yes.

A few seconds elapsed before I cautiously peeked through the palm fronds. Several small groups of men dotted the room, but no one group lingered nearby. The two men had moved away. I slipped on my heels. Bradford needed to know about this latest information that would crack the case wide open.

I found him chatting with District Attorney Randy Fallon. Bradford, with an uncanny awareness of something amiss, managed to convey the need for discretion with one luscious sweep of those long, black eyelashes.

He caught my hands, drawing me into his arms. "I'd like you to meet Jolene Claiborne."

Fallon smiled. "I'm glad to finally meet you. Sam was just telling me about your whirlwind romance."

Before I could respond, dinner was announced, drawing our attention.

I'm starving," Bradford said heartily. "Please excuse us."

"Of course," Fallon responded as Bradford took me by the elbow and escorted me toward the dining room.

"Saved by the bell," I said when we were out of earshot.

He laughed. "Always keep them guessing, Jolene. Now what's up?"

I checked for listening ears and then said in a low, composed voice, "I heard two men talking about the flash drive. One of the men was addressed as Blackstone. Could it be the same man? You know—the loan shark—the man that threatened to kill Daddy?"

Bradford eyeballed me. "What men? Are you positive they were discussing the missing evidence?"

"Pretty sure. Mr. Blackstone referred to a mole in the police department slipping it to him."

"Do you think you could identify them?"

"I didn't actually see them. I was sitting in the small alcove just off the main living room. You know, the one sheltered by the miniature forest? I couldn't hear very well over the music and loud conversations in the background. They were talking real low, but one voice sounded very familiar, although I haven't been able to put a face to the voice yet."

"Anything else?"

"They're going to meet in the library...I believe during, no after...sometime during the mayor's speech, I think. God, I'm not sure what time. But the package is gonna change hands then."

"Okay. The mayor is giving his speech later in the evening which gives us plenty of time to eat and do a little mingling. I have to work, so you keep your eyes open and your mouth shut. And whatever you do, don't approach those men if you come across them. Alert me. Understood? Please stay out of trouble."

"Are you calling me a troublemaker?"

Bradford leaned closer. "No, I'm calling you a trouble magnet. A very beautiful trouble magnet," he amended when I scowled at him. "Promise me you'll come get me before you do something stupid like shoot someone in the foot. Hey, wait a minute. You left your gun at home, right?"

"Of course I did." The lie came off easily—and it wasn't entirely a lie. It was Billie Jo's derringer strapped to my thigh, not Mini Pearl.

Satisfied with my answer, Bradford led me over to the end of the buffet line. I excused myself to the powder room, promising to return shortly.

Finding the nearest bathroom occupied, I wandered around until I found a vacant one in the back of the house. I'd just finished re-strapping the derringer to my thigh when Scarlett's ghostly image flashed in the mirror.

"Crap, Scarlett," I gasped. "Can't you find a gentler way of announcing your arrival?"

"Okay, here's my warning—I'm joining you in the

ladies' room," she said. "And you don't have to worry about a thing. I brought back-up."

I scanned the room. "What back-up?"

"Just take my word. Other heavenly beings are here."

"You mean angels?"

"Yes. Big kick-ass ones with swords of light."

My brows took a hike. "Really, Scarlett? Swords of light? That sounds Hollywood."

"Hey, you look great!"

Her tactic to distract me worked. I switched my attention to the burgundy ball gown Vivian Leigh had worn in the birthday party scene which was horribly out of date and not really Scarlett's style at all. What I wanted to say was she should've taken her heavenly hatchet to it and brought it up to date like all the others she'd worn, but I refrained, knowing she wouldn't take my suggestion quietly.

"Back at you," I said. "I take it you're joining the party?"

"Was there ever any doubt?"

"I never know with you, Scarlett. But since you're determined to tag along, keep a low profile. Bradford warned me to stay out of trouble, and I don't need any extra help finding it."

"The party will be over before you open the door, Jolene."

I lingered for a moment, questioning her sincerity. Not seeing any guile in her candid expression, I unlocked the door and stepped into the hall, colliding with Detective Grant. The solid strength of his arms locked us together in a tight embrace. His eyes strayed from my face to my revealing neckline.

"Oh, excuse me." I pushed my hands hard against his chest. He released me, and I staggered backward. He stared at me like a dog eyeing a T-bone steak. I grew uncomfortable and tried to walk around him, but he blocked my path.

"Ah, if it ain't Bradford's little woman." His words were loaded with ridicule. "I figured it wouldn't take him long to dip into your honey pot. Yes sirree, no time at all. I sure would like a taste of that honey."

I tensed at the insult. "Move out of my way," I demanded, my hand inching toward the derringer. Alarm and anger grew unchecked. If the man didn't get out of my way, I'd shoot his balls off.

He smiled with tobacco-stained teeth. "Now that's no way to speak to a police officer, Miz Claiborne."

"This one's going to hell," Scarlett said. "It's tattooed on his forehead."

With growing agitation, I scrutinized the detective's appearance. Appropriately attired in a black suit and tie, he looked presentable, yet the sharp smell of cigarettes and alcohol clung to him. Scarlett was right—evil radiated from him.

"Stay away from me." I pushed past him, his suggestive laughter chasing me all the way down the hall. Only when I was again at Bradford's side did I learn Grant had been hired as security. That left me feeling a little uneasy, so I shadowed Bradford.

Dinner turned out to be uneventful. Scarlett hovered close by as an invisible guest, only a shadow. Grant gave me a wide berth, but every few minutes, I would catch him staring. The guy gave me the creeps. Bradford noticed my nervousness and assured me he had warned the detective to keep his distance. After that, I found myself relaxing and enjoying the lively conversation.

Around nine, the gambling tables were opened and quickly filled. Bradford moved from table to table with a careful eye. I watched him work for a while but grew bored with the whole setup—not being a gambler myself. Thankfully, the hour passed quickly, and everyone was ushered into what appeared to be a spacious drawing room. Richard Payne introduced several important-looking men to the crowd. They each spoke of the political aspirations of the party, and Mayor Payne's rightful place as leader, before launching into the real reason we were here—money.

Since I had no intention of donating to the cause, I tuned out their voices and watched in amusement as Scarlett worked the room. Her ghostly antics were wildly amusing as she pinched and poked her way among Whiskey Creek's top families. Soon afterward, the mayor stepped up to the podium to fill the room with his deep, charismatic voice.

Bradford slipped through the crowd and made his way to the front, talking into a small microphone attached to his wrist. Grant mimicked Bradford's movement at the opposite end of the room. With Grant occupied, I turned my attention to the impassioned words the mayor effectively spun from a brilliantly written speech which captivated the audience.

I glanced at my watch, and then back at Bradford working security. The flash drive would change hands soon. Knowing that he would be right behind me, I assumed it would be safe to slip away unnoticed. For assurance, I touched the slight budge at my thigh. The derringer gave me added confidence to move away from the crowd.

The library was located in another wing of the house away from the drawing room. Earlier I'd scouted it out after my trip to the ladies' room so that I'd have no problem finding it later. A twinge of unease settled over me as I realized how far I'd distanced myself from the other guests. None of the sounds from the main part of the house penetrated this wing of the mansion. Complete silence. There wasn't even the ticking of a clock to shatter the insulated feeling I had. Cautiously, I turned the knob, peering inside the softly lit room. Finding it unoccupied, I entered, closing the door behind me.

Scarlett materialized at my side. "Why are we here?"

I gazed around the warm, cozy room, splendidly decorated in vibrant autumn colors. A wall-to-ceiling bookcase dominated one side of the room. "To eavesdrop on your killers. Now help me find a good hiding place. They'll be here any minute."

"I take it you didn't tell lover boy?"

A wide window seat caught my eye. "I told him. He'll be here. Don't worry."

"He doesn't know you're here," Scarlett stated.

"Well...I didn't exactly promise not to." I crossed the room to stand before the window seat. "I wonder if this opens."

It didn't, so I shifted my attention to the tall bookshelves lining the pine paneled walls.

"I'm going to hide in plain view," Scarlett said.

Stopping my perusal of the bookshelves, I turned around to see her perched on the back of the leather sofa facing the fireplace, the red velvet of her gown draped against the mahogany brown leather.

"Get your Little Red Riding Hood butt down here and help me. The big bad wolves can see me, remember?"

"How about under that table over yonder?"

"Funny. I'd stand out like a sore thumb."

"You stick out anyway in that dress."

Of course, she was right. If I hadn't been so vain and set on impressing Bradford, I would've dressed more modestly for this event. Just hearing her say out loud what was on my mind, and probably everyone else's too, caused heat to flood my face.

"Suck it up, Jolene. I'd have done the same thing if I had a good-looking man panting after me."

"He's not panting after me," I shot back. "We're working together, remember?"

"So you say, but I've noticed the way you two look at one another."

I paused in my search. "I don't have the hots for him. Now, if you want to spend eternity in some place other than my beauty shop, you'd better help me find somewhere to hide."

She floated toward a blue print chair. "What about here? You squeezed into that dress, so this should be a snap for you."

"Thanks for pointing that out."

The blue chair sat catty-corner to the wall, providing a small space behind it. The ruffled skirting around its edges would shelter a person from the rest of the room. I started toward it when I noticed the custom drapes lining French doors on the far wall. Dark brown and heavy, they offered better coverage than squeezing behind a chair, and they puddled on the floor, so even my heels would be hidden. Muffled voices sounded outside in the hall. Without hesitation I dashed to the drapes and disappeared behind them.

Chapter Twenty-Nine
The Mastermind

Silently uttering every prayer stored in my brain, I froze as approaching footsteps echoed on the hardwood floor. I held my breath as someone paused by the French doors then moved away.

"You have the package?"

"Mr. Blackstone delivered it as scheduled," another voice said.

Hmm. Sounded very much like Robert Burns.

"As I promised, your involvement ends here tonight if that is your wish. With this in hand, we're safe."

"What about the money? Detective Grant won't wait much longer for the second installment."

Well, I'll be. Richard Payne. He must be the mastermind. I hadn't seen that coming. The revelation of Grant being the police department informant failed to surprise me, however—and it explained the Rolex watch. The creep!

"Then you'd better pay him off tonight," Payne said in a dismissive voice. "We can't afford any further screw-ups. Everything is falling into place. The Brotherhood is solidly behind Henry's political future, and Scarlett's report is now history."

"I'll have a meeting with Grant as soon as you give me the last installment." Robert's voice sounded rough with anxiety. "After that, I'm out. That pesky Claiborne woman has been snooping all over town."

"Don't tell me you're feeling skittish?" Payne laughed. "Seeing ghosts?"

"Forget ghosts," Burns said. "Let's get finished with this business so I can rest easy."

The tinkle of ice cubes falling into a glass broke the silence. "Would you like a brandy?" I heard a second glass being filled.

"Henry's just what this country needs," Robert said. "Glad to know the Brotherhood is backing him. He's going to make a great governor someday."

"Yes, my boy's going places. I've big plans for him." A glass was set down on a hard surface. "Too bad you want out. You could ride to the top with us. But you've served us well over the years. Are you sure I can't talk you into staying?"

"Now's not the time. I'm concerned about the Cantrell murder investigation." He chuckled. "I've decided to take Cherry on a long vacation."

"You've earned a rest," Payne said. "Shame about Scarlett. The Brotherhood had hoped to recruit her into their ranks. She would've been an asset, but Henry couldn't stay out of her bed. He ignored my warnings."

"Well, her murder is the police's problem, not ours," Burns said. "I need to get that money to Grant."

A drawer opened and the sound of a stack of bills being slapped onto a desk top filtered back to me. "Here's the last of it, Burns. Now, let's get back to the party."

I waited a minute or two after the door closed before emerging from my hiding place.

"Oh God, I remember now."

Scarlett's voice startled me in the hushed stillness. I sank down into one of the overstuffed chairs, my knees shaking, and let out a long breath. I was back at square one. I'd been wrong in assuming that Scarlett had been murdered because of that investigative report. One by one, the names on my suspect list had been crossed off. Robert Burns had been the last.

Crap. What had I missed?

"Henry refused to leave his wife for me," Scarlett was saying. "I loved him. I would've sacrificed my career for him. But he wanted me as his mistress, not his wife. Ironic. He did to me exactly what I did to Deena. God, I'm sorry for the pain I caused her and the others."

I half-listened as my mind retraced every thought, every rumor, every note I'd written on this case. In my mind's eye, I replayed the autopsy report, each interview, each piece of gossip, the pictures Deena had taken of the crime scene, and my lengthy conversations with Bradford. My conversation with Mrs. Eisenberg, and then later, Nancy, when she also mentioned Magnolia Manor. I also recalled the light, ocean breeze scent of the facial room—the same scent I'd smelled earlier on the mayor's wife. The diamond brooch!

Suddenly, all the pieces of the puzzle fit together and I knew the killer's identity. With a sudden burst of strength, I jumped to my feet and ran to the door. I had to get to Bradford. My hand was on the knob when the door opened, and Linda Payne shoved me back into the room.

A gun appeared in her hand.

"Have a seat," she said softly, her eyes narrowing. "Do as I say. My patience is running thin. I will shoot you."

I obeyed as the Glock pressed into my side reinforced her words. I had to stay calm and not give into the cold, hard fear welling up inside.

Her frosty smile matched her eyes. "I knew you guessed the truth when you recognized my brooch."

"You're wrong, Mrs. Payne. I didn't recognize Scarlett's brooch until just a few minutes ago," I said. "She had it on the day she died. I wouldn't have connected the incident, had you not worn it tonight."

"My idiotic husband gave it to her as a token of his affection. Can you believe he would give a valuable piece of heirloom jewelry to his mistress? I won't be made a fool of."

I measured my options. Screaming was out—no one would hear my cries. I couldn't outrun a bullet. And I wasn't a fast draw. Linda would shoot me before I could reach the derringer. What's keeping Bradford? And where the hell is Scarlett with those big kiss-ass angels?

"You should've minded your own business. Surely you understand that I can't allow you to live." Her voice held a rasp of excitement.

The door pushed open, and a sound of shock issued from the newcomer. "Linda, have you lost your mind? Put the gun down. You've had too much to drink tonight."

A numb sense of relief came over me when I turned to see the mayor standing in the open doorway.

"Shut up you fool," Linda said. The gun swung back and forth between me and the mayor. "She knows everything."

The door closed behind him with a soft click. With

his hands held out in front of him, he took a hesitant step. "I can't let you kill another innocent human being."

Her eyes blazed green fire. "Innocent? Scarlett wasn't innocent. She bragged about her pregnancy. Pregnant with your child. She taunted me with it for weeks, saying I couldn't give you a child. You were going to divorce me and marry her—she would be the First Lady of Georgia. She's the reason I lost my baby." She broke out in sobs.

He stood awkwardly for a moment. "No, it's my fault. I'm sorry for hurting you. I should have sent you away to Magnolia Manor the same morning you showed me the diamond brooch. If I had, you'd be getting the help you need. Why did you do it?"

Linda shook her head. "Revenge. I broke into the salon and planted the poisonous tea bags, the plaster powder in the facial room. I even gave her another chance to give you up. She had to see you one last time, she said. Ha. My plan carried itself out flawlessly." Her hand closed over the brooch possessively.

"You murdered Scarlett just because you thought she was pregnant?" I asked.

"I ran into her at the doctor's office," she said. "She bragged to me that she was pregnant with Henry's child. I wanted her to know the pain of losing a child as I had." She looked at her husband. "And I wanted to scar her pretty face. Maybe then you'd lose interest in her."

I thought back to my conversation with Becky the day of the murder. My daughter had witnessed the confrontation between the two women, but she'd had no idea why they were arguing.

"Scarlett lied about the pregnancy," I said.

Henry took an abrupt step toward his wife. "Let me help you. Please give me the weapon."

The gun swung back to the mayor. "Stay away from me. You're not sending me back to Magnolia Manor. That's what Scarlett planned all along, you know. That bitch was snooping into my past. She was there. I know. I have connections."

The tension in the room escalated. I had to do something to defuse it, or I'd be pushing up daisies, and I was way too young to pass through the pearly gates.

"Listen to me, Mrs. Payne," I said as calmly as I could manage. "Scarlett wasn't at Magnolia Manor to dig up your past, but to track down a source for a story she was working on." I paused, taking a deep breath to steady my shaking voice. "Detective Bradford is going to be coming through that door any minute. It would be best if you put the gun down."

Insanity stared back at me. "This is your fault," she said, inching the gun closer. "Why couldn't you mind your own business?"

"Darling, please listen to reason. I'm begging you, my love."

Henry's pleading voice momentarily captured Linda's attention so I sized up my chances of escape without incurring bodily harm. Scanning my surroundings, I measured the distance between me and the door. Too far—I'd never make it before taking a bullet in the back. If only I could grab the derringer.

As if she could read my thoughts, Linda's gaze, and gun, swung around. Thankfully, I hadn't moved, but I watched in horror as the mayor lunged for the gun. The muffled *whomp* of a gunshot froze my feet to the floor. In appalled shock, I watched him collapse. Not thinking of my actions, I rushed to his side.

"Call 9-1-1." I jerked a small cozy from a nearby table and pressed it to his wound. Immediately, I was covered in warm, sticky blood.

Startled, Linda brought the gun around, pointing it directly at my forehead.

"Get up," she said in a raw, harsh voice.

"What are you going to do?"

"Finish the job I started the other night in the hospital."

The shock of her confession hit me full force. "It was you?" I gasped, climbing slowly to my feet, tottering dizzily. Then I slipped on a large white feather which suddenly appeared on the floor and smacked into Linda.

The Glock clattered to the floor, sliding several feet from us. Stunned and breathless, I struggled to my knees and lurched forward, only to find myself entangled by her grasping arms. Blood poured from a gash on her cheek. Our screams of rage filled the room as we both wrestled for the gun lying several feet away. Gathering my failing strength, I grabbed a handful of hair and jerked her head backward. I fumbled for the derringer strapped to my thigh, but it failed to dislodge from its holster.

Linda gasped and kicked viciously, her nails ripping into my arm. Pain streaked up to my shoulder, but I hung on, giving her hair another hard yank. Again, the derringer snagged as I tried to pull it from its holster. Then, mysteriously, it was in my hand. I brought it up and aimed at her torso as my finger tightened on the trigger.

"Don't do it, Jolene," a voice ordered from the door.

Bradford's arresting face swam into my view as I turned toward his deep-timbred voice.

I looked at the derringer held tightly in my shaking hands. "She shot her husband."

"It's over now. You're safe. Just place the weapon on the table and move away."

Linda slumped to the floor. I set the gun down as directed and heard the guests rush into the room. Someone screamed, and I looked up to see the mayor's parents standing over their son.

"Linda killed Scarlett," I choked out.

DA Fallon led me to a chair and placed a glass of water in my hand. "Here, drink this. You don't look so good."

"I don't feel so well," I said. The encounter with Scarlett's killer had unnerved me. For the second time in my life, I had known true fear—had shown my backside to the death angel, and had come out alive.

One of the guests escorted me to the bathroom so I could wash my face and hands free of the blood. EMTs and half of the police force had arrived and were working the scene when I returned to the library. Bradford waited for me with a frown.

"Officer Clark will take your statement in another room," he directed in a crisp authoritative voice that left me chilled. He turned to help the officers arriving on the scene.

I followed Clark out of the library and to an informal parlor down the hall. I told him everything I'd witnessed between Richard Payne and Robert Burns, then everything that had transpired between me and the mayor and his deranged wife. He wrote it all down, asking pertinent questions. When we were finished, he disappeared, leaving me in the welcome silence of the richly decorated parlor.

An hour later, Bradford walked into the room. He stood with his hands shoved in his pockets, his face angry.

"You could've been killed. I asked you to stay out of trouble and you ignored my warning. Then you lied about being armed."

Hurt and frustration radiated from him. Feeling utterly miserable, I reached out to him. "I do things without thinking." He didn't take my hand. I let it drop back to my side.

"The stolen thumb-drive was found in Richard Payne's possession. We now have the evidence to charge him and his cohorts with several major crimes in this town, including the murders of Judge Cantrell and his wife. He and Burns have been arrested, as has Mr. Blackstone. Further arrests will be made."

"Good. How's the mayor?"

"He's in surgery, but the doctors believe he'll make a full recovery. However, his political career is over."

"And Linda?"

"She collapsed after confessing to planting the tea bags and plaster powder at Dixieland Salon. She had hoped to induce a miscarriage with the arsenic and disfigure Scarlett with the plaster powder. She also confessed to attempting to silence you. She's mentally disturbed. Who can say if she meant to murder Scarlett?"

I pushed a wayward strand of hair from my face. "She shot her husband and would've killed me if circumstances hadn't intervened. Linda's a dangerous woman."

"We'll leave the details for the D.A. to work out. She's been transported to the hospital under heavy guard."

"What about Grant?"

"He's being interviewed downtown for evidence tampering. Turns out he's a dirty cop. He confessed to being on the Brotherhood's payroll. He's also the driver of the dark blue sedan that caused your accident. You've been cleared of any wrongdoing, so let's get you home."

I stood on shaking legs, numb with the reality that this nightmare had ended. Bradford offered his arm and helped me to his car. He drove me straight home and let the engine idle.

"You're out of danger, but for precaution, a patrol car will be parked out front for the night." He unlocked the door and handed me his key. "Get some rest now. I'll pick up my things tomorrow."

From the living room window, I watched his headlights back out of the driveway. With a weary sigh I followed Tango to my bedroom, where I took a hot shower and dumped my new blood-soaked dress into the garbage. The phone rang just as I was climbing into bed. Phones ringing at that early hour are seldom good news, and after my nightmare night on the town, my heart was beating a steady tempo when I snatched up the receiver.

"Hello?" I listened as my son-in-law's voice cracked over the line with the news that Becky had gone into labor. The hospital intercom blared in the background. "I'm on my way."

I bolted out of bed, threw on some clothes, and headed for the hospital in my rental car. Amazingly, the rest of the family showed up just minutes after I took a seat in the family waiting room. While we waited for the baby to arrive, I gave an abbreviated version of my role in solving Scarlett's murder, downplaying any heroics on my part. After assuring them I was never in any real danger, Mama settled down and turned her attention to the birth of her great-granddaughter.

Deena and Billie Jo pulled me aside.

"So it's over?" Deena asked.

"Yes, we can get back to normal." I yawned. "And Daddy can finally come home for good."

"And Scarlett?" Billie Jo asked.

"Gone."

"You sound sad," Billie Jo said. "I thought you'd be relieved that she'd moved on."

"I guess I am. Funny, how you think you know a person and then they show a side of themselves you never guessed existed. Scarlett was like that. Beneath that hard shell was a grain of good. Everyone carries a hidden hurt—even Scarlett. She taught me not to judge a book by its cover. I'm gonna miss her."

Another hour passed before Jacob came in with an update. Hannah Grace Fairchild had been safely delivered and would be making her first appearance as soon as she was cleaned up and dressed to meet the family. Becky was tired but doing fine.

I met my seven pound, three-ounce granddaughter fifteen minutes later, and with one look, I knew that she, like me, had the "third eye". Her life would be filled with visions of people who'd passed over to the Other Side. And I would be there to direct her steps

328

along this difficult path. But for now, my long night had caught up with me. I gave her butterfly kisses before handing her back to Becky, promising to visit after catching up on some much-needed rest.

Back at home, I changed into my nightie and climbed into bed, glad my grand adventure had ended on a positive note. Bradford's angry face came to mind. Losing him was my biggest regret. Tomorrow I would think about change. Yes, tomorrow would be soon enough, because after all, tomorrow is another day.

Chapter Thirty
Dangerous Habits

I had just drifted off to sleep when Tango's sharp claws dug into my leg, bringing me straight up in bed. With a hiss, he sprang from the bed and shot out of the room. There, floating at the foot of my bed, was Scarlett—clothed in a tan trench coat with a golden belt cinched tightly around her tiny waist. An aura of overwhelming joy surrounded her. I tore my eyes from her beautiful countenance to the glorious angels standing behind her, their massive wings a golden umbrella over her rich, brown curls. They, too, smiled down on me.

"I wondered where you'd gotten off to," I said. "You have a habit of skipping out just when the action is starting. I could've been killed!"

Her laughter rang like the tinkling of porcelain wind chimes in a delicate summer breeze. "Who do you think sent the feather your way and freed your gun from its holster? I timed it perfectly."

"You?" I questioned doubtfully. "I thought you said there were angels watching over me. 'Backup' is the word you used, and now you're telling me you were lying?"

"Only a little white fib to bolster your courage. It worked, didn't it?" Scarlett cocked her head heavenward. "I came to tell you goodbye and to thank

330

you. My trial is over. They found me guilty on all counts."

"Oh, I'm sorry. Now what? Do you have to move really far south where it's hot?"

"No, nothing like that, I'm happy to say. I have to take amendment classes."

I laughed. "I won't even ask you what that means. So where's your usual getup? The southern belle wardrobe."

"Oh, that's so yesterday," she twittered. "There's a Celestial University offering criminal investigation classes. I'm thinking of hiring out my services once I graduate."

I had to ask. "You want to be a detective in heaven?"

"No, of course, not. I'm thinking PI. You never know when you might need my help again."

"Oh no, I'm finished with investigating," I protested. "We can't take credit for solving your murder. We stumbled into the answers, so don't get any ideas about future sleuthing."

"We'll see." She tucked flyaway strands back into the thick bun fastened at her neckline.

"You seem happy."

Scarlett reached out and touched my face. "I am. But I have regrets. Take my advice, grab up that delectable police detective and taste the sweet things in life while you can. Life is short, you know."

"I'm afraid that door has been closed."

"It is only if you say it is. Well, gotta run. Goodbye."

"Stop in sometime and say hello. Remember, my friends are always welcome."

And then, in a blaze of light, she was gone.

****

The doorbell rang at eight. I had just finished my morning coffee and was stacking breakfast dishes in the dishwasher before getting ready for work. Short on time, I hastily hung up my apron on the inside of the pantry door and hurried to answer the second peal. I opened the door to see Bradford, cowboy hat in hand, waiting on the other side of the panel.

"I'm not too early, am I?" He shifted his hat from hand to hand. "You know, to get my things? I wanted to catch you before you left for the salon."

Words failed me. I'd been longing for, and dreading, this moment since our tense parting last night. Fixing relationships was never one of my strong points. The second I opened my mouth, all the wrong words tended to fly out. So I did the next best thing and opened the door wider, and with a motion of my hand, invited him in.

"This shouldn't take long," he said in the continuing silence of the foyer. "I left my belongings in the guest room." He crossed the foyer and started toward the hall.

"Wait."

I hadn't realized I'd spoken aloud until he stopped and turned around to face me. "Yes?"

"About last night."

"Quite a night."

"Yes. It was." I swallowed hard. "I was less than truthful with you."

"You lied about being armed."

"I stretch the truth on occasion."

He took a step toward me. "Yes, you do.

Dangerous habit."

"I don't always listen to advice."

Another step. "Almost never."

"I'm stubborn."

"Infuriatingly so."

"Pushy."

"That's a given."

"I do have a good side, if you're interested," I countered.

"I am."

I took a step toward him. "I could show you."

"You'll be late for work."

"I could say the same for you."

He returned my smile. "Actually, the chief gave me the day off."

"I could call in sick." Another step. "Of course, that would mean I would have to spend all day in bed."

"Want some company?"

I stepped into his embrace. "Yes, but only if you show me your gun."

"Handling guns are another dangerous habit."

"Yes, I know, Detective Bradford." I slipped my hand into his and we started down the hall toward the bedroom. "But that is one dangerous habit that I'm very, very good at."

Please turn the page for a sneak peek at
Utterly Deadly Southern Pecan Pie
coming soon from The Wild Rose Press, Inc.

Utterly Deadly Southern Pecan Pie

by

Penny Burwell Ewing

The Haunted Salon Series

Chapter One
The Key

The man leaning against the ornately carved mahogany mantelpiece had been dead for one hundred and fifty years and appeared as if he had stepped from the pages of an antebellum romance novel. His hair, dark and flecked with silver, flowed back from a high forehead—eyes darker than sapphires were set in a face bronzed by wind and sun. His lips, firm and sensual, pressed together in a cynical twist, and the gray frockcoat and vest fit snug over a pristine white shirt with a black stock expertly tied at his throat. Black boots shone from beneath gray trousers, and in his large, tanned hand, a smoking cigar.

He belonged to another time.

We stared in frozen surprise at one another. I stood in the open doorway of the library, my hand on the brass doorknob and a group of tourists at my back when my sister Deena noticed my hesitancy to enter the spacious room.

"What's the holdup?" she asked in a hushed voice. "Did you forget your lines again?"

The acrid aroma of tobacco smoke stung my nostrils. I nodded, my gaze glued to the ghostly specter at the fireplace.

Deena brushed past me in her blue cotton hoop skirt and motioned for the group to follow. "The

Rococo Revival furniture was placed in the house by Josiah Redding around the time of 1836 when he built Pineridge Plantation for his bride-to-be, Savannah Childs." She pointed to the dark, heavy pieces. "Josiah's portrait hangs over the chimney, and you can see he was a handsome and wealthy Southern gentleman planter. His wife later wrote in her journal that he would retire to this quiet haven after dinner to smoke his imported cigars."

Automatically, my gaze lifted to the portrait. The likeness of the man in the painting failed to capture the sense of mystique in the fathomless eyes of the man himself. The man in the portrait and the one standing beneath it were one and the same. Josiah Redding. And of course, I was the only one in the room who could see him fade away into nothingness.

Perhaps I should explain.

I see dead people. Celestial citizens of inner space. Transcendent realities. And yes, I suppose in certain circles they are referred to as ghosts. Most are friendly. Some not so much. And then every once in a while I run into a real pain-in-the-ass spirit.

It all started back about seven months ago after a client, Scarlett Cantrell, with some help from an outside source, joined the Other Side. It happened in my beauty salon. Scarlett needed help bringing her murderer to justice, and she picked Dixieland Salon as her earthly headquarters. As all of this unfolded, I found myself drafted into helping her. Yep, me, Jolene Claiborne. Hairstylist extraordinaire.

Not everyone in my life is happy about my special gift inherited from my Granny Tucker—namely, my younger sister Deena, and my boyfriend, Detective

Samuel Bradford, who happens to be her old high school sweetheart. But that's a long story and Deena's signaling for me to pick up where she left off.

Careful not to brush against the tables, and upset the delicate porcelain quail figurines, with my bulky hoop skirt, I glided deeper into the room until I stood beneath the portrait of Josiah Redding.

"The legend of Piper's Gold is well known in these parts," I said with an exaggerated southern drawl. "On July 19, 1864, a small band of Confederate soldiers under the command of Major Travis A. Piper were quietly transporting a cache of gold from a bank in Thomas County to headquarters in Macon, Georgia. As evening approached, they arrived at Pineridge Plantation and were graciously received for the night. The officers were given rooms in the main house, and the others pitched tents in a nearby field. As they retired for the night, a message came in alerting of an advancing Union troop. Immediately, the officers gathered to discuss their orders to hide the gold and retreat south. When the Union troop moved on, they were to retrieve the gold and proceed to Macon taking every precaution to elude capture.

"The orders were carried out. Unfortunately, at dawn on July 20, 1864, the Union troop struck and massacred Major Piper and his small band of soldiers. Heady with victory, the Yankee soldiers stormed the house and killed Josiah. His youngest son, Asa Douglas Redding, mysteriously disappeared from the plantation and history on that same night."

I paused as expressions of horror and gasps of dismay sounded from the group. When they settled down, I continued with my story. "The house and its furnishings were spared as an officer spotted a portrait in the front parlor of Josiah's father wearing his Masonic ring. The officer, a Mason himself, ordered the house placed under guard. But the damage had been done. The eldest son, Randall Josiah Redding, was reportedly killed two days later on July 22, 1864, in the final battle for Atlanta. Savannah Redding, and her young daughter Adelaine, died that winter when they both contracted pneumonia. The remaining son, John Milton Redding, survived the conflict and is the ancestor of the present owner, Victor Redding."

Here I paused again and lowered my voice to achieve dramatic expectation from my listeners. "The gold which they hid has never been found. Rumors abound that Major Piper and his soldiers are still guarding their Confederate bounty. And watch out for Tempy, the old slave woman. Many visitors claim to see her throughout the main house. Beware. You have been warned."

Muffled cries of anticipation rang through the group of tourists, and I could see several heads swirl to peer into the corners of the richly ornamented room.

"I saw something when I came in here," a man said.

"As did I," echoed another.

And on it went for several minutes until Deena, with a worried frown directed at me, began ushering the tourists toward the opened library door.

"I wish you wouldn't do that thing with your voice, Jolene," she said as I joined her at the rear of the group. "It triggers their imagination."

"In defense of myself, my dear darling sister, it's in the guide brochure, and it's what they expect to hear.

People love haunted houses, and I can't help it if Josiah presented himself over by the fireplace when we came in. I get the distinct impression he doesn't like strangers in his house," I teased.

"Please keep it light, not real," she pleaded. "And please don't let anyone see you talking to them. They'll think you're crazy."

"All right, Deena." I closed the library door firmly behind me. "Let's finish this tour so I can get out of this dress and corset."

We with the tour group now stood outside the library, which occupies the northeast corner of the principal floor. The walls were painted cream, reminiscent of ancient parchment paper, with electric wall sconces fashioned like candlesticks casting their soft yellow light over worn pine floors.

I took the lead again. "As you have noticed, the manor house has been modernized by the Redding descendants, but still retains its distinctive historical flavor with nineteenth century period furnishings. Before modern lighting however, the plantation mistress oversaw the making of candles for the main house and slave quarters. During the 1850s candle manufacturers made it possible for the richer families to purchase candles instead of making them. Savannah's household ledger, dated in 1860, details purchases of candles from a general store in the nearby town of Albany. Now if you will follow Deena to the front entryway, another guide is waiting to take you on a tour of the sole remaining slave cabin restored to its original condition."

As the group trudged past me, I let out a long breath and plucked the damp cotton dress from my sweating torso. Even though it was November in South Georgia, the coolness of fall had failed to arrive, and the manor house had air-conditioning only in the upper living quarters. My dark blue gown buttoned up to my throat, and the sleeves were long and tight around my wrists. Underneath the heavy cloth, all kinds of female paraphernalia had me cinched up tighter than a horse's saddle. All historically correct for the time period, but I was hot as Hades and ready to shed the tightly laced ankle boots pinching my toes with every step.

Bringing up the rear, I could hear my sister's voice drone on about the hand-painted wallpaper depicting a classic English garden gracing the entrance hall of the manor house. She spoke of the spacious circular room with a large square rug made threadbare from years of traffic and the original French crystal and brass chandelier which still hung over the center of the room.

I made my way to the front door with its delicate tracery in the fanlight and sidelights and thanked each tourist for their visit as they stepped onto the large front porch where a man dressed in period clothing waited to take them on a tour of the grounds.

As soon as the door closed behind the last straggling tourist, I turned to Deena. "Thank God, that's over. My feet are killing me, and I feel like I'm going to bust the seams of my stays. Let's go change and stop by Sonic for a cherry coke on the way home."

Deena eyed me critically. "You're the one who volunteered us for this gig. Which, I'm glad you did, I should add."

"Of course, you are. You're like a cat lapping up cream in this environment."

She performed a playful pirouette. "An age of

enlightenment."

I grimaced as ankle boots bit into my flesh. "More like the age of confinement."

A small bedroom in the back of the house had been set aside as a changing room for the volunteers, and as we passed by the library, a soft thump sounded from behind its closed doors.

"There shouldn't be anyone in there," I said, and we turned back to investigate. When I opened the door and peered in, the room appeared empty, but I noticed a small book lying on the floor next to one of the cherry bookcases. "You go on ahead. I'll only be a minute."

"Okay, but hurry," she said. "We have a tight schedule for the rest of the day. It's eleven-thirty and Billie Jo will meet us at your house in thirty minutes to decide on a recipe for the contest tomorrow night. And we have to be at the salon by four to do hair and make-up for tonight's Miss Pecan Festival Queen Beauty Pageant."

I groaned. "Don't remind me. It's going be a long week."

Deena left and I returned the book to its place on the shelf. A cold chill swept over my body, as the scent of cigar smoke wafted in the stale air. Slowly, I turned around to meet the appraising gaze of Josiah Redding. The hair on the back of my neck prickled with static electricity.

Once more our eyes locked in frozen tableau; his stare compelling, magnetic, and I lost all fear as he reached inside his front vest pocket, withdrew a key and held it out toward me. Without hesitation, I crossed the room until I stood directly in front of him. The shiny key glistened like new—its design heart-shaped with interlinking lines within the heart. He dropped the bronze key into my outstretched palm, and my fingers closed around it.

"What do you want me to do with this?"

Silence met my question.

I opened my hand and stared down at the key, now scratched and dull with age as if the past one hundred and fifty years had accumulated on its surface in a few seconds of time. I snapped my head up with the violence of uncertainty, but I stood alone in the cozy room.

I shivered in the warm air.

A word about the author...

Penny Burwell Ewing was born and raised in Fort Pierce, Florida. Growing up in a southern coastal town gave her the best of small town living where the residents look out for one another.

Her interest in writing began in the 1970s when she consumed every bodice-ripper published and decided to try her hand at entertaining herself. It worked, and she is now working on her fourth novel.

Once a professional cosmetologist, Penny draws on her humorous experiences behind the chair to add spice to her Haunted Salon series. She now resides in Tifton, Georgia.

Thank you for purchasing
this publication of The Wild Rose Press, Inc.

If you enjoyed the story, we would appreciate your
letting others know by leaving a review.

For other wonderful stories,
please visit our on-line bookstore at
www.thewildrosepress.com.

For questions or more information
contact us at
info@thewildrosepress.com.

The Wild Rose Press, Inc.
www.thewildrosepress.com

Stay current with The Wild Rose Press, Inc.

Like us on Facebook

https://www.facebook.com/TheWildRosePress

And Follow us on Twitter
https://twitter.com/WildRosePress